RECKLESSLY
YOU

By J. Morales

Playlist

"How Do I Say Goodbye"—Dean Lewis
"Holding Out for A Hero"—Nothing but Thieves
"You Broke Me First"—Tate McRae
"Dead Man Walking"—Jelly Roll
"I Am Woman"—Emmy Meli
"Outta My Head"—Khalid with John Mayer
"Damn I Wish I Was You Lover"—Sophie B. Hawkins
"Power Over Me"—Dermot Kennedy
"Drive"—The Cars
"Slow Hands"—Niall Horan
"Wildest Dreams"—Taylor Swift
"Use Somebody"—Kings of Leon
"Make You feel My Love"—Adele
"Outnumbered"—Dermot Kennedy

Complete list on Spotify
@J.Morales

For those who wipe your tears with the swipe of their thumb and kiss your tears.

To my husband

Dear Readers

Recklessly You is the second book of the Delgado brothers. Although I highly advise reading the first book, *Always You,* to become acquainted with the character, it can be read as a standalone. *Recklessly You* does follow *Always You's* timeline. While you can read book one later, expect to encounter spoilers for Book 1 in Book 2.

PROLOGUE
LIAM

Six years old

My tennis shoes pound against the asphalt, and my chest heaves with each breath. My legs burn as I run into the night. All I can hear is the wind howling and the rumble of passing cars. I ran like Papá said to do when the bad guys shot him. Coming to a halt, I hide behind a large, tall bush to catch my breath. I cover my mouth to contain my sharp breath and panting. The sound of boots pounding along the pavement has me shaking. Be brave, Liam, I tell myself as I feel a quick poke in my hips. I pull out my ninja turtle from my pocket and stare into Leonardo's eyes, hoping some of his powers will seep into me. I rub his shell again like it's a magic genie lamp.

The voices of the men sound closer with every passing minute. They speak in a mix of English and Spanish. I recognize one of the voices. He spoke with Papá before Papá asked me to hide.

"Find the boy. We leave no witnesses behind," shouts Pablo, the man with the familiar voice.

"Pablo, he's just a boy. I doubt he will remember. He was too

scared. And he wasn't the only witness. The place was filled with people," the other man says in a gruff voice.

"We just need to scare the shit out of him. Dead or alive, I don't give a shit," Pablo snaps.

Dead or alive. No, no—I need to find Mamá. I need to tell her. I need to keep her safe. Papá said to take care of Mamá. I pass a couple of restaurants and a laundromat close to the pizza place. I must be getting closer to home.

My legs pump faster and faster as I run like the wind, leaving a trail of dust behind me. I hear the shouts of men and the pounding of their boots behind me. I zigzag through the neighborhood. I gasp in pain as I stumble over a sharp rock, but I quickly regain my footing and continue running. The neon light on my front porch shines through the night, guiding me home.

Mamá runs out when she spots me from the living room window.

"Liam, Liam, what happened?" Mamá cries.

I wrap my arms around the swell of her pregnant belly. I clench her cotton shirt.

"Liam? What happened?" Mamá repeats. She peels me off her, scrutinizing me from head to toe.

She gasps. "Liam, you're bleeding."

I didn't notice the blood trickling down my leg and elbows.

After a few seconds, I catch my breath and glance over my shoulder. The men who chased me are not visible.

"Mamá, the bad guys shot Papá; he—he told me to run. The men chased after me, Mama. We need to leave," I say, choking on each word. I hold her gaze, pleading with her to listen.

Her body shakes, and her voice is barely above a whisper when she looks into the dark street. "Hide, Liam. Hide, and do not come out, no matter what you hear."

"Hide with me, Mamá, please." A tear runs down my cheek.

I can't lose Mamá; I've already lost my Papá. Be brave, be strong —those were my Papá's words. Mamá reaches for my hand, dragging me inside the house, and shoves me into a cabinet.

"Please, Mamá, hide, please."

I beg one last time before she says, "I don't have time, Liam. I love you. Stay and do not come out."

She closes the cabinet door as the familiar boots stomp into the house. The men's shouts echo through the walls, asking for me. Mamá's piercing screams slash through my heart, and my lungs tighten with each strangled breath until I pass out and darkness consumes me.

CHAPTER 1
LIAM

I jolt awake, angry that I fell asleep. I glance at my phone, cursing under my breath. It's two in the morning. Ten minutes have passed since I dozed off, yet it felt like time has dragged on for hours. I glance over to see the redhead still sound asleep. Lindsay or Linda—whatever her name is—passed out after I've given her multiple orgasms. Quickly, I slide my jeans and shirt on and take off before she wakes up. My number one rule is never to sleep with the same woman twice. Two times and they develop feelings and want more from you. Relationships are messy and too complicated for me.

Thirty minutes later, I pull into the driveway of my small two-bedroom home, which I scrimped and saved for months to purchase. I open the door, and my fifty-pound white boxer, Duke, runs to greet me.

"Hey, big guy." Stooping down, I ruffle his ears, and with his wet snout, he sniffs me and growls around my body. I chuckle knowingly. With Duke's keen sense of smell, he probably detects the lingering musk of sex on me.

"All right, I'll shower, Duke, and then bedtime, buddy. I have to be at work in five hours."

He barks and jumps on my bed. I turn the faucet on, and the beads of lukewarm water spray down, washing away any lingering remainders of a woman I don't care to remember. Turning off the water, I dry myself, then slip a pair of boxers on and crash the fuck out.

THE NEXT MORNING, the police station smells like it always does—sweat and stale coffee—and my head pounds from the previous night's activities. I pour myself some coffee and close my eyes for the first sip.

"Good morning."

I cringe as I open my eyes. "Not so loud, John. Good morning."

He chuckles. "How was the redhead last night? Saw you take off after you sucked all over her neck."

I shrug, leaning against the marble counter of the break room. "Good. No complaints. Only screams of pleasure."

He throws his head back in laughter. Last night we kicked it at Rocko's bar, played pool, and drank some beers with a couple of guys from work. He shakes his head as we walk to our patrol SUV.

"You plan on ever having a girlfriend...settling down, man? Don't you get tired of the bachelor life?" he asks.

I don't have to think twice about it. I answer him swiftly, rubbing my fingers along my stubbled chin. "Nah, relationships are messy. Too much drama. It isn't for me."

He sighs as if I'm missing out on being tied down to one woman. "Maybe you haven't found the right one."

He looks at me as if he's found the reason I'm still single, as if I'm searching for the right one. John and I met at the police academy. When we met, he was single. He was my wingman, but now he's a married man with a baby.

"I'm not looking for Mrs. Right," I proclaim as I start the engine.

"I wasn't either until I bumped into Beth and was a goner. It could happen, man, when you least expect it."

A call comes into the radio, a robbery at the liquor store. Fuck. This early? It's ten in the morning. "10-4," I say into the radio, turning on my light.

We rush to the liquor store. When we arrive, we jump out of our vehicle and find a young boy pinned against the wall by the store's owner. The child is trembling, and tears are streaming down his face.

"What's going on here?" I ask the bald man holding the boy.

"He was stealing a bottle under his shirt." The store owner grips the collar of the young boy's shirt and glares at him.

John shoves him away.

I drop to my knees so I am face-to-face with the boy, who appears to be about nine or ten years old.

"You drink?" I ask.

He shakes his head. "No," he whispers.

"Then who are you stealing this for? You realize this is a crime?"

He nods.

I wipe his tears with my thumb. My heart breaks for the kid. He's so young.

"My d-dad," he stutters.

Fucking bastard piece of shit father, the poor kid has.

"Where do you live?" I ask sternly.

"At the apartment next door."

"I'm going to take you back home, okay? I need to talk to

your dad. I never want to see you steal again. Do you understand me?"

He nods and wipes his tears. John escorts him to the SUV.

The old bald bastard owner runs up to me. "Are you taking him in? Kids like this start young. He needs to go to juvie."

I snap at the idiot, "He's ten, and his dad had him steal it. I'm going after the father." I leave the store, and we go to the apartments to find the asshole dad waiting outside for the kid. Stepping out, I slip on my aviator shades.

"Is there a problem, Officer? What did my kid do?" He fists his hand on his hips, and he reeks of liquor and cigarettes.

Motherfucker, I hate men like him. Men who take their children for granted, treat them like a burden, like scum on their shoes.

"He did nothing. It's what *you* did."

He blinks, attempting to appear innocent. "Don't know what you're talking about."

"Yeah, you do. You had your son steal a bottle of whiskey. Child services are on their way. Men like you don't deserve children. From the records we pulled up, this has happened numerous times." I take my handcuffs out and push him against the SUV.

After a long-ass fucking day, John and I make it back to the station at the end of our shift. Walking to my locker to collect my belongings down the corridor, I glance at the fallen officer's memorial. The photo of my father reads "Manuel (Manny) Rodriguez—Detective" with several medals surrounding it. I swallow the lump that forms every day when I see his photo.

The man I lost. The man my mother lost.

Under my breath, I say, "I will find them."

I STEP inside my mom's house, and the sound of the metal screen door clangs behind me. I find her in the kitchen, gently rolling out a dough sheet with a rolling pin while humming an old tune. She shapes the dough into a perfect circle. For years, my mom has mustered a smile, a laugh. The pain in her eyes never stops seething, though. I know the feeling too well. When she feels me near, her head lifts. And she smiles a genuine smile, her eyes sparkling with love.

"Hey, Mamá." I kiss her cheek.

"My Liam, how was work, mijo? Hopefully, nothing dangerous."

When I achieved my eighteenth birthday and graduated from high school, I immediately pursued an undergraduate degree in Criminal Justice. Three years later, at the age of twenty-one, I put myself into the police academy. I understand why my mother worries for me every day. It's a risky line of work.

"I started my morning off by arresting a man who had his son steal liquor for him. Social services picked him up. He had no family. Mom, it broke my heart. I hope he gets a good foster home." I sigh. My heart aches when I see cases like these. It has me thinking of little Rosa.

"Let's keep him in our prayers," she says as she flips a tortilla over the skillet.

"What's for dinner?" I usually come over for dinner and join her.

"I made your favorite pollo *chicken* and rice." She winks with a soft smile.

We eat in silence for the first five minutes. This is always how it's been. The empty chair next to us—she always glances at it. I clear my throat.

"Have you spoken to Rosa?" I ask as I scoop a mouthful of rice.

"This morning. She's doing good, finishing her last year in art school. She was thinking of returning to be an art teacher or opening her own art studio."

A grin creases her face with pride. When Rosaline was three years old, my aunt dropped her off at my mom's and never returned. She disposed of her like trash on the side of the road. My mother worked two jobs to support us. Rosaline is more of a little sister to me than a cousin. She brought light into our lives when we were in a dark place.

"I'm proud of her," I say.

She nods as she takes a sip of her drink. "I bumped into Dominic."

I lift my head and meet her wide smile. I chuckle and shake my head. "Oh, yeah? What did he tell you?"

"Well, he introduced me to his son. I'm so happy for him. His son looks just like him—adorable. He's so happy."

"He's whipped," I say, throwing my head back in laughter. I've known Dominic since we were seven years old, when I changed elementary schools. We became best friends. We always hung out at his house since my mom worked a lot. No woman has had Dominic by the balls like Mila. They were high school sweethearts. He's been pussy-whipped since the day he met her. I'm glad; she's good for him.

My mother narrows her eyes and glares at me. "I'm telling you, Liam, one of these days, a woman will put you in your place. *You'll* be whipped." There's a teasing glint in her eyes. She gives me an enthusiastic smile. "It's true, sweetheart. Put your money where your mouth is." Then she gasps dramatically. "I've *never* seen you with a woman." Her eyes widen in thought.

"Trust me, I like women. Just because you haven't seen me with one attached to my hip doesn't mean I'm not into them.

Mamà, I'm not interested in having a family and such. I like the single life."

She huffs, clearly frustrated. "Love is a special thing to experience, Liam. Never hold back from falling in love."

I know she's thinking of my dad when she hums with a smile. Love is not something I'm looking for. I'm content with my life and my career. My goal is to become a detective, like my father. I don't need the added weight of a relationship on my shoulders. I'm not a player, but I am a man with needs. I respect women. A powerful, devoted mother brought me up. I'm just not relationship material.

"I better get home, Mamá. I need to check on Duke and hit the gym." I kiss her cheek as she hands me an empty butter container filled with leftovers. "Thank you for dinner. See you tomorrow."

"Take care of yourself, Liam." My mom waves as I slip into my Camaro.

ONCE I GET HOME, I change into my gym shorts and tank top then release Duke to the backyard to take a dump, then I make my way to the gym.

I'm greeted by Dom lifting weights and watching me from the mirror as I walk in.

"What are you doing here?" I ask. He hasn't been coming to the gym as much, ever since he and Mila revived their relationship.

"I don't want to get a dad bod."

"What!" I chuckle.

"A gut, you know. It happens to dads, is what I heard."

"You just found out you were a dad a couple of months ago."

Dominic found out about his five-year-old son Dante when he and Mila found each other again. Mila disappeared from his life five years ago. His mother was to blame for the years they lost together.

"I know, but the way Mila looks at me like she wants to rip my clothes off...I need to stay in shape." He smirks, his ego bursting from his chest.

"I know the feeling," I say as a couple of women stand around us, practically begging for our attention.

I stand behind him to give him a spot.

"Sophie and Ryder broke up," he says, eyeing me with a stupid grin. I met Sophie, Mila's best friend, at Mila's studio months ago. "Well, I don't think they were technically together, but just seeing each other." He shrugs.

Sophie's gorgeous, but I wouldn't sleep with her. She's part of Mila's life, and unlike the other women I've been with, I would have to see her again because Dom is like a brother to me. If I had to see her after sleeping with her, we'd have a connection. I'm not interested in going that route. Once, I invited Sophie for a drink—a friendly drink. Maybe in that moment, my mind drifted to other possibilities, but the good thing is she refused me. She's the only woman to ever deny me. It bruised my ego. I don't know what the hell I was thinking about inviting her for a drink.

"You know I'm not looking for a relationship, bro. That has never been my thing."

He raises his hands up. "All right, I just thought I'd let you know. Since you were eye-fucking her at Dante's party."

I roll my eyes. "I was not."

He snorts. "Tell yourself that."

I do a couple of sets of bent-over rows and bench presses. A sheen of sweat trickles down my spine. My eyes drift to Dom, and I am reminded of the agony we have both lived with since learning that Dominic's mother was the one who started a fire at Mila's home seven years ago. I'm still in shock. I practically lived in their home. When my mom worked long hours, I would stay at their place or with my grandmother. Rachel, Dominic's mother, treated me and Rosa like part of her family.

"Have you told Mila yet?" I ask. I know he's been avoiding telling Mila the truth. He's terrified of what will happen. I understand where he's coming from.

"No, not yet." His shoulders deflate as he takes a heavy breath.

We continue our workout just as Dominic's brothers, Santiago and Mark, arrive. Working out has always been my way of releasing stress and tension. But it's not working right now. I wish fucking Dominic hadn't mentioned Sophie. Her rejection still stings, and no amount of bench presses will let me forget the sound of her voice when she told me no.

CHAPTER 2
SOPHIE

My screen flashes twenty missed calls and a shitload of text messages. I sigh as I get dressed for my date, splashing some color on my face and curling my long blonde hair. I honestly don't know what the hell I'm doing. This is not me. I've never gone on dates through a dating site. I used to be a relationship kind of gal.

Until Eric. I gave him three years of my life, and he threw it away. My faith in men was destroyed. They take what they want and then leave you alone or betray your trust. He left me high and dry, and then he dropped me like rubbish on the side of the road and fucked my friend.

After that, I decided no more relationships. I downloaded all these dating apps, figuring, why not? Meet new people, date casually, just get to know another person without the pressure of a relationship. It would be fun, right?

Wrong. Last week's date was a failure. He canceled an hour before we were supposed to meet. Before him, I dated a guy for two months. I wouldn't call what Ryder and I were doing dating, though. We were definitely not *an item*. He was sweet, kind, and sexy, but he wanted serious, and that's not what I wanted. I couldn't see myself marrying him or going farther.

I reach for my keys from the counter when my adorable nephew Dante, startles me.

"Where are you going, auntie?" Drops of sweat glisten on his face. He's dressed up in his Spider-Man costume. He's an avid admirer of Spider-Man, and he has memorized all the lines from the first three movies. So, have I. Unfortunately.

"Out with a friend," I say as Mila, my best friend and room-mate, enters the room. Dante makes his way back to the living room.

"Who's the guy?" she asks.

I press my lips together. She's not keen on me going out with strangers I've met on dating sites. She watches too much *Dateline*. And, well, she knows I'm not the type to go on dating sites. Until now, of course.

"Kirk."

Her forehead creases. "Is he cute?"

"Y-yeah," I say, with little enthusiasm.

"You don't sound too excited. Are you nervous?"

I sigh. "I don't know what I'm doing, Mila. I feel like I can't find my place. Eric really fucked me up."

She glowers and shakes her head as she grabs a water bottle from the fridge.

"I hate Eric. He was always such an asshole," she murmurs as she sips. "You and Eric dated for a little over three years. It's normal you're still hurting even though you broke up months ago. You'll get there. He never deserved you, Sophie."

"I know, and I'm over him."

She narrows her green eyes at me, wanting to call me out on my bluff. Instead, she says, "Have a great time with Kermit."

I shake my head, chuckling.

I park my car at Eddie's Seafood and Steakhouse, and my phone pings again. *Eric.* I put the phone on silent. Asshole has some nerve calling me. Opening the speed dating app, I glance at Kirk's profile once more before getting out of the car. I exhale, long and slow, and my breath fogs the cold air.

My eyes widen when I spot Kirk. He looks up and smiles widely. Kirk seems utterly different from the photo he posted on his profile. He looks older. Maybe mid-thirties. I'm positive I read he was in his twenties. He must have used a picture from when he was younger. He has sandy brown hair and bags under his eyes, and he is a little too polished for my liking. And he's wearing penny loafers.

"Hi, Sophie, nice to meet you. God, you look beautiful. More so in person." He licks his lips and yanks me into a hug.

The smell of Brut cologne stings my nose. I push from his hold, brushing my fingers under my nose, getting a whiff of my coconut lotion. The cloying scent of Brut wafts around us.

"Hey, Kirk. Nice to meet you. Should we go inside?"

He guides me in as the host seats us. God, he smells like my granddad—a major turn-off. My granddad practically *bathes* in Brut. My grandma would say he smells manly. Sorry, Grandma, but Brut smells like skunk pee.

"You look different, Kirk. Nothing like your photo," I say, honestly, as he pulls out a chair for me.

He picks up the menu and flips through it. "How about an appetizer?" He's nonchalantly ignoring my statement.

I press my lips together and hold my breath as long as I can. His cologne is making my eyes water and my throat burn. I exhale. "Sure. Sounds good."

The waitress takes our drink order, then Kirk says, "So, tell me, Sophie, what do you do for a living?" He scoots his chair closer to me.

Oh, God, no.

"My best friend Mila and I own a photography studio," I respond, my smile stretched with pride. The waitress returns with our drinks. Thank God. I reach for mine and take a gulp. My throat stings like a mother-fucker. "What do you do?"

"I work from home. I'm in marketing." His gaze bores into mine, and he frowns. "Is everything okay? Your beautiful eyes are glassy."

"Oh, yeah, allergy season," I lie. It's your damn cologne, you idiot. *Be nice, Sophie.* "I'll be right back—heading to the lady's room."

Once I'm in a stall, I dial Mila.

"Hello, how's it going with Kermit?" Mila's cheerful voice beams through the phone.

"I need help. I want to leave. This isn't very pleasant. He smells like Grandpa and wears penny loafers. No muscle in his body. My nose stings, my throat burns."

She's giggling.

"Stop laughing," I groan.

"I can't help it. What's he smell like?"

"Brut. It isn't very pleasant, and he looks older than the photo he posted. He might be looking for a baby mama. I need to leave. What do I do?"

I keep clearing my throat. I sound like a cat coughing up a hairball. She laughs even harder—that little witch.

"All right. I'll call you in five minutes. Make yourself panic, like it's urgent." She's breathing heavily from her belly laugh. "What happened to my ballsy BFF? What happened to Ms. Straightforward, Ms. New Yorker, who doesn't take shit from no one?"

"Well, biatch, she's still in here. I just don't want to be a complete bitch to the guy. Maybe he just likes cheap cologne." I groan in frustration.

The old Sophie would not dare to do shit like this, period, like speed date, or hide in a bathroom. But here I am on a date and ready to bail.

"Arggh, just call me, will ya? Don't take too long, or I'll turn blue from holding my breath."

"Fine. You're so dramatic."

I huff. "Am not." I stick my tongue out at the phone, then end the call and return to the table. Even from a distance, I can tell he's scooted my chair closer to his. Fuuuuuuuck.

Kirk beams as I take my too-close seat. "You're beautiful. How about after dinner, we head back to my place?" He hums, the whiff of his cologne collapsing my lungs.

My phone rings just in time, and I answer it like it's a miracle. "Hello, oh God, really? Okay. I'll be right there," I shout and try to look frantic by widening my eyes, then I hang up the line.

"Is everything okay?" Kirk says, worried—poor guy.

"My friend needs a ride to the hospital. Got to go." I grab my purse. "I'm so sorry, Kirk."

"No worries. Rain check?"

I muster a smile, shake my head, and run out the door. I make it back to my townhouse in record time, so damn relieved.

Then my phone pings. Eric. I read the message.

Eric: *Please, baby, I'm sorry.*

I'm so close to texting back and saying, "Fuck off," but I don't. I won't give him the satisfaction of a response. He can't think I give a damn about him. I'm not the ball-busting New Yorker I used to be.

I THROW my keys on the kitchen island, then shove a slice of pizza in my mouth. Mila and her boyfriend Dominic walk down the stairs. He kisses her cheek and whispers in her ear. She blushes. Makes my heart burst to see her happy. For years, she was a shell of herself. She loved him fiercely. I never understood why she couldn't move on within those five years. I begged her. I wanted to see my best friend happy. She had endured so much pain and lost so much in her life. My family loves Mila and Dante. They became part of our own instantly. Now I understand the love they have for one another. She looks at him as if he's her world, and he looks at her like she hung the moon. I'm in awe they found their way back to one another after Dominic's mother lied and kept them apart for years.

I dated Eric for a long time. He was my first boyfriend and the first boy I gave myself to. I loved him, or so I thought. I still don't know. The entire scene is still fresh in my head. I walked in on Eric in his apartment, fucking a friend I'd known since elementary school. Their groans and moans still echo in my head.

"Hey, you're back." Mila frowns.

I hadn't realized I was staring at my pizza, reliving the awful memory. "Yup. Thanks, by the way. You saved my life."

She chuckles.

"Good night, Angel," Dominic says to Mila as he kisses her and waves bye to me. He steps out, and her shoulders drop.

"What's wrong?" I ask.

She shakes it off. "Nothing, I'm just tired. I'd better get to bed. We have a booked day tomorrow." She wraps me in a hug and makes her way upstairs.

I snag another slice of pizza and retreat to my bedroom. Slipping into the shower, I wash the stench of Brut off my skin and out of my hair. Once I'm freshly showered, I jump into bed and snuggle into the blankets. I have fond memories of New

York, but I cherish my fresh start in California. Moving here with Mila was the right choice. Had I stayed with Eric, I'm sure he wouldn't have wanted to relocate with me. It was always his way or the highway. His betrayal really hurt. I pick up my phone when it vibrates, and my heart warms up when I read the text from Alex.

Alex: *Hey, you. How are you doing? I miss you guys like crazy.*

Me: *Doing good, big brother. I miss you too. How are you and Liz doing? How's London?*

My one and only brother moved with his wife to London a year ago. He's seven years older than me. They moved to London without even thinking twice. It was a ballsy move to pick up and go like that. I admire him for it.

Alex: *London is great. Come visit, little sister, and bring Mila and little rugrat.*

Me: *I will soon, promise.*

Alex: *I'll call you tomorrow. I'm sure it's late there. Love you, sis.*

Me: *Night. Love you both.*

After shutting down my phone, I doze off. Tomorrow is a new day. Maybe my next date will turn out better.

CHAPTER 3
LIAM

I raise the hood of my father's '65 GMC step side pickup, a truck that has been idle for many years. Every time I open the hood of the truck, I'm reminded of him. It was his truck, and now it's the only memento I have of him. When Friday evenings rolled around, he would take my mom and me out for a joyride and then stop for some ice cream.

Not a day passes without me thinking of him. His jovial laugh filled any room he was in, and Mom's face lit up when he was near. I wish more than anything I could still make her smile, make her happy. Sometimes, I think it should have been me who was taken away that night.

"Papá, Mamá asked if you want to go out for ice cream."

Papá is under the hood of his truck. He glances around the hood to look at me. I giggle, looking at my papá. He has grease all over his face. My papá always smiles wide when he sees me.

"Liam, my ninja, tell Mamá we'll go for ice cream as soon as I'm done changing the oil in the truck. Did Mamá tell you we have some special news to tell you, Liam?"

I nod while pulling my ninja turtle out of my pocket. "Yes, Papá. Mamá said she has special news to tell me. Papá, can we stop at the store? I want to get a ninja turtle. I don't have Leonardo?"

"Sure, tell your mamá I'm done. I'm going to wash up, and we can go."

I jump up and down, excited to hear the good news Mamá wants to tell me and get my ninja turtle.

Minutes later we get to the ice cream shop, and I order a double chocolate cone. It's a beautiful night. The stars are out and there's a light breeze in the air. We make our way to a bench. Papá has his arms around Mamá. He's always staring at her with a smile, kissing her all the time. Yuck.

"Sit down, mi bella," Papá tells Mamá. He always calls her his beautiful. I lick my ice cream, savoring the dark chocolate.

"Liam, Papá and I have some special news. Guess what? You're going to be a big brother."

SHAKING OFF THE MEMORIES, I crank the engine of my GMC. It gives a satisfying roar as it revs to life. I wait a few moments, and then I hear a *click, click* sound as the engine sputters and dies.

Fuck.

For the past few months, I've been working getting this baby running and on restoring it to its former glory. With work being hectic, I'll have to work on it in what little free time I have. Duke barks when he spots Santiago driving up. He gets out of his truck and strolls toward us.

"Hey, asshole, what are you up to?" Santiago teases, a smirk on his smug face.

"Hey, shithead."

He chuckles and smacks me on the back then stands in front of the truck, hands tucked into his pockets. His eyes light up as he takes in the beauty of the pickup. Santiago is the master mechanic we all call when we have car trouble. "Is it still turning off when you crank it?" He dips his head into the hood of the truck.

"Yeah, I crank it, and it purrs for a second then dies off."

He hums. "It looks like the carburetor flooded. Do you want to take it to the shop? I'll check it out for you, and I'll work on it." Santiago owns his own automotive shop. His business has boomed in the last year since he opened. He's a master at fixing anything.

"Nah, don't worry about it. You have plenty of work on your hands. I kinda want to restore it myself. I want to make my father proud, knowing I fixed it myself."

His lips twitch downward.

"Liam, brother, he is proud of you. You're a police officer with a degree in criminal justice. You applied for the detective position. I'm positive you'll get it."

"Thanks, man," I say, swallowing hard.

He nods and leans into the truck. Santiago is the big brother I never had. He's always looked out for Dominic, Mark, and me. Even Rosa, when she was with us—she hung on to him like a monkey.

His head drops like he's lost in thought. He rakes his hands through his hair when he mutters, "Dominic told me." His shoulders drop with a sigh.

I toss the wrench on the floor, getting up from under the truck. I can't imagine what they're going through—coming to find out their mother is not who they thought she was. In some ways, I can understand only because I grew up in their home.

"I'm sorry. I can't wrap my head around it myself. I was at

your house all the damn time. Never would I have thought your mom could commit a crime like that."

"I know my mom was never the nicest person. She had an evil side, but never to the extreme of wanting to kill Mila's father. How do I sleep knowing the woman who tucked us in at night and fed us was capable of such a gruesome act? I don't even know if she really loved us, come to think of it. She used Dominic's disease to control him. She used me in so many ways." He chokes on the last words. "Your mom looks at you with love, a twinkle in her eyes, Liam. My mom looked at us with annoyance. We were only ever bodies to control to her." He inhales and exhales.

My eyebrows furrow. The day Detective Johnson sent me to Mila's old neighborhood to get information about the deadly fire that killed her father, I was ready for justice to put them in jail. All because I love Mila like a sister, like a best friend. She deserved it to have that kind of closure. I know the feeling of losing a parent all too well. I felt sympathy for her. At least I had my mother, but Mila lost both her parents. Never would I have thought Rachel was the culprit—the lady who let us kick it at her house twenty-four seven.

"I'm sorry, man," I say because what can I say? I'm lost for words.

His phone pings, and he glances at the screen. "I'd better go. It's Mark. He's moving in with me. I'm going to help him move his stuff."

I pat him on the shoulder. "See you, bro. Let me know if you need anything?"

He walks back to his truck, and I get back to working on the GMC.

I'm about to walk into the meeting room of the station when the chief pulls me aside. "Rodriguez," he calls out. Chief Moreno has been here for many years and was friends with my father. His bushy gray caterpillar brows crinkle.

"Good morning, Chief," I greet him with a nod.

He points to his office, and I follow his gesture. The office door clicks as it closes behind us, and he collects a manila folder off the desk. His solemn demeanor makes me uneasy. I roll my heels back and forth.

"As you know," he says, "the crime rate in the city has recently escalated. But we are dealing with something different. Drug trafficking has increased along with the number of murders and kidnappings. The Serpents have been quiet for years, since the night we lost your father. We thought they'd moved their territory, gone into hiding, knowing the penalty for killing an officer—a detective at that."

My breath hitches. For years I've wondered where the motherfuckers were. I needed to avenge my father's death. He scratches his goatee and continues.

"We spotted them. Our investigation team, back in the city. Some of our agents in the city have seen them lately—big guys with serpent tattoos all over 'em. They're working with the Tijuana cartel. Pablo's son Marko is the leader of the gang—Los Serpientes—now." He spits the name out in an emotionless voice.

Fury fills me. I recall the name Pablo with clarity.

"I can't imagine what you went through as a child. Your father was a great man and a hell of a good detective. He would have been a good DEA agent. It's only right that I give you this case. I know you're capable of it, and you're just as good as your father. You'll be working with the DEA. You have been selected to be on the task force to take on this mission."

My eyes burn. Pride fills my chest. I've been waiting all my life for this moment to take them all down.

"Thank you, sir. It means a lot to be part of the task force and to get to work with the DEA. I'll do everything in my power to bring them all down."

He nods. "I know you will." He pats me on the back.

"Oh, and by the way, you're partnering up with a rookie today, Ashley. She's in her last weeks of training."

"You got it, sir." Stepping out of his office, I head to grab a cup of coffee before we head out on patrol. I can't fucking believe I'll be part of the task force. *Fuck.* I've been waiting for this moment my whole life.

Ashley's fingers brush their way up and down my back to my shoulders. "Hey, Liam, been a while. How have you been?"

I look over my shoulder as I stir cream and sugar into my coffee. "Hey, Ashley. Nice to see you. Ready for a long day?"

Her chocolate eyes twinkle as she scans my profile. She's been gunning for me since I first met her.

"Ready to spend the day with you," she purrs.

Taking a sip of my steaming coffee, I wave her out the door.

The conversation from this morning with the chief still lingers in my head. For years, my mom would call and check on progress in my father's case. But the noise of the Serpents had silenced. After decades of searching for them, I'm honored the chief asked me to be a part of the mission. When I do find them, I will make them pay for how they took out my father and took, so much from our lives. My mother struggled day in and day out to provide for us. I'm going to chase Pablo down, just like he chased me down the night my life changed forever.

"Hey, so, what do you think?"

I haven't heard a word Ashley's said. I zoned out. "Sorry, what did you say?"

"Are you going to the gala?" She flutters her eyelashes. She has no clue I'm the one who organizes the gala. I started helping years ago in college with my classmates.

"Yeah, I'll be there." I turn left on a gravel road and park the car then point the radar at speeding vehicles.

"I was thinking we could go together." Her brown eyes sparkle with hope.

Ashley is a beautiful woman, with her doe eyes and mocha-colored skin. She looks hot in her uniform. But I don't mix business with pleasure. She appears to be the type who's looking for a serious relationship.

"I'm not sure it would be a good idea. I never take a date to the gala," I say, earnestly.

She nods and looks out the window. "I get it. Maybe some other time."

After a couple of hours and a handful of speeding tickets, I'm hungry. For the second half of our shift, we have a drug bust planned, and I'm crossing my fingers a Serpent will be involved. I want to interrogate the fuckers until I get the whereabouts of Pablo. I park the SUV at Go Burger, and Ashley and I make our way in. The place is pretty busy. We sit close to a window that lets the beaming sun in.

My head jolts up when I hear the voice that makes my dick twitch. I scan the room, looking for the face that goes with the familiar New York-accented voice. When I meet her ocean blues, they're already on me. Damn, she's beautiful—a goddamned bombshell. She's wearing a tight black skirt that hugs all her curves. Her blouse shows just enough of her breasts, and my mouth waters. When my eyes travel back to her red lips, all I can think about is how they would look wrapped around my cock. She licks her lips.

Fuck me.

When I met Sophie Summers at the studio three months ago, my heart hammered against my chest. It felt like a thousand grenades exploded, and I had no fucking idea what that was about. Her beauty held me hostage then and hasn't let go since. I've come across plenty of beautiful women, and I've never reacted like this. I tried to shrug it off, but—fuck—shit had to go deeper when I saw her at Dante's birthday party two weeks ago. When Santiago was fucking with me, leaning to kiss her...he knew how to strike a nerve, and he was testing to see how I'd react. Like a complete idiot, that's how. She's like a damn magnet, a fishing line pulling me in for some goddamned reason. I asked her out for a drink.

Fuck me.

I've never asked a woman out for a drink. She rejected me, so I shut it down real quick. The woman's a damn grenade.

I notice the asshole sitting next to her. He's staring at her like he wants to fuck her. Which has my blood boiling. It has no business boiling in the first place. It needs to simmer the fuck down. Why do I care? Dominic said she broke it off with Rake, or whatever his name was.

Ashley trails her fingernails along my forearm as I lean them on the table. "Who's the girl?"

I look away from her. "Huh?"

She motions at Sophie.

Fuck, she's nosy. "A friend of a friend."

The waitress comes and takes our order just in time. Ashley was acting jealous, like we're a thing.

"Why did you decide to become an officer?" Ashley asks, sucking on the straw of her iced tea. The question makes her jealousy noticeable, like she wants my attention solely on her and not on Sophie.

"Since I was a kid, I always wanted to become an officer," I say flatly.

I'm not the type to talk about my personal life with anyone, especially a woman who wants more than friendship. Especially when she's scrutinizing me seductively. I return my attention to the blonde who has my blood pumping recklessly. My fingers tighten around my glass as the guy she is with moves closer to her. Red-hot anger burns inside me, and I shake with rage I never knew existed. I have to control myself and shut it down.

CHAPTER 4
SOPHIE

It's been a couple of days since my last date, with the brut guy. He should have scared me off casual dating for good, but I convinced myself to give it another shot. Maybe Kirk just wasn't my type. When I step out of my red Mustang and spot Milo, tonight's date, I'm glad I didn't give up. He leans against his white Kia, a long brown trench coat wrapping around his tall frame. His smooth olive skin stretches over high cheekbones when he grins—and he's cute. He waves at me.

"I'm rooting for you, Milo," I say under my breath.

He's texted me a couple of times. He's from Chicago, and he moved to California to help his grandma, who recently had knee surgery. He seems sweet. I traipse toward him, and the bitterly cold breeze makes me shiver. The aroma of burgers fills the air. My stomach grumbles. I asked him to meet me here at Go Burger, one of my favorite restaurants—a classic burger joint.

"Hey, beautiful." His chocolate eyes take in my appearance. With a lick of his lips, he leans over to kiss my cheek.

The smell hits me. *Mothballs.* Fucking mothballs.

"Hi, Milo. Nice to finally meet you," I say, massaging my temples.

Why do I get these stinky guys? I'm positive it's his coat. He smells like my grandmother's old cedar chest. My grandma would always put mothballs in her cedar chest. The smell's not great, but it isn't as strong as Brut, so I can handle it.

"Shall we go inside? I'm starving." Without hesitation, he places the palm of his hand on the small of my back and guides me in. He's so close I can feel his hot breath fan my neck.

He pulls a chair out for me to sit. He carefully slips out of his coat and folds it over the back of his chair. I stand to free myself from my heavy winter coat, but he beats me to it as his hands quickly find the zipper beneath my chin and helps to glide it down. I give him points for being a gentleman.

The waitress comes and takes our order.

"I'll have the bacon classic and an extra side of pickles, please," I say.

She nods and looks at Milo then takes his order.

I throw my head back in laughter when Milo tells me he watched a marathon of *The Golden Girls* with his grandmother. Don't get me wrong, I love *The Golden Girls,* and I love Betty White. I laugh so hard because Milo is not a fan of *The Golden Girls*, and I can imagine him bored for hour after hour of Golden Girl fun.

I stop laughing when a hard, muscular body passes right by me. The masculine scent of his body wash sends a tingle right to my core.

Holy guacamole.

He carries himself with a commanding air of self-confidence. His powerful shoulders strain the seams of his polo shirt. He's hot in his uniform, snug in all the right places. His tan skin is flawless, and his chiseled jaw, peppered with stubble, has me envisioning licking him all over.

Damn. I wet my lips. Those gorgeous gunmetal eyes are different. I've never met a man with such beautiful eyes, and with the sun shining right past him through the window, I can see the small brown specks in them. Yeah, I'm very observant when it comes to Liam Rodriguez. He's built, and I mean built. I'm enjoying the way he's watching me, like he's in a trance. Sparks of jealousy hit when the woman next to him trails her fingernails down his arm.

What the hell. Does he date his coworkers? I shake my head. Why am I feeling jealous when we've barely exchanged words and I've never touched him? We made small talk at Dante's party, and that's all. Now that I think about it, I didn't feel this jealousy when I caught Eric. It hurt me, of course. But this is ridiculous. I ignore the tingling and return my attention to Milo, who is watching me with a smile. He is a cutie. Maybe I'll offer to wash his coat.

"Tell me about yourself, Sophie."

I open my mouth to answer when he interrupts.

"I'm opening my own comic store. Oh, I'm sorry, I asked you a question and interrupted you."

Uh, yes, you did. "No, that's fine. Wow, amazing. Congratulations. My friend and I opened our photography studio a couple of months ago, and business is great—"

"I came to take care of my grandmother and ended up opening a store with the comic books I found in her garage." Every time I try to get a word in, he interrupts.

The waitress hands us our food, along with my side of pickles.

I can't help it. I keep glancing at Liam, and I catch him staring at me. He doesn't acknowledge that we know each other, and it's fine because we really don't. I turn my attention back to my mothball date. I hear the desperate officer girl laughing so hard. What the hell is he telling her to make her laugh? I realize I'm strangling my burger. I will not look like a desperate thirstbucket. And I will not show signs of jealousy.

I smile at Milo. Pretending I'm interested in his comics. "Wow, that's amazing. My nephew is an obsessed Spider-Man fan."

He reaches for my hands and kisses my knuckles, each one. Milo's breath hitches as his eyes go hooded. "You're beautiful, Sophie. I'm enjoying your company." He keeps kissing my knuckles, then he intertwines his slender fingers with mine.

When I feel a tap on my shoulder, I turn. He's so tall and so close, the bulge of his dick is at eye level. Slowly, I look up at his narrow waist then his broad, wide shoulders and muscular forearms. He's massive. His eyes look murderous.

"Hey—" I squeak. Yes, I squeak like a mouse. I've never squeaked before.

Pathetic, Sophie.

"Is everything okay, officer?" Milo asks. He gulps frantically.

Liam doesn't glance at him. His eyes are still on mine. "I need to speak to Ms. Summers...outside," he says in a clipped husky tone.

I stand up. Maybe this is about the break-in we had a few weeks ago at the studio. He places his hand on the small of my back, sending tingles down my spine. No, a massive electric shock. I think I just squirted in my panties. He guides us outside. The chill of the cold air nips at my skin, causing goosebumps. I'm pretty sure it's actually the Greek god standing next to me that's brought them on rather than the crisp air. Liam stands close to the brick wall, his stance powerful and inviting. His broad shoulders beg to be touched, and I have to consciously stop myself from resisting the urge. His free hand slowly drifts up to stroke his stubbly jawline.

What would it feel like if it brushed across my cheek?

Liam's lips are full and inviting, yet the intensity in his gaze roots me to my spot. He seems to possess an invisible force that holds me captive, and I have to remind myself I will not be one of those women who succumbs to his charm.

But holy mother of hotness. The power that radiates through him is alluring.

"What can I do for you, Officer? Is this about the break-in?" My words come out as a demand. My lips pucker in a sneer. I can feel the heat rising in my cheeks, and I almost allow my eyes to flutter involuntarily, but instead, I harden my stare, meeting his gaze with a challenge. The usually hidden flecks of brown in his steel-gray eyes appear as he sizes me up.

"No," he growls.

A single word is enough to make me shiver, but I'm determined not to show it. Hell, I can be intimidating too. I take a step forward and give him the coldest glare I can muster, resting one fist on my hip.

"Then what can I do for you? You interrupted my lunch." My heart thuds against my ribcage, and my hands tremble, sweat dripping from my palms like raindrops. When my phone slips from its grasp, his reflexes are quicker than mine, and he scoops it up, pressing buttons without warning.

"Hey! What are you doing?" I hiss through gritted teeth.

"Getting your number just in case I need to reach you if we need any more info on the break-in."

His phone vibrates in his pocket, and without breaking our gaze, he slides it out and checks something on the screen. His pink tongue swipes at his lips. Oh, how would that tongue feel dipped into my mouth? I clear my throat. It's getting a little too dry...

He continues looking at my phone. I reach to grab it, but he looks right at me with a pissed off glare. "Speed Date... Sophie...really?"

What the *actual* fuck. He's getting all up in my business like he's my lover and I'm cheating on him.

I grab the phone. "It's not any of your business, Liam!" My skin goes hot with embarrassment.

"It's dangerous, and you don't even know Milo."

The audacity of this man, to make it his business to click on the dating app and scan Milo's profile.

I make fists with my hands. "Well, Officer Rodriguez, that's what I was doing—getting to know him."

His brows furrow. He exhales. "Not anymore." His voice is full of haughty disdain.

My eyes widen. He has some balls. And they're probably quite large. *Oh, God, stop it, Sophie.*

"It's dangerous," he says again.

I feel the cold November air brushing past us, and my nipples tighten in response. I cross my arms to hug the warmth back into my body, but his gunmetal eyes are already roving over my chest, and his smirk tells me he noticed.

"Look, Officer," I say, tearing my gaze away from him and gesturing to the wall behind him, "you're telling me it's dangerous for me to meet up with a complete stranger but potentially less dangerous for you to take a strange woman home for the night? I'd say something about sexually trans-mitted infections, but it looks like you already know the risk quite well."

Oh, God, and how do I know Liam is a one-night stander? Because Mila told me, of course.

His smirk widens as he lets out a throaty chuckle, and his husky voice drops to a lower register. "Concerned about my sex life?"

My heart quickens at the way he drags out the *sss* of sex, and my eyes snap back up to his. His long eyelashes flutter slightly against his cheeks as he stares back at me with a knowing glint in his gaze. He hasn't moved from against the wall yet. His palms still press flat against the brick behind him. I want nothing more than to step closer, bury myself in the warmth of his neck, and breathe in his scent.

"Not at all. It seems you're concerned about *my* dating life."

He shrugs. "Doing my job, grenade. I am an officer."

Grenade?

Whatever, my ass. He's doing his job? It sounds more like he's jealous—*Don't be ridiculous, Sophie*—and the man is a sex God. Why would he be jealous of me? He hardly knows me.

"Liam, are you ready to go?" Officer Desperate asks, bringing me back to reality.

"I'll be right there, Ashley. Just hold tight in the SUV." His voice is soft and gentle. The scent of him brings warmth and comfort.

He leans in to close the gap between us, his face close enough I can feel the warmth of his breath on my skin. The aroma of ivory and a hint of spice coming off him is mesmerizing, and I have to remind myself to stay focused despite my heightened senses.

"I'll grab your coat." His voice is smooth as velvet.

I fist my hands on my hips and raise my brows. "I can get my own coat. I don't need your help." I'm determined to stand my ground. His offer is sweet, but I'll be damned if I allow him to think he can boss me around. I puff out my chest and hold my head high, hoping he will get the message. "Besides, I'm not leaving. I'm finishing my date." A slight smirk tugs at the corner of my lips as I spin on my heels.

He grabs my arm gently. "That's not happening, grenade. He's getting in his car, and I wouldn't have let you either way." He points to Milo, who really is leaving the date without saying a word. Well, that's not embarrassing.

I huff and my breath condenses in a cold cloud between us. "You're to blame for pulling me away for no reason." Not that I care. Milo smelled like mothballs and only talked about himself.

Liam licks his lips, surveying me with lust in his eyes. "If he were man enough, he would have come looking for you." He turns on his heels and walks into the restaurant.

My gaze goes straight to his buns of steel, and I swallow hard. *Damn.*

He returns with my coat and slips it on for me, taking me by surprise.

"Thank you," I whisper.

The cold has chafed Liam's cheeks, and the tip of his nose is pink. He takes a heavy breath. Shoving his hands in his pockets, he looks at me, puzzled.

"Stay away from dating strangers," he says flatly.

I massage my temples. I swear, this man is going to give me high blood pressure. "The next date I have, I'll make sure to let you know so you can do a background check. Have a good day, Officer." I walk to my car with a smile. I'm pretty sure I heard him growl. For some reason, it irks him I'm going on dates, which I like.

As I ARRANGE the props and equipment I need for a family photo shoot, my thoughts drift to the attractive police officer with muscles bulging out of his uniform.

My stomach grumbles. Milo and I didn't finish our lunch because of Casanova. Liam could have at least gotten me a take-out box or even brought me my side of pickles. I grab a granola bar from my desk and pop it into my mouth.

My mind wanders to Liam and how his eyelashes fluttered,

how his icy breath brushed against me. I felt something inside my chest I've never felt before, not even with Eric. Did I react that way because of his visible jealousy? Or was it his chiseled, clenched jaw and his eyes dancing with lust?

He reacted so weirdly. Why does he care who I date? Of course, he said it was his duty as an officer of the law, but does he go around pulling all women on dating apps away from their dates? Of course not. He simply enjoys pestering me in the hottest way possible. I met Liam months ago at the studio. We stared at each other for a hot second before I turned and walked off to grab lunch for Mila and me.

My phone buzzes—it's Eric. He's been calling and texting me for months, and I've not answered a single one. Until today.

"Eric, stop calling and texting me," I say sternly.

"Sophie, please let me explain."

"You don't need to explain. I caught up quickly when I found you in bed with her." *Fucking asshole.* I hang up the line. It rings again, and I silence it.

The door chimes. Mila walks in with a cage full of baby chicks.

"Don't tell me we are going to have a baby chick in our apartment. Are these Dante's new pets?" I ask, wide-eyed. Dante has been asking for a pet pretty much nonstop lately.

She giggles. "No, I borrowed them from a feed store. I needed them for a photo shoot. A client wants to do a farm setting with her toddler. I think it's adorable."

I agree. It *is* adorable. My best friend smiles sweetly. My phone vibrates. Thankfully, it's not Eric. I haven't spoken to Mila about Eric's phone calls. She's had plenty of drama going on in her life since Dominic returned. It's my mom, and I smile at the silly photo I have of her.

"Hey, Mom, how are you doing?"

"Oh, my sweet pea. I miss you so much. Tell me, how's

California life treating you? You lucky girl. You don't have to deal with the snow in San Diego." Mom's voice is soft over the phone, like a soothing blanket warming me up.

"Is that my sweet pea?" Dad shouts from the background.

A smile stretches across my face. My dad always spoils me. He would let my mom do the scolding.

"Doing great. I love it out here. Business is going great."

"That's great, honey. We have you on speaker."

"Hi, Dad."

"Hi, honey."

"Ahh, Jerry, help me!" I hear my mom scream.

Then I hear her panting like she's running from something.

"What's going on, Mom?" I ask.

"The geese are after me!" she shouts breathlessly.

Geese? What the hell? "Are you at the park?" She has to be. We have no geese at our place in the city.

"Clair, stop screaming; they're just hungry," my father shouts as the door slams shut in the background.

"Oh, lord, sorry, honey. That was a close one."

"What is going on out there?"

"Remember the farm we were flipping? We loved it so much that we bought it and sold our house. And it came with animals."

My eyes expand. I've got the speaker on, and I look across at Mila, who is laughing so hard she's choking. My father is a contractor who flips houses, and my mother is a real estate agent. They function as a tag team. They've spent their entire lives in the city. How on earth did they obtain a farm? With animals?

"Wow, Mom, that's just crazy. Do you even know anything about animals?"

"Well, not really. As you heard, a goose was chasing me. Don't worry, I'm hiring someone who does. You're going to love the house when you visit. I'm sure in the summer it's gorgeous. I called to let you girls know we won't make it for Thanksgiving because your aunt twisted her ankle and needs my help. I'm sorry. I looked forward to seeing you all and my little Dante."

"I understand your concern, Mom. I miss you guys. Mila's Nana and Uncle are coming down." I'm a little bummed. This will be my first year being without my family for the holidays.

"That's great, honey. I'd better let you go. I'm going to help your father milk the cows."

"What!"

She chuckles. "Just kidding. Give my love to Mila and Dante."

I say my goodbyes and end the call, then I hop off my desk and look up at Mila.

A smile curls the edge of her mouth. "A farm, huh? Are we Old MacDonald now?" she singsongs.

I throw my head back in laughter. Mila ducks down and feeds the baby chicks some grain. All you hear is little chirps as the chicks eat from her hand. I lean down and pet the cuties.

"Wow, chica, I think you would make an excellent farmer. Maybe you should go help Mom and Dad."

Mila raises an eyebrow.

"I wouldn't mind milking a cow. I've always wondered how it would feel squeezing the udders on a cow."

I scrunch my nose. "Eww."

She shakes her head, chuckling. "Hey, so how was your lunch date?" Mila asks as she moves a bale of hay out for her shoot.

I throw my head back in laughter.

"Mothballs?"

She scrunches her nose. "You mean he smelled like mothballs?"

"His coat. I think he might have gotten it from his grandad's closet."

"Wow, you'd think he would've smelled himself—unless that's just him."

I'm leaving the whole incident with Liam out. I don't want her to think anything about it. She will try to set us up, and he's a man who doesn't make commitments. And I feel the same.

"Who knows? All Milo did was talk about himself."

Her emerald-green eyes bore into mine, scrutinizing me. She sighs. "I love you, Sophie. You're my best friend. I have to ask. If you didn't want more with Ryder, and now you're online dating—this is not you. I'm not judging you. I'm just worried. Is this because of Eric? Are you looking for a serious—?"

I run my hands through my hair. "No, I'm not looking for anything serious. I don't want to give a man my time only to have him break me. I don't want to get hurt again. I'm just casually dating. I gave Eric my virginity, which meant a lot to me. I've only been intimate with two men in my life. Maybe these guys are just distractions until I can get over the betrayal. Deep down, I knew Eric and I wouldn't be together forever. We were drifting apart, but what he did and how he did it has left a mark."

She pulls me into a tight hug.

Soon after, our clients and Dahlia show up. With shot after shot of babies and family holidays, the rest of the day goes by relatively quickly. I lean my head back and collect my breath, slouching in my office chair. Grabbing my phone, I scroll through social media. My fingertips itch, urging me to search for Liam. I type in his name, and my eyes widen into a lustful haze.

Holy guacamole. Absent-mindedly, my finger traces the width of his sculpted shoulders to his biceps. His muscles are so cut and taut that his shirt sleeves are straining to contain them.

Scrolling down, I see he's wearing a pair of sweats, a plain white T-shirt, a backward baseball cap, and a pair of aviator sunglasses, his white boxer dog at his side. My breath hitches. Liam is a fine specimen of a man. I close my eyes, envisioning how my hands would feel roaming his body. Does he have tattoos, maybe scars? What is underneath all the clothes? God, it's getting warm in here. My thoughts go haywire when Mila walks in on me.

"Hey, do you have..."

Startled, I throw my phone up in the air. My heart feels like it stops, and I react instinctively, my arm shooting up to catch the phone before it can land on the floor. I teeter for a moment, off balance, before tumbling out of my chair and landing on the cold tile floor with a thud. As I scramble to my feet, embarrassed heat rising in my cheeks, I'm painfully aware of Mila in the doorway, eyes wide with surprise. I grab my phone before she catches me fantasizing about Liam.

"Ugh, what are you doing? What did I walk in on?"

I feel like a kid who got caught with their hands in the cookie jar. "Nothing." I fix my skirt, avoiding Mila's curious gaze.

"Ugh. Uh, you *were* looking at something. Your face is crimson. And your eyes were closed like you were daydreaming."

I scoff. "I was not!"

Her eyes widen with a massive joker grin. "Were you watching porn?"

I throw my hands up in the air. "God, no, Mila, sheesh."

She snickers and walks into my space. Brows raised. "You're lying, and you're buggin'."

God, it feels like porn. Liam is the definition of porn. I can't get his Greek god form out of my head. He's brolic. I flip her the bird and rest my hands on my hips.

"I'm not buggin'." Yup, I am freaking out.

"You can lie to yourself all you want. So, what was it? A threesome? Was it reverse harem like the book I let you borrow?" She sits on the corner of my desk. "I mean, you were flustered. Must have been some hot stuff you were watching." She raises her brows up and down.

I can't deny it was hot stuff. So hot that I feel the moisture in between my legs.

"Yes, it was hot stuff." I surrender to her stubbornness.

"I knew it."

"I guess all those romance novels are getting to you." She sighs as if in a cloud of lust.

Once Mila walks out of my office, my mind wanders back to Liam. What would it be like to casually date him? I've never casually dated up until now. I know I'd end up with a broken heart all over again because the lust I have for him is stronger than I've ever felt. The best thing to do is ignore it. Shut it down and go on another date.

CHAPTER 5
LIAM

After parking in my driveway, I emerge from my car and unlock the gate to the backyard, letting Duke out.

"Hey, buddy, how was your day?"

He gives his balls a good lick then runs straight toward me. Guy's got priorities.

"Don't you even think about licking me with your ball breath."

He barks, not pleased with my demand.

I unlock the door, and we both make our way into the house.

"Half of my day was good, buddy. The other half was shit." I toss my keys on the table and grab a beer from the fridge.

"Come on, boy." Collapsing onto the leather sofa, I sigh.

My body aches from a raid at an abandoned warehouse-turned-meth lab. I had to chase down two men and tackle them, though they put up quite a fight. We interrogated them and checked for the Serpents' mark, but it wasn't there. Still, we were sure one would eventually crack and tell us where to find them. Tomorrow I'm meeting with the task force. Two under-cover agents are going in.

I step into the steamy shower, and beads of warm water seep into every muscle. All I can think about is that vixen. The second I saw the dickhead's lips on her hands, I lost it. It's so fucking unlike me to give a shit and feel jealous. I've never experienced it before. And I hated it.

That mouth of hers has no filter. She is different from any woman I've ever met. The majority of women I come across throw themselves at me. She's different in how she puts herself together—and there's something about her sassiness. I know she felt the chemistry between us just like I did, even if she didn't acknowledge it, even if she ignored our lust and tension. Those damn lips were plump and red, and I was so tempted to taste them. I stroke myself as I think about how she would feel underneath me, her blonde locks wrapped around my fist as I kiss her hungrily...I stroke until I come all over the wet tile.

Fuck me. I need to keep my distance from this woman. She weakens me. I should be thinking about tomorrow's meeting with the task force, not jerking off to thoughts of a woman I don't really want. She's a distraction I don't need right now.

As soon as I enter the meeting room, my fury erupts like wildfire. My rage intensifies when I spot the photos of the top ten most dangerous and wanted Serpents on the bulletin board. The full image of Pablo, the leader from eighteen years ago, and a rendering of him as an older man now. Next to his photo is one of his son, who looks to be around my age.

Suddenly, a memory from the night of my father's death resurfaces. The motherfucker who killed my father said, "*A life for a life, blood for blood.*"

I never asked what it meant before I shut down. I never questioned why my father was taken brutally in front of me or why the gang leader was after my father. I know my father was about to transfer to the DEA just before he passed. Even though he was off duty that night, something about the situation has always felt wrong. After all these years, I can't shake the feeling something isn't right. I know after today, many pieces I've buried are going to resurface.

"Good morning, Rodriguez," Detective Cain says, walking up shoulder-to-shoulder with Officer Franco, the leader of the task force.

"Good morning, Detective Cain. Thank you for having me."

They nod. The room fills up with highly experienced officers. I'm honored to be part of the team.

Detective Cain takes the podium at the front of the room, and the buzz of conversation dies out. "Good morning, team. We have received some information from our informant. Our two undercover agents have been persuasive, convincing the Serpents to trust them. Pablo Marquez has been working with the cartel in Tijuana, Mexico, for the past few years. He's moving into the U.S. to import drugs—cocaine. We were informed of two possible drop-offs, one here and one in Long Beach."

My breath heaves. My father was a man many admired... respected. He was a hell of a detective. He would still be alive if I hadn't been with him that night. He held back because I was there. Pablo was a fucking coward to ambush him when he was with his son. Like all gangs, they don't give a shit; they're cold-hearted bastards.

"When our informants give us the signal, we will move in on them as soon as the shipment hits the docks. Remember, we keep this quiet. We'll take them off the streets and get vengeance for Manny and all those affected by the gangs," Detective Cain says, his voice booming through the room.

My chest aches at hearing my father's name. He was my hero—and still is. My stomach churns with excitement and burns with fury to finally meet the eyes of the man who killed my father.

"For those who don't know, Officer Rodriguez is Manny's son. He's a hell of an officer, and I'm positive he will become a skilled detective and agent like his father one day."

They all turn to glance at me. Some nod, some smile, and some look at me with pity, knowing the story. I muster a smile and square my shoulders.

———

AFTER A LONG DAY, I arrive at Rocco's and slide onto the stool. The chatter of the crowd ricochets through the walls of the busy bar, and the smell of smoke and beer lingers in the air.

"What can I get you, Liam?" Will, the owner, asks as he surveys me. We've been coming here for years.

"Two beers, please."

"Everything okay?"

I run my fingers through my hair. "So much shit going on, with the case against Rachel and an old investigation we are working on." I take a deep breath.

"Yeah, I bet it's a lot on your shoulders. Many don't realize what you do is hard as hell. You deal with so much shit." He hands me two beers, and a couple wave him down.

I nod and thank him as he leaves. I take a long swig of my beer, letting the icy stream relax me.

A woman slides over to the stool next to me. Her long cinnamon hair trails down to her ass. Her brown eyes scan me like I'm her favorite treat as she licks her lips. "Hey, handsome, what are you doing here alone?"

I smirk. "Waiting for a beautiful woman to join me." I wink, and she beams.

The door swings open. I glance up and groan. Of all people, grenade walks in, accompanied by a woman with pink hair—the girl who works with her, I think. I bite my fist. Fuck, Sophie's hot. She's wearing a short blue skirt, tall black boots, and a tight blouse. Her breasts are perky and look firm. Her creamy white skin glows. She's sculpted to perfection, curvy and beautiful. Her blue eyes sparkle in the light. Every head turns toward her, mine included. I watch her like a creep. She's walking to a table, but she stops and turns as if she can feel me. Eyes the color of sapphires stare me down. Sophie's gaze shifts to the woman beside me who's raking her fingers down my chest. She's so close I can smell her cheap perfume. A spark of disappointment, or maybe disgust, flashes in her eyes. She turns and sits with her friend. I have the urge to push the woman away from me.

"Tell me your name, handsome," the flirtatious woman says.

But I never get to answer.

Sophie squeezes between me and the woman at the bar, pushing the woman to the side. "His name is Liam, and"—she turns to me—"by the way, Liam, the pharmacy called—your penicillin and cream is ready for your rash...*down there*. The last woman you were with must have given you syphilis."

I stifle a laugh from erupting from my chest as the other woman's eyes widen, staring at Sophie.

"Good thing I warned you," Sophie says, turning back to the woman. "It's very contagious, you know." Sophie's tone holds a thread of challenge when she returns her attention to me, cutting the other woman off from view entirely.

The woman walks off without a word, and I shake my head at her with a vast fucking grin.

"Jealous, Grenade?" I tip my head, taking a drink of my beer.

"Nope. Just repaying the favor. You ruined my date, so I ruined your one-night stand." I don't miss the way her jaw tightens. I don't know why I feel the need to say this to her, but I do.

"I wasn't going to sleep with her."

She scans my profile. I like the way she looks at me.

"Sure, you weren't." She stands, and we just stare at one another like we're in a trance. "I should go back," she says, breaking the silence.

Pulling out the chair beside me, I point for her to sit. It's a bad idea. "Let me buy you a beer."

Her eyebrows rise. "Okay." She sits, and her cheeks turn pink.

I wave Will down, and she orders a Vanhattan, whatever the fuck that is, but Will knew just what it was.

"Syphilis, huh? You couldn't think of anything else?"

She giggles. "That's the only way I could get you back for ruining my date." She shrugs.

"Fair."

"You come here a lot, Casanova?" Her accent is thick and sexy.

I raise my brow at her. "Casanova?"

"Huh. Yeah. So, you come here a lot?"

"I do. Been coming here for years. It's where Dominic, Santiago, Mark, and I shoot the shit. And sometimes with the guys from work." I can't help but stare at how she grips the glass, how her plump lips press against it.

Damn, do I want to lick the saltiness of those lips.

"Oh, that's nice. I used to go to this bar in Manhattan. I would listen to jazz and have a couple of drinks with friends."

Did I mention I love her accent? My dick twitches every time. I've never met a sexier woman than Sophie...never met one who drives me crazy like this. She's feisty and straightforward.

"You miss Manhattan?"

She licks her lips, and I drool. "I do miss Manhattan. It's been my only home. Never been anywhere else. Until now. Manhattan has a unique energy I miss. Broadway shows and jazz music are such a fun part of life there. People here in California are different... Well, in San Diego. They're more outdoorsy and more relaxed."

A man enters the room, his eyes fixated on Sophie with a longing gaze. A wave of intense jealousy floods through me. He must be Rake—or whatever his name is.

"Who's that?" I tip my beer toward the man.

"A guy I was seeing. Ryder. We were casual. He wanted more, though...something serious. I didn't. So, he called it off."

So, she doesn't want a serious relationship. Interesting.

"From what I've heard, you don't do relationships either. Have you ever had a girlfriend? Or been in love?" Sophie's cheeks turn a little pink.

Having her this close isn't just frying my circuit, it's sucking the oxygen from my lungs.

"No to both," I admit. And will never happen. "If you're not wanting serious, then why are you going on dates?" I ask.

She arches an eyebrow at me. "You're very nosy, Officer," she teases as she sips from her mixed drink, letting me glimpse her pouting lips.

Damn it, I'm getting aroused.

"When it comes to you, I am," I reply before I can stop

myself. This woman has bewitched me. I take a deep breath and clear my throat, playing it off.

Fuck me.

"When it comes to your safety," I clarify.

She tilts her head, and her eyes sparkle. "Oh, I see. So, you interrogate all women about whom they date and how they date. For their safety." She makes air quotation marks.

"No, not all women. You're Mila's best friend. You're important to her, and Mila is important to me."

She stays quiet for an awful minute. Her shoulders drop. "Have a good night, Officer. See you around." She walks off without saying another word and joins her friend playing pool —not even a glance.

My heart deflates. Fuck, I feel like a dick. I want to apologize for making it seem like I don't give a shit about her. I have nothing more to offer her. We are both not into relationships. I've never had such a mirthful conversation with a woman as with her. I'm about to approach her and offer her pool lessons, make my apology, but the asshole Rake beats me to it. He looks like a fucking wanna-be biker. Fucking wild hog. He draws her in for a hug. Her smile widens. My stomach churns with jealousy. I hate the feeling, so I shut it down quickly. I pay for my tab and walk out the door.

I'VE SPENT the last two days searching for Rachel, Dominic's mother. Shit has hit the fan. Mila found out that Dominic's mother is responsible for her father's death. She closed herself off and broke it off with Dominic. I've tried calling her and Sophie, and they've both rejected my calls. I completely understand. I blame myself for not arresting Rachel immediately. I felt obligated to tell my bros first. And I never thought she would run.

It's been four weeks since I've seen Sophie at the bar. To say she hasn't been living rent-free in my head would be a lie. I've stroked myself numerous times, thinking of her. She's messed with my head and doesn't even know it. A couple of weeks ago, I went to a bachelor party, and a gorgeous brunette took me home with her, but my dick wouldn't cooperate. She wasn't the blonde I desired. Damn grenade knows how to create chaos in my life. Fucking hell. I haven't even touched her yet.

John and I prowl around Rachel's work, hoping she'll show up. My cell rings, and my eyebrows jog up—it's Sophie.

"Hello." She's breathing heavily.

"Sophie, what happened? Are you okay?"

"Liam s-she has a gun...Rachel."

Fuck, my heart rate speeds up. "Where are you? Where's Rachel?"

"In the house. I just got home with Dante, and I saw her through the window pointing a gun at Mila."

Goddamn it. Nauseating fear rolls in my stomach. "Stay in the car, Sophie. Keep Dante safe. I'm close by, okay?"

She's panting and wheezing.

"Breathe, Grenade." I click the line on hold, turn my light on, and speed to Mila's.

She is like a sister to me. I can't lose her. She's Dominic's entire world. I park my SUV and run to her door. John calls for backup. I'm about to open the door when there's an enormous crash. Screaming. Then the apartment goes quiet and still. When I open the door a few inches, I see Mila pointing the gun at Rachel. Mila is shaking, shoulders quivering, hands clenched, and eyes scrunched. Rachel stands with a blank expression, her arms low at her sides.

The last time I was this frightened was the day I lost my father. I'm not sure what I'm walking into, but I walk in anyway, calm Mila down, and take the gun from her. She's shaken up, so I help her find a seat. The officers take Rachel. I walk outside to check on Sophie and Dante. Dante is lying in the back seat of Sophie's Mustang, watching videos on her phone. She's distracting him, thankfully.

"She's okay?" Sophie's chin trembles, and a tear skates down her cheek.

I wipe her tears with my thumb. As shaken as she is, I pull her into my arms and hug her. I know it's what she needs right now.

She sobs. "I was so scared, Liam," she mouths into my shoulder.

I stroke her back. "Me too."

She pulls away and wipes her tears. John waves me over just as Dominic walks over to Dante.

Sophie's eyes narrow, her lips tighten, and her jaw clenches as she glares at Dominic. *Damn.*

"Can I go check on Mila?" she asks as I walk over to John.

I nod. "Yeah, she needs you."

Holding Sophie in my arms felt like heaven and hell. The sweet scent of her perfume had me hooked like a drug wanting more of her lingering scent. Releasing her from my arms tugged the strings in my heart. I wanted to hold her, comfort her, but I knew I had to let her go—for so many reasons. Letting her go is more terrifying than anything. That alone scares the hell out of me for having such strong feelings for her.

CHAPTER 6
SOPHIE

My head has been spinning from everything happening in the studio lately. Things always get hectic around the most festive time of the year. Now that Christmas has come and gone, there's been no let-up in our bookings. Mila left for Manhattan last night, and I've been scrambling to catch up. It's been a couple of weeks since the incident happened with Rachel. I've never experienced such terror in my entire life. When I got to the house, I felt something was off. I asked Dante to stay in the car while I checked inside. When I saw Rachel aiming a gun at Mila, I sprinted and dialed Liam. Thank God Mila was unharmed and that I had taken Dante shopping. Despite having anxiety for days, I managed to maintain my composure because Mila needed me.

I hear the front door chime. It must be my last client of the day, from a new law firm opening. I'll be taking headshots of the attorneys for their website. Daliah walks up with a shit-eating grin.

"OMG, Sophie, there are three men waiting for you," she

whispers, fanning herself. "So hot it will make your popsicle melt. And they're ready for you."

A throaty laugh escapes my lips. When I see them, I stop and gape. Damn, she wasn't joking. They are hot.

An hour later, I finished up with the last guy of the three. He clears his throat and rubs the back of his neck nervously. From the looks of it, he's contemplating what to say.

"Umm, I was wondering if you're free for New Year's Eve. I'd love to take you out." He exhales a long, nervous laugh.

I gaze at his profile for a while. Although it's not summer, he has perfectly natural brown skin, as if he was kissed by the sun. His long and slicked-back sandy blond hair has one flawless side-swept strand. His hazel eyes highlight his skin's bronze color. He is muscular, but not overly so, and slender.

Not bad. And my only other plans are to watch my favorite classic movies, *Dirty Dancing* and *Sixteen Candles*, and loathe myself while I stuff my face. The only friend I have made since I moved here is Daliah, and she already has plans for New Year's Eve.

"You know...I would like that. My best friend is out of town. I was planning to stay home."

He smiles coyly. "Great." He reaches for his dress shirt pocket and pulls out a business card, handing it to me.

I read his name. "Chad..." I raise a brow at him. Jeez, Sophie, smooth... you agree to go out with a guy, and you don't even know his name.

He chuckles, raking his chin. "Fuck, I'm horrible at this. I should have introduced myself before asking you out." He looks over his shoulder at the guys watching him embarrass himself. His cheeks splash with a tint of pink.

It's adorable.

I shrug. "Hey, no worries. Maybe I am too."

His shoulder slumped, relieving his tense muscles, and

when he grins, a soft dimple appears on his sun-kissed cheek. "How about I get your number, beautiful? You can decide if you want me to pick you up or meet me somewhere."

Chad hands me his cell, and I type in my number. It's been a couple of weeks since I've been on a date. Not because Liam threw a fit about my safety, so he says. But after the last few dates, I needed a mental break. Eric is still blowing up my phone, sending old photos of us, attempting to reel me back in.

"It was nice meeting you, Sophie. I'll text you tonight so we can get to know each other a little more before our date or whatever you want to call it." He winks as he walks back to his coworkers.

I hope this date goes better than the last two. Chad seems to be a sweet guy, and he's hot...but in no comparison to Liam.

I'VE SPENT the last two hours slipping in and out of different dresses. I started with a red dress and moved on to blue and then black. I finally decided on the red—a V-neck wrap mini-dress with a side slit. I stare at myself in the mirror, admiring the curves I worked hard to get. As a teen, I was always under-weight. In high school, kids teased me, telling me to eat a sand-wich and calling me bony. So, I ate, and by the end of high school, they were calling me fat. I couldn't win. I've spent the last couple of years working out, building muscle, and adding more protein to my diet.

Two nights ago, Chad called me, and we talked for a couple of hours. Surprisingly, he's easy-going and funny. He opened up a bit, telling me about his life. His older brother and another colleague started their legal practice, and Chad recently passed his bar exam. At twenty-nine years old, he's joining his broth-er's firm.

I finish by adding red lipstick and then call an Uber to pick me up. We're meeting at the Hard Rock Hotel. I slip on my red heels. A text beeps—my Uber has arrived.

At dinner, Chad throws his head back in laughter when I go over all the slang we use in New York.

"So, bag means to get a number or secure a date?" he repeats what I just said, taking a sip of his beer.

I mimic him and take a drink of my sangria. I smile into my glass. Chad is a charmer. I'm enjoying his company. Our waiter arrives with our dinner. The Bolognese smells fantastic. Later there's a band playing on the rooftop, and Chad mentioned heading up there after dinner to see it.

"Yup, you bagged me up for New Year's Eve," I say as I twirl my fork in the spaghetti Bolognese.

"What do you miss about New York besides family?" Chad inquires with his silky-smooth voice. He studies my profile, his gaze caressing me head to toe.

I tilt my head to the side in thought. "I miss the food... bagels, pizza, halal carts. I miss subway travel—and the weather. Most of all, I miss how straightforward people are. Don't get me wrong, I love it here. Have you lived here all your life?"

He nods. "Yeah, all my life. I've never been to New York. It's at the top of my list of places where I'd like to travel."

I swallow the bite full of spaghetti. "You should definitely vacation there. You'll love it."

He takes a bite of his ravioli. A splatter of sauce gets on his chin. Without thinking, I wipe it away with a napkin. I'm a little too close, my breasts practically on display as I lean in. He chews the rest of his food then swallows hard as his gaze goes to the deep V-neck of my dress and then travels to my lips.

"Damn, you're gorgeous." His long fingers tuck my blonde locks behind my ear.

I straighten back in my chair.

"Thank you," I mutter into my wine glass.

We stay quiet for a minute too long before he says, "Maybe you can be my tour guide."

"Huh?"

"New York," he replies with a smirk on his charming face.

"Sure." I take another long gulp of sangria. Maybe I should make it clear it's too soon.

He breaks the silence while I'm lost in thought. "How do you like your dinner?"

"It's really good. How about yours?"

He leans in with his fork, feeding me a bite of ravioli. Okay, I wasn't expecting to be spoon-fed...and it seems a little too intimate.

I swallow the steamy pasta burning my throat. "Good, wow, really good."

He smiles sheepishly.

My eyes widen when I see gun-metal eyes staring at me over Chad's shoulder. What the fuck? Does he have a sixth sense for finding me when I'm on a date? Fuck, he'd better not come over here and ruin it with his officer bullshit. Playing good cop. With a furious expression, Liam clenches his jaw and grips his silverware so hard, his knuckles go white. What the hell is his problem?

Liam sits with a couple and an older woman who must be his mother. They're having dinner, and I don't know how long he's been sitting there. I return my gaze to Chad. He hands the waiter his card.

"Oh, I can cover my part," I offer, not wanting to feel like a freeloader.

Chad reaches for my hand and places a kiss on my knuckles. "Absolutely not. I would never let you pay."

"Thank you for dinner. I'm having a great time," I say honestly.

"The night is not over, beautiful. We need to head to the rooftop to bring in the new year." He winks as he stands and reaches for my hand.

I take it and feel Liam's stare burning right through me. Why the hell does he care? I'm not doing anything dangerous. I met a man at my job, and now I am on a date with him. Countless other humans do the same every day. Either he's entirely unreasonable or...worry is not his reason for overreacting at all. Jealousy is. No. No, he made his motivations very clear—he worries for my safety because I'm Mila's friend. He's just an unreasonable dickhead.

Besides, Casanova only has one-night stands, and he wouldn't be interested in me. Chad holds my hand as we walk out of the restaurant and take the escalator to the rooftop.

I shiver as we walk into the cool night air. Damn, it's cold. Not as cold as New York. But cold enough to make me want to go home and cuddle on the couch with a comfy blanket and some hot cocoa. My coat is not heavy enough.

We shuffle over to a small table by one of the outdoor heaters placed around the space. As we sit, it engulfs us in warmth. Chad shifts in his seat, edging closer and closer to me with each passing moment. A waiter interrupts our conversation with a tray lifted high in the air, offering glasses of champagne, Sangria, or golden-hued bourbon. I study Chad out of the corner of my eye. His thick sandy-brown hair, square jaw, and hazel eyes make me wonder why he's single, why he lacks experience in the dating game.

As straightforward as I am, I blurt it out. "Why are you single? You're smart, handsome, funny, and successful."

He grabs the bourbon off the tray and takes an extended nip of it. "I had a long-time girlfriend. We dated for five years.

She cheated on me two years ago. Since then, I haven't really dated or been in a relationship." He stays quiet for a hot minute. After another sip, he places his drink gently on the smooth glass table. He turns to look at me.

"I realized she wasn't the one. We had just been going through the motions since we had been together so long. I think we just felt forced. It hurt me when I found out, and it took me time to see it was for the best. We both loved each other at some point, but we fell out of love. I didn't even realize it until she left. She's married now and has a kid. She looks happy—the happiest I've ever seen her." He shrugs it off.

I wonder if that's how things were with Eric and me—going through the motions. Although he wants me back, or so he thinks.

"I'm sorry you went through that," I murmur.

He chuckles. "It is what it is. You want to dance?" He smiles boyishly.

Crimson Flowers, the live band, starts playing something vaguely pop and country at the same time. A swarm of people start dancing in front of the stage. Chad clasps his arms around my waist as we dance, undoubtedly influenced by the alcohol. We're not good, and we giggle at ourselves, having fun anyway. As we move together, he twirls me around, and our heads accidentally collide.

"Oh, shit, sorry."

I rub my forehead. "I'm okay. I think it's the alcohol and all the twirling. I'm fine."

We walk back to our seats. He licks his lips hungrily and lifts my chin, skimming his soft lips over mine. A chilly breeze passes between us as I long for warmth. It's too damn cold. I wrap my arms around his neck, letting him pull me into his heat. He kisses me, slow and steady. Our tongues tangle. It's sweet and warm.

I pull away as he kisses my cheek and whispers in my ear, "That was nice."

It was lovely. However, just like with Ryder, I felt nothing. It was dry.

"Yes, it was. I'm going to run to the restroom."

"Okay, beautiful. I'll be waiting." He kisses my cheek.

I turn on my heels and head down a long hall toward the restroom.

After using the restroom, I reapply more lipstick. The door swings open. I pay no attention. Then I hear a clearing of a throat—a man's deep voice. I straighten up, pressing my back against the tile wall.

Liam's steel gray eyes blaze fiercely, his arms rigidly folded across his torso. He stands like a statue. His hard muscles flex beneath the fabric of his clothes. His jaw is clenching, his eyes are narrow, and he looks like something out of a Greek myth. Liam's dark hair is meticulously combed over, and he is impeccably dressed in a perfectly tight black leather jacket, a fitted button-down shirt, and a pair of dark jeans.

My eyes roam slowly over every inch of him, shamelessly drinking in the sight before me. The heat between my legs becomes unbearable. After a few drinks, I've lost control over myself. It's like a force from within me is telling me what to do. I lick my lips. He stalks toward me with a glare that could cut through glass. He leans in with the palms of his hands above my head. His demeanor is powerful and intimate. My heart pounds rapidly. The heat of his minty breath intoxicates me. The masculine scent of his cologne sends me into a whirlwind of arousal that spikes throughout my body.

"I thought I told you not to go on dates," he growls. He's breathing heavily, his nostrils flaring.

I cluck my tongue in irritation. My eyes burn fury-hot. Who does he think he is to tell me who not to date?

"And I thought I told you to mind your own damn business. You don't need to be concerned about my safety. I can care for myself, Casanova. If you'll excuse me, I'd like to get back to my date," I bite out. I'm trying to maneuver my way out, but he's a solid brick wall of muscle.

"Not happening, baby."

Baby.

His lips are so close, millimeters from my mouth. "Tell me why you are going on speed dates. You don't come off as a one-night-stand type. You're not looking for anything serious, so what are you doing? What are you looking for, Sophie?"

Having Liam so close, I can't register what he's saying. I hear only the vibration of his rough, husky voice. He's intoxicating. He's like gasoline, and I'm the fire he's igniting.

The noise outside fades as Liam keeps his gaze pinned on me. The only sound in the room is the dripping faucet and our breathing. His hooded grays penetrate my soul. His beautiful, godlike sculpted face reflects rage, lust, and jealousy.

"Tell me," He repeats.

He's so close, his hot breath moistens my lips. Right then, my phone vibrates in my purse. I jolt up, startled, and fish for my phone. It's Eric, of course, calling at the worst possible time. I shove it back into my purse after I silence it.

"Who's that? Your date?" His jaw ticks. God, he's jelly.

"No, it's not."

"Then who is it?" His voice thunders so loud it echoes.

Fuck, he's nosy. It must be the cop in him, interrogating me for everything. Shit. I'm hesitant to tell him about Eric. He's not my date or anything. But before I can stop myself, I blurt out everything. The New Yorker in me has to be straightforward, dammit.

"My ex."

His brows furrow. "Rake?"

I don't know why he calls him Rake. I roll my eyes. "No, it's not Ryder. He was not my boyfriend. He's an ex from New York."

He stands tall, shoving his hands in his pockets, probably because he keeps fisting his hands, staring at me, surveying me with such intensity. His intimidating glare has me shivering like a dark knight ready to strike. He's not here to save me but to torture my soul. To take me to an unknown place I'll never return from.

CHAPTER 7

LIAM

I rest my gaze on Sophie's luscious curves, devouring the sight of her body. The way the thin red material clings to her, how she shivers under my watchful eye, and how the pebbles of her nipples swell through the material. I know my proximity affects her. Jealousy ripples through me like a hurricane, tearing me apart. Never in my life have I experienced jealousy to the point of losing control.

Never.

The minute Rosa, her boyfriend, my mother, and I walked into the restaurant, I heard a laugh. I knew. My eyes darted up, and there she was. I sat facing her. She laughed and smiled at the motherfucker she was with like he was a stand-up comedian. My blood boiled, and my pulse thumped every time the asshole laid his hands on her. For months, I have been avoiding my feelings for her, my need for her. I need to get her out of my system. I've been relieving myself for days, weeks, imagining how her creamy flesh would feel under mine. How she would taste when my tongue christened every curve, every layer, every inch of her. I'd brand Sophie with my touch as I thrust savagely into her, marking her mine.

Fucking hell, what's wrong with me? I shake it off.

Eric. She has an ex. If the asshole is calling her, he must want her back.

"How long were you with him?" I prod. My eyes drift to her swollen red lips.

She's hesitant to answer. "Three...close to four years." She presses her lips together.

Four fucking years. Did she love him? Dammit, why should I care? I try to remain impassive when all I see is red. Flames of jealousy seep into my bones.

"Why did you break up?" I run my fingers through my hair, trying to keep my cool. And my hands away from touching her.

She places her hands on her hips and narrows her beautiful ocean-blue eyes at me. She takes two steps toward me. She's pissed. My dick swells against the zipper. I like her feistiness.

"What the fuck, Liam? Why in the hell do you care who I date? And why my ex and I broke up. What's it to you?"

Yeah, Liam, what's it to you? I should walk out and mind my own damn business and go find a woman to take my edge off for the night. And stay the hell away from Sophie. But no, I'm like a fucking thief seizing her from the asshole pretty boy waiting for her. I stalk toward her, pinning her against the wall. I'm like a predator staking my claim.

"W-what are you doing, Liam?" she stammers, breathlessly. Her breasts rise and fall.

"What's it to me, baby? Why can't I get you out of my damned head? I know you feel the chemistry between us. Neither of us is keen on relationships. So how about we relieve the tension between us? Get it out of our systems."

Her eyes widen as if my proposal is the stupidest shit ever.

Because it is. We would be playing with fire. But we both have an itch to scratch.

"I'm not sleeping with you, Liam." Her blue eyes narrow to slits.

Fucking hell. My ego deflates along with my dick. She's fucking stubborn as hell.

"I'm not a one-nighter. Or a hooker," she bites out.

My lips twitch into a grin. I lean the palm of my hand on the cold tile wall, and with my free hand, I stroke the softness of her cheek. I tuck a golden lock of hair behind her ear.

"I know, baby. We would need more than once to get it out of our systems. You know very well it's what we need." I lick my lips, contemplating how her soft lips would feel against mine. Her coconut scent pounds through me like a drug overdose.

"Do you do this to all women, lock them up in the restroom, and offer them sex with no strings attached?" She wraps her arms around her chest, absent-mindedly pushing up her breasts.

Fuck me.

I chuckle. "No, never have..." Because I'm entirely out of my mind asking this. I'm doing this for my benefit. Hers, too.

She scans my profile, scrutinizing me. I like how her glistening eyes shine in the moonlight beaming from the skylight. She's so damn beautiful. Stunning.

"So, how would this work?"

Good, she's contemplating my suggestion.

"Simple. We fuck when needed until we get it out of our system, then go our separate ways." I shrug.

She bites on her bottom lip.

"And no more dates with other people," I add.

Her brows furrow as she tilts her head, looking right into my eyes. "Fine, but the same goes for you."

My galloping heart beats wildly, and my dick thickens painfully in my jeans. If she only knew I hadn't had sex in weeks. I skim my lips onto hers. I can feel her heartbeat quicken. I lick her lips. So soft. I whisper into her mouth,

"Same goes for me, Sophie."

Before I kiss the fuck out of her, I have one more request. I lick her lips once more and trail a kiss on her neck. She gives me perfect access. Her breathing picks up. I love how my touch affects her. I step back.

Her eyes widen—maybe disappointed my lips are no longer on her perfect soft creamy skin.

The thought of that prick Eric calling her has me wanting to check his background and find something on him to get him locked up. Good fucking thing he's in New York. She spent four years with him. The dates she's been on are redundant. It all makes perfect sense. She's not looking for relationships. She's looking for a rebound. Who knows what the asshole did to make her go on a dating rampage? I won't be fucking her when she still has another man on her mind.

"This guy, Eric—you still think about him? You so hung up on him that you're looking for rebounds?" I ask, slipping my hands into my leather jacket, to keep from touching her.

She turns to grab the coat she left on the sink. She slips it on and avoids contact. Yeah, that's what I thought. The fucker still has a hold on her. "No," she says, grinding her teeth.

Liar.

I rake my hands around the stubble of my jaw. "You're lying, baby." I run my knuckles along her cheek. "Confess it, baby. The fucker Rake didn't satisfy you as much as you needed, did he? That's why you're on the hunt for something casual and temporary. You haven't had someone give you pleasure. When I touch you and kiss you—when I fuck you with everything I've got, you'll forget your ex ever existed. You won't be able to think of anyone else. You won't want to. I'll be the only man whose name you beg for and whose touch you crave when I make sure to leave you satiated. You'll be coming for more because you've never had this—" I press my swollen hard-on against her.

She gasps. I lean her against the wall, grinding on her, leaving featherlight kisses on her collarbone. My fingertips trail up her dress. She shivers when I slide her underwear to the side.

Fuck, she's soaked.

I brush a finger back and forth up her clit.

"Liam," she moans breathlessly.

That's it, baby, moan for me.

I want her to crave *my touch, my mouth.*

I move my fingers quickly in circular motions around her sensitive bud, causing her to arch her back in response. If she has another man on her mind, I won't fuck her. I won't grant her the luxury of an orgasm. I will give her the luxury of being properly kissed, though. I brush my fingers faster in a swift motion. I pinch her clit, capture her lips, and let my tongue explore the inside of her mouth as if it's a foreign land. I devour her mouth like a starved man.

For a taste. A kiss.

My mouth works with urgency, desperate for every second of it, and I bite down lightly on her bottom lip before pulling away. I can feel the need radiating off her body, filling me with a desire I don't have room for in my heart. She whimpers. I claim her lips, erasing the fucker who kissed her.

Kissing Sophie is reckless, so fucking reckless.

The minute I saw the shithead kissing her, though, it brought the beast out of me. Brought out the male chauvinist too. I pinch her clit as she moans. A feral growl leaves my mouth. I pull away. She's panting, and I'm panting.

Our mouths are both swollen. Lust engulfs Sophie's dazzling blue eyes. By the looks of it... this is the best kiss she's ever had. I feel like I should high-five myself for giving her a proper, mind-blowing kiss. She hasn't seen anything yet. Or should I say she hasn't felt anything yet? When my dick thrusts into her, sending her into an unknown dimension, she'll feel an electric shock like no other. I lick my drenched finger, savoring her taste. Bad fucking idea because now I want to feast on her, but that will have to wait. Fuck, she tastes like heaven and hell.

I need to leave before I'm tempted to fuck her against the wall.

"You have my number, Sophie. Call me when I'm the only man clouding your head." I step back and turn to leave her in a lusty haze. I unlock the door, but before I leave, I turn to her. "Lose the bastard date of yours. I don't want to see another man touching what's mine. See you soon." With that, I walk out and rearrange my dick, who's begging to be set free.

I step onto the rooftop where the band is playing. The crowd grows by the minute, circling around the makeshift stage. I walk toward my mom, Rosa, and her boyfriend. My mother stands under a heater. "Liam, where did you run off to?"

"Restroom." I jerk my head to the side of the long hallway leading to the restrooms. She reaches into her purse, takes out a tissue, dabs it into her glass of water, then grabs my chin and scrubs my lips. I pull back.

"Mamá, what are you doing?" I feel like a kid getting his face washed by his mother in public.

Rosa and her boyfriend Ivan bark with laughter.

I groan.

"Lipstick, Liam. You have lipstick all over your mouth. I'm

trying to help so you don't look like the Joker." She goes back to scrubbing hard.

Fuck, I was on cloud nine and forgot about lipstick. Of course, little Rosita has to put her two cents in.

"What is this, high school? Did you go lock yourself in the utility closet to make out?" She throws her head back and laughs so hard, she snorts.

Ivan watches her grinning with growing intensity.

I growl at Rosa—leave it to her to always bust my balls.

My mom smiles, tossing the tissue back into her purse. "Who's the girl?"

The last thing I need is to be questioned. Nothing will come of the agreement I made with Sophie. We both need to get this out of our systems and go our separate ways. I'm not the kind of man who gives a woman status and marriage. I'm not the kind of man who falls in love.

"Just a woman I know," I say to my mom, and her smile drops to her toes.

"So, are you guys ready to go?" Rosa asks. "It's getting colder. We can bring in the New Year at home." She knows me so well, she's studying me like I'm a damn textbook.

I nod to Rosa. "Let's head on home."

We push through the crowd, and I spot Sophie whispering in the pretty boy's ear. He nods, looking worried. They walk toward an elevator and disappear.

The chilly breeze swirls through us, the fog moving in from the coast as we step out into the cold air. We make our way to the hotel garage, and I catch Sophie standing in the rideshare lane. Waiting for her ride, I assume. Hell, I can't let her get into a rideshare when she's had too much to drink, and she's alone. I guess pretty boy left.

I look at Rosa. "Can you take Mom home? I'm going to give

Mila's friend a ride home." I shove my hands into the pockets of my jacket.

Rosa leans in and whispers, "Is that the girl you were making out with?"

I glance over my shoulder to where Sophie is standing and shake my head at my nosy cousin. "Just take Mom home. I need to give her a ride. She's been drinking."

She taps my nose with determination. "You don't kiss women. You've never kissed a woman on the lips. She must mean something to you," she whispers, her little brown puppy eyes gleaming in the light.

"You're overthinking it, Rosita," I say, using the nickname I've used since childhood.

She turns on her heels, gives me a knowing grin, and hooks my mom in her arms. I roll my eyes. Rosa's more than a little cousin to me—she's a sister. Always up in my business.

I stand behind Sophie, observing her as she huffs and puffs, hitting buttons on her phone.

"God, this would not happen in Manhattan. You would get a taxi at your feet within seconds." She groans, still unaware of me watching her, a smirk on my face.

"I guess you're right. No taxis here. Life is much different in California."

Her head jolts up from her phone as she turns and scrutinizes me with an intense glare. "Why are you lurking there in the darkness like a weirdo?" She scowls, her steely blue eyes narrowing.

"I'm here to give you a lift." I quickly downplay the situation, acting as if it's no big deal.

"I'm good. Uber should be here in"—she looks at the time on her phone—"thirty minutes."

I blow a hot breath of air. "Cancel it. Come on. Let's go. It's too cold to be waiting outside."

She shakes her head stubbornly. "No, it's fine."

I pinch the bridge of my nose. Damn, this woman is so fucking stubborn. "You've been drinking. It's not safe for a woman to be in an Uber alone with a strange man."

"What if the Uber driver is a woman?" she says matter-of-factly.

I roll my eyes at Miss Sassy-pants. "Is it?"

"No."

"All right, then. Let's go. My balls are fucking freezing, Sophie. Stop being so damned stubborn, or I'm going to throw you over my shoulder."

She grumbles, pressing on her phone screen roughly. "Fine, but only because my tits are freezing." She snickers with a grin as my gaze drops to her fantastic rack.

Yup, her round tits are pointing right at me.

Fuck me.

I open the passenger door to my '67 Camaro, and Sophie hops right in. I rev the engine and crank up the heater. Sophie squirms and giggles at the vibration of the car. When she bites her lip and her legs clench, my dick twitches with an unmistakable need to grab her and sit her on my lap, to straddle her legs around me. Her eyes shine with the moonlight as she stares at my lips with need.

Yeah, baby, I want it too.

I reach over to grab the strap to buckle her in. Her potent scent intoxicates me. Cherries and coconut. Her breath heaves at my proximity. I let my lips skim her cheek.

Breathlessly, she grabs the seatbelt. "I-I can do it."

I shake my head. "I got it, baby." I smirk, knowing I got her where I want her. She wants more, and I'll gladly give it to her when she stops thinking of her fuckhead ex.

I PULL into a local mom-and-pop coffee and bakery shop.

"Why are we stopping here?" Sophie's eyelashes flutter, and her eyes go to the coffee shop, then turn to look at me.

"You need to sober up. We can get coffee and a pastry," I drawl as I turn the engine off. I honestly don't know why I brought her here. Sitting together and having a cup of coffee like lovers is not part of our agreement, but it feels wrong to drop her off at home alone while she's intoxicated. Friends have coffee, right? Are we friends? I'd say yeah.

"Oh, I'm sober. You did a fine job barging into the women's restroom, assaulting me." Her eyes darken with lust. And that lust suggests she didn't mind the bathroom barging as much as she wants me to think.

"You didn't seem to mind when you moaned for me." I step out of the car and walk around to open her door before she can respond.

Her eyebrows furrow, and she shakes her head. "Poor Chad. He was a nice guy. I felt bad sending him off."

I growl, gritting my teeth. "Fuck Chad and his pretty-boy doll face."

She stops and spins on her heels at the entrance to the cafe, laughing. Her beautiful golden locks glow under the light, making her shine. "God, you're such a caveman. No wonder you and Dominic make such great friends. He barged in on Mila as well and sucked on her neck like a bloody leech."

I shrug apathetically. "Now that's what you call a real man, baby." Fuck, is she right. I laughed my ass off when Dominic cornered Mila. "And what kind of name is Chad? Like chadder cheese."

She giggles, and my smile widens at the beautiful sight of her.

CHAPTER 8
SOPHIE

My entire body tingles. I've crossed and uncrossed my legs what feels like a million times. Liam's actions in the restroom left me speechless, needy, and wanting more. Kissed...oh, I've been kissed numerous times, but it never felt like that. It was an in-and-out-of-body experience. The way his lips rolled onto mine felt magical, and when his tongue tangled with mine, it was ecstasy. And his firm, thick fingers brushed me in the most penetrating way. He left me hungrily unfulfilled and wanting more. So now here I am, having coffee next to Liam while my lady parts are aching. And the smug bastard knows it.

"I grabbed a sample of different desserts for you to try—we have lemon drop cake, coffee cake, red velvet cake, and dark chocolate cake."

My eyes grow wide.

He digs his fork into the red velvet. "Try this one. It's good," he mumbles as he chews.

"This is a lot of sweets." I wave my hands over the delicious cakes.

My mind wanders to Eric. He would always comment on

what I ate, telling me I should watch my weight. My weight was always a problem for him. Either I was underweight, or I was eating too much. I could never find a balance he approved of.

"It's New Year's, Sophie. Enjoy. I'll work it off at the gym, anyway." He shrugs and digs his fork into the coffee cake.

Men. No wonder he's built like a machine. He must work out a lot. He's bigger than Arnold Schwarzenegger in *The Terminator.* I guess I can run it off tomorrow morning. I dig my fork into the red velvet. Oh, my heavens, it's good. I wash it down with a pumpkin spice latte then lick the frosting from my lips and glance at Liam.

"Do you come here a lot?" I ask, breaking the silence.

He chews, then takes a sip of coffee. He looks up at the ceiling as if searching his brain for something to say. Has he never been with a woman without the involvement of his dick before?

Okay, that's harsh. If he's never been in a relationship, then he's never sat and had a conversation with a woman.

His eyebrows furrow and his forehead creases. "Yes, my parents would come here a lot when I was a kid. The owner's kids have taken over now."

There is a hint of sadness in his voice, and it makes me want to know more about him. I've never asked Mila about Liam's life, and if I did, she would want to know why I asked. It would make me look interested. I'm still not comprehending why I'm so captivated by Liam. In all ways, too, not just in bed.

"Was that your mom and sister with you tonight?"

A warm smile stretches to his ears, and his eyes shine at the mention of his family. "Yes and no. My mom and my cousin Rosa and her boyfriend. Rosa came down to visit for the holidays."

Mila mentioned his cousin Rosa before and how she would hang out with them when she was in high school.

"What about your dad?" I ask. "Are you close to him?"

He grips his fork and glances out the window. "No. How about we get a refill, and I'll drive you home." He runs his fingers through his hair.

My eyes widen at the edge in his husky voice. My big mouth and my curiosity always get me into trouble. Liam had not mentioned his dad yet, so, I asked. Big fucking mistake. It clearly upset him.

"Sorry." He still looks out the window. "Didn't mean to raise my voice. Touchy subject."

I clear my throat and stand. "I shouldn't have been prying into your personal life. Sorry about that. We should go."

He stands and rests his hands on my shoulder. "I wasn't trying to be a dick." He huffs a breath.

I get it. Something happened. He can't talk about it. I'm just a fuck buddy to him. I change the subject and take his cup.

"I'll refill our coffee, and you can clean the table." I smile, letting him know we're good. I'm not hurt.

He leans in and whispers in my ear, "I love how you say coffee in your accent. It's so fucking sexy."

My body is burning with an intense heat. A powerful craving seeps through every vein. I turn to glance at him. He winks and walks off, collecting the plates and napkins and dumping them in the trash.

We speed off in his gorgeous Camaro. The powerful engine hums under me, and it's as if the body of the car controls a giant vibrator between my legs, one that turns on each time I glance at Liam. My need grows stronger by the minute. I have to get out of this car. He said he wouldn't fuck me unless I stopped thinking of Eric. He turns onto a back road I've never been on. The engine revs into the night sky and turns into a stream of light as it reaches for the stars. The city lights shine like shards of glass surrounding the city. The moment *Drive* by The Cars fills the air in the surround sound speakers, he turns up the volume. He drums his fingers on the steering wheel to the beat of the music.

He's been quiet and pensive since we've gotten in the car, as if a war is raging in his mind. There's a mysterious gloom in his gunmetal eyes. I can't pinpoint what it is, and, well, obviously, we are not close friends. The car stops in front of my townhouse. Liam gets out, leaving the engine running, and swings the door open for me. He scans my profile as if he's seeing me for the first time, as if he hadn't touched me intimately hours ago.

"I'll walk you to your door," he says after he clears his throat.

To spite him, I say, "Thank you, Officer Rodriguez. My hero." I flutter my long eyelashes at him.

He tilts his head in a solemn manner. "You're something else, Ms. Summers."

His gaze lingers, and our eyes connect. I'm unable to peel my gaze from him, and he seems unable to take his from me. Fireworks explode into the night sky, startling us. I fish for my keys in my purse as he lifts my chin.

"Two minutes until the new year, Grenade," he says in a low, husky voice. He traces my lips with his thumb then dips his tall frame down until our noses touch.

"I've heard if you kiss a confident woman at the stroke of midnight on New Year's Eve, it will bring you good luck." His lips are so close I can feel the heat between us.

I lick my lips, preparing for a kiss.

"Have you kissed many women on New Year's Eve?" I ask, jealousy churning in my belly.

He wraps his arms around my waist, lifting me up. I wrap

my legs around him. His lips skim mine, and he kisses me just before he says, "Never. You're my first."

Butterflies swirl in my belly as I grip his jaw and devour his lips and mouth. Liam's tongue swishes around in the most rhythmic way. He tilts his head to the side, pressing his lips against mine in a kiss that makes me feel like he is tasting me from the inside out. His well-muscled body moves with easy grace, pinning me to the wall. Fireworks blaze through the night sky, raining down light and color like petals from a flower garden. He takes my mouth with a savage intensity, and his hips brush against mine. Oh, God, the feel of his erection building against my core makes me cry out. I press harder into his pelvis, feeling up his size.

He pulls away, and both of us are panting, our gazes locked together.

"Happy New Year, Bella. *Beautiful.*" His voice lands in my ear an octave below a whisper.

He stares at me, his face unreadable, then he looks away, and his eyes seem to search for something, his brows furrow in confusion. He looks...unhinged. He spins on his heel and rushes to his Camaro, fumbling with the keys in his pocket. He stumbles into the car and drives off into the night, leaving me alone and confused in a cloud of exhaust fumes, my mind spinning with questions. What the hell just happened?

It's been two whole weeks since the entire charade with Liam. I haven't spoken to him since then. I find myself confused, my emotions reeling out of control. Does he still want our agreement?

Do I?

He's been living rent-free in my head since that night. One

touch from Liam Rodriguez, and I was a goner, lost in the clouds of heaven. He did say he wouldn't relieve me unless I stopped thinking of Eric, and boy, have I forgotten him. I mean, yeah, I forgot about Eric months ago, but every time I had sex with Ryder, I thought of Eric and all the sex we had. I was going through the motions with Ryder. Sex with Eric was great, although he was always in control in a way that wasn't fulfilling. Come to think of it, it was always about his needs.

Oh, but Liam is a god, a mythical creature. Those hands work magic, and his mouth has me wondering what else he can do. He ignites me in a powerful way. He's offering a casual relationship, which is exactly what I want, but what if my feelings catch fire? If that happens, he won't give me anything beyond that. I'll be crushed, with a broken heart.

I have been running three miles every morning, relieving the tension, and contemplating whether I should call him, wondering if the agreement would make me look desperate.

"What the heck are you doing pacing up and down the kitchen?" Mila waltzes in, holding Dominic's hand. She has been moving into his place since they got back together. I'm happy for her. She deserves the world.

"Is everything okay? Are you still, you know, dating?" she whispers as if Dominic can't hear.

Dominic chuckles. "Brut, huh? Damn, couldn't he have used Old Spice? What type of dating app are you using, Grandpas.com?" He slaps his hand on the counter and bursts into a full-blown laugh, and Mila follows right behind him.

Honestly, it's funny as fuck, so I join them in the belly laugh, too.

"Seriously, is everything okay?" Mila asks, catching her breath.

I sigh. I look at Dominic, searching for any sign that Liam has mentioned something to him about me. But there is none.

I'm still blown away and confused about the erotic kiss he gave me at the stroke of midnight. Confusion and regret seemed to be written all over his face. What had he been thinking? Should I take a chance and call him, risk being rejected like an idiot?

I grab a water bottle from the fridge and twist the cap.

"Nothing's wrong. I'm going to miss you guys."

Mila's eyes water, and I immediately regret saying it. Yes, I will miss her, of course I will, but I am also using it as a cover-up.

"No, no, bestie, don't cry. I'm going to miss you guys, but I'm happy for you. I'll be fine."

She runs to hug me. Now I feel like shit.

"Oh, Sophie, I brought you here to California, and now I'm leaving you alone. I'm a horrible friend." She sniffles on my shoulder.

I rub her back. "I'll be fine, Mila, I promise. You're my only best friend and not a horrible friend. You're my B," I say honestly. She's my only true friend. We're like peanut butter and jelly—we stick together.

"She'll be fine, baby. She has Grandpa.com to keep her busy. She probably needs her privacy." Dominic wraps his arms around Mila's waist.

I roll my eyes but grin. Dominic has grown on me. More than once, I wanted to strangle him to death, but he's proved himself. The love he has for Mila is unconditional and special in many ways. I long for the love they have. Maybe someday. But now all I want is casual.

"What the fuck, asshole," Santiago shouts from upstairs to Dominic. "Are you going to help us carry the dresser down the stairs? Mark's noodle arms aren't helping."

"Noodle arms? Really, asshole? You're the one with a noodle dick," Mark shouts at Santiago.

I laugh at the brothers talking shit to each other. Dominic growls. "I'll be right up, asshole. What the fuck is your problem, Santiago? You've been all pissy since the night you argued with little Rosie." Dominic runs up the stairs as Santiago grumbles curse words.

CHAPTER 9
LIAM

"Knock, knock." I pound on my grandma's door. It always takes her a while to answer. She usually has the TV on so damn loud. The door swings open. Her eyes brighten at the sight of me, like they always do.

"Abuelita, how are you doing?" I kiss her cheek, and she blesses me like she's done since the accident.

I step into my grandmother's living room and inhale the familiar scent of freshly brewed coffee and the faint aroma of baked bread. She un-pauses her telenovela and flashes a warm smile as she greets me in her native tongue.

"Bien. Cómo estás, hijo?" she says as she practically sprints back to her rocking chair.

She grabs her concha—sweet bread—from the coffee table and takes a bite. Her tired eyes focus on her Spanish soap opera. I chuckle, place the bag of leftovers on her table, walk toward her, and move to the loveseat across from her. She glances at me with tender eyes as I settle in.

"Doing good, Abuelita. How a—"

She lifts her finger to her lips to shush me and raises the volume.

Sprawling my legs wide, I lean back and watch the drama unfold in her daily telenovela. A woman stands with her back toward a man. She's clearly pissed at him. He declares his love to her, apologizing for how he treated her and gets on his knees, telling her how sorry he is for not seeing sooner how much he loves her. He was blind and did not see the true meaning of love. The woman turns and kneels next to him, and they hold one another. I roll my eyes, but my grandmother places the palm of her hand on her heart and shakes her head. I chuckle at the dumbass drama unfolding. Love is for chumps. Suddenly, I'm being whacked on the head by a cushion pillow. My grandma is a hopeless romantic and lives for her telenovelas.

"Liam, hijo, why haven't you fallen in love? Are you saving yourself for a special someone?" She wags her eyebrows playfully.

What is with everyone in my family wanting me to fall in love? Love is beautiful, Liam, yada, yada, yada. What the fuck? Who wants a woman all up on your nuts telling you what the fuck to do when they do the complete opposite?

"No, Abuelita," I say firmly, shaking my head and shuddering at the thought. "I don't plan to fall in love." Never. "All this is drama, Abuelita. It's fake what you watch. Love is betrayal, loss, heartbreak, and unattainable expectations."

She gets up from her chair, her shoulders hunched as she makes her way to the kitchen. She sighs as she fills a cup with steaming coffee, the aroma wafting through the air. I lean in the kitchen doorway, watching as she opens a kitchen drawer and pulls out a photo, gazing at it for a few seconds before returning it to the drawer.

"Liam, you are so wrong, my love. Your grandpapá was the

man of my dreams. He is the definition of love for me. There's not a day that goes by I don't think of him. I miss him every day. Your mamá will tell you the same. She loves your papá. He treated her like the queen that she is."

She takes a long sip, then dips a chunk of her concha into her coffee. My abuelita is my father's mother. I know how much my father loved my mother and how much my grandpapá loved my grandmamá, but love will not exist for me. I have my reasons.

She chews and continues talking as she walks toward me and cups my cheeks. "You, my Liam, have chains, shackles wrapped around your heart, your beautiful, precious heart. It will take a special woman to undo those shackles. And when it happens, you will feel the power of love, and oh my, what a beautiful thing to feel." She smiles and looks into my eyes.

I place a kiss on her forehead. "Love is for chumps." I'm joking, but she swats me with a kitchen rag.

"Then you'll be a chump someday." She winks.

I WOKE up at the crack of dawn on my fucking day off since I found out little Miss Sassy Pants jogs every damn morning and night. I made it a mission to stalk her like prey. It's been two and a half weeks since I've spoken to or seen her. The kiss lingered on my lips for days after I left her standing on her doorstep, yet I could not bring myself to stay. Being around her is intoxicating. I was losing control of the situation.

A part of me wanted to take her there and then and have my way, and another ached to be the man she craved, not just a replacement for her ex. I freaked the fuck out and ran off like a pussy. I asked her to call me when she was no longer thinking of her ex, but what if she changed her mind? I didn't think it would take this long.

My damn forearm is sore from all the hand jobs I've been giving myself. Like now, I stroke it as I lean on the shower tile, picturing her naked creamy skin all over mine, my mouth capturing every part of her body, tasting her desire for me. I groan when my mouth covers her breast. I spill all over my hand. Fuck me. Getting out of the shower, I dry myself, only to put on workout clothes to run with Sophie. Who fucking does that? Takes a fucking shower so that they can see the woman they want to fuck while jogging. What the hell am I thinking?

Duke barks and wags his stub of a tail when he sees me reach for my keys.

"Sorry, bud, I would take you with me, but I fucking know you. You're an attention stealer. She will fawn all over you. Not today, Duke."

He barks repeatedly. His head tilts to the side, giving me innocent eyes.

I lift my hands in defense. "My dick needs attention right now. I need to see if our friendship with benefits, or whatever you call it, is still on."

He tilts his head, looks up at me, and barks again when I grab my keys.

I park my Camaro close to Sophie's neighborhood near a trail leading to a park and a small pond. This was where I saw her run one morning when I was on patrol. I've been taking this route to see her since then.

I do some leg stretches before running along the trail. A couple of yards away, I spot her in some tiny pink shorts and a white tank top, taking a sip of bottled water. I jump behind a giant willow tree and pinch the bridge of my nose. What the fuck am I doing? What the hell am I supposed to say? Hey, I decided to park my car around your neighborhood and take a jog.

Fucking lame, Liam. Fuck.

I need to think of something. Maybe I can say I'm getting ready for a marathon and ran from my house. Fuck it. She won't know. I've never reacted this way toward a woman. It's insane.

I dash down the dirt trail as soon as I notice her picking up speed. She is sexy as hell in those tiny shorts, especially with her toned legs. Goddamn, her ass is perfect. I run faster to catch up to her, but she speeds up like the fucking boogie man is after her. She runs like a gazelle, light and airy with lightning speed. She pumps her legs, gaining momentum with each push. I pick up my pace. Fuck me, I'm a fast runner, or so I thought, but this woman can run.

I finally catch up to her. She's startled when she sees me running alongside her.

"Hey, Sophie. Why are you running like the devil is chasing after you?"

She continues running at lightning speed and snickers. "That's because he obviously is."

I grin. "The devil is chasing you because he wants to play, baby."

She stumbles to a stop on the trail, and I can't help but stare. Perspiration runs down her neck and soaks her tight white tank top. The white top clings to her body, dark patches of sweat showing where it has soaked in. Her nipples are hard and prominent, pushing against the fabric of her sports bra. I feel my stomach tighten with desire.

She puts her hands on her hips. "What are you doing here, Liam? You don't live close by, do you? I would have seen you around." She sasses as if she's irritated by my presence.

She could be pissed off from the other night, but not too

pissed. Her blue eyes drink me in like I'm her favorite wine. I'm dripping in sweat. It's January, and it's still fucking cold as fuck. This woman does not seem bothered. It could be because she's from New York. I peel my shirt off just to watch her unthaw. She bites her lip, watching the sweat glisten and drip down to the V line; she swallows slowly as her gaze travels back to my face.

I smirk and say, "No, I don't live around here. I'm training for a marathon." *Lie, lie.*

Her eyes brighten at my words. All sassiness gone. "That's awesome, Liam. I've done a couple of marathons back home. When is it? Maybe I can sign up?"

Oh, fuck.

I scratch the back of my neck and avert my gaze to the pond where kids are feeding some ducks. "Um, well, it's for work. Only for officers."

Her shoulders deflate. She takes her air pods out of her pocket. "Oh, I see. That's too bad."

I clear my throat. "You're a fast runner," I say, trying to change the subject.

"Yes, being from Manhattan does that to you. Speed walking is the norm, so running comes easy."

My gaze stays pinned to her tank top, her pink nipples peeking. My dick throbs. Her body is covered in goosebumps.

"You're cold?" It comes out as a question more than a statement.

She looks at her nipples, which are clearly visible because of the white tank top and sweat dripping down from them. She blushes, causing her ears to go red.

Adorable.

"Yeah, it's cold when I'm standing around. So, I'd better get going." She takes a couple of steps back and places one of her air pods in her ear. Panic seeps in. I've never felt so damn needy for a woman. It freaks me the fuck out. I don't want her to fucking go. I want to fuck her.

Without thinking, I blurt out, "Why haven't you called?"

Her brows furrow, and she rubs her palms up and down her thighs.

Silence.

I take a long-exaggerated breath. "Look, if you changed your mind about the deal, it's fine."

No, it's not fucking fine. I want to feel her, taste her.

She wraps her arms around herself in a hug. Her mouth opens and closes, and she gives me a haughty stare. "What was I supposed to think when you ran from my doorstep like your ass was on fire?"

"Fuck." I rub the stubble on my chin. "I've never done this before." I gesture with my hands to her and me.

"What do you mean? You said no strings attached. You clearly sleep with women all the time." Her eyes drift away to a bare stretch of grass.

I could be mistaken, but I think I see a hint of jealousy on her face. Oddly enough, I rather like it.

"Kissing," I say.

Her head jerks up and her eyes widen, like a deer in head-lights. "W-what do you mean? Like you never kissed before, or our kiss...that you regretted it?"

I didn't plan on confessing this, but I don't want her to think I regretted the kiss. I ball my t-shirt to my chest and shake my head. "I've never kissed a woman before, Sophie. I never felt the urge to. With you I feel reckless, demanding things I've never done or wanted." I hate to admit she's bewitching me.

I take a couple of steps toward her then run my fingertips along her cold pouting lips. "Kissing you was like breathing in an ocean breeze. The freshness and calmness only intensified as I ventured further. The deeper my tongue thrust in you...it was fucking *fire*. Every exhale was an electrifying surge, every thrust of my tongue unleashed a raging inferno."

She gasps, her eyes widening further.

Fuck. When did I become a poet? I want to chuckle at how surprised she is. She has no idea the power she has over me and we have only known each other for a short time.

"Y-you never kissed, but how...I mean—"

I step so close to her, her words drop off like they'd been cut through with a knife. She's confused, and it's adorable. She steps away from me, scanning my profile like she's trying to figure something out.

"Like I said, baby, I never had the urge to kiss anyone. I'm into one-nightstands, and kissing would make it complicated."

She's quiet, taking it all in like I just confessed a sin. Her mouth is gaping open, and her eyes are wide.

"Baby, close that mouth of yours before I thrust my tongue in there." I lean in to grab her, wrapping my arms around her. I can feel her pebbled nipples rubbing on my bare chest. My dick swells with the feel of her body close to mine.

"Why did you kiss me and run off?"

"Because kissing you was making me lose control. I wanted you. Fuck, did I want you. My self-control was deteriorating. I needed you to be in on this thing with us. I need to be the only man you think of when I touch you, bury myself in you." I want her to submit to my touch, to the feel of my body when I pleasure her. I cup her cheek. "Am I the only man you think of?"

She nods, and a breathless whisper leaves her lips. "Yes."

I kiss her collarbone all the way up to her ear and whisper, "Then let's go back to your place to relieve some of the built-up tension."

The trail is clear of all other runners. It's just us, so I dip my fingers into her pink running shorts. "Baby, are you wet for me?" With just a fraction of my fingertips swiping her clit I feel the need to come in my shorts like a teen.

"Yes, Liam, just fuck me already."

I let out a husky laugh. "Not here, Sophie." I'm growing hard with each second that passes. I lift her up, throw her over my shoulder, and run toward her townhouse. She squeals as I pick up speed.

CHAPTER 10
SOPHIE

My breath hitches as we fumble into the foyer. I'm still finding it hard to believe I'm his first kiss. *Me.* Liam, the hot sexy Casanova, has never been kissed. He's kissing me as if he's experienced and kissed a million women. God, he's naturally good at everything he does, I assume—at least, based on the way he's pinning me up against the living room wall. His lips consume me, stealing every breath from my lungs, my soul. Dangerous is what this is, playing with fire. It makes the adrenaline burn through my whole body. His strong arms lift me up.

"Shower, baby," he pants.

I shake my head.

"You're cold. We can warm up," he says as his mouth wanders all over my neck.

"I'll warm up when you're under me. I need to feel you now!"

He groans. I let the palms of my hands roam his chest, abs, down to his V line. His vast bulge is visible through the thin material of his workout shorts. His fingers hook under my sports bra as he gently pulls off my tank top, and because the bra's built-in, I'm now bare-chested before him. My breasts bounce out, and I'm suddenly feeling embarrassed and not so sexy. His gunmetal eyes are pinned to my breasts.

"Perfect," he groans as his mouth covers first one, then the other.

My eyes roll back with the slight friction of his mouth on me. I rock my hips to get a feel of his erection. He's huge. I've never felt such electric bolts of chemistry for a man, not even with Eric. I never felt with him what I'm feeling now. My hands, my mouth, want to roam every inch of Liam. I already obtained his very first kiss, and I want to be the one to experience all of his other firsts.

Liam peels my shorts and panties off, and now I feel vulnerable, completely naked before him. I squirm uncomfortably. He's been with plenty of women with much fuller bodies.

"Don't hide from me, Bella. You're stunning."

Bella sounds so fucking sexy. Coming out of his hot lips. I know it means beautiful. He lifts me up with his broad masculine shoulders. I wrap my legs around his torso, grabbing a fistful of his dark hair, my demanding lips caressing his with urgency.

When he lays me on the loveseat, my legs dangling off the armrest, he curses under his breath, bending down. When his tongue hits my center, my eyes roll back again. Damn, it feels like I'm being possessed by his soul. I rock my hips back and forth on his face. Grabbing another fistful of his hair, I watch as he nips, sucks, and lavishes my sensitive area. His hooded eyes flicker to mine, and his tongue never stops working. The thick thrusting only intensifies. I moan and call out his name. He groans with pleasure as if he's feasting. I come undone on the tip of his tongue.

"Goddamn, baby, you taste so fucking good," he says, nibbling on my inner thighs, leaving hickeys. "Fuck. I don't have condoms with me. They're in my car. In my wallet." His voice is raw and overworked.

"I have some in my bedroom," I say, flipping my legs over and getting off the sofa.

Before I can stand, he swiftly picks me up and carries me upstairs. I rush to my panty drawer and grab a condom. When I turn around to face Liam, he's naked. I take him in, and damn, he is a *masterpiece*. I feel as if the air is knocked out of me. A breath leaves my lips. Maybe it's a sigh or maybe it's me trying to breathe steadily. When my eyes drop to his very large...you know... dick—God, it's mouth-watering.

He smirks. "Come here, baby."

I walk toward him, handing him the package. He tears the wrapper. My insides are throbbing, begging for him to be inside me. He lifts me up with one arm, the palms of his hands on my ass. He lays me on the bed, and his mouth nips my nipples. His hands tremble with eagerness as they trail down my breasts to the curve of my hips. I arch my back into his touch when he swirls at my nipples, feeling their hard peaks. His hand runs down my waist. Liam presses his palm against the curve of my hip, and his finger inserts between my thighs.

"Oh, Liam," I moan as the friction of his fingers picks up speed and hits all the right places.

A fire of heat burns through his eyes, a dark lust like the moonless night sparkling there.

"That's it, baby, moan my name, only my name. I've been dying to see you like this, sprawled out for me, fucking naked and beautiful. Damn, it's like an offering, and like hell, I'm taking it. Every inch of you, baby," he rasps, his eyes devouring me.

My heart races like a stampede of wild horses in my chest. I shift my weight, arching my back and craning my neck so I can reach him. My hands explore his muscular thighs, up to the veins pulsing beneath his skin. His arousal is evident as I grasp his hard length, already slick with anticipation. My eyes slowly wander up his muscular body, and I admire the way his disheveled hair falls over his forehead. His chest rises and falls quickly as my tongue softly traces the veins that run down his hardening shaft. I can feel the anticipation and excitement radiating from him. Liam's head falls back as he holds onto my ponytail.

"Fuck. Feels so good." His hips move at a steady rhythm.

I'm a straightforward person, but when it comes to intimacy, that's a totally different animal for me. Eric was my first in everything. It took me a while until I was ready to give him a blowjob. For some strange reason, it feels right with Liam, and how could I not take full advantage of his gorgeous, godlike body? He tastes of salty goodness, and I moan as my mouth works his length.

He takes a step backward, pulling out the condom and slipping it on. Our mouths collide, and intense energy spreads through both of us. Our kisses are wild and passionate, as if we have abandoned all rational thought. I can feel waves of desire radiating through my body as he enters me. My muscles stretch to accommodate him. Emboldened by my reckless desire, I guide him in. He slams into me then out, in and out, and I cling to his thick muscular shoulders, my nails digging into his pillar of a back.

"More," I cry as he swells inside me.

His big hands cup my breasts, taking each one. When Liam said that once I had his cock, I would never want another...oh, boy, was he right. I meet his driving rhythm beat for beat. The heat of his body seeps into my pores and into my bloodstream.

"You feel so damn good, Sophie. So tight."

I gasp when he pulls out, leaving only the crown of his tip

before he plunges in all the way. His mouth covers my screams as my body radiates with each deep thrust.

"Look at me, bella, I want to watch you come for me. I want you to feel how my dick swells inside your tight pussy, how it fills you in."

Oh, fuck.

He presses harder, more profound, and my entire body vibrates in response. The sheer power and intensity of pleasure we feel sends us into a trembling, blissful state of euphoria. It's like the moon and the stars have come together in this moment. But there is no together, not beyond the physical. I can't help feeling like more than our bodies are connected now, though. Damn. I'll be in a lot of trouble if I allow myself to continue thinking that, to become emotionally attached to Liam.

We lay in a pool of sweat, panting, still reeling from our euphoria. As the high begins to wear off, he rolls over to look at me. God, he's the most handsome man I've ever seen or been within in the dreamiest way.

He clears his throat. "Damn, this was the best sex of my life."

I snort. "Yeah, right! I doubt it. You probably don't remember. You've lost count."

He leans his elbow on the bed, holding himself up. His gaze sweeps down my naked body. "Those women...I don't remember their names. I've never slept with the same woman twice. But I'll remember your name. And believe me, this is something worth remembering."

My heart does this funny thing, and oh, he can't say things like that. I swallow the ball of nerves. "It was the best sex of my life, too." My voice is a mere whisper as our eyes lock briefly before he tears them away.

He brushes his hair with his fingers, and an awkward silence envelops us. He reaches for his shorts. My eyes stay hypnotized on his bare ass, hard, firm, and muscular, as he shims his shorts on.

He looks at me over his shoulder. "I should go. I'm sure you have work today."

I nod. "Yeah."

"Let's keep this between us. You know the way Mila and Dom get."

I reach for a throw blanket to cover myself. A repressed laugh escapes my lips. "Oh, I know. They would think we're an item, and we know that's not happening."

He gives me a curt nod. "Yeah." He swallows nervously as he walks to the door. The deep frown on his handsome face is etched with confusion. He scratches the back of his neck absentmindedly before turning back to me. "Umm, so I guess if we get the urge, then...um, we call—"

"Yeah, I'll call you. Or you call me." I bite my lip. This is sooooo awkward. It feels like a booty call. We clearly don't know how to go about it. As awkward as it is, it changes every-thing for me, for us. I want Liam and not in a casual way anymore because damn now I wish he was my lover. Although I know it can't happen—it's not what he wants. I have to keep myself from catching feelings for him.

I'm TOSSING my purse on my desk and reaching for my appointment book when Mila rushes in.

"Good morning!" she singsongs, throwing her hands up in the air.

My gaze bounces back and forth between the hickeys on her neck. "Aren't you chirpy this morning? Could it be the marks on your neck?"

She digs into her purse, pulling out a mirror. She growls,

dabbing foundation on the bruises. "I swear, Dominic is such a caveman. And you know I can say the same thing about you. You're glowing and have a heaping number of hickeys on your neck."

My eyes widen, and I reach for the mirror in her hand. Oh, God, it's like a necklace of hickeys. He mauled me like a savage beast. I hadn't noticed. After he left, I laid in bed, wanting him to come back for another round of sinful sex. There's no coming back from this. It was *amazing*. Once or twice would never be enough. His ivory and spice aroma lingered in the air and seeped into my flesh. His body was a work of art.

"So, you had a hell of a night, morning, or something, huh? You're on cloud nine. Was it that good?" Mila asks.

"So good."

"Amazing. You needed it. Anyway, our morning appointments canceled. Let's go to Bath and Body Works for their semi-annual sale. On our way, you can tell me all about him."

"Bath and Body Works for what?"

She smacks some lip gloss on her lips. "Candles and body creams. Candles always set the mood, and Dominic sniffs me when I wear my cherry lotion."

Oh, that spikes my interest. "It sets the mood?" Should I be setting the mood for Liam and me, though?

She nods, waving at me to follow her out the door.

An hour later, my hands feel smooth as butter after sampling more lotions than I realized existed. I pick up a candle that reads "Strawberry Pound Cake." Nope, that will only make me hungry. I sniff lavender, and espresso smells good. I add two of those and some other scents to my basket. For some reason, I've never been a candle person. Setting the mood for Liam and me, though...it feels sexy and hot.

"Tell me, is this guy better than Eric?" Mila asks.

I chuckle. There is no comparison. Liam is breathtaking. I

want to know more about him and who he is under all the hard layers. It's a bad idea, but I do.

"Oh, yeah, way better," I say with a grin.

Mila asks where I met this hot guy. I feel guilty lying, but I tell her we met through a dating app. She's my bestie. I've never lied to her. After my arrangement with Liam is over, I'll tell her.

The thought of our arrangement ending has me feeling... heartbroken. *Dammit, Sophie, don't think with your heart.* He doesn't want anyone catching feelings for him.

"Are you going to see him again?" Mila asks as she sniffs different scented candles.

"Yeah, but he doesn't want a relationship. It's only casual, a no-strings-attached thing."

She frowns. "Sophie, be careful. You don't want to fall in love when he wants the opposite. You already like him way too much. I can tell. And it's only been one night."

She's right. Mila knows me so well. The minute I caught a glimpse of him in my studio speaking with Mila, I wanted him. My heart sinks to the pit of my stomach. I knew I was playing a dangerous game when I agreed. I know I will get my heart broken again, but I know this time it will be different because Liam is no match to the men I've been with. The chemistry I felt from the beginning was fire. Let's just hope I can put the fire out before I'm the one getting burned.

CHAPTER 11
LIAM

"What can I get ya, Liam?" Will bellows over the blaring music and chatter in the bar.

"Corona with lime," I reply as he starts to fill a pint glass.

The chairs next to me are quickly pulled out, and Santiago and Mark wedge into them.

"How's it going, bro?" I tip my head up and give them a strong handshake.

"Did you manage to get the truck running?" Santiago asks, signaling Will for a beer.

I squeeze the lime into the corona and look at Santiago. "Not yet. I bought a 454 big block engine. All I need now is a lift to swap out the old engine and rebuild the carburetor."

Will returns with drinks in hand and offers beers to both Mark and Santiago.

"If you need a lift, you can always use the one in my shop. I'm happy to help," Santiago drawls out as he takes a swig of beer.

"Thanks, man, I appreciate it," I reply.

He pats my shoulder and gestures to the unoccupied pool

table.

Mark takes the first shot, leaning onto the glossy mahogany table as he aims his cue. "Has Rosa returned to Oregon? I didn't get a chance to see her or meet her boyfriend. Your mom mentioned she might move back."

Rosa and Mark are the same age. They've been friends since childhood, although Rosa spent her time constantly by Santiago's side.

I glance up at Santiago. He stiffens at the mention of Rosa. When I returned from dropping Sophie off on New Year's Eve, Santiago showed up to hang out and drink some beers. Later that night, Santiago and Rosa had a fallout in the backyard. We couldn't hear anything when Santiago walked in. He grabbed his keys and drove away. Rosa always followed Santiago around like a big brother, and Santiago always looked out for her. We always ran off any boyfriends Rosa had, anyone who was interested in her. I'm sure he's being the protective big brother as I have always been to her.

"She left the day after New Year's. She plans on moving back when she graduates in May. Rosa and her boyfriend are getting an apartment together. She hopes to open her own art studio." Mark grins. "Remember when she would have her bucket of crayons and draw and paint for hours?"

I laugh. "Yeah, and she would only let Santiago see her drawings."

Santiago grumbles and aims his cue. A tall redhead leans into him, wrapping her arms around his waist, the palms of her hands brushing his chest.

"Hey, Santi," she says, her voice dripping with lust.

I snort. *Santi.* Her two friends approach us. One gazes at Mark, and the other, a blonde, comes toward me like she is walking the runway seductively. Her eyelashes flutter, and her hand runs over my biceps.

"You're so muscular and hot. What's your name, handsome?"

I brush her hand off. "Liam, and I'm not interested."

She pouts. "You have a girlfriend?"

"No." I walk off, reaching for my beer. Mark dismisses the woman hitting on him. Telling her he has a girlfriend. The only blonde I have on my mind is grenade, who came to explode shit up in my life.

Santiago whispers in the redhead's ear and she giggles, twirling her hair around her finger. I'm sure he'll sleep with her tonight.

Santiago saunters toward me, smirking like an idiot. "Never seen you dismiss a woman before. Especially one who is hot as fuck, her breasts spilling out."

I shrug. "Not in the mood tonight."

He studies me, then says, "Hmm." He shakes his head then takes a sip of his beer before setting the bottle down. "Your mom said on New Year's Eve you left with Mila's friend." His eyebrows rise as he grins.

I roll my eyes, leaning against the wall. "She needed a ride home. She'd been drinking."

He's not buying it. "Oh, I'm sure you gave her a ride." He laughs. "A ride on your dick." He thrusts his hips.

Mark spits out a mouthful of beer.

"Fuck off," I retort, sticking out my middle finger with a cheeky smirk. I line up my shot, making sure to send the cue ball into three other balls on the table.

Thoughts of Sophie run through my head, her porcelain white skin so soft and buttery, caressing mine. Her eyes are like sapphires, sparkling with each passionate thrust. She was like nothing I'd ever experienced before. I long to be inside her again. I won't forget how stunning she looked with my cock in her mouth, giving me the best damn blowjob I've ever had. It's been a week since I've seen her. Work has been hectic.

"I thought you didn't do relationships, fucker?" Santiago says.

"I don't. We're only...how do I say it...releasing tension? Getting it out of our systems with a no-strings-attached agreement."

He snorts. "So, you're fucking her. Like a fuck buddy?"

I scratch the back of my neck. When he puts it that way, it feels wrong, even though she agreed to it. "Something like that." I point to them. "Don't fucking tell Dominic or Mila."

They lift their hands and say, "We won't," in unison.

Right as Dominic bursts through the door, Santiago mumbles, "You're getting yourself into a rabbit hole."

I ignore it and give Dominic a strong handshake.

"Sorry I'm late," he says, oblivious to our stares. He grabs a pool stick. His hair is in disarray, and his shirt is on backward.

Santiago laughs. "Damn, you think you would have fixed yourself up after having sex..."

Dominic shrugs. "I was running late, and I'm making up for lost time, and she's been through hell."

He's not wrong. Mila deserves every bit of happiness Dominic can give her.

Santiago ruffles his hair some more. "Yeah, little bro, she has."

An hour later, after our game of pool, I text Sophie. I know it isn't the alcohol making me feel daring because I only drank two beers. We agreed that when we felt the urge to call one another, we would.

. . .

ME: *Hey, are you up?*

When I see the bubbles appear, I'm relieved.

Sophie: *Yes, I'm up. It's not too late.*

Right, it's only ten.

Me: *Are you up for it tonight?*

I stare at my phone for four whole minutes leaning against my car at Rocko's.

Sophie: *Are you asking if I'm up for a booty call?*

Christ, why does she have to make it so awkward?

Me: *Booty call? Let's call it a craving. So, is that a yes?*

I can already see her rolling her eyes.

Sophie: *I think it's the other way around. You're texting me!! Yes, come over since you're craving me.*

I hate how a grin appears on my face, how ready I am to see her.

Me: *On my way.*

Twenty minutes later, I'm at her doorstep. I rap my knuckles against the door twice, and she swings it open, wearing a crop top and shorts. *Damn.* My body reacts instinctively.

"Hey," she squeals.

Walking in, I shut the door behind me. I greet her with a kiss, my mouth covering hers, and my legs wedge between hers as I deepen it. She needs this as much as I do. I can feel it by the way she slides her fingers through my hair and moans into my mouth. Her kiss feels like a heart-stopping plunge from the highest point of a roller coaster. I step back, catching my breath. I shuck off my shirt and jeans and stalk toward her.

She's biting her lip, watching me. "Liam," she purrs when I slip off her crop top.

Perfect—no bra. I take each breast in my mouth and suck until she whimpers. My dick throbs with need.

"Take off your shorts, Sophie, and lay on the couch," I demand, unable to wait any longer. I need to be in her.

She takes off her red silk shorts in a rush, matching my thirst for her. It knocks the air out of me. I need to fuck her then leave. She makes me feel things I'm unfamiliar with, and I don't like it.

Her creamy skin is flawless, and the shape of her body is divine. She lies on the couch, ready for me, as I slip off my briefs and stroke my hard cock. My fingers trace the line of her pussy. She's so damn wet and ready for me. I'm too aroused for foreplay. I need her now. I grab a condom from my wallet. Once I slip it on, I glance up at Sophie. She's watching.

"Baby, spread your legs for me."

She moans when I insert a finger.

"So wet for me."

She nods. I slip into her wet entrance. She's so damn tight. Fuck, she feels good. Ramming myself faster and harder into her. Sophie raises her hips, wanting me to go deeper. I grunt into her hair, sucking on her beautiful slender neck. I can feel she's at her peak by how she claws on my back and tightens around my cock as she milks me dry.

Slipping off her, I shuffle to the restroom, tossing the condom in the trash. When I make my way back to Sophie, she's still trying to catch her breath on the couch. I grab her clothes and hand them to her.

"Fuck, you feel so damn good, Sophie," I admit because she fucking does. I slip my clothes back on. I've done this shit so many damn times. Fuck her and leave her. Sophie's different, though. Maybe it's because she's Mila's friend. I feel like an asshole fucking her and leaving. I shake off those feelings. We are both adults, and this is what we want. We released tension, and now I can go. I reach for my keys on the floor and glance over my shoulder at Sophie.

"I'd better go. See you later?" I raise an eyebrow, waiting for her reply.

"Yes, Liam, see you later," she responds in a low voice.

I walk out the door feeling like an ass, because I can see she's not the type to sleep with a man and not want more.

———

THE POLICE OFFICERS and our task force are ready, their raid jackets and armored vests reflecting the dim light of the harbor. We're standing in a line wearing bulky black armor and masks visible even in the shadows. In the distance, I hear two limousines pulling up to the docks, and the sound of conversation floats across the cold night air. They are close enough that we can see two men emerge from the limousines and move toward a third man with a bag over his head. Every officer tenses as they watch silently, waiting for their cue to move in. John passes me the binoculars. One of the men is Pablo's son. A surge of anger vibrates through me, the need to pin the fucker down and demand he tell me where his bastard of a father is. One of his men takes off the bag covering the man's head. I gasp when I see who it is. Pablo's son looks right at us in the dark shadows and smirks.

Fuck.

He points the gun and shoots at one of our undercover men. His body jolts back from the recoil, droplets of blood spraying the crashing waves. Suddenly, men burst from the building with guns blazing. Our squad launches out of the shadows in response, shots erupting in utter chaos. I look for Pablo's son, Marko, and spot him scurrying away from the scene in his car.

Coward.

I lean against a cold metal crate, my gun cocked and ready.

When I spot two men beside a pillar of metal, I take aim and bellow through the chaos, "Drop your guns. Hands up." They toss their guns on the filthy cement floor, raising their hands. As one of the guys lifts his arms, the hem of his sleeve drops, revealing a serpent tattoo.

My anger boils into a raging inferno with my gun in hand, the metal cold against my palm. "Get down on your knees," I command.

Before I can take another step, a mountainous figure slams into me, knocking me off my feet. My gun and cuffs clatter to the ground. Two men tower above me, snarls on their faces and violence in their eyes. I feel every jab and blow as they thrash me, despite the thick body armor I have on. One punch lands squarely on my jaw, causing stars to flash before my eyes. In a burst of adrenaline, I grab the leg of one of the men and pull him down with me, throwing punches to counter each hit he lands until I knock the bastard out. The other two men flee like a bunch of pussies. I reach for my handcuffs, clamping them on his wrist.

Later, I stand in front of the two-way mirror window of the interrogation room, listening in as Detective Ryan questions Julio, one of the serpents.

"Where are Pablo and Marko? Who informed them about our operation?"

The Serpent leans in his chair, legs spread, with a don't-give-a-fuck look. A smug smile spreads across his malicious face. "Pablo sent a message. Don't fuck with his shipment. Next time you send a spy, the aim will be straight to his head." He makes a *puff* sound, mimicking blowing his brains out.

I want to beat the shit out of him until the truth spills from his venomous mouth.

I FEEL a sharp pain as I climb out of bed this morning—it feels like an invisible vice is squeezing my shoulder. My muscles are tense and knotty, like large balls of lead attached to my sides. The bruises from the three men who ambushed me the night before made my abdomen sting, but it would have been worse if those assholes had grabbed my gun when they ambushed me. Dumbasses.

I grunt as dull, sharp pain needles its way through me when I slide off the sofa. I look at the clock hanging on the wall. Four o'clock. I've laid on the couch for five hours, going over the interrogation in my head. I grind my molars, infuriated. We have a rat on our force. A fucking snitch, dirty cop.

What plays in my head is how the fucker claimed to be Marko's cousin and how he looked straight at the mirror window, saying, "I heard Detective Rodriguez's son is on the force, a pig just like his father. What a shame he didn't die that night." A sinister laugh erupts from his mouth. "Back off our shipments, pigs, or you'll have fallen officers."

All I want is closure for my father and mother. I know she worries I'll be next. In my line of duty, we never know what can happen.

———

I GO DOWN the aisles at Lucky's grocery store carrying a basket. I sort through all types of creams for sore muscles. I've been walking all afternoon like my grandma when she rolls out of bed. My strained shoulders and sore abdomen make it hard to straighten up. I grab some Vicks and toss it in the basket. My abuela swears by this shit. I reach for different types of pain and muscle relief creams. Music plays over the store speakers, and someone nearby is singing along with it. A familiar voice. My head jolts up, causing my lower back to ache in pain. But my lips turn up in a smile at that voice. That sexy New York accent has my blood scorching hot, streaming down to my cock.

Strutting toward her, I watch as she sways her gorgeous hips, her round ass jiggling to the music, and the fabric of her leggings shaping her ass to perfection. The need to have her has only intensified since the last time I had her. I just have to make sure I don't fall under her spell.

She bends to grab a box of popcorn. Her ass is in mid-air, and my dick stirs, pressing against my sweatpants. All I can envision is my cock pounding into her firm ass, her moans echoing through the walls as I fill her in when her tight pussy clenches on my dick.

Fuck me.

I shake the thought out of my head and slap her ass. After all, it's my ass to slap at the moment. She jolts up when my hand meets her ass. When she sees me, her eyes widen, but then she relaxes. Her beautiful sapphire eyes roam my body with heat.

"Liam," she says, her voice straining to suck in a breath. Sophie gently brushes her fingers along my jaw where a bruise has formed, and tingling courses through my body, a feeling of electricity passing over my skin. I shaved, so now I can feel the softness of her touch.

"What happened?" she asks, her eyes filled with concern.

It's a new feeling—no woman has ever worried about me before. They usually only care about using my body for their own pleasure. She gently runs her fingers down my arms, pausing to touch the small scrapes on my skin.

"Shit went down at work during a drug bust at the docks. When I had two guys down, a fucker ambushed me, knocking me to the ground."

She hisses as she traces each visible mark. She shakes her head. "Liam, didn't you have a partner with you?" She's angry.

"Well, yeah, I had my team with me, along with the entire task force. I ran off when I saw the man we have been after—he's the head of the gang. But he left like a coward. I went after one of his men to get information, then another couple of guys ambushed me, and we tumbled to the ground."

She tippy-toes to kiss my chin on the bruise.

I inhale sharply at the feeling of her soft lips on the bruise, and even that small breath sends pain cramping through my abdomen.

Her eyes widen at the realization of what she just did. "Sorry, I'm used to kissing Dante's boo-boos," she utters, flustered.

"It's fine," I say, holding back a wince of pain. "Just hurts a little."

"What else hurts?" Sophie scans my body, and her eyes drop to my basket.

"My abdomen, shoulders, and back. Everywhere the fuckers kicked me. I'm good, baby. This shit will help relieve my knotted muscles."

She nods, reaching for my small basket and throwing it in her shopping cart. I cock my head, but she ignores me.

"I just need to grab a couple of sweets and snacks for a movie night I have planned with my guy. You're coming to my place so I can rub cream on your back and shoulders." She throws the words over her shoulder while looking for some popcorn flavoring.

Guy! Who in the fuck is *her guy* because it sure as hell is not me. Did she plan a movie night with someone else? Jealousy ripples through me like a scorching hot iron. No sign of guilt is written on her beautiful face. Nonchalantly, she throws butter, nacho cheese, and caramel flavoring into her basket. She moves along, pushing her cart, while I trail behind her, pissed enough to become a ticking time bomb.

In the bakery aisle, she grabs a pre-sliced container of cheesecake. She peers at me with those hypnotizing eyes. I know I should get my basket and leave. She has plans with another man. I'm not going to be her side bitch. It's obvious she's already taken what she wanted from me.

"What kind do you want? Cheesecake, chocolate double fudge, any of these?" She points at the rows of cakes.

I stand in front of her, my arms crossed over my chest. "Are you asking me?"

"Well, who else would I be talking to, Casanova?" Sophie rolls her eyes.

I grab a chocolate double fudge and place it in the basket. "Maybe the guy you have plans with." I'm grinding my teeth.

She throws her head back and laughs. "Oh, you mean Patrick. Well, he won't be having any dessert."

I growl and look around, making sure no one is watching. Cupping her cheeks, I peer into her gorgeous face. "We had an agreement, Grenade. You want to see other shitheads, we're done."

"Oh, lord, you're hot when you're jealous." She fans herself, then adds, "You got nothin' on Patrick Swayze. No need to get so, jealous, big guy." She snickers, grinning.

This woman knows how to get under my skin, making me look like a complete dumbass.

I lean in to whisper in her ear, "You're going to pay for it, baby."

Sophie's eyes widen, her mouth opens slightly, and her lips become moist with anticipation. Lustful chemistry saturates the air around us; she likes it. She loves it, my naughty girl. God, what am I saying? She's not mine. I shake my head.

"How?" she asks breathlessly.

"You'll see."

CHAPTER 12
LIAM

"Liam, get in my car," she commands. "You're not driving in your condition. You're all fucked up."

I lift an eyebrow at her. "Nah, I'm good to drive," I drawl while lifting a grocery bag from the cart. I grunt as I lift an enormous bag of cat food—and she doesn't even own a cat. She claims it's for the strays.

"See? You're in pain, Liam. Stop acting like a macho man."

I snort. "Baby, I'm not *acting* like a macho man. I am one."

She rolls her eyes.

"Get in my damn car, Liam. I'm not taking 'Nah, I'm good to drive' for an answer." She scowls at me, and it's fucking hot.

My dick twitches.

We make it to her apartment. The last time I was here was when I called her to have rough, dirty sex. This is the third time I've been at her place. She gestures to the sofa for me to sit. The place looks empty now that Mila and Dante have moved in with Dominic.

"Have you had anything to eat? I made lots of pasta for lunch since it's only me now," she says sweetly.

My heart speeds up at her close proximity. She's all I think about—and it's been a week since I last touched her. Goddamn, I've never wanted a girl more than once. I want Sophie day in and day out. She weakens me—she's like a drug. The sweet scent of coconut and the taste of pure heaven in her body have me bending to my knees. I've had to turn off that switch more than once. I'm only going to take her body a couple of times more and end it, and then we can both move on. I'm sure our needs will come to an end and we will no longer crave one another.

"Sure, I'll have some. I haven't eaten since this morning."

What the hell am I doing? *Dammit, Liam, get your shit together.* I'm about to tell her no thanks, say it's better if I leave.

But she smiles and says, "Great."

All chirpy and shit, she rumbles through her fridge, taking out a container and popping it into the microwave. She gracefully moves around the kitchen. Her blonde hair is tied up in a ponytail, but strands of it fall free to the sides. The way she holds herself is strong and powerful. She doesn't see what I see. I can tell that much by how she covers her naked body and how she tries to keep from eating too much. Her confidence is in there, hidden in the shadows of her mind. I'll work to get it out of her so she can see how powerful and gorgeous she is. Even though we've only shared a few encounters, I feel I know her better than anyone else.

I creep up behind her, my skin tingling with anticipation for the warmth of her body. My erection is thick and ready for her, a volcano ready to erupt. I plant kisses on her collarbone.

"Liam," she says, breathlessly scooping the warm pasta from the container onto a plate and adding a warm breadstick to the side of the fettuccini.

"Hmm," I say as I continue tasting her.

My tongue strokes up and down the nape of her neck. She

tastes of coconut, a fruity taste that intoxicates me. Rubbing my erection on her ass, I let my hands move freely, cupping her breasts. Good thing I'm wearing sweats so she can feel my throbbing shaft. Her head falls back onto my shoulders, giving me more access to her delicate neck. The pulsing vein under my tongue solidifies how much I affect her.

"Liam, not now. You need to eat, and you're hurt. After dinner, I'll rub the cream on you," she pants.

"I'd rather eat you," I groan as the blood rushes to my cock.

Sophie spins around, her eyes wide with surprise, arousal blushing over her cheeks. She is so beautiful that it hurts to look at her. My mouth crashes onto hers, demanding more from her red lips than she can give. Our tongues tangle, sucking the oxygen from one another. Kissing this woman is heaven. I never thought I'd be addicted to kissing. It never felt right to kiss any of the girls I've been with. The soft warmth of her lips unmans me. I only want to explore them further.

She pants, pushing me away. "No, not now, Liam. When you're better. Eat before it gets cold."

"Baby," I whine, my dick aching.

She looks at my enormous erection and licks her lips. I don't even think she realizes she's doing it. I groan, grabbing my plate and placing it on the table.

AFTER I FINISH EATING DINNER, Sophie streams her favorite movie on Netflix, *Dirty Dancing*. Although I've only watched *Dirty Dancing* once or twice, I'm a fan of Patrick Swayze in *Roadhouse*. I can watch that one movie over and over.

"Take off your shirt," she shouts as she pops a bag of popcorn into the microwave.

"Damn, Sophie, if you wanted me naked, you should have

said so. I would have gladly given you a striptease." I smirk and peel off my shirt.

She gasps as she over-analyzes my torso and back. Sophie's hands gently roam the maroon bruises, then her lips press against each one on my chest, sides, and back, and she runs her lips to my jaw. Just a small fraction of her warm lips on my skin sends me to an unknown dimension where it's just us. But it just can't happen. It feels too domestic, being here with her, having dinner at her table, popping popcorn, watching movies, and now her lips on me, soothing the pain away.

"Poor baby," she murmurs. "Lie on the sofa so I can massage the cream on your back." Her eyes are soft and sympathetic.

"I'd better go, Sophie. I shouldn't be here. We didn't sign up for this." I gesture around the house.

She averts her gaze. "Oh, I see. We're friends, aren't we? Friends with benefits, right?" She crinkles her nose. "No harm in me trying to help you out." She sighs. "Lie down. I'll put some cream on you, then you can leave."

I nod and do as she says.

Her thin, gentle fingertips work like little drills, probing and kneading deep-seated muscle tensions. She works her fingers into the knots of my neck, kneading and pressing with a gentle but firm touch. My eyes flutter closed as she works, the tension flowing away from my body with each breath. Her hands are cool from the cream but warming quickly, and she moves from my neck and shoulders to my back, kneading and pressing, feeling the tension flow out of me.

"Am I hurting you?" she asks softly.

"No, it feels good." Too fucking good. My dick is rock-hard.

I ignore the nagging voices in my head about how this is something lovers do...the domestic side of a relationship. Not what I agreed to, but with her, for some unknown reason, I want to feel what it's like before it all goes to shit. Because it *will* go to shit. Sophie and I can't happen. I've never experienced a woman's touch and kindness like this before. I guess I've never wanted it. Until now.

"All right, turn around, and let's do your chest and abdomen."

I turn, along with my dick, on the verge of springing free. Her gorgeous ocean-blue eyes, which hold me captive, roam my body down to my swollen shaft.

She sighs. "You're making this really hard, Casanova."

I bite my lip, drinking her in. She's stunning. She changed into black shorts and a white T-shirt. Her simplicity is alluring. She wears light makeup, enhancing her natural beauty. Her red lipstick makes her look divine.

"Then ride me, baby. I'll take you for a wild ride."

Her eyes flutter. I can see the pulsing of the vein on her neck. I love how I affect her as much as she affects me. She swallows hard. "Not happening. We need the cream to...penetrate really well." She continues rubbing the cream, ignoring my bulge, giving me a bad case of blue balls. She clasps her hands. "Okay, all done. I'm going to wash my hands, grab my popcorn, and finish the movie. Let the cream soak into your skin, and if you want to leave, you can. Or you could just hang out."

She moves toward the bathroom while I sink into the soft couch cushions, feeling relieved and tranquil. It's been a long time since I've felt such peace. Since the night my father was taken away from me and my nightmares started.

Sophie appears with a bowl of popcorn and cheese flavoring then takes her spot next to me. She carefully places my head on her lap. You would think we've known each other for years by how well we click together. This unnerving feeling is scaring the shit out of me. She mindlessly runs her hands through my hair.

Damn, this feels good. I close my eyes and enjoy the touch of her hands. A part of me wants to stay.

Tilting my head up, I glance at Sophie. With her other hand she pops a piece of popcorn into her mouth. Her eyes are focused on the movie. She chews and pops another one in her mouth.

Cute. Adorable.

Her eyes flutter when Patrick Swayze lifts Baby or whatever in the fuck her name is into the air. She sighs.

"You know, I've watched this movie a million times. It's one of my mom's favorite movies. When I was a kid, I would watch it with her. I would practice the dance moves and ask my brother to lift me up in the air." She laughs.

"You have a brother?"

"Yeah, it's just my brother and me. He's older. He lives in London with his wife." She's still focused on the movie and running her fingers through my hair. "And you? Any siblings?"

I feel a sharp pang in my chest. "No," I bite out, not meaning to.

"Oh," is all she says.

I feel like an ass being snippy with her. "Sophie—"

She kisses my forehead. "It's okay."

I don't know how she does it, but she understands without even knowing. I don't think Dominic has mentioned my life story to her or Mila, and Mila keeps personal things private. If she knew about my childhood, she wouldn't tell. They know it's *my story* to tell. Glancing up at her, I find myself drowning in her. Breathtaking. I wouldn't mind getting lost in her, drowning in an abyss, as long as she was with me, bringing me into the light and the waves of her blue eyes. I watch as she licks one of her fingers, cheddar staining them from the popcorn. The light from the TV reflects off her face, lighting up the little brown freckles dotted across her cheeks.

Twenty-five.

I count twenty-five freckles, making her look flawless. She throws the palm of her hand over her chest when Patrick Swayze says, 'No one puts Baby in a corner.' I hold in my laugh. She would get along with my abuelita and my mom. They're suckers for anything romantic.

I wonder if she watched movies with her ex. Were they close? Does she still think of him and wish for him? Jealousy burns in my chest, so I reach for her chin to press a kiss there. She tastes salty and cheesy. I don't mind at all. I want to feel her lips. Call me desperate, but I can't help myself when it comes to her.

Sitting up, I wrap my arms around her and bring her in to snuggle with me. Yeah, snuggling is a foreign word to me, but here I am, initiating it. She looks up at me with a goddess of a smile, snuggling in, her fingers gliding up and down my bare chest.

Slipping my fingers into her shorts, I feel the moisture between her legs. My naughty girl is not wearing underwear. I insert two fingers, and she tightens around them, causing her to buck her hips. She wants more; I'll give her as many orgasms as she needs.

"Take off your shorts, baby, ride my face. I need to taste you. It's been way too long. Fuck the chocolate fudge cake. I want *you* as dessert. Your pussy tastes sweeter. Tastes like heaven." My voice is raw and demanding.

She blushes, and man, does my cock want to be set free. She stands, slipping her shorts off.

I groan, watching her undress. "Your shirt and bra, too. I want you naked when I taste you. I need to feel your body and memorize each curve, down to each freckle and mole." My blood pumps rapidly with a need to touch, taste, and feel her.

She ignites a fire in me that only she can tame. In a hot second, she's naked before me. No words can describe how beautiful she is bared to me like this. I can tell she feels uncomfortable.

"Sophie, you're stunning, the most beautiful woman I have laid eyes on. You're breathtaking."

She shakes her head dismissively. "You've been with many women, Liam. I'm sure beautiful knockout women."

I lift my hand up, cutting her off. I hate the word *many*. It makes me sick to my stomach to know I've bedded so many women, but not because I'm a manwhore or some shit like that. I have reasons, but now it feels wrong when Sophie says *many*.

"Stop talking about other women I don't care to remember, Sophie. They knew it was a one-night thing, knew that if we ran into each other, I wouldn't remember them, clothed or naked. But I'd remember you. You're engraved in me. My body only reacts to you." *The truth.* "Now, get your sweet ass over here, baby. I'm thirsty." I lay on the sofa, lifting her up. Fuck, she's wet. I grab her firm ass with both hands, squeezing them even as I moved my head between her legs.

My tongue tentatively explores, tasting her delicate flesh. I circle her clit with slow precision and then increase the pressure. I flick my tongue against her arousal, occasionally adding a gentle bite as she gasps and moans in pleasure. My name is a whisper on her lips.

"Fuck, Liam." Her voice is raspy—and sexy.

She rocks faster, grabbing a fistful of my hair as my dick pulses, blood rushing with heat. Fuck, I could come just by tasting her, my hands roaming her body. I blow a hot breath into her clit just before biting and thrusting faster. She cries my name in pleasure right after she orgasms on my tongue. Fuck, she tastes like my new favorite flavor. One I won't be able to live without. I ignore the tugging feeling. She scoots down to my chest, our eyes meet, and fuck me. I shake the feeling again and remind myself I can't get hypnotized by her spell.

CHAPTER 13
SOPHIE

"Bedroom," I say tugging on his arm.

He doesn't hesitate. I drag him up the stairs to my bedroom. Fuck. Liam knows how to give me an ocean-wave orgasm, the type I've only felt with him.

We lock eyes; his gorgeous gunmetal eyes burn passionately, and my orgasm glistens on his lips. I close my eyes and try to keep my heart from fluttering as I look at Liam. He bites his lip and makes me weak in the knees.

"Ride my dick, bella," he commands softly. His choice of endearments like bella,' grenade,' and baby ignite a fire within me.

Holy guacamole.

Rubbing his thick erection over his gray sweats, I fall to my knees, drawing out his thick cock. Liam Rodriguez is hot and sexy. He waits for me to take him in my mouth, putting his hands behind his head. Anticipation is written all over Liam's handsome face. My mouth waters, tasting the saltiness and precum spilling from him. I moan, and my tongue glides freely up and down his pulsing veins. He bucks his hips with every thrust in my mouth, my hair intertwined with his fist.

"Oh man, fuck baby, you take me so well." His voice is raw and husky.

I slurp, feeling him swell in my mouth.

He pulls me from his length and says, "Ride me now, bella, it's time for your payback," he orders.

The tingling between my legs grows stronger, and I need him to be inside me. Chewing on my bottom lip, I look up at him, getting off my knees. The way he says bella in his native tongue is hot.

"What do you mean payback?" I ask, not knowing what he has in mind.

He smirks. "Don't fucking come until I tell you to." He slaps my ass, and I jump up. "You got it?"

I nod. "You're such a brute."

He slaps my ass again. I moan, liking it.

"I'll show you brute, baby."

I push him onto the bed and straddle his hips, my body in perfect alignment with his. My breath grows shallow as I sink into him, relishing how his girth fills me. Our movement finds a gentle, instinctive rhythm that has us both lost in pleasure. My breath strangles in my lungs as I ride him like he's my wild stallion. I want to tame him and keep him as mine.

"Fuck, Sophie, you feel good, but, baby, I forgot to put a condom on. I'll pull out."

I rock back and forth, panting as I answer him. "I'm on the pill." But...shit...he's been with other women.

As if he can read my mind, he says, "I've never been without one, Sophie, and I'm clean. You feel so damn good."

Relief washes over me. Bucking my hips, I drive deeper into him, the pressure building up. I need to come.

"Please," I beg. "Liam, I need to."

He slaps my ass, making it harder to keep it in. "Not yet," he says in a strangled breath.

He rolls us over so he's on top, and with each heavy, powerful thrust, the bed creaks in protest. His muscles tense with each forceful thrust as he increases the intensity, pushing us both closer to the edge of pleasure. His teeth gently graze my shoulder while his soft lips seek mine out in an enticing whisper of a kiss. I'm helpless under his expert touch, every nerve afire from the heat radiating through him into me. All I want is more of this pure bliss.

"Come for me, baby," he says in a raspy voice.

Within seconds, we both come together, and it's earth-shattering. Waves of pleasure crash over our bodies like a tsunami hitting the shore. His lips seek out my breasts, taking each one in his mouth.

"Fuck, baby," he says in the sexiest voice.

There's something in his tone that I can't piece together. He lays his head on my chest, and our bodies glisten with sweat under the light coming in through the bedroom window. My heart melts when he looks at me, his hooded eyes filled with lust.

Exhaustion washes over me. I'm about to crash, and he looks like he's falling asleep too. Will it be too much for him, sleeping with me?

"Hey," I say, my voice drowsy. "You can sleep in Mila's old room if you want. I know you—"

"Later." He wraps me in his arms and falls asleep in what must be record time.

Despite my exhaustion, I don't fall asleep, and soon it's three in the morning and I'm watching his chest rise and fall. Liam's body is machine-like, with solid muscles and soft skin.

His tan, olive skin glistens in the moonlight coming in through the window. He's beautiful.

Would staying enveloped in this love haze in my bedroom be virtuous? Love. It's such a strong word, but I used it several times with Eric. A word not meant for him, though—a word he didn't deserve to hear from me. He never made me feel beautiful, worshiped, or worthy of love, inside and out. Eric always sucked the life out of me, confidence, and all.

It only took being with Liam twice to see it. How ironic that this man can make me feel things in such a short amount of time. Is it possible to fall for Liam have fallen this soon? From the beginning, I knew I sought him out at my and Mila's studio, the chemistry wrapping around us like a soft blanket. How he played with my body like a string on a guitar was...mind-blowing. No man has ever made me feel this way. Ever. He's ruined me completely. No man can take me to the height of ecstasy like Liam can.

I lie back in bed, trying to fall asleep without ruminating too much about Liam and me. When I'm about to close my eyes, Liam tosses and turns. His breathing suddenly upticks, and he mumbles something that sounds like, "No, no." Liam has nightmares.

Under all his hard exterior lies a broken man. I saw it in his eyes—under all the lust is pain. I noticed this when I mentioned his family, particularly his father, and asked if he had siblings. Something happened. I understand things are temporary for us, but I don't want to be a BandAid, to be the one to fix him like a broken doll. I want to be the one *who brings him up for air, who brings him back to life.*

Kissing the bruises on his soft chin, I wrap my arms around him and soothe him. "It's okay, you're okay," I say until his breathing calms down.

He tightens his hold on me, still in a deep sleep. I lie on his chest and fall asleep.

———————

LISTENING to Mila and Daliah talk about sex has me reminiscing about two nights ago with Liam. Two nights since I last saw him. That following day, I woke up to him in between my legs. I'll admit it was the best way to wake up. I made us coffee and offered breakfast, but he refused. He said he needed to stop at his mom's house to work on something. I drove him to his car, and he texted last night, asking how I was doing.

"Hello," Daliah calls out, snapping her fingers. "We've been talking to you." I've been staring for the last couple of minutes at a sheet of models we have to shoot.

"She's been in a haze lately. I think it's about some guy she's seeing," Mila says with a raised eyebrow. She studies me like a book.

I clear my throat. "So, what is it you were talking about?"

"We were talking about where we've had sex in public," Daliah declares with a cheesy grin. "Mila said she's had sex in a couple of places, and I was telling her the craziest place I had sex was in the restroom at a football game."

I frown, cross my arms over my chest, and lean back in my seat. Thinking. All those years with Eric, and we only had sex at his place or mine. When I was seeing Ryder, it was the same —at his place.

"Nope, I can't say I've had sex in a public place. Eric was never that adventurous," I say, feeling annoyed.

Eric has not stopped calling. He has even called using different numbers. Mila jumps out of her chair and runs to the restroom with her hand covering her mouth. I trail right behind her. Pulling her hair up, I soothe her back while she pukes.

"Do you think you have the stomach flu, or are you pregnant?" I ask, feeling concerned.

Her face is a little pale. Mila has cream porcelain skin like mine. Only her raven black hair makes her stand out. She rinses her mouth, and her green eyes widen.

"I-I don't think I'm pregnant. I mean, I could be. So much has happened in the last few months. I lost track of my period." Mila looks at her reflection in the mirror.

"Go home and get some rest. I'll take care of the hottie swimsuit models," I drawl, wagging my eyebrows.

"Oh, I'm sure you'll love that." She snickers.

Closing my eyes, I inhale the crisp air and the saltiness of the ocean breeze, feeling the sun's warm rays on my face. There isn't a cloud in sight. It's a perfect day in San Diego. Kicking off my sandals, I savor the cool sensation of sand between my toes before withdrawing my equipment from my bag.

A couple of models arrive, and lucky for us, Mila's Uncle Roger is a well-known photographer in Manhattan for high-end models and celebrities. He passes a lot of gigs on to us, which is helping our fairly new business boom. It gets our name out. All the men crowd around, some in Speedos, others in swimming trunks or boxer briefs. It's quite a sight, I'll admit. Handing them the massage oil, I give them instructions on the poses they will be doing. The oil helps the photos stand out and makes their skin glisten in the sunlight.

Last summer, Mila and I did a photoshoot for a European publication. I'll admit their site overheated me. Now I'm like, ehh, no big deal. Liam's body is God-sent. He's like my own personal Adonis. Angling my camera, I take the first shot of a tall guy with sandy-blond hair wearing a red Speedo.

"You're beautiful, sweetheart," he mutters and winks.

"Thanks," I mutter back.

I move on to the next guy. We have twelve models, one for each day of the month since we're shooting for a calendar. The next guy leisurely walks toward me wearing white boxer briefs. I swallow hard. I'll admit he's hot. He unclips a pin from his man bun and shakes his hair into a mane that rivals Mufasa's from *The Lion King*. I quickly scan his body. He has thick muscular thighs. Not as good as Liam.

"Hey, Sophie," he breathes out, so close. "Would you be a good girl and rub some of the oil on me, babe?"

Oh, Lord.

"She won't be oiling shit on your body. Do it your fucking self," Liam's voice booms.

I stumble backward, in shock at the threats I hear in Liam's husky voice.

Mufasa lifts his hands up. "Officer, I'm sure it's not illegal to ask a beautiful woman to oil me up and ask her out for dinner." Mufasa offers a cocky grin.

Turning slowly, I glance up at Liam's tall frame, glimpse his murderous scowl. My breath hitches. When Liam is in full cop mode, his demeanor is solid and protective. Good God, he's hot in his uniform, and his ass looks great too. A shiver runs through my body and pulses between my legs. Liam stalks closer to me, my back hitting his front. *Oh, heavens.*

"I'd say it's illegal when you're hitting on my girl. She's not yours to call *babe*, and definitely not your *good girl*. She's mine."

My stomach does this strange thing that feels like butterflies fluttering inside. Liam wraps his warm arms around my midsection protectively.

"Sorry, man. I didn't know she was taken." Mufasa steps back.

I turn to look at Liam's infuriated face. "What are you doing here?" I'm still confused by his outburst.

"I wanted to see if you would like to go to lunch, but apparently, you are getting ready to oil models up." He stiffens his square shoulders and locks his jaw.

I place my hands on my hips and tilt my head.

"You didn't give me a chance to answer him, Liam. I was going to tell him no." I refrain from asking if I'm really his. And, of course, I spit out the wrong words. "And I'm not yours, even if I did agree to stay away from other guys until we call it quits."

Silence.

"You're right. You're not mine," he retorts.

My heart feels like it's being squeezed in my chest. That was not what I wanted to hear. I feel it. I'm falling a little at a time. Now would be a good time to tap out and save my heart.

"If you want out, Sophie, just say the word. This is not a relationship. We can move on."

I watch as his throat visibly constricts. He's so fucking jealous. He wants nothing more than what we have going on between us. His gaze shifts away from me, and I behold the anguish in his captivating eyes, which ignites my heart. His walls are so high up, his demons caging him in. My heart aches for him. I can sense the weight of a thousand secrets dragging into his soul like an anchor tied to his feet.

What is it, Liam? What's holding you down? I want to ask, but I can't pry into his personal space. He needs to let it out on his own willingly. For now, I can only hope—for the short time being, I can crumble his walls and free his heart.

"I don't want out. Not yet," I admit. Getting on my tiptoes, I place a kiss on his lips. "Not yet," I whisper into his lips.

"Sophie," he says with a strained voice.

"Give me, let's say, thirty minutes to finish up. And we can go have lunch." I lean in to kiss him again.

He responds by pulling me closer and deepening the kiss. Our tongues dance together like waves crashing against one another. The passionate embrace feels like he's staking out his territory, telling all other men in the vicinity that, even though he says I'm not, I'm his.

CHAPTER 14

LIAM

I made a left at a hole-in-the-wall burger place that Dominic and I discovered years ago. Sophie's been awfully quiet since my jealous rampage. Maybe I had no right to claim her as mine when, in reality, she isn't. But seeing another man want her...an unexpected surge of jealousy ripped through me. I'm possessive of her, wanting her to myself. When I asked her if she wanted to end this, I swallowed the fear that crept up the back of my throat.

The night at her place plays on repeat in my head. Sophie warming dinner for me, Sophie's attentiveness as she massaged my sore muscles, her soft hand caressing my hair with affection as if we've done this a million times, her body tangled in mine all night, the warmth of her body seeping into my flesh. As she lay on my chest, her blonde hair cascading around me. Unfamiliar sensations coursed through my body as I awoke to the warm embrace of another person in my arms. Never before had I awakened with someone snuggled so close. Anxiety raced through my veins.

Deep down, I liked it, which scares the shit out of me. But I know she is never mine to keep, so selfishly, I'll take what I can —what she will give me. I know I'll never experience this again, and when we go our separate ways, I'll have something to remember her by. The ghost of my past will always anchor me down like the abyss of the dark sea. I have no right to give away my cold, dark heart, let alone to fall in love, so I shackled it down years ago, carrying the weight as a reminder of the night part of me died.

Parking the SUV, I glance at Sophie. She's staring out the front window, chewing on her perfect red lips.

"Are you pissed at me?" I ask.

She turns to look at me, her eyes sparkling in the sunlight. "No. Why?"

"You've been quiet the whole time."

Her lips curve into a smile. "I was just giving you time to cool down. You scared the shit out of Mufasa. And all the other guys." She shakes her head and laughs. "First it was mothballs, followed by Chad-der cheese, and now my clients." She reels off, as she shimmies her black leather skirt down from riding up her toned legs.

I shrug. "I go for what I want, and what I want is you."

Sophie's head jolts up to look at me with a wandering gaze. She sighs. "Liam, you're impossible to understand."

Our shared stare feels like it lasts a lifetime, even though it's only for a few moments. Sophie scrutinizes me like she can tell what I'm thinking, like she can see right through me. She's the first to break our stare. Before I can ask who mothball guy was, she nods, maybe to herself, before getting out of the SUV.

While in line, I gently tuck a strand of hair from her pony-tail that has fallen to the side of her face behind her ear. She glances away from the menu to meet my gaze with an expression full of joy. Sophie's smile is like a ray of light in the middle of a dark cloud. The way her tight skirt emphasizes her curves, and the sky-blue off-the-shoulder blouse makes her look stunning.

Maybe we should take the food to-go, head to my place. That way, I could trace my tongue along her soft, ivory-skinned shoulders, connecting the dots of her light brown freckles. My cock hardens at the thought. I haven't seen her in three days, and it feels like a lifetime.

She reaches for my hand, intertwining our fingers as if we're lovers. She does it mindlessly. Staring at our intertwined hands, I relish how she molds into one. An unfamiliar feeling rattles my chest. I said I'd take anything she gives, but Sophie *will* be the death of me.

Those lips curve ever so slightly as she goes up on tiptoes to reach my height. She brings her free hand up to my jaw then whispers, "You look so damn hot in your uniform." She steps back, tilting her head back to look at my ass, our hands still intact and bites her lip. She lowers her heels to the floor, but her hot breath still rushes across my neck. "Uh-huh, just like I expected, your ass makes those uniform bottoms look hot. I had a fantasy of you fucking me in your uniform," she says in a sultry voice.

My eyebrows jog up, and I choke on my spit while laughing. "Good to know," I manage to say in between each choked laugh. I squeeze her hand.

I take in the bustling crowd in the tiny restaurant. The owners painted the place in a variety of hues and provided bumper stickers so patrons could paste them on the walls, giving it a distinctive appearance.

Once they call our order, I walk toward Sophie, who is waiting at a table tucked in a corner. I lean in and whisper in her ear, "Maybe we should take this back to my place or yours so I can make your fantasy a reality."

The air and the surrounding noise evaporate as if we're

alone in the room. My heart gallops in my chest as her lust-filled gaze rakes over me. Sophie inhales deeply, allowing her lungs to fill with air before she exhales, the breath leaving her body. The pulsing vein on her neck manifests how much she wants me. I now realize I'm obsessed with her, with anything Sophie. Her eyelashes flutter, but she doesn't break her gaze. My cock swells. She bites her lip, something I've noticed she does when she's nervous or turned on.

"As much as I would like to say, 'Hell, yeah,' I have to get back to work. I'm booked with clients. Mila left to go home early. She wasn't feeling well. Can I get a rain check?" she pouts.

I give her a charming grin as I pull our food out of the bags. "Sure, how about tonight?" I ask, sounding desperate to be close to her.

Fuck me.

I pop a fry in my mouth and pass Sophie her burger and fries.

"Sounds good to me, Officer," she says flirtatiously, just before her eyes widen at the sight of the amount of food.

It's really not much. I can see the gears grinding in her head, just like they did that night at the coffee shop.

"This is a lot of food. The burgers are huge."

I grab her burger, unwrap it for her, and pass her a side of pickles. "They're not that big, baby, and I got you extra pickles. I even got two burgers for myself. This is how small they are." I mean, they're not small or too big, just in between.

Her head tilts and her eyes soften. "You...you got me extra pickles. How did you know?" she croaks, as if the gesture is too much for her. It makes me wonder if her asshole ex treated her like shit. Maybe he never did anything kind for her.

"Yeah, the day I saw you at the restaurant, I noticed you had extra pickles." I shrug it off as if it's no big deal and unwrap my first burger. The hot steam of the burger wafts in the air, making my mouth water. The juices from the burger run down with two thick beef patties settled onto the hot bun, topped by a layer of oozing melted cheese, thick strips of bacon, and a pile of shredded lettuce, tomato slices, and jalapeños. I like my food to be extra spicy. When I was a kid, my dad once told me chile would put extra hair on my chest, adding that we all need some spice in our life.

Well, I have a spicy woman right in front of me who is looking at me like I hung the moon by giving her a side of pickles. Taking a bite, I then groan. Damn, it's good. I don't know what they put into seasoning the meat, but it's good.

Sophie's nibbling on her burger like a mouse nibbling on cheese.

"What's wrong?" I ask.

Her brows knit together, and she chews on her lower lip. She's nervous. I wipe my mouth with a napkin and wait for her to speak. Sophie places her burger on the wrapper in front of her and glances up at me. Her nose crinkles in embarrassment, and she can't help but look away as she mutters, "It's embarrassing."

"Try me, baby. What is it?"

"When I was a kid...and until high school, I was super thin. I was always called names like skin and bones, twig, and other stuff. I got teased for it—a lot. I weighed a hundred pounds. Senior year, I began working out, trying to gain muscle, eating more, adding protein shakes. I started gaining weight. I was happy until I started hearing kids at school call me fat." She exhales heavily, looking out the window.

"When Eric and I were dating, he was always commenting on my food choices. Dropping comments, telling me not to eat too much, reminding me I didn't want to gain weight."

Fucking asshole. Anger whips through me like a violent storm.

"It really messed me up. I don't like eating in front of people. Except for Mila and my family."

I take an angry bite of my burger. I'm going to look up this fucker and strangle him.

"Baby, look at me."

She slowly turns toward me. God, she's beautiful and sexy.

"First, that ex of yours is an asshole. That fucker doesn't know shit. People like him have self-esteem issues and enjoy diminishing the confidence of others. He wanted to stay superior by putting you in a subordinate position. You're a beautiful woman, Sophie. You. Are. Perfect. Any. Shape. Or. Form." I drawl the last words out so she can hear every word.

Her lips curl into a shy smile. "He never remembered my extra pickles," she whispers.

"What a dick," I say.

She throws her head back and laughs. My heart thunders in its cage and bangs my ribs as if to break free with the vibration of her laugh, and it rings through me and *lights up my world*.

"Yeah, he is."

I like that she acknowledges it.

"Thank you," Sophie whispers softly.

I nod, not wanting to say more to make her feel uncomfortable. "Eat, baby. It's getting cold."

She takes a big bite.

"That a girl."

She groans, and a soft moan leaves her red-stained lips. All I can think of are those lips on my body, wrapped in a particular place.

"God, you weren't kidding. This is so good."

I can't get over how the asshole made her feel. He stripped her of her confidence. Who knows what else he's done to her or why they broke up? No wonder she is self-conscious of her naked body. She's so oblivious to how beautiful and hot she is.

After we devoured our burgers, we sat and talked. I knew she was hungry, and I'm pleased she felt comfortable eating in front of me after she revealed what she went through in her youth and with her ex. I wash down the rest of the fries with Dr. Pepper.

"What happened to your partner? Don't you always have a partner?" Sophie asks.

"I dropped my partner, John, at the station. He needed to get some paperwork done, and I needed to go help Dominic and his brothers go through their mom's house. That's how I knew Mila went home, and how I knew you were here. I came and got you for lunch."

"Oh, I appreciate it. Thank you for lunch."

I nod. "No problem. Anytime."

I knew asking Sophie out for lunch was more than what we agreed on, but I needed to see her. It was the perfect excuse. Now that she has given me a piece of her past, I feel the need to protect her and be around her more than I should. The honest truth is I enjoy being around Sophie, I can't seem to get enough of her.

AFTER DROPPING Sophie off at the studio, I return to the station. I have a meeting with the task force to review new intelligence and devise a plan for our surprise attack on the drug bust at the Long Beach docks without alerting them in advance. We'd also been questioning Marko's cousin, who is loyal to his kin and the gang. No matter how much we interrogate him, he won't give them up. He's a dead end, but now that the Serpents are in bed with the cartel, we will be able to get more intel on them by setting a trap and leading them to believe the Serpents betrayed them.

First, we need to find the drug dealers connected to the cartel; with the Serpents, one is always bound to talk. The word on the street is that the Serpents have started recruiting young teens to join them. They start them young and use them at their disposal, taking advantage of them. As fucked up as it is, unfortunately, some of these young kids are homeless, or they're troubled kids looking for money or simply a place to belong. Gangs and cartels will use this opportunity to initiate them into their organizations.

I sit at my desk to catch up on paperwork. Later, I'll head to Sophie's to devour her stunning body. She wants me to fuck her with my uniform on, and I'll gladly do it. I've been trying my best not to think about her, to keep some distance, but Sophie's like a siren tugging on my chains, pulling me to her.

I reluctantly meet John's gaze from behind my enormous stack of paperwork. He drags his chair, squeaking along the floor, and snickers as he settles himself down, legs kicked out in front of him.

"What the fuck are you snickering about, snickerdoodle?" I drawl.

He leans in his chair with an amused grin on his pretty-boy face. "You've been smirking into your paperwork."

Have I? "No, I haven't," I grumble.

"Sure, glowworm, you've been in a great mood lately. Smiling, laughing, not your typical broody self."

John taps his fingers on my desk with a lazy grin, waiting for I don't know what.

"I didn't know it was a sin to laugh and smile." He's right, though. It's been years since I smiled without it being forced.

"Who's the girl?"

"Huh?"

"Don't play dumb, Liam. It's written all over your face."

Is it? I guess I have been smiling and laughing more. "I'm not seeing anyone."

I'm half lying. We're *not* really seeing each other. It's more like hanging out and fucking. Honestly, I hate the way it sounds —like she's not worth it, but she agreed. I have never regarded her as any less than the goddess she is, and I worship her accordingly.

"You know how I know? You look just like how I looked when I started seeing Beth."

"How's that?"

"Glowing sunshine," he replies, not missing a beat, smirking like a fool.

"Fuck off," I retort, grinning. "I'm not really seeing her. She's Dominic's girlfriend's best friend. We have been messing around. No strings attached. But not seeing anyone else, either. It's an itch to scratch."

John's a good friend. I can trust him.

His blue eyes dim in the light, and his smile fades. "You think this is a good idea? I mean, you've never slept with anyone more than once. You're getting yourself into a shitload of trouble. You're truly fucked now. If you don't watch it in the end, she'll be the one hurting if you back out. If you like her, and I think it's clear you do, then don't settle for less."

I let his words soak in. Do I want more than a no-strings arrangement? No. She agreed to do the same. Raking fingers through my hair, I look back at John.

"She's just out of a bad relationship, and she doesn't want to be in another one. She wants casual."

He brings his elbows to his knees and chuckles. "You don't know shit about women, do ya? They always catch feelings. Maybe you will too."

I shake my head. I highly fucking doubt it.

"You're so fucked." John slaps the palm of his hand on my desk with a grin.

Am I fucked? My phone pings with a text. I grin when I see it's Sophie.

Mi Bella: *Hey, so you want steak and potatoes or chicken? Does that sound good?*

When I dropped her off, she offered to make me dinner since I'd taken her out to lunch. I couldn't refuse after the kiss she gave me in front of those naked dudes. I wanted to fuck her in my SUV.

Me: *Whatever you want, baby.*

Mi Bella: *Okay...oh, and come in your uniform. I'll take it off for you.*

Fuck me. I love how straightforward she is. When I look up from my phone with a grin, John's watching.

"Told ya," he mouths.

Yup, I'm fucked.

CHAPTER 15
SOPHIE

My gaze hits the rows of workout machines and weights, searching for Daliah. I spot her in the back of the gym. Yesterday, she asked if I wanted to join her in some workout class. I didn't bother to ask what kind of class. Maybe yoga? Walking toward her, I scrutinize the place. It's a mid-sized gym, not too big or too small. I expect a separate room for the classes, but no, it's all out in the open. It's a good thing I don't know anyone here. I usually get up early and go for a run, but since Daliah invited me to join the class, I decided to change my routine—I'll go for a run tonight.

"Hey, Daliah. Good morning."

She looks half-asleep at six a.m. "Morning."

"So, what class are we doing?"

"I think it's called heat high-energy athletic training."

My eyes bulge out like a fish. I've never worked out with equipment. I enjoy running. Just the name of the workout makes it seem pretty intense. I hope I don't make an ass of myself.

"Have you done this class before?"

She shakes her head. "No, it's actually my first time here. I need to get myself in shape," she says with a yawn. Most of the people in the class are women, of all ages. Some whisper about how great the instructor is, fawning over him.

"All right, ladies, let's get in our stands and start with stretches. For those who are new, my name is Luis, and I'll be your instructor."

I understand why the women are fawning over him, with his peppered hair, sharp cheekbones, tanned skin, and well-built physique.

Twenty minutes in—O.M.G. I'm dying. My body is screaming as I finish my hundredth burpee. Muscles quivering, heart pounding, and sweat dripping from my forehead, I gulp frantically from my water bottle, desperate for relief. Daliah, just a few feet away, looks in a similar state of exhaustion, with her hands resting on her knees and chest rapidly rising and falling.

"We still have thirty minutes to go," Daliah cries, panting between breaths.

"Oh, God, what did we get ourselves into? Am I really this out of shape?" I whine, splashing water on my face.

Luis comes toward us with a smile of satisfaction. "Ladies, ladies, hands on the back of your head and take a few deep breaths. Do you feel the burn?"

"More than that. I feel death near," Daliah cries out.

"Awesome, ladies. It means you're doing good." Luis claps his hands. "All right, everyone, grab your kettlebells and watch for your neighbor. You don't want to knock them out." He laughs.

"I can do this," I say to myself when Luis instructs us to do three sets of twenty kettlebell swings. With a deep breath, I grab the black kettlebell off the ground and lift it up to chest level. As

Luis counts down from twenty, I swing it back and forth between my legs, feeling the muscles in my hips and arms burn with each repetition. When he finally tells us we're done, I'm relieved but proud of myself for pushing through. Luis gives us a five-minute water break. I chug a stream of water. Grabbing a towel, I wipe the sweat trickling down my chest into my sports bra.

Feeling eyes on me, I glance around the now-crowded gym. My gaze comes to a complete halt as it lands on Liam, squatting in front of the rack of weights. His white tank top is completely soaked with sweat, and his arms are straining beneath the heavy barbell he's holding. His muscles ripple as they span across his chest, bulging in all the right places, holding up a multitude of weights. My breath hitches, watching him squat effortlessly. And he's staring at me.

Holy guacamole, mother of God, sweet baby Jesus.

After I'm done praising the lord and guacamole for this man, I turn my gaze to Luis, who's shouting for us to get jump ropes.

Oh, God, what is Liam doing here? I mean, I know why he's here, but why couldn't it be another gym? Has he been watching me make a fool of myself? Sweating like a pig and gasping for air as if my lungs were being retrieved from my body. He's not alone. He's with Dominic, Santiago, Mark, and some other guys. Reaching into the box of jump ropes, I stand inches away from Daliah, who's red as a tomato, and I'm positive I look the same.

Luis claps his hands and shouts, "All right, guys, let's get our hearts pumping with a hundred jumps."

Everyone groans. A hundred will definitely have my heart pumping until it explodes. The last time I jumped rope was back in elementary school with Margaret and I jumped and sang the song Cinderella while jumping. Margaret, who is now my ex-friend, slept with Eric. Yup, it was Margaret. The audacity of that woman.

I turn my gaze back to Liam, who is still staring at me while spotting the other guys. A chill runs down my spine. For the last days, every night after work, he's arrived at my place with a change of clothes and a dessert.

Since the day at the restaurant when I told Liam about Eric criticizing me for how I ate, he's acted strange, in a way I can't quite put my finger on. Different. More, I don't know, I guess, more vigilant toward me, protective of my body, caressing me with his hands and eyes. Making sure I feel beautiful. Then he would show me just how much he wanted me by giving me the fantasy I wanted. Him fucking me in his uniform every night. Fucking me in the kitchen, living room, up against the wall, in the bedroom. We would shower, then return to the kitchen to make dinner together. Liam chopped the vegetables, or whatever we were cooking, and we ended each night watching Netflix. It has become our nightly routine. It's like we're doting lovers.

My breathing quickens as my feet tap the concrete in time with the swish of the rope. Sweat drips from my forehead, but I keep jumping—my arms steady, my heart racing. I close my eyes, hearing the thump, thump, thump, the drumming in my chest. The burning sensation in my body intensifies ten times like a summer fever. I can go through cardiac arrest at any moment, not because I'm jumping like a mad woman...no, it's because of the man who is slowly capturing my heart unknowingly.

"Jeez, woman, are you training to be the next Rocky Balboa? I've been calling your name. We stopped five minutes ago," Daliah says in a raspy voice.

I stop, sweat dripping down my forehead to my breasts. Looking around, I notice everyone is putting their ropes back in the box, and Luis is talking to all the elderly women fawning over him. My gaze goes back to Daliah, who is standing with her hands on her hips, watching me. I want to laugh at how strange she looks in athletic gear. I've only seen her in graphic rock band shirts, skirts or jeans, and combat boots.

"So, you want to tell me why Dominic's bestie is staring at you like he wants to eat you out?"

"Jesus Christ, Daliah." My voice strangles in my throat. Glancing across the gym where the weights are, I spot Liam watching me, grinning.

Then he mouths, "Come here," and beckons with his finger.

"Oh lord," Daliah whispers. "Is something going on with you two?"

"No," I say defensively. I lie through my teeth.

"Yeah, whatever, Rocky. I'm going to the bathroom to wash up. Go check on your buns of steel of a man." Daliah snickers, wagging her eyebrows.

"Look, don't tell Mila anything. She'll either worry about me getting hurt, or she'll go over the top, acting like we are a thing and wanting to plan a double date. When were not. A thing." I'm rambling.

Daliah lifts her hands and says, "I don't know anything." She smiles and heads to the bathroom.

———

GRABBING A HAND TOWEL, I wipe the sweat off my forehead and make my way toward Liam. He's surrounded by women, and the other guys are hot on their tails. Except for Dominic, who ignores them completely. Good.

I hate how close Liam and I are getting. I guess I shouldn't say close. He doesn't share anything about his life, which is infuriating. I want to know what demons are hiding in his shadows. He knows more about me than I know about him. Hell, I don't even know where he lives. He falls asleep in my bed and wakes up early to go back to his place and get ready for work. I huff an irritated breath at how all the women are doing squats right in front of him, lusting over him like cats in heat.

Bitches.

Why is it that men can get all territorial and stake a claim? I know we are not a couple, and I can't stake a claim, although I let him do it when I was doing the calendar shoot. So, how in the hell am I supposed to get these women away from him? Just as I approach him, a woman jumps right in front of me. What the fuck?

"Hey, Liam, you're looking good." She hums like a hummingbird, all sweet and sugary.

Annoyed and pissed, I make my way to Dominic, who is packing his gym bag. I hate how jealous I feel and how it makes my chest cave in. I just got out of a bad relationship, and the last thing I need is to feel like a broken doll with Liam. I don't want to feel anything, but I do feel like a stupid idiot after he told me what he wanted, and I agreed like a desperate slut. I don't bother to glance back to see if he's talking to the woman, whom he probably slept with.

"Congratulations," I say to Dominic. We just found out Mila is pregnant.

His smile widens. "Thanks, I can't fucking wait until her belly swells."

I smile in awe; the guy has seriously won me over. When Dominic and Mila reunited, I threatened to seriously hurt him if he ever hurt her. He said he would prove he was here to stay with her and Dante, and he has.

"That's so cute, Dominic."

He scoffs. "Whatever, Grandpas.com."

He lifts his head up to the person walking up behind me. I know it's Liam. I can feel him. "How's the dating life going? No more Brut or mothball guys?" he asks, laughing as he grabs his gym bag.

"Brut guys? Mothballs? What the fuck is that?" Liam asks behind me.

I roll my eyes.

Dominic laughs harder. "She dated some guys who smelled like her grandpa. You know, the cologne old guy's wear."

"Ha, ha." I mimic the guys laughing, including Santiago and Mark, who are nearby, bench-pressing.

"Got to go, guys. I'm going to check on my girl." Dominic swings his bag over his shoulder, waving to his brothers and patting Liam on the back.

I look up at Liam for the first time since he snuck up behind me. "Hey." I force a smile, jealousy still dripping from my lips. His female admirers are still watching him with interest. He must talk to them when he comes to the gym since they clearly know him by name. Oh, of course, they're staring at his ass. The man has the best ass I've ever seen in my life.

"Hey, Sophie!" His beautiful eyes scan my profile. "You looked great out there. Not only do you run like a gazelle, but you jump rope like you're training for a competition. May I add that your tits bounce to perfection?" He offers a cocky grin.

Well, I can be cocky, too, a little ray of sunshine. "Ugh, yeah, I'm sure it's what all the guys thought when they were staring at my tits."

God, you sound like an idiot, a total bitch because you're jealous. He moves toward me until I can feel his breath on my face. His body is so close, I can make out the beads of sweat forming on the side of his cheeks and trickling down his neck onto his already-damp shirt. My hands itch, as I desperately want to reach out and trace the contours of his arms with my fingertips.

"Watch it, Sophie," he says, his voice full of authority. "I made sure no man was looking at you but me." Well, someone is territorial, so why can't I be too, right?

"Stay put," I command, and he raises one dark eyebrow in response.

I step around him and let my palm crash against his left meaty butt cheek. The heavy sound of my palm connecting with his toned ass cheek vibrates on my fingertips. His skin feels hard beneath my hand, and a wave of pleasure rushes through me as I remember how tight his ass is when we have sex.

Satisfaction floods my veins as he tenses. I have marked my territory. I can hear Mark and Santiago laughing, as well as some other guys I saw Liam talking to earlier. Glancing up at those guys, I notice they're wearing tank tops that say SDPD. They must be officers. I return my gaze to Liam, who is looking at me, confused. Squaring my shoulders and standing tall to hide my embarrassment, I turn my gaze to the three women looking at me in shock, whispering to one another like school-girls gossiping in a locker room.

A soft grip around my neck has me startled. Liam's hard callous hands keep me in place. I look into his gunmetal eyes, and he's laughing.

"You slapped my ass?" he says in a deep husky laugh.

"I did." My voice strangles in my throat. God, I can't think straight with him looking at me. He's just so handsome. I feel my face flush hot cherry-red. I never blush. Never until him. He looks up at the women in their tight little elastic shorts. Then he glances back at me. His thumb caresses my soft skin in an up-and-down movement.

"I see," he says before his lips crash onto mine. The kiss

sends a shock of electricity through me. My arousal spikes as he tightens his hold around my neck. His tongue slips into my mouth, exploring, and I melt into him. He's kissing me in a way I've never been kissed before. Deep. Passionate.

He's letting me stake a claim on him, even if it's for a short time. Letting my hands trail to his hair, I grab a fistful, deepening the kiss more. Liam tastes like my perfect temptation, my sin. His free hand rubs my ass, then he smacks it and pulls away.

"There," he drawls out with a grin of satisfaction on his handsome face. All I hear is whistling in the background. I'm still staring at Liam in shock and aroused. He kissed me at the gym in front of the guys. Oh. My. God.

"You—you kissed me in front of the guys."

"Santiago and Mark already know, and the guys from work —who gives a fuck?" He grabs his bag and swings it over his shoulder. "Let's go."

"Why? Where?"

"To the alley in the back, baby. Now. Hurry your sweet ass."

I chase after him as he walks to the back, where the restroom and lockers are. The guys are yelling for Liam, but he simply ignores them. The alley. Why the hell is he in a hurry to get to the alley? Then it hits me. There must be someone getting jumped. No, someone getting jumped in the alley doesn't really make sense. How would he know it was going down? He's been inside for at least an hour. But what else could he need to do in the alley? It has to be that, right? My tennis shoes smack into the cement floor as I jog after him.

"Maybe you should get the guys."

He turns to look at me while he's still scurrying toward the back door. "Why the fuck would I want the guys?" he grumbles, his eyebrows scrunching.

"Well, maybe because you're not armed, and you don't know how many guys are out there." My heart is beating like a drum. I saw a gun pointed at Mila. I can't handle any more crazy shit. Sure, I've seen plenty of crazy shit living in New York, but it hits differently when you see it happen to people you care about.

Liam stops, and I run right into his hard chest. "What in the hell are you talking about?"

"The alley. Is there someone getting jumped or something? You're running out the door like a bat out of hell."

My eyes widen when he throws his head back and laughs—full and throaty. A smile breaks on my lips at the sound of his gorgeous laugh. His Adams apple bobs with each hearty laugh. He rests his hands on his thighs, bending slightly to catch his breath from the roar of laughter.

"Oh, man, baby, I haven't laughed so hard in a long time," he says.

My heart squeezes at the thought of him holding back from living, laughing, loving, from happiness. I've always believed happiness is the recipe our soul needs. I might be going through hard times, but the damage Eric did to me left me feeling self-conscious. He stripped me of my confidence. Liam has made me feel sexy and worth so much more these last couple of days. I want to leave him with a kaleidoscope of laughter and smiles.

He grabs my hand and continues leading me through the emergency exit. He pushes the gray door open, and the soft breeze hits my sweaty skin.

"The only one getting jumped out here, baby, is you. By my cock."

"What?"

"You said you wanted sex in public places, didn't you?"

Well, fuck. I did tell him that the other night in bed, explaining the conversation I had with Mila and Daliah. He said, "I'll give you all your fantasies, Bella," right before he fell asleep.

"Yes, I did," I say, "but right now, I'm all sweaty."

He shrugs. "So am I, and I don't give a shit. I'm so damn hard right now. My little grenade was about to combust with jealousy, so I had to kiss the fuck out of her to calm her ass before she spanked me again."

Oh, God. I want to die of embarrassment. I turn from him and walk toward one of the buildings in the alley, leaning up against the wall.

"I wasn't jealous," I shout.

He chuckles and walks toward me. My face heats up when he leans into me, the palm of his hand resting on the wall above me.

"Sure, you weren't. Now give me what I want."

Oh, my heart, my poor heart. His soft lips and strong hand trail down my neck. He slides my leggings down all the way to my ankles with the other hand, unhooking one of my legs.

"Wrap your legs around my waist." He says it in a raspy, lust-induced voice.

I scan the area. It's empty and quiet. "What if someone comes?"

"Then we'd better hurry." Then he shoves his hard, wet length into me.

My eyes roll back with the sensation of his pounding cock. Our lips meet, sucking the air from my lungs. The rush that someone might come makes it so much of a thrill. He brings me to life with each hard, rough thrust. His hand grips my ass as he thrusts faster. Harder.

"I'm so fucked," he murmurs as he spills his hot seed on me.

CHAPTER 16
LIAM

Sitting in the meeting room at the station, I glance through the files of my dad's old case. I've never had the urge to look through it. I knew it would bring up a lot of dark memories. Memories I don't want to relive.

Yes, my dad killed others in the line of duty. Only when it was necessary, when his and others' lives were at risk. His record shows no evidence that he killed any of the Serpents by his own hand. What reason did Pablo have for targeting him, then? The only asshole who can give me that information is Pablo himself. Like the coward he is, he's remained hidden for years and is now taking the cartel under him for his protection.

"Hey, lover boy." John walks into the meeting room with an amused grin on his stupid face. "So that was the girl at the gym, huh? The one you kissed like a die-hard poet."

"Fuck off."

I flip him the bird as two more guys walk in, Jasper and Greg. Jasper, my partner in the task force, fans himself. I knew they were going to give me shit for kissing Sophie in front of everyone. I don't give a shit. The way she looked all hot and bothered by the girls there made my dick twitch over and over.

"What the fuck do you guys want?" I snap, annoyed.

"Down, boy. She's beautiful. What's her name?" John asks.

"Sophie," I grumble, getting up from my seat.

"I didn't know you had a girlfriend," Jasper chimes in.

"I don't. She's just a friend," I say, clearly annoyed by my answer. I'm not sure why the fuck I'm annoyed. She's not my girl, not entirely. Only for the time being, right? *Fuck.*

"Damn, is that how you kiss friends? Pass her over when you're done being friendly. I'll be sure to take her for a fucking wild ride on my d—"

Before Greg, the recruit, can finish, I shove him against the whiteboard and grip his pressed uniform. "Watch your fucking mouth, asshole. She's not some fucking slut to be passed around. If I ever hear you talk about her again, I'll kick your ass. I don't give a shit if I get suspended. She's worth more to me than letting some asshole like you talk down to her. What we have going on isn't any of your damn business."

John stands behind me, peeling me away from the greasy airhead. Letting him go, I reach for my keys on the table and walk out. I need air. Leaning into my patrol SUV, I dial Dominic.

"Hey, man," he says when he answers, "I was about to call you. How are you doing?"

I swallow the lump blocking my airway. "Hanging by a thread, bro," I say honestly.

Today marks eighteen years since my father passed away. Not a day goes by when I don't think about how I lost so much in the span of a second. I spent years telling everyone I didn't remember much of that night. I lied. I remember it all. I relive it every fucking night. Dominic is the only one who knows the story. I shared it with him when we were kids.

"Come on over to the restaurant. I'm about to have lunch. It will help you get away for a bit."

"All right, I'll be right there. Thanks."

"No problem, brother. I'm always here for you."

Hanging up, I shove the phone in my pocket, then drive off to Dominic's restaurant. He's a chef—and a hell of a good one.

Delgado's Steakhouse is booming with people. It's lunch rush, and Dominic's place is very popular.

I walk into Dominic's office, where he sits, cursing under his breath at a stack of papers. "Hey, brother."

He looks up from the mountain of paperwork. "Hey, glad you made it." He stands and gives me a bro hug. We walk into his private dining space reserved for family and special occasions. "How's your mom doing? I know it's so damned hard for her, especially during this time."

"I stopped by her house this morning. She was leaving for the cemetery. She wanted me to come with her, but I said no. I haven't been there in years. I just can't fucking do it, bro. It's too much for me. My conscience is heavy with the knowledge that if I hadn't been present, he would have reached for his firearm in a matter of moments."

"Liam, you don't fucking know that. You were just a kid and did everything you could that night at such a young age. Don't put this on you. I might not know what it's like to have a father, but I know for sure that your dad would not want you to live with this guilt. You did what he told you to do that night, Liam, and you are still going after the men who did this to you guys. I'm so damned proud of you."

I slump in my chair just as Mario, his head chef, walks in with drinks.

"Thanks, man," I say.

"What can I get you?" Mario asks.

"A burger of any kind. Surprise me," I say.

He nods and walks off.

I sigh, frustrated and pissed about Pablo, and answer Dominic's question.

"Next week, we have a mission in Long Beach. There's a shipment coming in. I have a good feeling about this. I know bringing them down won't bring my dad back, but I need this for my mom and me."

Dominic is watching me, slumped back in his chair. "Do you remember in first grade when we first met? You were sitting under a tree, and I went and sat next to you. It was your first day."

I laugh. It was such a long time ago. We had moved to an apartment because my mom couldn't afford the house. I had just started a new school. I was so fucked up in the head, after going through so much. Dominic was my only friend. His friendship saved me. I was in a dark place, not that I'm not now. I've just learned to live with it.

"Yeah, I remember. You helped me get through a lot of shit. I'm grateful to have you as a friend." I sip my Dr. Pepper and slump back in my chair.

"How are things going? Hooking up with any chicks?"

He raises his brow inquisitively; clearly, he hasn't heard about what went down at the gym yesterday. It's hard to keep this much of a lie from him, and I wish I could just tell him the truth: that I'm absolutely infatuated with Sophie. Dominic is the kind of guy who values relationships. He's made mistakes, but his heart was always for Mila.

"Nah, I'm taking a break from chicks," I say just as Mario arrives with burgers.

Dominic bursts into a fit of laughter. "You taking a break? I fucking don't believe that shit. Is there something going on with your dick?"

If only he knew how fucking alive my dick has been. Just

the thought of Sophie's cream-toned skin, her full breasts, and her warm liquid tone have me swelling in my slacks. Her voice was heavy with lust as she moaned my name right there in the alley. Sophie arched her body up against the wall, ready for me. I slid into her, desperate to be inside her. The soft, lilting tones of her voice filled my ears, and I felt transported to another world. I forgot about our surroundings as I stared into her eyes, mesmerized by the exotic cadence of her accent. It was my first time having sex in such a public place. As an officer, I knew it was illegal. Breaking the rules to give Sophie what she wanted was worth it.

"My dick works just fine. I'm just tired of the random chicks. It's getting old."

He takes a bite of his bacon burger and shakes his head. Once he swallows, he says, "Take it as a sign. This usually means you're ready to settle down."

"Hell, no, I'm not ready for that, nor will I ever. You're a family man. Shit, you have baby number two on the way. I'm not meant for the life of a family man—wife, kids, all that."

Dominic groans. "Dammit, Liam, you're so damn stuck into the past that you'll miss the beautiful things in life. I could easily hide, terrified of cancer consuming me all over again, afraid of leaving Mila and my kids. But I won't let the darkness take me again. I want to see my kids grow. I want to have *so many* kids with Mila. I spent five years away from her, and fuck it, I will not make that mistake again—letting her go and not trying harder. I won't."

He takes a sip of his water and points at me angrily. He's clearly a dad. He's certainly acting like one.

"You're sucked into this dark cloud, Liam. You don't see yourself as a family man who can have everything. When you speak of your father, you speak of him as an honorable, amazing, loving father. When your mom speaks of him, she speaks of him as a man worth remembering—one-of-a-kind. And that is who you are, Liam—an honorable man. You just need to get your head out of your ass." Dominic stands and taps the table. "I'm going to check on how things are going in the kitchen. Remember what I said, Liam."

"Fuck, you sound like a dad already."

He laughs. "You want to go to the house later and have some beers?"

"Nah, I have some shit to do," I drawl.

"Of course. With Sophie."

My eyes bulge.

"It's only obvious, Liam, and no, Mila doesn't know." Just as he's about to walk out, he turns to glance at me. "Don't let this drag on. If you don't want a relationship, then let her go. It will only make things more complicated. You'll end up hurting her." Then he leaves.

I stay right where I am, though. I'm not ready for the kind of change he spoke of. But I'm also not ready to let her go. Just a little longer...

―――――――

AFTER LUNCH, I head back to the station to finish my shift and review our new mission. It turns out we have an informant who ratted out the Serpents and who is willing to provide us with intel if we grant him and his family protection. The Serpents are planning on receiving crates full of drugs from the cartel next week. If everything goes smoothly, we should take them down. From what we heard, Pablo should be there, but I think the fucker will send his son.

Pulling into Sophie's apartment, I park my car along the side of the street. After the shitty day I've had, all I want to do is get lost in Sophie and numb the pain this day brings me every year since my father's passing. Every year, I relive that horrible night, the night I lost a part of myself.

I KISS my mamá and get into Papá's car. Mamá stayed home to rest. On our way to the pizza place, Papá turns up the radio when a song he loves comes on.

"This song, I sang to your mamá years ago in high school. She's my high school sweetheart."

I'm not sure what it means, but it makes him smile. "What is the name of the song, Papá?"

"Drive by the Cars," he says and sings each word.

I close my eyes and listen to each word.

"It's about a man in love who's willing to do anything for that one person." Papá smiles brightly. He must be thinking of Mamá.

"I'm never getting married, Papá. Gross."

Papá laughs so much his body shakes. He sings the last lyrics of the song as it ends.

"Someday, when you're grown up and find the right girl, you'll want that, Liam. You will want her by your side."

I cross my arms and lean back in my seat as my stomach grumbles. Good thing we made it to the pizza place in time.

I SHAKE off the memory when I make it to Sophie's door, and I hear a man's voice.

"Baby, please listen to me. I love you so much, Sophie. For months, I've been calling you. You blocked my damn calls. Soph, just hear me out, baby. I came all the way out here for you." The fucker. It must be her ex.

"It's too damn late, Eric. Tell me how long you've been sleeping with her, huh? How long? Because I thought she was my friend, and I thought you were my boyfriend, and you both made a fool out of me. So how long had you been screwing her?" Sophie's voice booms.

So, the asshole cheated on her with her friend. Cocksucker.

It's quiet for a split second.

"It was only that one-time, babe. I've never been with anyone else. I promise. I'll move here. We can start over, Soph."

Sophie huffs. "Just go, Eric. I can't even look at you."

Good—she wants him out. Rage burns through my veins when I hear it... kissing and a moan from him. I step into the doorway since it's open slightly. I see his lips forced on Sophie and her pushing him away. A storm brews within me to protect her from the asshole who hurt her. I burst into the room, rage boiling in my veins. I grab the idiot by his collar and drag him away from her. He lands hard on the floor with a harsh thud.

"Liam," she says, bewildered, wiping her mouth, then rubbing the palm of her hands on her tight leggings.

Eric, the lame idiot, stands up looks at me with his sandy blond curly hair. "Who the fuck are you? And what the fuck are you doing here, Officer?" Eric leans onto the kitchen island.

"Eric, leave now!" Sophie shouts, yanking him by the arm and escorting him out the door.

He shoves her off, walking toward me.

"She said to leave," I snarl, and shaking my head. "After you treated her like shit, you have some nerve showing up here."

"This is why you've been ignoring my calls, Soph. You've been fucking this cop; a damn pig."

My hostile glare swings toward the dumb fuck. Sophie rounds herself from the island at flash speed toward me.

"Liam...um, he was just leaving. I didn't know he was in town." Her voice is soft and pleading—pleading for what? I don't fucking know. She didn't do anything wrong.

"Get your stuff, Sophie, we're leaving. You're not staying here with this asshole around."

"Wha'd you say, Hollywood?"

God, what a fucking idiot. This is San Diego, not Hollywood. I get in Eric's face and shove him up against the wall.

"Get the fuck out of my face! You lay a hand on her, I'll fuck you up!"

Eric cries. Just what I thought. He's a pussy. Sophie's small hands come around my waist, pushing me off him. Shoving her hands away, I storm out, slamming the door behind me.

"I'll be outside, Sophie," I shout. I need to get away from the asshole before I end up kicking his ass. I'll always protect her.

A deep-seated hatred surges up inside me. Not for her but for how I feel, my stomach churning with knots and the chains around my dark heart rattling. An unknown feeling tugs at my chest. I hate the power she has over me.

"Liam, wait," Sophie shouts as I jump into my Camaro, slamming the door. She bangs on the window. "Roll down the window," she bellows, banging on the window as drizzle of rain slides down.

Fuck. I curse under my breath. Rolling down the window, I look at her beautiful face.

"Where in the fuck are your clothes, Sophie?"

Her eyebrows furrow. "Why in the hell are you talking to me like this? And what happened to baby, Grenade, or bella?" She places her hands on her hips. Her beautiful blue eyes dim in the dark, cloudy sky.

If I weren't so pissed off, I would laugh at how much she loves the names I've given her. The day the words mi bella slipped from my lips—the exact words my father called my mother, his beautiful—I didn't regret it. It felt right. And she's the grenade who came blasting into my life without warning.

"Because I'm pissed his lips were on yours. I know it's not your fault, Sophie. It's starting to rain. Go get your stuff."

I start the engine and rev it.

She leans into the window. "Liam, I blocked him when we started up. I haven't spoken to him since the day I walked in on him in Manhattan. It's been months. He just showed up. He kissed me, it was a split second before my brain reacted. I feel nothing for him, Liam. *Nothing.*"

I run my hands through my hair. "I know—I heard what you told him before I walked in. Seeing him here...him forcing himself on you—it has me seeing red. I don't like another man's hands on you. I don't like how he treated you, forced himself on you." Opening my door, I walk to the trunk of my car and pull out a hoodie. "Here, it's raining. You're getting wet." I hand her a SDPD hoodie.

"Why, Liam?" She yanks the hoodie out of my hands.

"Why what?"

"Why do you care if he kissed me, or if another man touches me? When you clearly just want to fuck me to relieve the tension. Isn't that what you said? You don't do commitment. So why do you care, huh?" she shouts, shoving her finger into my chest.

I grab her finger and nip at the pad of it. Sophie takes steps back every time I take a step toward her. We keep going until I have her pinned to the car.

Leaning into her, my body pressed on hers, I say, "I don't fucking know why I care, Sophie. You're right—I don't do commitment. It pisses me off that you affect me and that I want to protect you. It pisses me off that I want to be near you every damn second of the day. It pisses me off how obsessed I am. What pisses me off the most is how I don't want to feel any of it." My mouth skims along her neck. I lick and suck so hard, it makes a popping sound. My protectiveness for her has me rock-hard.

"What pisses me off is that I want to decorate your sexy neck with my mark, so all men know who you belong to. I want to protect you from that asshole in there. We are only temporary, baby, but during this time, you belong to me. No man touches what's mine. Those lips belong to me." I dip my fingers into her slick leggings. Dipping my finger into her wet pussy. "This belongs to me, bella, only me. No one touches it." I plunge my finger up and down and she moans to my touch. I like that I make her feel this way. That I have the power over her body.

"Y-you think of—"

"Don't overthink it, Sophie." The last thing I want is her thinking more of this, thinking I'm in love with her. I plunge my finger deeper into her. She tilts her head back, resting on the car. "Did he ever make you feel this good, baby?"

She shakes her head, panting. "No, never."

I pull my fingers out of her tight pussy, licking them, tasting her sweet flavor. She whines and tries to kiss me.

"I'm not fucking kissing you when just minutes ago, another man's lips were on yours, not yet, at least."

Her eyes widen.

Fuck.

"What! I didn't do anything."

"I know, baby. Get in the car. We're going to my place." The last thing I want is to be here where that mother fucker is. I'm so damn close to fucking him up. But obviously a bad idea. I'm an officer, in uniform.

"Why, Liam? I'm not going anywhere with you. You're acting like a maniac." She stomps her foot like a petulant child. A cold breeze picks up. I lift her hood and tuck a golden blonde lock behind her ear. I lower my hips into hers, and her eyes flutter closed in response. The heat of my arousal radiates through the tight fabric of my slacks, and I can barely contain it. She looks stunning in my hoodie, her golden hair spilling over her shoulders. My lips brush against the soft flesh of her earlobe, and I whisper assurances to her as our bodies press closer together.

"You make me act like a fucking brute, baby." Protectiveness has always been part of my nature. Although I've never experienced such a drive to protect a woman I'm with until now. It's like a thunderstorm erupting in me. Taking Sophie to my house is a bad idea, but the blazing volcano in me needs to have her close and away from the little bitch of her ex inside. A *need* to protect her.

"Would you rather stay here with your ex?" I ask, grinding my molars to dust.

She grumbles, cursing under her breath. She pushes me back, her warm body distant from mine.

"No, I'm not leaving Eric here at my house. He needs to leave. Which is what I was telling him when you got here. Eric and I were done a long time ago."

"I'll have him leave. Get in the car. It's pouring."

"I need to get clothes."

I nod and cup her cheeks. "I'll grab some for you. Although you don't need anything. I prefer you naked on my bed," I point out, my voice low and husky.

She shivers and whispers, "Fine," and gets in the passenger seat.

I make my way inside the house. The shithead is lying on the couch, flipping through the channels as if he owns the place. If he loved her, he wouldn't have forced himself on her. No real man would have laid a hand on a woman without her consent. I grab him by the shirt and yank him up.

"What the fuck, man?"

"Get the fuck out of here. She wants you out. If you walk out without a word, I won't have your ass arrested for forcing yourself on her. This is the last fucking time I want to see you here with my girl. She's mine to touch, mine to fuck, and mine to protect. She's all fucking mine! She doesn't need a scumbag like you who treats her like shit. You're not good enough for her."

He slips his hands in his pocket and sneers at me. "No, I'm not good enough, but neither are you. Or else she wouldn't have returned my kiss."

A malicious laugh erupts from my chest. "Think whatever you'd like. I don't stoop that low and kiss a woman who doesn't want me." I point to the door. "It's my thick dick she wants."

He sneers, but he steps out, getting into his car.

I know taking Sophie into my home and into my space will change things. She'll worm her way into my heart, but it's a price I'm willing to pay to protect her from the asshole coming back. The fear rattles me—if I had not been there, would he have hurt her? I'll protect Sophie with my life, even if it costs me in the end.

CHAPTER 17
SOPHIE

I watch the drops of water trickle down the window. What the hell just happened? I was about to order pizza when there was a knock at my door. I thought it was Liam because I never get people over besides Mila. But it was Eric standing in my doorway in his polo shirt and denim jeans, his beautiful curls draped over his face. I used to love seeing Eric standing in my doorway, use to love how his golden sun-kissed hair covered his eyes. But tonight, all I felt was disgust. It wasn't so much his betrayal, sleeping with another woman. It was more how he made me feel for years. I hadn't realized it until Liam came around. We are not an item. We are straight out fucking, nothing else. But he never makes me feel any less; he makes me feel *more*. My insides melted like a hot wick candle on a dark night when he said he wanted to be next to me every second of the day.

My stomach dropped in agony when he walked in on Eric's kiss, I thought he would think I wanted Eric to kiss me. Liam protecting me with such rage is hot. My head jolts when I see Eric storm out of the house. I don't feel the need to run after him; he's not who I want. Obviously—I'm sitting here waiting for Liam like an obedient dog.

Five minutes later, Liam strolls out of my house with a bag and my purse. He looks like an angry god, hair wet and shirt soaked as the rain comes down harder and thunder rattles the night. He hops in, tossing my stuff in the backseat of his Camaro. Without a word, he starts the engine. The car roars to life, his beautiful gray eyes look to mine, a strand of hair draped over his eye. Leaning in, I brush it to the side. God, I want to kiss him. It hurts that he rejected my kiss earlier. Will he ever kiss me again?

"Let's go," he fumes, protectiveness coursing through his veins.

Is it wrong it turns me on? Liam tossing Eric off of me was the sexiest thing I've ever seen. He drives angrily on the highway until we take an exit into Mission Drive. We drive up into a beautiful neighborhood surrounded by green trees and beautifully landscaped flowers. Liam has been silent the whole way. He should have left me at home if my presence is too much for him. He clearly doesn't want my company, but he wants me here with him.

He parks the car in front of a small home with a beautiful patio and a small garage, a white fence surrounding the place. It's cute. When he stops the engine, I reach for my bags.

I step into his home, and my eyes immediately dart around the spotless room. The color palette is dull, with no splash of color, but there are hints of warmth in the cozy blanket draped over the leather sofa and photos of him as a small child lining the walls. It certainly looks like a bachelor pad. A huge white dog bounds up to me, tail wagging uncontrollably. I kneel down to pet him.

"Hi, Duke. You're a cute guy."

"How do you know his name?"

Fuck. I shrug. "You told me."

"Liar. You looked at my social media pages, didn't you? Didn't know I had a stalker." He smirks and walks to the fridge to retrieve a water bottle.

I roll my eyes at his hulking back. "I had to look before I agreed to anything with you. How would I know you weren't some crazy fuck?" I scratch Duke's ears, and he nuzzles into me.

"Sure, whatever you say. Do you want water?"

"No, thanks."

He leans into the gray marble counter and swallows a stream of his water. "I'll give you something else to drink." His deep-timbred voice sends a shiver down my spine.

He's pissed Eric touched me forcefully after I told him to leave—and not because he's jealous. It's because he's being protective. And it turns me on.

"Let's go to the bedroom. You're wet, and so am I." He walks off while I trail behind him nervously. "Stay, Duke," he says without looking back.

He slams the door shut. Standing behind the door, I bite my nails, an uneasy feeling crawling in the pit of my stomach. How many women has he had in his room, on that vast king-sized bed? He unbuttons his uniform shirt, dropping it to the floor, leaving him in only his white tee. His muscles tighten under the shirt, showing every bit of his six-pack. His eyes scan me with possessiveness, fire dancing in their gunmetal depths.

"Come here, Sophie," he demands, his voice even and gruff.

I can sense the fury simmering in his rigid posture and sharp eyes. His clenched jaw and flared nostrils show his blatant displeasure at Eric having forced his lips on mine, but a part of me is strangely pleased to see him so protective of me.

Once I'm in front of him, I say, "Liam." My voice comes out pleading.

"Shut the fuck up, Sophie."

I shoot him a narrow look. "Excuse me!"

"Unbuckle my belt and pull out my cock."

Holy hotness.

My eyes widen, and the tingling between my legs burns with need. Without a doubt, I can't refuse this demand. God, who would? My hands tremble as I undress him. His eyes track me closely, never leaving my body. My fingers slip past the button of his trousers, and finally, freed from his trousers, I take out his huge cock. I stroke it up and down, feeling veins pulsing underneath the palm of my hand.

"Suck my cock, bella. I want those pretty red lips wrapped around it. I want my cum spilling on those lips and seeping into them. Demolishing any evidence of the fucker whose lips were on yours. Now, get on your knees. Suck it like a good girl."

Oh, hell.

Why do I like this so much? I bite my lip and kneel, taking him in my mouth. My tongue traces up and down his pulsing veins. He groans at my touch. My mouth worships at his altar, taking him in with devout desire. His shaft enlarges in my mouth, the saltiness running down my lips as he comes.

"That's my good girl. So good." His fingers tangle in my hair as he bobs my head deeper, grunting his release.

My eyelashes flutter when I look up at him, watching me.

Licking my lips, I say, "Better?"

He smirks. "Not even close, baby." He lifts me up, placing me on his bed, then tugs off the hoodie along with the shirt I'm wearing underneath, leaving me with only my bra and jeans. "I'm going to fuck you raw." He unclasps my bra. "I'm going to show you how no one can make you feel as good as I do," he says, confidence oozing out of him.

His hot breath fans my skin, stealing away the chill of the night air. My body stiffens as his mouth closes over my breast, and I am caught in his grip. He teases me, pulling at the edges, then following with a slow lick that circles my nipple.

Does he not realize what his words do to me, what he does to me? *I'm falling in...no, no, you're not, Sophie, you can't.* I arch my back, and a low moan escapes my lips as his tongue caresses my hardened nipple. His hungry mouth laps and sucks as I tremble under his touch.

"Take off your shirt and pants," I plea, my voice strangled in my throat.

He steps back, peeling off his shirt. His pants are already hanging halfway off. He kicks them to the side, leaving him completely naked before me. My breath hitches at how beautiful he is. He's magnificent, a naked god. This man is a fantasy come to life.

"You're hot." The confession spills from my lips without thought.

His mouth curls into a cute smile.

"And you're stunning," he drawls, shimming off my pants and underwear. "On your knees."

He enters a finger into my slick opening. My body convulses with pleasure just by the friction of his touch. One night would not satisfy the appetite I have for him. I will always crave him.

"You're fucking wet, baby. Have you been fucked in the ass?" He spits and enters his thick, callous finger into my hole.

Panting, I shake my head. "No." I've never had anal sex before.

"Good, because it's my first time too," he admits in a strangled voice.

I moan with desire, my body heating with the thought of him never having had a woman in this position.

"It's going to hurt at first, but I'll make you feel so good."

He brushes his warm fingers lightly across the twin indention above my ass, then he spits on my butthole, lubricating it. His fingers thrust into my pussy as his thick shaft enters my butthole. I squirm with pleasure and pain. He pinches my clit, distracting me from the pain as he goes deeper. He's gentle, then picks up speed. My body shakes with each thrust as I arch my back, pressing deeper into him.

I cry in pleasure and cry for this not to end. I've never felt so whole with a man—and so alive. My need for this moment to last forever is overwhelming, to be trapped in this cocoon of ours. To be entangled in lust in another dimension where it's just us and nothing can distract Liam from wanting me. Mila always talked about being destined to be with Dominic. If there is someone out there destined for me, let him be it. I'd die a thousand deaths just to have him. I know it sounds dramatic, but it's true.

He withdraws from me and kisses my back along my ass. "Are you all, right?"

I look over my shoulder. Our eyes meet. A sheen of sweat glistens on his chest. I can't help but melt over him. I finally get the word out that is lodged in my throat.

"Yeah."

He grabs my ankle, flipping me over on my back. Liam leans in to latch on to my breast, and my body shudders. "Don't come until I tell you."

"I need you inside me, Liam, please."

He chuckles. "You want my cock in your pussy, grenade? You're my fucking grenade who just had to combust my life, didn't you?" As he speaks, he plunges into me.

My body is on fire as his thrusts grow deeper, and I arch my back, curling my toes. His skin tingles beneath my nails as I dig them into his muscular back. His cock swells inside me, sending waves of pleasure coursing through me. With each thrust, my clit tightens around him.

Our eyes meet—fire and lust swimming in pools of desire. His gaze never drifts from mine. I can't seem to look away. With each thrust, the feeling in my chest deepens.

"Sophie," he whispers, then nods to himself, as if he's battling something within. It almost feels like he wants to make love to me, but just then, he looks away and tucks his head in the nape of my neck, kissing it. He grips the headboard, and his thrust picks up speed. Fucking me raw, working me into a frenzy. Pleasure rocks through me with the need to come.

"Liam, I need to..."

He groans. "Not yet, baby." His body jolts up, and his hips thrust back and forth. "This pussy belongs to me." He thrusts harder. "Your ass I fucked—it's mine, baby. I claimed it." His mouth latches onto one breast, then he takes the other into his mouth. Liam's tongue swirls at the tip of my peaked nipple. "These are mine," he mouths into my breasts. He looks up at me, and his thrust keeps a steady rhythm. "These lips are fucking mine." Just as his lips crash onto mine, our tongues tangle, hot and desperate for one another. I cling to his soft, silky hair and cry into his mouth. "Come for me, bella."

The power of our orgasms send us into a shivering ecstasy.

THE SUNLIGHT BEAMS through the window, causing me to stir from my deep sleep. After last night's sexual marathon, I'm drained and bone tired. Protective and angry Liam is hot as hell. Snuggling into the sheets, I take a whiff of Liam's masculine scent. Turning, I pat the bed in search of Liam, but it's empty. Just then, the shower turns off, and Liam steps out with a towel around his waist. Beads of water drizzle down his olive-tanned, toned skin. I'm tempted to lick every drop. His black hair is silky wet. I lift my eyebrows and bite my lip. God, my body aches, and in between my legs, my ass stings, but not even that could stop me from wanting more of him. He's watching me with enthusiasm. Uh, yeah, my mouth is gaping like a fish out of water. Suddenly, I feel my cheeks burn. Blushing is so unlike me; no man has ever made me blush. *God, Sophie, get your shit together.*

He smiles as if he can read my thoughts. "Morning, mi bella. How did you sleep?"

"Umm, good, good, and you?" My words stumble out of my mouth. Something shifted in the air last night. Liam seems different. I can't grasp what it is, but something changed.

"I slept great." He runs his fingers through his wet hair and drops the towel.

Good, lord.

My heart stutters, and my body heats, and I struggle to breathe. His ass is on full display. He shows it off with ease and confidence. "Take a warm bath, baby, and I'll make us breakfast." He opens a drawer to grab underwear.

"Sounds great," I say to his toned, sculpted ass. So firm and not even a dimple there. He turns to face me, and whoa, if my heart was stuttering, now it's palpitating. My eyes widen, and I clear my throat. "You should change in the bathroom."

"Why in the hell should I change in the bathroom? It's not my fault you can't control yourself." His lips twist arrogantly.

I flip over and groan into the pillow, then yelp when he flips me back over unexpectedly and lays a kiss on my lips. The blue silk sheets slide down, and his eyes darken with lust as he scans my profile.

Liam's thumb swipes at my engorged nipple. "I would take you right now, but unfortunately, you're sore, and I need you ready for me tonight. I have to go to work for a bit."

I moan when his tongue circles around my nipple.

"And I don't want you staying at your place for a while. I

don't want that fucker looking for you because, I swear, I'll fuck him up. I would have done it last night if I hadn't been in uniform." His voice is laced with possessiveness.

His perfectly shaped eyebrows rise, challenging me. I could fight him over it. I know Eric won't come back. Part of me wants to stay here with Liam and get to know him. He hardly shares anything with me about his life. I'm surprised I'm sitting in his bed. We've been messing around for a couple of weeks now. His possessiveness and jealousy make me want more, not just casual, but all of him. I know it's too much to ask, and if I say anything to him, he'll freak out and push me away. So I'll settle for the little he gives me.

Cupping his cheeks, I lean in and peck his lips. "I'll stay a couple of days if it makes you feel better. I don't have work today, so if you don't mind, I can hang around."

"Of course, I don't mind. I'm telling you to stay. We can get your car later tonight. There's food in the fridge—not much because I've been at your house. And Duke's probably—well, not probably. He *will* follow you around. He seems to really like you." He chuckles, lifting from the bed. He walks to the closet in his boxer briefs and points to the bathroom. "Bath, mi bella, *my beautiful.*"

I could get used to this.

CHAPTER 18
SOPHIE

Liam left thirty minutes ago, and I sit here thinking about an hour ago when I stepped out of the warm bath. I made my way to the kitchen where I found Liam cooking in jeans and a tank top that showed every bit of hard muscle. We ate breakfast together for the first time. Usually, he runs out the door from my place. He appeared to be more at ease, calm. I made some coffee, and we sat together as if we were a couple.

I asked why he wasn't in uniform. He said it was just a meeting he needed to attend because he had a mission in Long Beach in a couple of days and needed to get all their information together. Then he kissed me and left. It was the most I've gotten out of him. Now I'm walking around the house, trying not to pry into his business. His home gives off a cozy feeling. It's small but perfect. Roaming into his bedroom, I glance around. The thought of him having other women here bothers me. Come to think of it, I'm bothered more than when I found Eric with my ex-friend.

Duke trails behind me, wagging his tail in pure happiness. I kneel to pet him, scratching behind his white silky ears.

"Hey, big guy. You're a cutie just like your owner, aren't you?" He closes one eye in complete heaven. "Tell me, how many women has he had here?" He ignores me and lies on his back for a tummy rub. I scratch his tummy until he passes out, legs parted, paws up in the air. Well, he certainly is like his owner. I chuckle.

Opening one of his drawers, I look for, I don't know what, maybe women's underwear. In his sock drawer, I find a photo of him and his father. Liam looks just like him. He appears to be around four years old in the photo. Beside it, I find a ninja turtle—two of them. I'm in awe of how cute it must have been—his favorite toy as a kid. I still have my dolls and my bear-in skates in a box in the basement back home.

My phone rings, and I answer it.

"Hey there, sweet pea, how are things out there?"

I smile, hearing my mom's familiar voice. "Good, Mom, things have been fantastic. I have exciting news. Mila is pregnant." I can hear her gasp, then scream. I pull the phone from my ear.

"I'm so excited I get to be a grandma again!"

I chuckle.

My mom adores Mila and Dante. She's claimed them as her own. "I love it. The house is going to be filled with grandbabies. All we need is you now."

My mom's comment startles me. "What do you mean me, and what about Alex? He's way older, with no kids," I retort.

"Hold on, let me call your brother on three-way."

I close the drawers and walk into Liam's walk-in closet, hearing my mom dialing Alex's number. Poor guy. With the time difference between here and London, he's probably in bed.

"Hello." A sleepy yawn comes through the line.

"Hello, honey, I have your sister on the line. I can't believe you haven't told her the news."

Alex groans. "I was going to when I woke up. But since you woke me up, I'll tell you the news. Liz is six months pregnant. We just found out. We didn't even know. She had no signs of pregnancy, and she was getting her period."

My jaw drops. I can't believe it—more little boogers to spoil. "Congratulations! How exciting. I can't wait to meet her —or him. God, Alex, you're going to be a dad. Give my love to Liz."

The doorbell rings.

"Hey guys, sorry, but I have to go. Someone's at the door. I'll call you later, Alex. Go back to bed."

"Ok, sweet pea. I'll get back to you so we can plan a trip to London when the baby is born," my mom says in her chirpy voice. Once I hang up the line with my mom and brother, I make my way to the door. It could be Liam. He must have forgotten something.

Opening the door, I find a beautiful woman with black hair, brown-gray sparkling eyes, and high cheekbones. She's wearing a beautiful yellow summer dress. She looks so much like Liam —that smile.

"Hi, I'm Liam's mom, Andrea." She extends her hand for me to shake.

I extend my clammy hand into hers and shake it dumbly, feeling awkward. "Hi...I'm Sophie, a-a friend of Liam's."

She scans my profile, and I realize I'm in Liam's shirt. And not wearing underwear because the jealous beast didn't get me any. *God, how embarrassing.*

I scoot to the side to give her room. "Oh, come on in. Liam went to work for a bit. He said he would be back in a while."

Her lips curl into a smile of contentment. Her eyes gleam

like globes in the light. She reaches for the grocery bags lying on the porch outside. I hadn't noticed them.

"Let me help you," I say, reaching for a bag in one hand and pulling the shirt down from behind with the other. My cheeks flush with embarrassment as I set them on the wooden kitchen table. "I'm going to go change." I speed walk to Liam's room. Rumbling through the bag, I pull out a top and leggings. Surprisingly, he packed a bra.

Making my way back into the kitchen, I find Andrea stocking the fridge and pantry. Clearing my throat nervously, Andrea turns to me with a beaming smile.

"Hey, sweetheart, I'm just putting the groceries away. I usually come over and cook for Liam, or he comes over to my place." She glances over her shoulder at me.

"Oh, that's sweet of you."

From the laugh lines around her eyes to her easy smile, Andrea is the picture of kindness and warmth, the kind of woman everyone wants for a mom.

"Well, I try to feed the big guy since he's always on the run at work. And at the gym, too, you know." She waves her hand in the air, then raises an eyebrow. "You know, it's been a while since he's come for dinner. I see why now," she says teasingly.

My face flushes for what feels like the millionth time this morning. "Oh, I-I—"

She laughs, a hearty, genuine chortle. "Sweetheart, I'm not upset. I'd rather him be with a beautiful girl like you. So, tell me, how did you two meet?" She swings around, grabbing a bag of flour and a mixing bowl.

I pull out a stool and sit by the kitchen island. "I'm Mila's best friend, so that's pretty much how I met Liam."

She tosses some ingredients into the bowl and starts kneading. "Aww, you're Mila's friend; even better. So, you must be from New York. That explains your beautiful accent."

I nod and relax my tensed muscles. When I'm with Liam, I feel comfortable, as if I'm being embraced in the warmest blanket on a chilly night. His mother radiates the same aura—it's strong enough that you can almost touch it. I'm glad I had the chance to meet her—this is like getting a glimpse into a part of him.

"Can I help you with anything?" I offer, and her smile stretches to her ears. She's still kneading that dough.

"Yes, it would be great. You can dice the meat for me while I make these fresh tortillas. The pack of meat is in the fridge, sweetheart." She tilts her head to the side, pointing in the direction of the fridge.

Maneuvering my way around her, I fish out the package of meat and search for a cutting board and knife. I'm surprised Liam actually has a cutting board.

"You know, it's nice to have Liam's girlfriend help me cook."

"Oh, I'm not his—"

She shakes her head and laughs again, pulling out a rolling pin from her purse. My eyes widen, and I want to laugh at how she's carrying a rolling pin with her.

"I know you're not his girlfriend," she says. "Is that what youngsters call it these days? Liam has never introduced me to a girl he's into or brought someone to his place, so this must mean you're his girl."

I drop the knife.

Her confession has me swooning on the inside, melting like a stick of butter. I know he doesn't do relationships, although I had no idea he had never taken a girl home for his family to meet. She only knows about me because she showed up. Otherwise, he would have never introduced me to his family. Hell, he barely talks about himself. All I know about him is his body and the small conversations he has with me, which do not include talking about his personal life. If I'm really the only girl he's brought to his house, then I'll feel like a gourmet grilled cheese.

"How do you know he hasn't brought a woman here? I mean, he could have, since you don't live here," I say. Hopefully, I don't sound rude, but I want to know her answer.

She glances up at me, and her lips curl in a smile. I must look like a scared chihuahua. She begins rolling the dough into circles, stretching it to form a circle. "Liam has repeatedly said he doesn't want a girlfriend, for whatever reason. He's very private, so he won't bring just any girl into his home. If he has you here at his home while he's at work, then you must mean something to him. I know my son is stubborn as they come. It might take a while for him to admit it."

I'm not sure what she means by that, but a sense of relief washes over me, knowing he hasn't brought other women to his bed. I guess I can add it to *our* growing list of firsts.

ANDREA PLACES the last of the tortillas in the hot skillet and watches as they bubble, filling the kitchen with a heavenly aroma. She adds pieces of steak to the pan, followed by slices of peppers and onions, allowing their fragrance to mix with the smell of the cooking meats. The combination is familiar and comforting, like an invisible hug from a mother. I prepare a pitcher of ice-cold lemonade.

During our conversation, Andrea shares that she has been working as a receptionist at a doctor's office for several years. She also mentions that she used to work two jobs when Liam was younger. Although I am curious about Liam's father, I hesitate to ask, since I just met Andrea and don't want to overstep any boundaries.

I can't help but wonder what has made Liam so closed off.

It seems he had a good upbringing. He's a sweet, compassionate man with a heart of pure gold. He doesn't seem to see himself as I do. Last night he glared daggers at Eric and protected me. His possessive, protective behavior was undeniable proof that he cares about me and that even with blinding jealousy, he can't hide how much he cares.

His words are forever printed in my mind. *Take out my cock.* I still remember the taste of the smooth velvet of his skin, my lips wrapped around him. It was so erotic, the way his lips curled and his grip on my hair as I took him in my mouth, every inch of him.

"Did you find it, sweetheart?" Andrea asks.

Oh yeah, right—she wanted the bag of rice. Closing the pantry, I hand her the rice. Her smile is contagious. I can't help but return it. My tongue thickens with anticipation, and it slips out of my mouth before I stop myself.

"Um, is Liam's dad around?" I swallow hard at the mass in my throat.

She drops the bag of rice on the counter, her sparkling eyes —gone. Her shoulders slump, the glow in her beautiful face pales. I want to kick myself in the ass for being so intrusive.

"Liam didn't tell you? Oh, of course not...he doesn't like talking about it, although I wish he would. It might help him," she mumbles, the last part more like she's talking to herself. She grabs the bag of rice then pours it into a pan.

"I'm sorry. I didn't mean to pry."

She glances at me over her shoulder.

"No, it's fine, Sophie. My husband passed away. Yesterday marked eighteen years since my Manny left this world," Andrea says in a gentle, soft voice.

My blood drains from my face, leaving me pale as a bedsheet. My eyes sting with unshed tears, and my heart aches for them. Yesterday—oh, God, he was hurting, and he had to deal with my shit...with Eric. I feel like even more of an ass now.

"I would tell you what happened, but I feel it's Liam's story to tell."

I nod. "I'm so sorry, Andrea, for your loss."

She smiles and gazes out the kitchen window as if she's thinking. She stays quiet for a minute, then looks up at me. "Liam is so much like my Manny—handsome, kind-hearted, and caring. Every day I look at my son, I see a piece of his father. That's what has kept me going all these years." She stirs the rice. "Manny would be so proud of the man Liam has become. He takes care of me, my mother-in-law, and Rosaline. You have yourself a good man, Sophie. Maybe you're the key."

I'm unsure what she means by the key, but before I can think about what she means, the door swings open, and Liam walks in.

"Ladies," Liam says.

Andrea wags her eyebrows at him.

"Mamá, nice of you to drop in." He grins, and they share a look only they understand.

"Oh, yes, honey. Me and your girl made lunch. Sophie here is one of a kind."

He nods. I'm feeling a little uneasy, but Liam seems fine. He gives his mother a kiss, places a kiss on my forehead, and asks Andrea what's for lunch.

I wasn't expecting him to be so calm for a man who has never introduced a girl to his mom. And for him to place a kiss on my forehead in front of her.

What has me lost in thought is...what is Liam's story? He doesn't like talking about his father's passing. Hell, I didn't even know his father passed. Maybe I can get him to open up for me. I can't imagine the pain he must carry.

CHAPTER 19
LIAM

"Fuck!" I grunt under the hood of my dad's pickup. I've been working on it all morning, trying to get the carburetor in. Weeks ago, we rebuilt it at Santiago's shop, and I picked it up a week ago. Specifically, the day I walked into my house to find my mom and Sophie sitting at the dinner table, laughing like they were BFFs. My mom hardly ever shows up at my house. It's mostly me going over to see her. Finding my mom with my girl together was bewildering. It's been years since I've seen my mom laugh without faking it or putting on an act. But with Sophie, her smile stretched to her ears, and her eyes beamed like the sun. The aroma of freshly cooked food filled the house.

When Sophie excused herself to go to the restroom, my mom couldn't help whispering in my ear, asking if Sophie was my girlfriend. A fraction of me wanted to say yes—she's mine. I mean, she *is* fucking mine. She always will be, but she will never be mine to keep. Instead, I told my mom Sophie, and I were just seeing each other. No labels.

She cupped my cheek and said, "You look at her the same way..." She cleared her throat and shook it off with a lopsided smile. "Don't let the darkness haze you from the light, or you'll realize too late."

Even days later, I'm not sure what she meant.

Duke's throaty bark pierces the air, and my head jolts up, smacking into the hood of my truck. Sophie stands a few feet away, holding Duke's leash as she does every day—taking him for his daily walk through the neighborhood. It's been a week since I brought her to my house. I'm not going to lie—I love having her here. I come home to her every night, making her cum with just one finger, and then I salivate on her fine pussy. Then I assist by helping her make dinner, and by assisting, I mean by wrapping my arms around her waist while she cooks. She shoos me away. It's so damn hard to keep my hands off her; she's so fucking hot.

Duke wags his tail, prancing toward me. That little fucker has been stealing all the attention when we cuddle on the couch. Duke always jumps to sit in the middle, laying his head on her bare legs.

"Hey, how's it going? Did you get it running?" Sophie's eyes sparkle in the light.

My lips curve in a smile at the sight of her in a flowy green dress. The thought of not having her for life sends an arrow right through my heart.

"I think so. I just finished reinstalling the carburetor and topped off the fluids."

She nods, seeming very interested. "Do you plan on getting it painted?" She presses her hands on the truck, leans forward, and peeks inside.

"I was thinking ocean blue," I say, peering into her eyes, leaning in to kiss the lips I can never resist.

She opens up for me, giving me access to her perfect red lips. Her tongue swooshes like the ocean, sending bolts of electricity through every pulsing beat of my body. Pulling away, I look down at her beautiful face. She regains the air I sucked out of her.

Tilting her head, she retorts, "Ocean blue! Why is that?" she questions, obviously, or maybe fishing for more of an answer. Women are always fishing for more.

"Because it looks good on me," I utter, letting my eyes travel her body.

She smirks.

Yeah, she knows why. I jump into the driver's seat and start the ignition. The truck purrs, coming back to life. A satisfied smile cuts across my face. Damn, my dad would love to hear this—it sounds just like when I was a kid. Sophie jumps up and down, along with Duke.

"You did it, baby," she screams, causing nosy neighbor Inez to peek out from behind the curtain.

She's never called me baby, and I like the sound of it. My chest fills with pride. I step back, staring at the truck, wiping my hand with a rag, and scrubbing off the grease. Sophie comes behind me, wrapping her arms around my waist.

"Can I ask you a question?" she mouths on my back.

"Of course."

She's quiet for what seems a minute too long. "Um...who was your first?"

I'm startled by her question. Shit, it's been years. Grabbing her arms, I pull her toward me so I can look at her.

"Why are you asking?"

She shrugs. "Is it a painful question?" she snaps, eyeing me and narrowing her lashes.

I take a second to think. Crystal was my first. We went to high school together. She was the only girl I slept with more than once and the first girl I went down on. I finally answer her.

"Crystal. Her name is Crystal."

Her lips press into a thin line. I'm not sure why she's asking. She must have been thinking about it.

"Does she live around here, and was she a constant hook-up?" She kneels to pet Duke, avoiding any eye contact, it seems.

"No, she moved away a little after we graduated. And, well, I was sixteen, and she *was* a constant hook-up then."

She stands and dusts her hands together. I'm peering at her, wondering why she's asking, but she changes the subject. "So, are we still going to your mom's for dinner?"

Right, my mom invited us for dinner. My mom can't seem to stop talking about Sophie. Even my grandma called me asking questions. I gave up on telling them we were not an item. To them, we are.

"Nah, I canceled. I have somewhere I want to take you, and now that this baby is purring, we can take it on a test drive."

Her eyebrows scrunch up. "Where?"

"It's a surprise."

ONCE SOPHIE HAS CHANGED into jeans, we hit the road. Driving my dad's truck makes my stomach twist in knots. The last time I rode in this truck, was when I was a kid. As much as I love it, it also brings back those memories, the good and the bad. They replay in my head like a carousel—so much blood, my dad's last words, running for my life. Not a day goes by, I don't stop and think—what if we hadn't gone out that night? Would things have been different? It was me who held him back. He didn't draw his gun fast enough because I was with him. The guilt consumes me every fucking day.

"Are we almost there? It's beautiful out here." Sophie's sexy accent fills the truck, bringing me back to now—with her. Reaching for her hand, I pull her closer to me.

"Yeah, twenty more minutes." I wish she would have kept her dress on so I could run my hands up her legs. "It is beautiful." I stare at her luscious lips, thinking of the night I demanded she take my cock out. Fuck, that was a sight. Those lips wrapped, hugging my cock. Fucking sexy. I was so pissed the asshole touched her. Forcing his lips on hers as if they belonged to him. Never have I talked to a woman the way I did with Sophie, but she loved it, and so did I.

Twenty minutes later, we arrive at Tension Canyon Trails. I ease the truck through the open metal gate and park near a weathered redwood ranch house. Horses snort in the surrounding fields, their manes glimmering in the sunlight. Red brick stalls stand in the corner of the ranch house.

Hopping out of the truck, Sophie takes in her surroundings. A light breeze fills the fresh air with the scents of manure and pine. Not the best combination. The path to the spot is hidden from view, and only a few are aware of its existence. Lush pine trees surround it, creating a canopy of comforting shades of green. Down the trail, an inviting lake glimmers in the sun.

"It's beautiful out here, so quiet and peaceful." Sophie inhales, filling her lungs with the fresh air. I take her hand in mine, navigating her toward the horse stalls. "What are we doing, exactly?"

"Taking Monkey for a walk or run." My voice rings out as Monkey comes galloping toward me. She's a beautiful white palomino. I have been coming to Bill's Ranch since I was sixteen. It became my sanctuary, a place to think and clear my head. In the past, Bill made his horses available to those who wanted to ride along the trails. He closed a few years back, but he still lets me borrow a horse whenever I want.

"O.M.G., she's beautiful! She knows you, too, so you must come here a lot?" Sophie runs her fingers down Monkey's white, thick, coarse mane.

"I do. Since I learned how to drive. I needed a place to get away from the world. This became my place. I've never brought anyone here with me before," I admit, a little sheepishly. For some reason, I feel the need to admit it to her. I want her to know she's not just some other girl. She turns to peer at me, and her eyes soften.

"I'm honored to be the first to join you in your private place, Liam."

Once we put the saddle on Monkey, we follow the trail that takes us to the lake. Sophie's afraid to mount the horse, her hands clutching my waist in a firm grasp. All those workouts have been paying off at the gym. We've been going together every morning, but now I have her work out with me and not pervert Luis.

"I've never been on a horse before," she breathes, her hot breath fanning behind my ear. I chuckle as she states the obvious. She's practically clamping onto my nipples.

"You don't say, baby? I thought you were the rodeo queen," I tease, and she scoffs, pinching my nipple. I wince, gripping the reins.

I take in the peacefulness of the vast landscape, inhaling the smell of the lake offset by the crisp scent of pine trees. The rhythmic sound of the horse's hooves' trudging against the pebbles is a soothing accompaniment to the tranquil setting along the winding path from the ranch house to the lake. It takes about fifteen minutes for me to fill my lungs with fresh air and clear my head of all the stress of work. Once we arrive at the lake, I tie Monkey around a tree and let him grub on the tall grass.

Sophie inhales the fresh air, a smile spreading across her beautiful face. "I understand why you like coming here; it's so... refreshing—no cars honking, no loud noises, no city life."

I seat myself on the green patch of grass facing the lake. The sky is clear, and the sun reflects off the lake.

"Come here." I pat the patch of grass between my legs for her to sit. She lays her head on my chest. I pull her in close to me, wrapping my arms around her waist. The sharp pain in my chest feels like a toothache. Her closeness makes me feel things I shouldn't want to feel.

"It *is* nice to get away from the city."

"Tell me something about you," Sophie probes.

"Like?"

"Anything, Liam. Tell me something...I don't know."

I exhale a long breath. Talking about myself is not something I'm comfortable doing.

"My cousin Rosaline is like a sister to me. My mom raised her from when she was three years old. My aunt, my mom's sister, left her at our house and never returned for her. She lives in Mexico with her husband—he was her boyfriend when she ran off with him."

Her head tips up to peer at me. "That's sad. I'm glad she has you and your mom. Your mom is a wonderful woman for taking her in."

I nod and place a kiss on her forehead. "She has a big heart. She worked her ass off to support us. She always felt guilty about not spending enough time with us because she had to work so much."

She worked during the day at a doctor's office and part-time as a waitress at a restaurant in the evenings. The first couple of years were the hardest for her. I'd hear her cry in her room. I wished it was me who died that night: my dad would be here, and my mom wouldn't have struggled so much.

"She's proud of you, Liam. You have accomplished so much at a young age, and you're still growing." She turns to face me, wrapping her arms around my neck. "I'm proud of you."

Just as I'm about to swallow the lump in my throat, her lips press on mine as I part my lips, letting her take control. Her fingers slide into my hair, and her tongue thrusts deep against mine, like a snake letting out its venom. My dick tightens in my jeans.

"Take off your pants," I say, my voice barely more than a whisper.

She complies by shimmying them down her legs and stepping out of them. We are in a remote spot. I've been here many times and never run into anyone. This woman consumes my thoughts and my body, yet I want to keep her at arm's length. Right now, I'm dying to feel our flesh mold into one, to feel her heat on mine. I bite my lip, watching as she undresses.

I pant, just seeing her naked before me. On my knees, I grab her waist and bend lower to swipe my tongue between her legs. Pleasing her has become my new favorite thing to do. Thrusting my tongue deeper, pounding it—as deep as I can get.

She moans with every thrust of my tongue.

"Your tongue works magic," she cries out.

I chuckle. "Lie down, Sophie." I need to be inside her. Feel her.

My heart pounding in my chest as I lay on top of her, I embrace her tightly in my arms and begin to thrust inside her. The desire to protect her overwhelms me, and she becomes the focal point of my attention. As I move inside her, I want to keep her safe from any harm.

CHAPTER 20
SOPHIE

"Fuck, Sophie," he grunts just as he spills into me.

I honestly couldn't care if someone passed by. I am too seduced by the way his body moves with mine. His hard muscular body revs like a muscle car, driving me into the bliss of ecstasy. I can't help the feelings stirring in me—he brought me to his special place, and that itself is worth more than I could have hoped for. My body shakes with my release. Digging my nails into his bare back, throwing my head back, I cry with pleasure.

He nestles in my neck and murmurs, "Was it good?"

Oh my, he melts my world.

He gazes down at me, and the way he's peering into me makes my lungs tighten as if they are being squeezed.

Don't look at me that way, Liam. My heart can't take it. I close my eyes at his hooded stare.

"Perfect," I say, my voice barely audible.

He nods and climbs off me with a shit-eating grin. I want to say it was the best sex of my life. It always is *with him.*

He's such a charmer.

"Good—and we have an audience." He tilts his head to the side toward whoever is watching.

I gasp and grab my jeans. "Who?" I whisper.

He chuckles just as two bunnies run away.

I groan. "You scared the shit out of me. And they were probably staring at your fine ass."

His eyebrows rise, and he fans himself.

I roll my eyes. Egotistical man.

"Fine ass, huh? Of course, you're the one who smacked my ass in public. It still has your handprint on it."

"I'm surprised I didn't fracture my hand on your buns of steel. No wonder you're always doing squats with the barbell."

He laughs.

"I'm glad my hands are imprinted on your ass. At least now people know who it belongs to," I say as I button up my jeans.

He passes me a water bottle he brought with him. "It's all yours, baby." He winks, and I gush like a complete idiot.

Coming from New York, I'm used to the big city life. I've always lived in a fast-paced city. Moving to California has given me a sense of quietness. It is busy but not compared to Manhattan. I hardly stepped out of the city in Manhattan to enjoy the outdoors. I've never felt so content in my life.

"Almost there," Liam utters, holding my hand as we walk uphill.

My feet stop moving as I take in the expanse of rolling golden hills dotted with vibrant clusters of California poppies swaying in the breeze. I fill my lungs with the fragrant air, and a sense of peace overwhelms me. *Beautiful.*

"Wow, this is...just wow, Liam. Beautiful," my voice comes out in a whisper.

His arms wrap around my waist. He blows kisses along my neck. He searches for his phone in his pocket.

"Selfie?" he asks.

I'm taken by surprise. For a man who clearly wants less than casual, he sure has a strange way of showing it. I really don't think he realizes it.

We take photos of him kissing my neck, one of us smiling, and the rest he takes of me lying in a bed of poppies. The photo of us looks amazing—we look like a couple in love. I know it's wishful thinking. Initially, I wanted casual, but being with Liam makes me want more.

"Send them to me?" I ask.

He nods and texts them to me.

After a few minutes, we begin walking back to the lake, where Monkey is waiting. The weight on my chest has been heavy as I think about what Andrea said to me about Liam's father. We've been practically living together for the past few months, him at my place, and now I've been staying with him. I know what relationships are, although he fails to acknowledge we are anything but fuck buddies. I'm dying for him to let me in and tell me more about himself. In reality, I know nothing about him when he knows everything about me. I've told him about my family, friends, even my relationship with Eric was like. I'll admit it's frustrating.

He stops and places a poppy behind my ear. "Beautiful," he breathes.

My heart comes to a complete halt. Those beautiful eyes hold so much pain, and he has become a master at masking it. Only I can see through him. Getting on my tiptoes, I kiss the end of his nose.

"Liam," I whisper. "Tell me about your dad." My lips go into a straight line.

His demeanor changes as he steps back and shakes his

head. "Not now, Sophie." He picks up his pace, walking toward the lake.

"Liam, your mom told me your father passed away. I'm so sorry. She didn't tell me what happened. She said it was your story to tell."

He spins around, and I run right into his chest. "Exactly. It's my damn story to tell. And I sure as fuck don't want to talk about it."

"It will help if you talk about it."

A dark laugh drips from his lips. "You want to fix me, Sophie? Is that what it is? You think I'm some broken puppet who needs fixing?"

"No, Liam, of course not. I just want to help you...to be there for you."

Anger grabs him by the jaw, his fist tightening into a ball. "Help? Help me?" he bellows. "You don't know shit about me, Sophie. The only real problem you had was with your shitty ex. You've lived a cushy life with two parents, a brother. Soon you'll have nephews and nieces. A fucking family. You're a queen on a pedestal, never had to struggle in life," Liam spits, his nostrils flaring, burning with rage. The veins on his neck are visibly pulsing underneath the skin.

I see the pain within him. I understand his anger, some of it, but I don't know what has caused it.

"That's because you don't tell me shit about you, Liam!" I shout, my chest heaving. "We've been messing around for months now, sleeping in the same bed. You'd think you would have opened up to me. It's like I'm sleeping with a stranger every night!" My heart squeezes with pain at how he's looking at me.

"You're not my girlfriend or wife. You're just—"

"What, huh? Your friend with benefits? Your sleeping buddy? Your slut? Just the girl warming your bed? The one to give you a release, right? Isn't it what all men say? You know you're no different from Eric. He treated me like I was just his ragdoll."

He swallows hard as his Adam's apple bobs. I glare at him in disgust and pain, shooting in every direction. I step beside him, walking toward the trail and returning to the ranch house. I'll call for a rideshare. I'm sure someone can find me out here.

"Sophie," he calls out in a raspy voice.

My heart hurts—the pain of a thousand bee stings. Maybe I pushed too hard. I swear, all I wanted to do was make him feel better—make him feel alive. I'm not trying to fix him like a broken doll. I lo...nope, I can't say it. It will make it real, and he wants nothing more. My eyes sting with the unshed tears.

You're not my girlfriend.

"Sophie, wait," he calls out, but I keep my feet moving evenly through the tall spring grass. My footsteps crush the grass and dry leaves, the sound echoing in my ears as I trudge forward, determined to reach the distant ranch.

Minutes later, he catches up to me with Monkey. "Sophie, hop on." His voice is soft and velvety.

I shake my head. "No, thanks. I'll walk."

He sighs and jumps off the horse. He walks beside me in silence. For several unspoken minutes, I feel him cast a glance my way. I don't turn to acknowledge him. His words hurt. They made me feel as if I'm not important to him. We make it up a gravel dirt path. You can see the horse stalls and ranch from a distance.

"I was six years old when my dad died. That night, my mom stayed home, and my dad wanted to take me out to eat. A gang leader murdered my father that night."

My head jolts up as I glance at him, but he's looking straight ahead. I stay silent and look at my feet as we walk.

"My dad was a detective. My mom told me he had

accepted a position with the DEA. I'm not sure why they came after him." He clears his throat. "There's more, but I can't right now, Sophie. I'm not ready to talk about the rest. I went through therapist after therapist as a kid, and I couldn't talk to anyone."

He was just a baby—only six years old. My heart aches for him. I wish I could take the pain right out of him.

"I understand. And thank you for telling me. I'm sorry for your loss," I say.

He stops, scans my profile, and shuffles his hand into his hair. "I'm sorry about what I said. You're not any of those things. I can't offer you more, Sophie. Not right now, or maybe ever. Just give me time, please. I like what we have right now."

I want to agree, but it would be a lie. I *want* more. Why continue something that will never go further? "It's better if we sto—"

He covers my mouth with a kiss. "Don't say it," he says in a strangled voice. "Just give me some time, please." Past the pain in his eyes, there's desperation. He's pleading with me.

"Okay," I whisper, not understanding what he means by time. We make it back to the ranch. Liam removes the saddle from Monkey and then brushes him. We drive back in silence until we arrive at his house.

"At least we know the truck runs great," I say, breaking the silence with a lame joke.

"Uh-huh," is all he says.

Pulling out my keys from my purse, I peer up at Liam. "I'm going to go to my place to feed the stray cats."

The statement is not entirely untrue. I do need to feed them. But more than anything, I need to take some time alone to reflect and think. Does he even understand that, based on what we've been doing in the past weeks, we *are* in a relationship? Maybe he doesn't want to acknowledge it, or he doesn't want *me* that way. And I can't stop wondering if the reason he doesn't do relationships is because of that girl Crystal.

She and I are the only girls he's ever slept with more than once. Did something happen that left him incapable of moving on? All reasons why I need to go home and think, take a breather. Maybe it's his past and not Crystal that means he needs distance between us. He made a huge leap in telling me something so personal. I'm proud of him for that. I want more than he can offer, so I know there's a huge chance I'll get my heart broken.

"You want me to go with you?" He's watching me. He nervously runs his hand through his perfect black hair. The awkwardness envelopes us.

I fiddle with my keys. "Umm, no. It's okay. I'm just going to feed them really quick and grab my clothes."

"You have clothes here. I just did the laundry."

Yup, he did my laundry, hung my skirts, blouses, and dresses in his closet, folded my undies and bras, and placed them in the dresser—another reason why I'm falling in lo... nope, not saying it.

"I know, but I still need to feed the cats."

He nods and leans in to peck a kiss on my lips.

"See you in a bit?" he murmurs.

It's more of a question than a statement. He is waiting for my reply. He's worried I won't come back. There's a part of me unsure if I will.

CHAPTER 21
LIAM

The task force leader outlines the mission we are undertaking in the upcoming days. We are set to depart for Long Beach in Los Angeles tonight and will spend a full week there to get ready for the bust. We will also meet with the Los Angeles Police Department to discuss the details of the hit. According to our undercover informant, the shipment has already left Mexico, headed for the docks. Everything is running according to plan. I grab my paperwork and head straight for the coffee station once Jerry, the lead, wraps up the meeting. John walks in with a new rookie.

"Damn, what happened to you? You look like shit."

I grunt at his response and pour myself a hot, steamy cup of coffee. He's not wrong. I feel like shit. I stayed up last night waiting for Sophie, who never returned to the house. It felt like a knife to the chest. I don't blame her. I acted like a complete ass with her. She asked a question I should be able to answer, but I couldn't. The trauma is too deep. What if I did tell her the rest? Would she freak out? Would she think less of me?

"Couldn't sleep."

He leans back on the counter with his arms crossed. "Woman problems?"

"Something like that." The buzz of the station has me wanting to get out of here. I'm not in the mood today.

Fuck, I have never had women problems. I don't even know how to handle this shit. And the look on her face when I told her we couldn't be more. Goddamn. It's clear she wants more than the terms we initially agreed to.

John grabs himself a cup, pouring coffee. "Apologize, even if you did nothing wrong. Then buy her chocolates or something, take her out, and lastly, let her have it."

I raise an eyebrow at him and laugh. "Let her have it. What's that supposed to mean?"

He shakes his head and stirs the cream in his coffee. "You need a book for dummies on how to make a woman swoon? It means *fuck her.*"

I walk out laughing then turn to flip him off.

PULLING UP TO THE STUDIO, I grab the box of chocolates John suggested. Standing before her studio door, I watch her as she talks to the girls. She looks beautiful, wearing a red skirt with a white tank top. Her blonde hair sways as she shakes her head, laughing. My lungs constrict, becoming tighter and tighter.

I should be the bigger person and let her go if we can't be more, but it's not that simple. I'm selfish, and I don't want to lose her. When I open the door, the bell rings, and the three girls glance up. Suddenly I feel awkward, and my nerves spike. As soon as I spot Sophie, my stomach drops. My mouth goes dry, and a wave of heat floods my face. I shift on my feet, unsure what to do, while my racing heart pounds like thunder in my chest.

Who am I? Since when does heat flood my face? Fuck me.

"Hello, ladies," I say.

Sophie gives me a small smile, and Mila charges—well, more like, wobbles—toward me.

"Hi, Liam. What brings you here today?" Mila asks, hugging me.

"I needed to speak with Sophie. I'm heading out of town and need her to feed my dog."

She chuckles. "Oh, I see, gotcha." She winks and says in our native language, so Sophie won't hear, "I know what you guys are up to. I wasn't born yesterday. I'm not saying anything until she tells me, though."

I shake my head with a laugh and respond, "You sound just like Abuelita." That's her signature response. *I wasn't born yesterday.*

Mila waddles to the back of the studio, leaving me with Sophie.

"Hey, can I talk to you outside?" I ask.

"Of course."

Once we're outside, I ask what has been hanging over me. "You didn't come home."

Home. Fuck.

When she meets my gaze, her blue eyes melt. My mom's words hit me like a tsunami: *One of these days, a woman will put you in your place, and you'll be whipped.* She definitely has me by the balls—strangling them.

Her eyes expand. "Oh, I'm sorry, it's because I fell asleep on the couch after I made a bed outside for the cat who had her kittens. Umm, and I didn't know if you really wanted me to come back. You said you needed time."

Cupping her cheeks, I kiss her soft lips. "I did. I waited for you. I wanted to apologize to you with my tongue between your legs, lapping up and down, biting and sucking until you come on my face."

Her breathing picks up, and she squeezes her thighs together. I give her another kiss on the lips.

"I'm leaving tomorrow for Long Beach. The rest of the team leaves tonight, and I want you to spend the night with me before I leave for a week."

She wraps her arms around my neck, and our chests press together. The strings in my heart tug, and her body heat seeps into mine.

"Why do you have to go to Long Beach?"

I review everything that happened, with Pablo disappearing, returning to San Diego, leaving some parts out.

"How many days will you be gone?" she whispers onto my lips, which I can't seem to stop pecking at.

"Five days. Why? Will you miss me?"

She shrugs. "Maybe just your dick?"

I laugh and squeeze her peach ass. She moans softly. The sound of her moan has my dick hard.

"Sophie, I'm sorry for how I acted yesterday and the horrible shit I said. I didn't mean to hurt you. And you *do* know me better than anyone. Let me take care of you in the car and satiate you for now—until tonight...when I'll wreck your world, baby."

She shivers and mumbles, "Holy guacamole."

I laugh as I lift her up in my arms, taking her to my Camaro. Good thing my windows are limo-tinted. No one will see me buried between her legs.

THE PREVIOUS THREE days in Long Beach have felt like an eternity. We were busy preparing for the mission ahead of us, ensuring that all aspects of it will run smoothly. Our under-cover agent has been shadowing Pablo's son, eavesdropping on his conversations to pick up any vital pieces of information. It seems he will turn up at the drop-off as intended, so everything seems to be going according to plan. We've been at the shooting range all day and working out at the station's gym.

Once I arrive at the hotel shortly after five, I toss my clothes into a heap on the bathroom floor. A facetime call comes in, and Sophie's beautiful face appears on my screen. We've been texting back and forth for the last couple of days.

"Hey, baby, how was work?" I ask. Her eyes roam my body, then she bites her lip. I run my hands through my hair. I'm hard as fuck now.

"Why are you naked?"

I gesture with my hands to the shower.

"Oh, I can call you back," she says, her breath coming out uneven. Placing the phone standing against the wall, I walk toward the shower.

"Nah, you can watch." Giving her a clear view of my bare ass, I twist the faucet.

"Christ, are you trying to give me a heart attack?" Her sexy accent rasps through the receiver.

All I can think about is how I played with her body the night before I left, how her body hummed rhythmically against mine. I asked her if we were good after the blow-up we had. She said, "Yeah," so I continued making her body sing my name.

"Where are you?"

She moves the phone around the room, and now I can see she's sitting in our bed. I mean, *my* bed. *Fuck.*

"Take off your clothes, Sophie. Let me see your beautiful tits and my pussy."

She doesn't hesitate. That's what I like about her—she's

always ready for me. She sheds every piece of clothing with confidence and eagerness. My dick hangs heavy between my legs. She's so fucking beautiful. Sophie props up the phone and kneels on the bed, her long blonde hair hanging down to her ass.

I step into the heated shower, letting the hot steam waft around me, and leave the shower curtain open. My skin tingles as the hot water cascades down my body. I reach up and run my hands through my hair, massaging my scalp. With my other hand, I slowly begin to stroke my already aroused cock. As I do this, I hear a small moan from Sophie.

"Lay on the bed and touch yourself, baby," I command, looking into the screen. "Spread your legs and insert two fingers. Pretend it's me." I watch her as she watches me jerk off. And her fingers slide into her wet pussy. Sophie's chest rises and falls, her nipples erect, her legs spread open, and her mouth gaped open.

Hot as fuck.

"Pump harder, Sophie. Think of my cock pounding you." My voice is raspy and raw. "That's my good girl."

She moans my name as her back arches in pleasure. My hand moves in time with hers, keeping a steady beat. Our movements remain in sync as we move closer to the peaks of our pleasure. When she screams my name, my orgasm explodes like hot lava, a damn explosive fountain milking every drop. My eyes go heavy as I watch my girl glisten with wetness in between her legs.

"Wow," she pants.

Wow, indeed. I'd say I've never experienced something so erotic as this, but then again, with Sophie, it's all erotic. Turning off the shower, I dry myself and watch as Sophie grabs one of my shirts and slips it on.

A lazy smile spreads across my face. I like how she looks in it. Like she's mine. "Baby." My voice is barely recognizable. Christ, I'm turning into such a pussy. Ignoring my inner voice, I ask her something I've never asked anyone.

"Yeah," she says, tying her hair into a messy bun. Adorable.

"Uh, do you want to go to the gala with me for work?"

Her head jolts up, and she stares at the screen. "Really? Oh, I'd love to go with you." Sophie's smile widens. That smile melts, and my chest tightens.

"Good. Get some rest, mi bella. I'll see you soon."

"Will you stay on the line until I fall asleep?"

I nod, slipping on a pair of boxers. "Anything for you." I watch her tuck herself under the covers. She leans the phone on a pillow. Her eyes go droopy.

"Good night, Liam. I miss you." She mumbles the last part before she falls asleep. I lay in bed and watch her sleep.

For the last couple of hours, we've been quiet. Only the thump of my heart echoes in my ears. Jasper signals to me—it's time, just as the cargo arrives. I nod, heading for the car which just rolled in. We all slip from under the shadows and make our bust. Shots are fired into the night sky. Gun out, I duck down in search of Marko. When I spot him, I signal Jasper to spot me. Pablo's men hide in the shadows, waiting for the cargo to arrive. We are all suited up with our protective gear, ready for combat. It's past midnight, the sky is clear, and the night is quiet.

Jasper signals to me—it's time, just as the cargo arrives. I nod, heading for the car which just rolled in. We all slip from under the shadows and make our bust. Shots are fired into the night sky.

Gun out, I duck down in search of Marko. When I spot him, I signal Jasper to spot me.

Marko stands in the shadows like the complete pussy he is. I aim the gun at his head, chuckle darkly, and say, "Look who we have here—the man I've been looking for. Drop your gun, asshole."

He drops it to the ground, and Jasper collects it, then pats him down.

I give him a hard shove, and he slams into the brick wall behind him. His face is menacing, even with the sharp scar bisecting it. He looks as threatening as I know him to be.

"Where the fuck is Pablo? Such a fucking coward. Your father has been hiding for a decade. The Serpents must be ashamed to have a leader like him."

A sinister laugh erupts from his mouth.

"I agree with you, Liam. My father is a coward. This is why I'm taking over. And I've heard plenty of stories about you, Liam. How you ran home like a pussy after seeing your father bleed to death."

Venom runs through my veins, hot and ready to kill the motherfucker with my bare hands. My hands wrap around his neck, blocking his airway.

"Where is Pablo?" I add more pressure. He tries to fight me, but he's no match for me.

"Liam," Jasper calls out frantically.

I snap my gaze toward him.

A man with tattoos covering his skin towers over him, pressing a revolver against Jasper's temple. Just then, Marko attempts to reach for my gun. I throw a punch and send him tumbling to the ground. Jasper has the tattooed guy on the pavement, handcuffing him.

"Where's your fucking bastard of a father?" I repeat, hand-cuffing him.

Marko spits on my shoe. "You think I'd tell you? He'll show

up when you least expect it. After all, he has unfinished business." He laughs darkly.

A thunder of electricity runs through me. I ball my fist so
that I don't put a bolt through his skull. Unfinished business...
does he mean ending me or...? *Fuck.*

"Don't mess with the Serpents or you won't like what
happens next," Marko warns.

Not wasting a second, I punch his jaw and call for backup.

"Shut the fuck up!" I say, gritting my teeth and pushing
toward our vehicles.

CHAPTER 22

SOPHIE

"So, how are things with that guy you've been seeing?" Mila asks as she chews on a popcorn kernel and scrolls through Netflix.

My stomach sours and guilt eats at me. I hate keeping the truth from my best friend, but I know she will be anxious, knowing Liam's relationship perspective.

"Good. We're just seeing each other, nothing serious." I walk into the kitchen to avoid looking into her green eyes. We decided to have a girls' night at my place. It's been a while since we've hung out, with everything that has happened in the last couple of months between her and Dominic, then me and Liam. And now she's an engaged woman.

"Oh, that sucks. It seems like you really like him."

I shrug. "Kinda, but he doesn't want more," I admit, remembering why I came to my place that night. We had an argument. My heart said to give it more time. *Maybe he will fall in love with you.* But my big noggin said we were going to end up hurt. *Run for your life now.* The truth is, if I ran for my life, I'd miss him. I'd be heartbroken. Half of my stuff is at Liam's place my perfume, make-up, and clothes. I had to try Mila's set-the-mood advice with candles. Oh, boy, does it work. I thought the sex before had been mind-blowing. I had no idea. But then every moment with Liam blows my mind. Every night and every morning, whether I wake up cuddled in his arms or with his tongue between my legs.

"Earth to Sophie Summers. Pizza is here, or is she in sex heaven?" Mila's voice rings in my ears.

I burst out laughing. "What are you talking about? Sex heaven?"

She snorts. "Been calling your name. You were staring off into space, flushing with heat." She takes a bite of her pepperoni and jalapeño pizza. "And I do it all the time, thinking of stuff Dominic does with his tongue."

I make a gagging noise.

"He must be good at what he does."

Oh, she has no idea. And last night, Facetime was so damn hot. The way he was peering at me with lust in his eyes and the way he stroked his enormous shaft, soaked and wet. His biceps flexed with each stroke when he moaned my name. So. Hot.

"You're doing it again," Mila mumbles, walking to the sofa.

Grabbing our drinks, I follow her to the couch with heat pulsing between my legs. "So, what are Dominic and Dante up to?"

"Before I left, they were cooking together, then they planned to work on model cars. Dominic wants to teach him how to build one." Mila's smile stretches from ear to ear. She lets out a satisfying yawn, snuggles up on the couch, and with a gentle touch, rubs her pregnant belly.

"You're not going to pass out on me, are you?"

Truth be told, my bestie passed out on me an hour ago after watching two episodes of *The Night Agent*. The show actually reminds me of Liam. He is on a mission tonight. I just pray it all goes well and he's not injured. I keep my mind entertained by cleaning up the kitchen.

My phone beeps after midnight. My heart races when I see it's Liam.

––––––––

LIAM: *Hey, you're probably asleep, but I just wanted to let you know the mission went well, and I'm heading back to the hotel. I'll be back tomorrow.*

My body immediately relaxes. I'd been tense the whole day just, worrying about something going wrong.

Me: *I'm wide awake. I'm glad everything went well.*

The bubbles immediately show he's texting back.

Liam: *Why are you wide awake? It's two in the morning.*

Me: *I'm at a party, living it up.*

I laugh to myself, watching my pregnant bestie pass out at our sleepover party. I spent three hours cleaning my house since I'm hardly here. I've been with Liam at his house.

Liam: *Seriously? Doing what?*

I snort, reading his text. Would it be bad if I teased him just to make him jealous?

Me: *Been dancing the night away.*

Liam: *Who in the fuck are you dancing with? No man better lay his hands on you, Sophie!!*

Jeez, he even adds exclamation marks. He's so hot when he's jealous, it makes my insides throb.

Me: *Don't worry. When he grinded his dick on my ass, I moved away from him.*

Liam: *Excuse me? Fuck, Sophie, get your ass home!! LIKE NOW!*

Me: *But it's not over yet.*

God, I'm being horrible.

Me: *One more song, "Talk Dirty" by Jason Derulo, is pumping through the speakers. I have to dance to this one.*

Liam: *Are you testing me, Sophie? I'm going to spank your ass red for allowing them to get close to you...No one touches you but me. I thought I made that clear!!*

Is it bad I that want him to spank my ass? *Christ, Sophie, what's getting into you?*

Me: *Joking, I'm here at my place.*

I send him a picture of me in my room.

Me: *See, I'm home.*

Liam: *Better be, and just for pissing me off, I need nudes— several of them.*

Good, lord.

I CAME HOME a little early from work to cook Liam dinner. It has been five days since I've seen him, and I miss him. I'm so proud of him for telling me a piece of his past. What we have is so much more real since he's let me in a little more. He just doesn't see it—or maybe he doesn't *want* to see it.

I open a bottle of wine and wait for him to arrive. As soon as he appears, my heart begins to race. Possibly due to the half-bottle of wine I've consumed, I'm warmed up so well that I'm eager to jump his bones. He walks in, and it's like watching a supermodel walk through the door—everything happens in slow motion.

My heart races as he sashays across the room, his denim jeans perfectly contouring to the curves of his body. The t-shirt hugs the bulging muscles in his arms and shoulders, and a ball cap shades half his face. His sunglasses reflect the light streaming through the windows.

Then he tosses his sunglasses on the sofa and gently presses his hands around my neck, making me meet his tall frame. Without a single word, he kisses me, melding our lips together. I moan as our tongues dance, our heat seeping into each other. His kisses are deep, starved, and vicious. He lifts me up with one hand, wrapping my legs around his torso. My skirt rides up as he walks us to his bedroom, his mouth not leaving mine as he ravishes me.

Tossing me on the bed, he peels off his clothes, leaving a puddle of clothing, standing naked before me. Words will not come. Stars and lust fill my eyes. He still doesn't say a word. However, his gunmetal eyes never withdraw from mine. With his thick finger, he hooks my thong, and slides it off. A satisfied smirk curves his hot lips, seeing me dripping wet for him.

Then he licks his finger and finally says, "Fuck, you're wet, and you taste so good." His voice is husky and raw. He strokes himself mindlessly, not realizing what it does to me. "I'm going to fuck you so hard."

Excitement runs through my veins. He shoves his cock inside me with no warning. With his dick inside while he's propped on his knees, peering into my soul.

"I'm going to fuck you raw for pissing me off, making me go crazy thinking another man was touching you." He plunges in deep and hard while holding onto the bed frame.

I scream with his deep thrust. It hurts so good.

"I'm going to fuck you until you can barely see straight, Sophie, because I have no damn business missing the shit out of you. I have no business missing a woman."

The man dominates my body with ease. Liquid heat courses through my veins. He keeps his word. He fucks me throughout the night until I pass out.

Early the following day, Liam covertly presents me with a charm bracelet. It's made of shining silver and encrusted with minuscule charms—a camera, a poppy, and tiny dumbbells, symbolizing the activities we've shared. He's bashful as he hands it to me, evidently embarrassed that he'd purchased such an item for me, embarrassed by his genuine thoughtfulness.

When he hands it to me, he says, "I bought you this. A lady with a stand on the side of the street was selling it."

In the box is a price tag that tells the truth. The bracelet costs more than what a lady on the street would sell it for, and it's custom-made. A feeling of excitement tingles through my veins as if a hundred tiny lightning bolts are traveling toward my heart. I close my eyes and inhale deeply, savoring the sweet scent of hope that lingers in the air.

All day long, I smile at the bracelet dangling from my wrist. All day at work, I'm eager to get home to Liam. Just thinking of him sends my stomach into a swirl of emotions, like butterflies dancing around inside me. Frequently, I have seen him with a joyous expression on his face, laughing with a beautiful, genuine smile.

CHAPTER 23
SOPHIE

Weeks, days, and months have passed. Last week was Mila's wedding. It was such a magical night for all of us to see them come together. Liam and I danced to a couple of songs. He's not big on dancing, but we still had a great time. Rosaline, or Rosa, as she told me to call her, came home for Mila and Dominic's wedding.

"So, are you sure you and my cousin aren't seeing each other?" Rosa asks, fluttering her eyelashes as she lays her fluffy beach towel on the wet sand.

"Not exactly. We're just hooking up."

Rosa eyes me with her big brown eyes, raising her perfectly shaped brow.

"How long have the hook-ups been going on? You've been staying at his place, no?" She squeezes a good amount of sunscreen into her palm. "Auntie said he smiles and laughs more than he has in years. I'd say it's more than just a hook-up."

A rush of complex emotions washes right over me like a rainstorm. *Love. Fear. Hope.* If it all goes to shit, I can live knowing I did what I promised myself I would do for him —*bring him back to life.*

"He's not looking for more—"

"Oh, I've been there and done that, and at the end, we're the ones walking out of it with a broken heart," she softly says, gazing at the ocean.

My heart falters because she's so damn right. Who hurt her?

She clears her throat. "We're going to the club on Saturday —Ivan and me—if you want to come with us. Before we go back to Oregon."

"Sure, that would be fun. It's been a while since I've been to a club. Since I moved here, I haven't done much clubbing. In Manhattan, I went to jazz clubs, raves, you name it."

She clasps her hands. "Great."

Liam and Ivan arrive with a cooler full of drinks. Liam studies me, a hint of hunger in his eyes. When I went shopping for a swimsuit, I tried to find something that would catch his attention. I've never gone swimsuit shopping intending to attract a man's attention, and I've never felt as comfortable wearing a bikini as I do now in the one I just bought, with little triangles covering my nipples and the bottom just covering the front.

He kneels on the wet sand and grabs the sunscreen, moving my hair to the side so he can apply it to my back. A shiver runs down my spine at his touch. His big, muscular hands rub up and down my body, down to my ass.

"Your ass better stay rooted to this chair. No man better stare at your beautiful body. You're goddamn practically naked out here," he sneers.

I burst into a fit of laughter. "You know, there are plenty of women out here who are practically naked. I'm sure you're staring at them." My tongue coats with jealousy.

He continues applying sunscreen, moving to my arms and chest. "Nah, there's only one woman I want to stare at. And she has a small triangle cloth covering her pointed nipples and one barely covering her pussy. My eyes are very much hypnotized. I'm so close to finding a place to fuck her."

Butterflies flutter in my belly. I love how he talks to me and makes me feel like no man has. My eyes wander to Rosa and Ivan. He's holding her in his arms as the waves hit. They look so cute.

I turn back to Liam, who's staring at me. "Do it. Find a place to fuck me." It's a challenge.

He growls and sweeps his thumb across my nipple. A shiver shoots up my spine.

"Don't underestimate me, grenade. I've fucked you in the car, in the alley, by the lake, and locked you up in the restroom. I'd fuck you here in this chair. The only problem is no one gets to see you like that. Your moans. Your screams. Your breathing is only for me to hear." Liam's warm arms gently wrap around my neck, bringing me close to his lips.

Call me crazy, but having his hands wrapped around my neck is so hot. His soft lips brush mine.

"I'll fuck you, baby, as soon as we can disappear from these assholes. I forgot I had invited them."

I turn to see who he's talking about and see four shirtless guys. Santiago, Mark, and two other hot tattooed dudes walk toward us carrying red plastic solo cups. Santiago has a cigarette dangling from his lips. Liam cups my chin, bringing my gaze back to him.

Flames of jealousy burn in his eyes. I can't help but feel a sense of pride. I make him feel this way. I let my arms roam his masculine body, which is thick and hard. I jump when his finger hooks inside of me, stroking me. His hand is still cupping my chin, and his lips are swallowing mine. The kiss is gentle but possessive; it goes beyond jealousy. Moaning into his lips, I pull away, wanting to see if the guys are getting close, but Liam's still holding my face prisoner. My cheeks flush with embarrassment. His fingers slip out, leaving me aroused. I watch as his finger inserts itself into his mouth, sucking it dry. Damn, he's hot.

Then he leans in his hot breath, scattering around my ear; he pulls a loose strand of hair behind my ear and whispers, "Only I have the ability to make you feel good. Is that right, baby?"

"Yes," I say breathlessly.

He smiles boyishly, proud of himself. "That's my girl," he says just as he stands to greet the guys with a bro handshake.

My girl God, I wish he wouldn't say things he doesn't mean. He's oblivious to how he makes me feel and what it's doing to me. Rosa's words from earlier ring in my ears—*we're the ones who walk out of it with a broken heart.*

Smiling warmly at the Delgado brothers, I greet Mark and Santiago. Santiago introduces me to his friends, Damien, and Reese, who seem very flirty. They shake my hand, showing off their sleeve tattoos covering both arms. Their voices are gruff and husky, matching their devilish personalities. Santiago's eyes drift to the couple swimming. His jaw hardens, and his eyes go wild. He tips his head up.

"You didn't tell me they'd be here. I thought they were going back to Oregon."

Liam laughs. "I imagine if you had a sister, you'd be all on her shit about who she dates. Ivan seems to be a good guy." Liam shrugs as he reaches for two drinks in the cooler, handing me a soda. "She's always been glued to you, pestering you like a little sister."

Santiago rolls his eyes just as Rosa and Ivan approach us.

"Hey." Rosa smiles at Mark. "How's April doing?"

April is Mark's girlfriend, whom I've never met and just heard of her. Rosa dismisses Santiago entirely. I don't think anyone notices the tension between them. Strange. She and Mark chat, then she walks off to lie on her beach towel.

I catch Santiago watching Rosa. Out of all the brothers, Santiago seems to be the bad boy with tattoos decorating his skin. He's the protector type, watching out for his brothers and Rosa.

Liam snakes himself around me, grabbing a handful of my ass. "We'll be back," he shouts to the guys, guiding me to a deserted area where it's just us—keeping his promise.

THE MUSIC REVERBERATES off the walls of the intensely populated club. A heady mix of sex, alcohol, and sweat fills the air. Liam wraps his arms around me possessively as we walk to the bar. Rosa and Ivan dance among the bodies, swaying to the music. Liam is not a big fan of clubs, mainly because of his job. However, once he saw me come out of the room dressed in a short, blue silk, spaghetti-strap dress, my breasts filling the cups perfectly, with matching blue high heels, he changed his mind. I'm entirely out of my comfort zone wearing something so revealing, but the way he looked at me made me feel bold, so I promised him a gift later in the night.

The way his hand grips my waist, pulling my ass to his front and feeling him swell up for me, is so worth it. He does it without a care in the world, just like the day at the beach in front of everyone. He sneaked in kisses, then, when he leaned me up against a massive rock, taking me with significant force. On our way back, he held my hand, which caught me by surprise, but I ate that shit up. He's been more open with our relationship, if we should even call it that.

"Corona with lime!" Liam shouts to the spunky brunette bartender before burying himself in the crook of my neck and peppering kisses there.

"I'll have a martini," I say.

The bartender nods, and minutes later, she hands us our drinks.

We weave through the crowd, sidestepping gyrating hips and buzzing conversations until we reach an empty corner of the club. We cozy up in a corner, almost completely out of sight of the dancers and away from the music blaring through the speakers.

I call out over 'Lady Gaga's' Just Dance song, "Are you liking it?"

He wraps his arms around me and lifts me onto his lap. He nibbles on my ear as his hot breath seeps into me. His new cologne smells like cedarwood and spice.

"Beautiful, with you here, everything is better. You look hot as fuck." His warm, rough hands roam my bare legs. "All I want to do is take you home already. Have you all to myself. There are too many wandering eyes on you." He stares into the depths of my soul.

You're fucked, Sophie. You have been for a while now.

"Stop looking at me like that," he says.

"Like what?" I reply innocently. My hand aimlessly rubs his chest.

"Like you want me to—"

He's cut off when Rosa stalks toward us, holding Ivan's hand. She's wearing a black halter dress, tight around her curvy body.

She takes a swig of her cranberry vodka, groaning as she sits on the table.

"Take it easy, Rosaline," Liam scolds her like an angry brother.

She rolls her eyes at him. "Dancing makes me thirsty," she shouts over the music. "You guys need to get out there and dance. Take my moody cousin out on the dance floor." She winks, hops off the table, and walks away. But then she turns on her heel and looks at Liam. "That smile you've been wearing looks good on you." Then she's back on the dance floor.

Liam stays silent for a minute too long, staring at the dance floor. When his eyes land on mine, he gives me a boyish, shy smile, melting me in every way possible.

"Do you want to dance?" I ask.

His eyebrows jog up. "Honestly, I've never danced the way they are dancing out there." He points to the dance floor, where everyone is grinding on each other. "Sure, we danced at the wedding, but nothing like this, and you know I'm not big on dancing."

Jumping off his lap, I extend my hand. He takes it, sliding off the booth.

"All you need to do," I say, "is wrap your arms around my waist and sway to the music with me. I'll guide you." My voice comes out raspy.

He bites his bottom lip, eyes roaming my body hungrily. "Your ass grinding my dick...I can't say no to that, baby."

Music fills the air, and I move my hips in a slow, sensuous rhythm. My hips sway, and Liam's arms tighten around my waist, pulling me closer to his rock-hard body. Gently, he works his hands down over my hips as I lean my head back onto his chest, the alcohol fueling every shiver of pleasure that courses through me. His fingers dig into my flesh, demanding more, and I gladly oblige, arching my body into his as we move together.

I've never felt so free and alive as I do at this moment, or maybe it's been since Liam. Liam makes me feel sexy, confident, and wanted—something I've never experienced before. I feel like a new person. Liam's hands keep wandering around my body, and I grind deeper into him, relishing the electricity buzzing with each beat. His lips brush the slope of my neck. My body heats up with need. God, I'm not wearing underwear; I can feel myself getting wet.

One song finishes, and the next song plays. Fuck, I need a drink to cool down. He must feel the same—beads of sweat trickle down his face. He smirks when we step off the dance floor, leading me to the bar.

"That was fucking hot. Damn." He shakes his head. "I'll dance with you anytime if we can do it like that. My dick agrees."

I giggle like a schoolgirl with a crush. His face is flushed, and his lips turn into a smirk.

Liam grabs our drinks while I wait aside at the bar. My eyes roam around the bustling club until my eyes drop on two women pointing toward where Liam is. The woman pointing has hearts in her eyes, cinnamon hair, and an hourglass figure. She storms toward him with her short black dress showing her shaped ass. Liam walks toward me with our drinks just as she catches up.

"Hey, Liam, is that you?" she calls out, her voice dripping like honey.

Liam turns to meet her sparkling eyes, and he smiles. He knows her, that much is clear. I wonder if he's slept with her.

"Hey, Crystal."

Crystal. Crystal, his first. She must be the one who broke his heart, and now he wants nothing to do with relationships. She snakes around, wrapping him in a hug.

"Oh, my, gosh, it's been so long, Liam. You look good,

babe." Her hand brushes his chest up and down.

Liam makes no effort to remove them. A surge of jealousy twists in my stomach. I move a little closer. She has no knowledge of me or ignores my presence.

"You look good too, Crystal. Are you here visiting?" His arms are still wrapped around her in a hug.

"Yeah, I'll be here for a month." She finally notices me and gives me a tight, fake smile. "Girlfriend?" She tosses her head up, pointing at me.

Realization hits Liam, and he releases her. Hope spreads through me like a wildflower. *Say it, please.*

Clearing his throat, he shakes his head. "This is my friend, Sophie."

I've never felt so humiliated. Close to five months of being with each other day and night, and all I am is a friend. A fuck buddy. My heart deflates, and Crystal's shoulders relax.

Completely ignoring me, she turns to Liam with a beaming smile. He smiles at her the same way. What is he thinking? Maybe he's thinking of their first time and reminiscing about all the times he fucked her and went down on her.

"We should catch up sometime, Liam. We can talk about all the good times we had." She winks, and he laughs.

I can't take this any longer. Maybe it's her he wants. After all, I'm just a friend. They have a history together, and he and I have only known each other for five months. I excuse myself, walking outside for some fresh air, leaving Liam there with Crystal, whom he seems eager to see.

Standing up against the club's brick wall, I pull out my phone from my handbag and dial for an Uber to pick me up. A light breeze feathers past me. My eyes sting with suppressed tears. How can I be such an idiot for putting myself out there to be treated like rubbish once again? *A friend.* I thought I meant more to him than friendship. Apparently not.

CHAPTER 24

Sophie

THE NIGHT HAD BEEN GOING SO WELL before Crystal showed up that I could still fill his erection pressed against my ass. A part of me wants to go back in there and pull him away from her. But then why, if I'm only a friend? Not even a date. A friend you fuck and grind your dick on.

"Sophie," a familiar voice calls out from the parking lot.

Chad appears in front of me. It's been months since I've seen him. It feels like ages ago that Liam pinned me in the restroom.

"Damn, you look beautiful. What are you doing here all alone?" He shoves his hands in his pockets, unsure how to greet me. Chad's good looks would be incredibly hard for any woman to resist. He has that boyish handsome smile, although it does nothing for me—no sparks or chemistry.

"Thank you, Chad. It's nice seeing you again. I'm just

waiting for my ride." My voice comes out raspy as I swallow the knots in my throat.

"I'll wait with you—I can't leave a beautiful woman all alone. Or I can give you a ride—or we can go back in and have a drink." He smiles, a glint in his eyes. Chad is different—not a heartbreaker type of man. He's one of those men you would cozy up with by the fire and watch a cheesy rom-com with.

A robust and husky voice roars toward us. "She's with me."

I roll my eyes.

Liam reaches for me, wanting to wrap his arms around me possessively, but I swat him away. Liam raises his eyebrows and grinds his teeth.

Fuck him.

I glare at Liam with such intensity that if my eyes had lasers, he'd be dead.

I surprise myself when a laugh escapes my lips. "Oh, no, I'm not. My friend here was just heading back inside. We're just pals, nothing more." I chuckle some more. God, maybe it's the alcohol, or maybe this man just makes me crazy.

Liam's chest rises and falls.

I can see him from the corner of my eye. However, my smile is pinned on Chad. Rubbing my hands up and down his chest, I say, "I'd love to get a drink sometime, Chad. I'll call you." I don't plan on it, and it's wrong to lead him on, but part of me wants to see how the asshole reacts.

Poor Chad seems confused and uncomfortable from Liam's grimacing stare. Chad nods with a smile. Maybe he gets it, what I'm doing. "Talk to you soon." He walks into the club with a wink.

Liam

. . .

Wʜᴀᴛ ᴛʜᴇ ᴀᴄᴛᴜᴀʟ fuck is going on? Sophie stands with her arms wrapped around her chest, leaning against the wall. Fucking pretty boy Chad scans her body as if it belongs to him. He winks and walks into the club after she offers to have a drink with him. Her phone pings. She then looks at the message, removing herself from the wall. She walks toward a black Nissan car.

Without sparing me a glance, she shouts, "My ride is here!"

Hauling my ass toward her, I lift her and throw her over my shoulder, then spank her ass.

"Put me down, Liam, you fucking asshole. We are fucking done."

Absolutely fucking not.

"What are you doing, Sophie?" I shout, frustrated and angry at her. Things were going so well. We were all over each other. How did the night go to shit?

As we leave the club, the bass and laughter fade away until all I can hear is our footsteps on the pavement as I head to my car. Leaning Sophie against the Camaro, I pin her in place. My gaze shifts down toward her lips, which are pressed firmly together, and her look is one of sheer deadly anger.

"What the fuck is your problem, Sophie?" I bite out.

She stabs her sharp nails in my chest. "What's my problem? Seriously, you have to ask?"

I raise an eyebrow, lost in why she's being feisty and pissed at me.

"Why don't you just go back in there with your ex, Liam? You obviously enjoy having your arms wrapped around her waist, her hands raking over your chest. My mistake, we are only friends, Liam, so I'm sure it's okay for me to have others roam their hands up and down my body, and I'll do the same to them."

Realization hits me with a punch to the face. *Fuck*. I'm not good at this shit. I've never had a woman at my side. Sophie lowers her eyelids to hide the hurt I have inflicted. I press my hands firmly against the roof of the car, trapping her inside. Tilting toward her, I lean in to kiss her lips. But instead of connecting with them, she turns away from me. Skimming my lips along her soft, creamy skin, the scent of coconut invades me; she smells delicious.

I whisper in her ear, "I'm sorry, Sophie, Crystal is just an old high school friend. I'm not interested in her. I don't even want a friendship with her. She's in the past. She asked if we could be more before she moved, and I said no, I wasn't into her like that." I nibble on her earlobe and continue. "You left, baby. You didn't hear when I told her we were hooking up and you're my date tonight. I also told her I didn't want to meet up with her. I had another woman I wanted to spend my whole time with."

She stiffens, and I pull away to meet her eyes. They swallow me like a current. Fuck, she's beautiful.

"You had your arms wrapped around her for a hot second too long, and you let her touch you. And you said she looked good," she says dryly. She turns from me, her head held high.

I chuckle. "Baby, if you only knew what I was thinking. My mind was in a haze. I can still feel your ass grinding on my dick. I was smiling like an idiot because it was the hottest thing ever. Erotic is what it was. I mentioned to you I'd never danced with a woman so close. I didn't even realize my hands were on her or that her hands were on me. I was thinking. I just wanted to get home and do some more grinding." I can't help but grin, and she responds with a roll of her eyes.

She's still mad. I understand where she's coming from—it looked fucked up.

"And she didn't look good, baby. I was trying to be polite. No one matches you, Sophie. No one." I mean it.

I cup her cheeks, and her lips make a fish pout. I peck a kiss. "My first time, I wasn't looking for a memorable moment. I was a teen wanting to get my dick wet, and Crystal was the type to spread her legs for anyone. I went down on her once because I was curious, and let's say...it wasn't enjoyable. I never did again until you," I say honestly. Stepping back, I sweep my gaze down her body.

Sophie literally takes my breath away. She is sexy, gorgeous, intelligent, and has a big heart. Her creamy, soft skin melts underneath me every damn time. Her lips twitch into a smile of satisfaction. I take advantage and nuzzle her neck.

I whisper to her, "Mi bebé is jealous." I throw my head back in laughter when she pinches my side.

"Me...jealous? Whatever. And you were like, *she's with me,*" she mimics my voice.

We both fall into rolling laughter, realizing we both are jealous idiots. Smacking her ass, I gently put her in the back seat of my car in the empty parking lot, showing her how much I enjoy my tongue between her lips, swallowing every drop.

"Are you ready?" I shout to Sophie, who's been in the room getting ready for the fallen officer's charity gala tonight.

The last two years have been a success. My mother went through a lot financially and emotionally when my father passed. When you lose someone, the last thing you want on your mind is to worry about money. The charity event will help families with funeral services, rent for the first three months, counseling, and support for kids who lost a parent.

"Just a second, I'm coming!" she yells.

I shove my hands in my slacks, blowing out the candle in the living room.

Sophie fills the house with the lingering smell of her candles and coconut scent. The whole house has her touch; she's even changed my curtains because she said the room needed a splash of color. We go to my mom's for dinner—she insists on having Sophie over. My mom lights up and smiles wider when Sophie is around. I haven't seen her this happy in years. Sophie's presence is like a salve for the bones. She soothes the soul. She just seems to penetrate deep into her heart. My mom even has Sophie sit in the empty seat at the table that has been vacant for decades. Unvaryingly, my grandma appears as if she just dropped in, not knowing Sophie would be there. My grandmother stares at us like she's in a telenovela—crazy old lady.

Abuelita whispers her riddles to me. "She has the key around her neck; only you have the power to use it."

Whatever that means.

The clicking of heels grabs my attention as I turn to see the woman who's crashed into my life. My jaw drops to the ground, and my eyes fill with stars. My heart beats like a drum.

Fuck me.

She spins around, her cobalt blue silk dress flowing around her like a dream. The halter top shows off the smooth curve of her neck and shoulders, and the glittering high heels I bought her perfectly complete the look. When I saw them in the store, I knew they were perfect for her. The dress is the exact shade of her eyes—a bright, vibrant blue that could light up any room.

"What do you think?" Sophie inquires.

I can feel my arousal grow, and I bite my lip in anticipation.

Finally, I exhale a breath I'd been holding. What do I think? Fuck, I've never felt the need to drop to my knees and worship a woman *like I do now*. She has no idea the power she has over me.

Clearly, neither do *I*.

Taking a leisurely walk toward her, I say, "You look gorgeous." I softly cradle her cheeks in my hands so she looks directly at me. Sophie's lips are a deep red hue and form a straight line. "Stunning. Sexy and breathtaking." I peck at her red lips and add, "The most beautiful woman I've ever had on my arm."

Sophie's soft lips press on mine as I inhale her steady breath. She's too beautiful, a hidden gem who has managed to tug at the strings of my black heart with her tender touch. She deserves so much more than I can offer. My darkness would only weigh down her light.

I search Sophie's eyes, and I can see what I hoped to avoid —she's fallen for me.

"Liam," she whispers in her velvety, soft voice.

Closing my eyes, I swallow the knot in my throat and step back. "We should go before it gets late," I mumble, adjusting my tie. The damn thing is squeezing the breath out of me, and I can't bring myself to look her in the eye.

Sophie's gentle touch swats my hand away and adjusts my tie. She smiles widely.

"You look handsome, Liam, and very edible." She winks, and my lips curl into a mischievous smile. Of course, only Sophie knows how to put me at ease.

"Ready, mi bella?" I extend my hand for her to take, which she does.

Just as we're about to walk out the door, Duke runs out of the spare bedroom. He no longer pays me any attention. It's all about Sophie. He whines, and Sophie kneels down, scratching behind his ears. Damn, even the dog's whipped. I roll my eyes when Duke gives her a look of adoration.

Thirty minutes later, we arrive at the Bahia Resort, where the event is taking place. I rented Sophie and I a hotel room at the resort so we wouldn't have to drive home so late. As soon as I step out of the car, I get this airy feeling that something doesn't feel right.

CHAPTER 25
SOPHIE

As we walk toward the resort, the gentle breeze from the bay caresses our faces. The venue is set up beautifully outside, facing the bay. The tables are decorated with bouquets of wild-flowers and draped in pristine white cloths. Flickering tiki lamps illuminate the winding path leading to the resort, casting eerie shadows that seem to dance. Liam escorts us in, his hand resting on my exposed lower back, his thumb tracing in a circular pattern.

The room fills with soft, ambient music floating through the air. Several of Liam's coworkers approach us. Liam introduces me as Sophie, his date, to the woman officer, who looks at him like he's eye candy. He introduces me as his girl. I'll take that, unlike last time when he told Crystal bubble butt I was his friend. Once we reach the bar, Liam wraps his arms around my waist possessively.

"What do you want to drink, baby?"

"I'll have a Vanhattan."

He nods and gives our order to the bartender. Then he leans into me, and his lips brush past my cheek to my neck. A shiver rockets through me when his hot breath fans my earlobe, and he whispers, "All I can think of is taking you to the hotel room and stripping you down. And for you to show me how edible I am." Liam's hand slides up my leg. My dress has a slit up the side, allowing his touch to wander freely. "No underwear?" His fingers hook my entrance, and I gasp. "My naughty girl wants my fingers in her wet pussy."

Just then, the bartender comes with our drinks.

"Liam," I say with panting breaths.

He chuckles and bites my ear. He licks his finger, then he grabs the drinks.

John and his wife approach us as we make our way to the table where we're seated. I've met John a couple of times at the gym, but I've never really spoken to him. The room is filled with officers and their plus ones.

"Hey, you're looking sharp, Liam." John smiles. "Nice to see you again, Sophie. This is my wife, Beth. Beth, this is Sophie, Liam's girl."

Beth, a tall, gorgeous brunette, leans in to give me a warm, inviting hug. "So nice to meet you, Sophie. You look stunning— those eyes. God, girl, Liam is a lucky man." Beth offers a beaming smile.

"Thank you, Beth. Likewise."

John wraps his arms around her but looks at Liam. "Ready for tonight?"

"Ready as I'll ever be."

"Good man. Great idea doing this gala—it helps so many people," John replies.

We chat for a bit longer before John and Beth make their way to the appetizer table. Liam and I sit at a corner table just as the rest of the people began to sit.

"In a bit, I have to make my speech," he says, scooting his chair closer to mine.

I love how he doesn't shy away from holding my hand or kissing me in front of his co-workers. He's even possessive if they give me a look not to his liking.

"About what?"

"I'm the founder of the Fallen Officer's Charity Gala." His boyish expression melts my heart.

"Oh, Liam, why didn't you tell me? You just mentioned what the gala was for." I reach for his hand and squeeze. "This is amazing, Liam, it's...God, it's beautiful. So many people are here tonight. You have a heart of gold. You're helping so many."

Liam shakes his head, avoiding my compliment. "Sophie, my heart is nowhere near gold. My heart is black." He smiles weakly. "I'll be right back, baby. I need to make that speech." He places a kiss on my forehead before I can correct him.

If only he could see what I see.

He gracefully navigates his way through the sea of people, who pause to converse with him and give him a pat on the back. It's clear how many admire him. Who wouldn't? He's a special kind of person.

When he reaches the microphone, he smiles at the crowd. "Good evening, everyone. Thank you all for joining us in honoring our fallen officers at our charity event this year. This cause will help those grieving loved ones without worrying about their finances and give them the peace of mind to grieve while we support and grieve with them." Liam's husky voice booms with authority, filling the room.

My heart swoons with so many emotions filling it. One in particular. Love. Yes, I'll admit it. *I'm in love with Liam Rodriguez—wholly in love with him.* I watch as his lips move and his firm jaw tightens as he speaks—those soft lips, how his brows furrow, how a strand of his silky black hair falls to the side. What I love is how his eyes stay trained on me as if we are the only ones in the room. Maybe I can love enough for both of us. I just don't know for how long if he's unwilling to let the light in. His words give me time, which flows through my mind; How long can you give a person time before you burn to ashes?

"Thank you all once again for joining us. Have a wonderful night."

The crowd cheers. Liam steps down from the podium as more people swarm around him. Soft music begins to play, and couples dance. Liam shakes the chief of police's hand and then walks toward me just as a woman approaches him. I remember her—the partner he had with him when he interrupted my date. Ashley, I think her name is. She smiles brightly at him, fluttering her eyelashes. He shakes his head and points to me. She frowns and walks away.

"No one puts baby in the corner." He extends his hand, quoting my favorite line from *Dirty Dancing*. I can't help but hold my stomach in laughter. I take his hand once I can control my laughter. His lips turn into a smirk.

"Are you going to get all Patrick Swayze on me, throwing me up in the air?" I say, letting my admiration show in my voice.

He laughs as we walk to the dance floor. "I would if I knew his moves. Otherwise, I'd break your neck."

I smile as he wraps his arms around my waist, and I pull my arms around his neck, bringing him in for a kiss. "You did really good out there, Liam. I'm proud of you."

"Thanks."

I'm surprised he's open to my compliments since he usually changes the conversation whenever I offer one.

"You know, I don't agree with the name *Dirty Dancing* for Patrick Swayze's movie."

My forehead creases.

"Listen," he says, licking his lips as we sway to the music. "I don't consider it dirty dancing in the movie...now what we did in the club, that's what I call dirty dancing."

I snort, unladylike. "You're unbelievable."

"It's true, your ass rubbing on my dick, me close to blowing a load. That's dirty."

I laugh, swatting his shoulder. "You're an idiot."

He grins. "I'm *your* idiot."

"That you are," I say, looking into his eyes.

He tenderly kisses me, our tongues tangling with each other. "Let's get out of here, Sophie. I need to get you out of this dress. Our hotel room is close by," he murmurs into my mouth.

I nod, out of breath. "Let me just run to the restroom."

"All right, I'm going to let the guys know I'm leaving. I'll wait for you right here."

I nod. "Okay."

———

ONCE I FLUSH the toilet and wash my hands, I reapply my ruby-red lipstick. The loud, reverberating boom of gunfire startles me, and my heart races as my breath quickens. I need to get to Liam. I open the door carefully, sticking my head out to peer into the chaos. Gunshots pop off, and people run and scream in all directions. Leaning up against the cold tile wall, I drag myself until I find a safe spot to hide. Then I see five masked men, all in black, shooting in every direction. People are running out. Police officers point their weapons and take cover from the gunmen, and people hide under tables. I move cautiously toward a utility cart and crouch in its shadows. My heart pounds in my ears, and gunshots reverberate all around me.

"Sophie, Sophie," I hear a husky voice yell.

"Liam," I answer in a shaky voice.

Liam runs to me. His face is ghost white. He grabs my face, inspects me, and scans my whole body. "Are you okay, baby? Are you hurt?"

"I'm fine. Are you? Are you hurt?" I ask.

"I'm fine. Let's get you out of here." He swallows, his gaze stuck on me, reflecting pain and fear. "Listen. If something happens to me, don't stop. You keep running to safety, find a place to hide. You understand, mi bella?"

"Liam," I whisper.

He shakes his head and kisses my lips. "Do you understand?"

"Yes." But my voice is hoarse.

"Stay behind me."

Without hesitation, he takes the gun out of its holster and is ready to fire. The sound of the sirens becomes increasingly louder as they approach. Three masked men lay in a pool of blood. I spot three officers down. Liam holds my hand, looking in every direction. He scans the area, nods, and keeps moving. My hands shake in Liam's as we get closer to the exit. A swarm of officers rushes in to cover us until we make it outside.

Most of the people have made it outside safely. We spot John holding a crying Beth in his arms. Liam murmurs something quietly to one of the policemen. The other officer nods in agreement. We make our way to the back side of the resort, where cops are standing around trying to locate any of the suspects. Thankfully, no more shots ring out in the night sky.

"Clear," an officer shouts to Liam.

Liam nods as we climb the stairs to our hotel room. Fishing out the hotel key, he mumbles, "I'm sorry, Sophie."

"Baby, you have nothing to be sorry about. You did nothing wrong."

He stays silent for a couple of minutes, shoving his hands in his hair. Finally, he sits on the loveseat.

"C'mon here." He pats his lap for me to sit.

Carefully and deliberately, I approach him and settle down on his lap. I stare into the depth of his gunmetal eyes. He looks so lost. "Liam, are you—"

He cups my cheek and kisses me. First, my lips, to quiet me. Then my forehead and cheeks. Gently.

"You're okay, you're okay." His voice is barely above a whisper, as if he's speaking more to himself. He swallows and then says, "When I heard the gunshots, all I could think about was getting to you. I was so fucking scared I'd find you in a pool of bl-blood." He chokes on the last words. I've never seen Liam so fragile and vulnerable as he is now.

The recollection hits me—Liam's father was killed in front of him.

Tonight has opened all those wounds.

Wrapping my arms around his neck, I kiss all over his handsome face, leaving no place untouched. "I'm fine, Liam. A little shaken up, but we are both unhurt. You found me and brought me to safety. You saved us. You know you're a badass."

His lips turn up a little.

Slipping off his lap, I find a water bottle on the kitchen counter. My mouth is dry, and my nerves are shot. Hopefully, this will help some.

Liam glances out the window, red and blue lights flashing through the night. He closes the blinds and curtains. He sighs and walks toward me. He then kneels on one leg. "Leg up, baby, let me take your heels off. All that running...you're probably hurting."

Silently, I lift my leg while he unclasps the buckle. He then proceeds with the other leg. I curl my toes, and my feet immediately relax.

He wordlessly stands and goes behind me, gently untying the knot of my halter dress. It falls to the ground, leaving me standing in nothing but my skin. The dress didn't really work with a bra or underwear. His soft lips meet my jaw peppering all the way down to my neck, his thumb rubbing against my aroused nipples.

Liam gently turns me around, walking us to the king-sized bed. The pain and fear in his eyes are replaced with lust. If giving him my body will distract him from the pain he's reflecting on the inside, I'll gladly do it because this man has stolen my heart and my soul. And I let him—all because I'm in love with him. I've known for some time that my heart will only ever be for him. I'm ready to tell him how I feel. But not tonight; it's not the right moment.

His mouth covers each one of my breasts, sucking gently, making his way down between my legs. The way Liam's tongue works me, the way his heat seeps into mine, my heart comes to life. I want to be the remedy to his soul, to the pain that cuts deep within him. Electricity rockets into me as I arch my back.

"Spread your legs wider for me, baby. This is mine, right?"

"Yes," I say with a moan.

"Damn right." His husky voice vibrates, and his tongue working in a circular motion sends me over the edge.

"Not yet, mi bella."

Gentle kisses trail down my leg to my toes. Propping my elbows up, I watch as Liam fumbles with the buttons of his dress shirt, dropping it to the ground. My eyes follow his hands as he unbuckles his belt, then his slacks fall into the puddle with the rest of our clothes.

No underwear—lord, help me.

My pupils adjust to the darkness of the room, and I'm able to make out his broad shoulders and defined biceps. His arousal is evident in the thick veins running along his hard length. Even in the darkness, the size of his erection is unmistakable, and my throat goes dry as every inch of me tingles with anticipation. My heart races against my ribcage as he moves closer.

"Liam." My voice comes out raw and strangled. Moistening my lips, I ready myself to take him in my mouth.

"Not tonight."

My eyebrows jog up in disappointment.

He must see it because he chuckles. "After the night you had, you deserve gentleness, tenderness."

His lips cover mine, gentle yet demanding. A kiss from Liam is as intoxicating as the finest wine. I buck when his length enters me, wanting him to go deep and hard, but he doesn't. He moves in a circular motion, making me feel everything—the gentleness and the tenderness. I cry into his mouth. This is not fucking. He's making love to me. I place both of my hands on his cheeks, bringing him in so we're staring into one another's eyes as he makes love to me. I want him to see when he looks in my eyes that I'm in love with him. I want him to see that I want this. *Us.* I want more. But more than anything, I want to see what lies beneath those beautiful, rare eyes—does it match what I feel? All I see is fear and pain all over again.

My body shakes as waves of ecstasy roll in like a stormy night. He watches me as I scream his name. Liam grunts his release right after. I'm not sure if this is a new beginning or an end for us. In those eyes, on top of the pain and fear, a small part of me sees regret.

If it's our end, he must know it will crush me. Would he be so cruel, to end it this way? His name on my lips. His body covering mine.

CHAPTER 26

LIAM

I sprawl my legs on the couch, watching Sophie sleep, the sunrise shining through a slit in the curtains. Once Sophie fell asleep, I made my way downstairs, toward the gala venue. The investigation team is out, including the FBI and the chief of police. The whole area is wrapped in yellow tape, closing it off. When we unveiled the masks of the three men who lay dead on the cement floor, it became clear Pablo had sent his men to an event full of law enforcement. He sent a message, too—he wants us to release his son from custody. The motherfucker can rot in jail—soon, his father will join him.

When the seven hooded men poured through the entrance-way, gunshots echoing in the air, my only thought was to find Sophie. Losing her would be like losing the ability to breathe or live. I'd rather her be happy with someone else, and I'd rather watch from a distance than never see the light of her smile again.

I return to the room and lay beside her until sunlight pours through the window. Sophie's still sleeping. But not peacefully. Her body jolts and twitches. The pang in my chest deepens. I did not want her to experience such maliciousness last night—she's too pure. Being in law enforcement, I've been through shit like this more times than I can count, but not Sophie. I took her out only to traumatize her with blazing guns and falling bodies.

Lying beside her, I lift her in my arms and place her head on my chest.

"Liam," she moans in her sleep.

"It's okay, baby, I'm right here." I kiss her forehead, soothing her. It pained me to see her shivering in fear. It brought me back to the night I lost my father, reminding me why I've kept my corner tight and never allowed myself to be in a relationship.

Sophie's warm hand glides up and down my bare chest. With her groggy blue eyes slowly opening, she peers at me. "Morning." Her voice is sweet as honey.

"Morning. How did you sleep? How bad were the nightmares, Sophie?"

She lifts herself up, leaning on the headboard, shoulders touching. "I slept well. I'm shaken up. Don't worry. It will pass. I'll be okay, Liam." She gives me a weak smile and adds, "I didn't have any nightmares."

Liar, I want to call out. I've lived my whole life having nightmares—until Sophie began sleeping in my bed every night, and I stopped having them. She's like a lullaby.

"Did you sleep?" she asks.

"A little," I lie. I've been watching her all night.

The bed sheet slides down, revealing her cream breasts and pink nipples. My tongue darts out, and my dick immediately stands at attention. My nostrils flare, exhaling loudly like a bull ready to attack. I close my eyes, trying to tame the beast.

Now is not the time, Liam.

"Sophie, baby, get dressed. We have to check out, and I

need to go to the station. I have a meeting," I drawl, my voice raspy and raw.

"Oh, okay." The sheet slides further down. "Let me take a shower first."

I nod, unable to speak. She crawls off the bed completely naked and traipses her hot ass to the bathroom. The confidence she possesses would give any man a hard-on. It takes everything in me not to follow her.

THE CAR RUMBLES along the highway in oppressive silence. I can tell Sophie is still trying to wrap her mind around what she has seen. It was a difficult and traumatic experience that will stay with her for an eternity. A dull pain fills me. Her innocence was shattered by the cruelty of last night's event. A burning anger rises inside me at the thought that she endured such fear and terror. Sophie is strong, but no one can play it as if they're okay. Not even her. A fierce determination takes over as I vow to keep her safe no matter what, shielding her from all harm with my life, if need to be. As we approach her townhouse, she furrows her eyebrows in confusion.

"It's safer if you stay here while I'm at the station. I'm not sure if they're targeting a certain person." I clear the rock in my throat. "I'll have Mark drop off your car in case you need it."

She closes her eyes, taking a steady breath. "Okay, I understand." She reaches for the door handle.

"Do I get a kiss?" I ask like a needy little bitch.

She gives me a bright smile that could light up a dark night. "Of course." She leans in and pecks my lips.

Really, that's it?

Grabbing her by the face, I sink my lips into hers. My

mouth works with urgency, desperate for every second, and I bite down lightly on her bottom lip before pulling away.

Before shutting the door, she asks, "See you in a bit?" She raises a brow.

I nod. "See you soon."

I SLAM the front door and march into the living room, my keys rattling in my clenched fist. I throw them onto the kitchen table and slouch onto the sofa, pressing my hands against my forehead as I let out a long sigh of frustration. For the past twenty-four hours, my head has been spinning. I spent all morning at the station listening to detectives interrogate the man who survived a gunshot to the leg. He gave us Pablo's whereabouts in exchange for protection for himself and his family.

I spent the last hours with the task force and the DEA, outlining our plan to move in on him. We need to play it off, as if we don't know shit, before we move in on him. I'm certain he's expecting us to pounce on him. He knows that someone in his gang has ratted him out. Pablo wouldn't have sent his top people to a law enforcement benefit event without being aware they'd be significantly out-manned.

I know Pablos's location. I should be jumping for joy. Make no mistake, I want to redeem my father's death. For the first three years of my life without my father, my mother attempted to do whatever she could to mend me. She sent me to therapist after therapist, hoping one of them could help me talk about the night he passed away. But I was too shattered, and not even their efforts could put the pieces back together. I was broken beyond repair. Reminding me of my demons.

My phone buzzes in my pocket, bringing me back to reality as I stare at the black screen of the TV.

Sophie: *Hey, are you still at the station?*
Me: *Can you meet me at Luigi's Pizza on Mission?*
She immediately answers.
Sophie: *Yeah, what time?*
Liam: *In ten minutes, wait for me in the parking lot.*
Sophie: *Okay, see you in ten.*
Shoving my phone into my pocket, I grab my keys off the table. My Camaro roars to life as I drive to Luigi's with the windows down, inhaling the salty ocean scent and blasting my system. A light breeze feathers the night sky, relaxing my tense shoulders.

I park, waiting for Sophie. Two minutes later, I see her ruby-red Mustang pull in. It's the same color as her lips. I wave for her to jump in the passenger seat. My heart rattles in my chest, and my jaw clenches.

"Hey, you. How did things go?" Sophie asks, leaning in to kiss my cheek.

"Good. One of the men gave us Pablo's location."

She clasps her hands with excitement. "I can't wait till you guys get that motherfucker."

My lips turn into a small smile.

She sighs. "Okay, tell me what's wrong. You're not acting like yourself."

I blow out a harsh breath, staring out the window at Luigi's. I haven't been here in years.

"Sophie, there's something I need to tell you."

Her shoulders stiffen, and her beautiful blue eyes become glassy. She must sense where this is going. When she gazes into my eyes, it's as though she can see right into the depths of my soul. "What is it?" she whispers.

"The only people who know the entire story of what happened that night are Dominic and his brothers. My mom...I could never tell her. She knew some of it from the detectives who were there after it happened. Talking about it makes me relive the night that...part of me died."

"Liam, you don't need—"

"I do. I want to tell you."

She nods.

"This is where my dad died, inside Luigi's, having pizza." I close my eyes, exhale a long breath, and tell her everything.

———

I FIX *my gaze on the television and marvel at how Raphael and Michelangelo take the villains. I stand and try some moves the Ninja Turtles perform. I hear my papá chuckle as he watches me. I wonder if my papá fights the bad guys the way Ninja Turtles do.*

My papá reaches out and messes up my hair affectionately. At the same time, my mamá enters the room carrying my coat. I offer her a smile as she waddles toward me.

"Here, Liam, let's get your coat on so you can go have dinner with your papá." Her beautiful brown eyes always sparkle. I kiss her round tummy. In four months, I will be a big brother. Mamá is having twins.

"Okay, Mamá. You're not coming?" I ask.

"No, your little brothers in my tummy make me so tired. I'm going to get some rest." My papá kisses my mamá. I watch as he rubs her tummy and tells her he loves her.

"What do you feel like eating, Liam?" my papá asks as he straps his holster around his waist. He always carries his gun and badge with him.

I bring my finger to my chin, thinking. "Pizza, Papá. I want pizza."

"Pizza it is. Let's go so your mamá can rest." My papá leans in to kiss my mamá again.

Yuck.

"Get some rest, my love." Papá sweeps his thumb on her cheek.

I scrunch my nose.

PAPÁ PULLS UP to Luigi's Pizza, and we make our way inside. I get a cheese pizza for myself, and he orders a meat lover's plus some breadsticks. As soon as we sit down, I take my Ninja Turtle action figure out of my pocket. My father watches me with a kind smile.

"What do you want to be when you grow up?" he asks.

I shrug. "A ninja. I want to fight bad guys like you, Papá."

His head tips back, a roaring laugh escapes his mouth, and his chest shakes. I take a bite of my pizza and smile. Papá is a brilliant detective. I want to find bad guys like he does.

"You will be an amazing officer and detective one day, Liam. You're strong, smart, and courageous."

He takes a bite of his pizza when his head jolts up. His face goes pale. My head turns to look in the direction he's staring. Two men walk in, glaring at him.

Papá whispers, "Hide under the table, okay? I need you to be strong right now and have courage. Close your eyes. If you need to run, you run fast from the bad guys, okay?"

I stare into Papá's eyes. I've never seen him this scared. I nod. I duck under the table.

"Rodriguez," a man shouts, wearing jeans and black boots.

I watch from under the table, my father's hand on his gun.

"What can I help you with, Pablo?" My papá's voice is seething with anger.

I rub my ninja turtle, praying he will give me some magical power to turn into a ninja and help Papá.

"You took something from me, Rodriguez." The man's voice is filled with rage.

Papá told me to keep my eyes shut, but I can't bring myself to do it. I need to be ready to assist him if necessary. In a single motion, Papá rises from his chair.

"Let's talk outside," Papá suggests.

The men chuckle darkly.

"A life for a life. Blood for blood," one of the men sneers darkly.

The sharp crack of guns echoes in my ears and reverberates through the room. I curl up into a tight ball and wrap my arms around my head, my heart pounding as bullets rain down, shattering glass. People in the restaurant shriek in terror as I keep my trembling body covered, too afraid to open my eyes. The room falls quiet as the shooting stops, and I slowly peel away my arms to survey the destruction.

My heart's beating so fast, it wants to explode. I'm brave, I'm strong, I say to myself. I look for Papá. And see a pool of blood.

"Papá," I whisper. "No," I shout. I see another man in a pool of blood then. I see my papá. "No, no, no Papá," I cry. I run to him without thinking if there are more of them.

"Come on, Papá, we need to go." I shake him, and his eyes open and close.

He coughs out blood when he tries to talk. "My little Liam, I'm not going to make it. Will you take care of your mamá for me?" He wheezes and gulps. My hands shake. "You're going to become a great man, Liam. I see it in your eyes. Stay strong, my son. Run, Liam, and find somewhere to hide until the officers *arrive. I love you, Liam. Tell your mamá and little brothers I love them."*

I take a sharp breath. My body shakes. "Okay, Papá, I love you."

I hear footsteps and boots stomping behind me. I turn to see who it is. It's two bad guys. There must be more of them outside. He smiles and winks. I stare at his silver tooth and the serpent tattoo on his arm.

I turn to Papá.

"I'm sorry, mi hijo," he says. He gurgles and says, "RUN!" He takes one last breath, and he's gone. Gone. He's gone. My heart hurts.

"Papá," I whimper on his chest. His body is so warm. "Don't leave me, Papá. Who's going to play baseball with me? I need you. Mamá needs you, Papá," I shout. I wrap my arms around his neck. When I hear boots getting closer, I do what Papá said to do. I run.

CHAPTER 27
LIAM

Tears roll down Sophie's cheek as she hiccups and peers at me from behind her hands, which she holds fisted before her face as if she's praying. "I'm so sorry you witnessed such cruelty, Liam, but more than anything, baby, I'm sorry you lost the most important man in your life. If I could take the pain away, I would do it in a heartbeat." The words of a true queen with a heart of gold. I don't deserve her.

"There's more," I say, my heart beating a little faster.

"More?"

"Yes, there's more to taint my life."

She reaches for my hand and squeezes. "Tell me."

MY TENNIS SHOES *pound against the asphalt, and my chest heaves with each breath. My legs burn as I run into the night; all I can hear is the wind howling and the rumble of passing cars. I run just like Papá told me to. I halt, hiding behind a large bush to catch my breath. I cover my mouth to contain my* sharp panting. Boots pound along the pavement, and the sound makes me shake. Be brave, Liam, I tell myself as I feel a quick poke in my hips. I pull out my Ninja Turtle from my pocket and stare into Leonardo's eyes, hoping any of his powers will seep into me. I rub his shell again like it's a magic genie lamp.

Once I make it home, my mother runs out of the house. I tell her what happened at the pizza place, and that Papá is gone. I plead with her for us to leave, but we are out of time.

Her body shakes, and her voice is above a whisper when she looks into the dark street.

"Hide, Liam, hide, and do not come out, no matter what you hear."

"Hide with me, Mamá, please."

A tear runs down my cheek. I can't lose Mamá. I've already lost my papá. Be brave, be strong—this comes to mind when I think of my papá's words. Mamá reaches for my hand, dragging me inside the house and shoving me into a cabinet.

Holding my breath, I can hear the thump of their boots and then a gunshot. When I hear the front door slam open, I know they're in the house.

A voice that sounds like Pablo says, "This must be Rodriguez's bitch."

"Please leave. There's nothing for you here." My mamá's voice trembles, pleading with them.

"The boy!" one man shouts.

My mom screams.

"Where is he?"

"H-he won't say a word about this." My mom's cries get louder. "Please don't hurt my babies."

I have to keep my word. Papá wanted me to protect Mamá and my brothers. Darkness consumes me. The numbness in my body has me moving on autopilot. I step out of the pantry and *quietly go to my mamá's room, retrieving my dad's handgun. I've seen him hide in between the mattress.*

I don't hear my mother's cries, only a thump on the ground. I cock the gun, readying myself. I hear the voices of the men. I'm so far gone that I don't make out what they say.

My body runs cold when I see my mom on the ground, knocked out, a pool of blood between her legs. I don't think twice. I lift the gun and shoot one of the men in the head. His body falls to the ground just as the sound of sirens in the quiet night rings in the air.

Pablo steps back and says, "You have balls, boy." He runs off just as police cars swarm in.

"LIAM, YOU WERE SO YOUNG," she whispers.

Closing my eyes, I take the time to let it all sink in. I haven't spoken of this since I was seven, when I told Dominic.

"I'm tainted, Sophie. I don't regret killing the asshole. My mom lost the twins because of them. They kicked her so many times. I've killed men in the line of duty. It's different from killing a man in cold blood at the age of six."

She squeezes my hand twice.

"It has fucked me up for years, seeing my dad die, seeing my mom cry because she lost her husband and babies. Seeing my mother try her best to raise me. She worked her ass off to keep a roof over our heads, grieving the whole time." I grind my teeth.

"Liam, you're not fucked up."

Pushing my door open, I get out of the car, needing fresh air.

Fuck.

Sophie jumps out of the car and walks around to get to me.

I slide my fingers through my hair, blowing out a hot breath. She wraps her arms around me, but I peel them off, slamming my fist on the hood of my car. Fuck. I was certain that if I shared this with her, she'd distance herself from me, realizing just how messed up I am. She's too good for me.

Resting my hands on the hood, I stare at the dent I made to avoid peering into Sophie's eyes. Might as well tell her...why beat around the bush?

"It's over. We're done, Sophie." My jaw tightens. The words are like acid in my mouth, but we both knew it would come to an end.

"Did I hear you right? Did you just say it's over?"

"Yes, as in 'we' are done." The poison tumbles from my lips like lava, scorching everything it touches.

She lashes out, her fingers digging into my arm so hard, I have no choice but to turn and face her.

"The least you can do is to be a man and say it to my face!" she bellows.

My gaze lands on her, and I scrutinize her glassy eyes. "We are done. Remember what we agreed on?"

"So, it's over when you say?" She gets in my face, her voice cracking.

"I'm not what you fucking need, Sophie. You deserve a man who can give you everything. I'm not him. I'm too fucked in the head...when you see your dad die in a pool of blood, your mom bleeding, and men hunting you down...it messes with a kid. I'm a lost cause. My heart is not pure."

Sophie grabs my shirt by the chest, yanking me to her. "You're not a lost cause. You had a very traumatizing experience, but you have to be willing to live to move past it."

Stepping away from her, I shove my fingers through my hair, frustrated with how her coconut lotion makes me want to lose it. I need her to hate me so she can move on. The thought of her with another man has me seeing red. Sophie was never mine to keep, though. We were on borrowed time.

"It doesn't matter. Our time has come to an end."

A tear skates down her cheek, and I hate myself for making her cry.

"I thought what we had was special," she says. "We've been living together for the past few months. This was not some hook-up. It was more, and you know it." Her voice cracks, and her chin trembles.

I shove my hand in my pocket, distracting myself from the almost overpowering need to hold her. I can't let her have the life my mom and I had. If something happened to me or, worse, to her...Last night's incident proved how easily I could have lost her.

I'd rather set her free than lose her.

"It was, but it was temporary."

She shakes her head, determined, and wipes her tears off. "It wasn't...it was real. I felt it in here." She points to her heart. "I'm in love with you, Liam." Her voice is barely above a whisper.

Those words are a sledgehammer to my chest. My heart bleeds out with her confession. No woman has ever uttered those words to me.

No, no, she can't.

"You're not in love with me. You think you are, but you're not." I refuse to look at her; instead, I focus on the asphalt of the empty parking lot.

She steps closer, pressing my cheeks with her warm palms, and I can feel her breath against my skin. Her tears glisten in the streetlight, and I can hear the faint sound of her muffled sobs. The touch of her gentle palms is like fire coursing through my veins.

"I know what I feel. Don't tell me what I feel or don't feel. I know you feel something for me. Liam, I've never felt this way about anyone." Her voice is pleading. "I can love you for both of us. I love y—"

I shove her hands away and step back. A weight thuds on my chest, knocking the air out of my lungs.

I'll hate myself for this for the rest of my existence, but I need her to walk away hating me. I lock eyes with her and give her a disdainful look, shaking my head.

"It was fun while it lasted, Sophie. We were just fucking. You were nothing more than a good fuck. Time to move on." The bitterness thickens into a dry, sour sludge. My pulse leaps in my throat. The sound of my words disgusts me.

Her mouth hangs open, but she quickly regains herself. She lifts her chin, squaring her shoulders—that's it, baby. Don't let my words break you.

She bares her teeth. "Nothing more than a good fuck, huh? Now you can add me to your list of great fucks, and I'll add you to my list of assholes."

I turn to walk to my car. Watching the only woman who's ever mattered to me break, shatters my heart. I didn't even know my heart could break for a woman.

"Liam," she shouts.

I stop in my tracks, giving her my back.

"Please don't leave me." Her whisper is faint, but I hear it.

My eyes water for the first time in years. I didn't even cry at my father's funeral. I stood like a robot, trying to be brave for my mom.

"The day you wake up and see what we had was real, it will be too late. The second you drive out of this parking lot, *you lose me*. I never want to cross paths with you again. I'm sorry you went through so much at a young age. I pray that someday *you'll find peace and find love* to heal that broken heart. *I guess*

I wished it could have been *me, who you feel in love with.*" Her soft voice breaks on the last words.

Oh, baby, it will always be you. I want to turn around and wrap her in my arms, but I don't—in order to save her. I need to let her go. My heart thumps loudly in my chest. I want to turn and stare into those eyes and memorize her. I gave this woman my soul. She can keep it. I know I'll never find a woman like her. So, I do what I know will haunt me for the rest of my life. I get in my car and drive off into the dark night with my heart clawing at me. I leave her behind.

CHAPTER 28
SOPHIE

Is it possible to die from a broken heart? My heart shatters like glass as I watch Liam walk to his car without a backward glance. He slams his foot on the accelerator, and his car screeches out of the parking lot, spewing a shower of gravel. He speeds away, the red taillights fading in the darkness until they are only pinpricks in the night sky. I glance up at the twinkling stars as tears fall uncontrollably. Slowly, I walk to my car.

He left me.

Dumbfounded, I sit in my car and rest my head on the steering wheel. Last night, he made love to me. We danced before the shooting happened. I know what we had was more, or maybe it was one-sided. I poured my heart out and told him I loved him, and he left me. I figured we were moving forward once he expressed his horrific childhood. I meant what I said. I hope he finds peace. But the idea of Liam finding love with someone else cuts like a knife. His words echo in my heart.

You were nothing more than a good fuck.

The iciness in his eyes made it clear he didn't reciprocate my feelings. How could it be? I remember every sunset, the tickles of laughter, and the warmth of his embrace. We had that for five months. Every perfect moment felt like a dream until reality came crashing down. Now all I feel is excruciating pain in my chest, like thorns piercing through my heart. I grip the steering wheel until my knuckles turn white. I let out a wail. I can't remember the last time I cried like this.

I'm not sure how I make it home. I have no recollection. Stepping out of my car, I see Mila standing at my apartment door. Running to her like a child running to her mother, I wrap my arms around her and wail in her arms.

"I'm sorry, honey. You're hurting. He called and asked me to come check on you."

I choke out sobs, unable to speak. "He-he—"

"Come on, let's get you inside so you can tell me what happened. I'll make us some tea. I picked up ice cream. Unless you need a stiff drink. You can have that too."

I nod. Mila means the world to me. She has my back, just like I've always had hers.

"He called you?" I manage to ask in between each sob.

"He did. All he said was you needed me." She hands me a glass of wine and sits beside me on the sofa.

"I'm sorry I didn't tell you. I'm a horrible friend. We have been—"

"I've known for a while, Sophie. When you mentioned you were seeing someone, and he didn't want to commit. I knew it was Liam, and of course, your face has always lit up at the mention of him, just like it did the first time you met him."

I gulp the glass of wine and reach for the bottle, filling it to the rim. I've never needed to numb the pain as much as I do now. She's not wrong. Liam's presence has always made my heart beat a little faster, from the first day I saw him at the studio. I go over the last five months with Mila, filling her in.

"Just before he ended it with me, he told me about his childhood."

Mila looks into her hot tea and rubs her pregnant belly. I know Mila can relate—she lost both of her parents. "Dominic told me about it. I can't imagine; he was so small, the same age as Dante, to have to witness such cruelty, being robbed of his innocence." Mila frowns.

"I told him I loved him," I blurt out, and the waterworks come running down at full speed. "He told me I was nothing more than a...a good fuck."

She frowns, and her green eyes go glossy. "Oh, Sophie. I've never seen you like this."

I've never cried for a man, not even when I caught Eric in bed with another woman.

"I thought I loved Eric. Don't get me wrong, I cared for him and loved him in a different way. I didn't realize what love really felt like until Liam. I was never in love with Eric." I grab a tissue to wipe the snot. "Liam made me feel like rubbish, just like Eric. I never thought he would make me feel this way. I thought he was different."

Mila pouts and scoots closer to me, tears trailing down her cheeks. My emotional and pregnant best friend can't handle seeing me cry. "Liam is a great man. What he said to you—he's just trying to push you away. I know, deep down, he feels the same as you, Sophie. He loves you..." She shakes her head. "He just doesn't know it yet. As they say, sometimes losing someone makes you realize what you lost, and that's just what Liam needs. But first, he needs to battle those demons anchoring him down." Mila grabs a tissue and wipes my tears.

She does it so motherly that it makes me smile.

She continues. "Neither you nor anyone else can fight this battle for him. He has to be ready to fight to unleash himself from those weights in order to swim to shore and set himself free. I know what it's like to drown in a dark abyss. Dante was my light to fight for. And you are his."

"No, I'm not. He left me even after I said that once he left that parking lot, he lost me. He left me standing there, Mila. He didn't spare me a glance." My heart sinks. "I'm not waiting around for him, Mila. He broke me."

I stare at my best friend. She is so strong. She's been through hell from her teens up until recently. Now she's a married woman with a baby on the way. She's someone I look up to, like a big sister, even though I'm older than her by nine months.

Mila goes to the freezer and pulls out a tub of cookies and cream ice cream, and two spoons. We both dig in. "You're absolutely right. You shouldn't wait around. Sophie needs to work on Sophie."

I raise an eyebrow.

Mila sighs. "No more online dating, trying to find a rebound. I think maybe you need a breather. Men can be too much work. Good lord." She gives a faint laugh.

Her statement is accurate, and it hits me right in the gut.

"Uh, I'm such a slut." I burst into tears.

Mila pulls me into a hug. "Oh, God, Sophie, no, you're not a slut. Eric just made you feel like you were never good enough. He put you down. He made you feel like you couldn't have done better than him, like you had to find someone to distract you from how he treated you."

Mila's right, I need to work on myself. I need to heal my broken heart. But Liam left me shattered into pieces, and I'm not sure if I'll ever fully recover.

"I think I need to take off for a while—two weeks, maybe a month. I'm not totally sure yet. It's just that I don't want to stay here anymore." Everywhere I turn, there are memories of Liam. He haunts almost every corner of my house. "I'm thinking of going to London since Mom's going to be there with Alex. Liz is going to have the baby soon. Then maybe I'll head to Manhattan for a couple of weeks. But only if you're okay without me."

"Don't worry about me. I have Daliah to help me out. I'm positive getting out will help. That's a great idea. Spend time with your family and send me lots of pictures." Mila pulls me over to lean my head on her.

Tomorrow I'll sneak into Liam's house to get my clothes and board the next flight to London.

I feel like the ground has opened up beneath me, and I'm falling into a bottomless abyss with my heart in tatters. My throat closes up, my palms sweat, and I can't get enough air. Everywhere I look, there are reminders of him in the room—his smell, laughter, and warmth, all gone. All that's left is a creeping sense of dread that threatens to take over.

Is he thinking about me? Maybe he'll change his mind and come knocking on my door. Maybe.

"Thank you," I tell Mila. "What would I do without you?"

Mila smiles faintly. "I say the same thing about you, my friend. I wish I could have a drink with you." She pauses as she helps me up from the sofa. "Things will get better day by day, my bestie. I know how you feel. Come on, let's get you to bed."

As soon as I wake up, I dress and send Mila home to her husband and Dante. She whines, clearly worried about me, but I kick her out anyway. I'm just as eager to leave. I feel like I'm drowning in this apartment. I booked a flight to Westminster, London, and called my brother, letting him know I'd be visiting Mom, who left for London last week. My flight leaves at three this afternoon. Now I wait patiently around the corner from

Liam's house, and as soon as I see his car leave the driveway, I pull in and jump out of my car. My heart thumps so loudly that I can hear it as I turn the key in the knob. All I need are my clothes and makeup. I have to hurry before he returns.

As I open the door, the familiar scent of cedarwood and spice fills my nostrils, stirring a dull ache in my chest. Then I notice the bottle of tequila and a single glass placed on the coffee table. Duke runs to greet me like he always does.

"Hey, big guy, I'm going to miss you. I'm going to miss taking you for walks, playing fetch with you, having you sit between us while we watch TV, and most of all, I'm going to miss those belly rubs you love."

He howls as if he understands me and gives me sad eyes.

"Be upset with your owner, not me, bud." I go to Liam's room. Everything is the same as we left it the night of the gala. There are blankets on the couch. He must have passed out drunk. I grab all my clothes, shoes, and makeup, leaving my candles behind. I leave his house key on the coffee table and remove the charm bracelet he gifted me, placing it next to the key. I want nothing from the man who thinks I'm just a good fuck. He can shove it up his ass. Tears begin to fall once I shut the door for the last time. I miss him so damn much. The way his body felt next to mine when I'd wake up in his arms. The way we'd curl up together on the couch to watch Netflix, but we never made it all the way through a show because his hands were always exploring my body. We inevitably ended up in the bedroom, with him going down on me. I start the car and head back home to finish packing.

Two hours later, I'm ready to go. I gave Mila instructions for her and Dominic to feed my adopted cats and water my plants. My phone dings with a text from the rideshare saying my driver is here to take me to the airport. My stomach churns with nerves. My heart clenches as I realize that once I'm gone, everything familiar will be wiped away in my absence. The thought of leaving behind the precious memories sends shivers down my spine. Every moment, every word, and every kiss will slowly fade away. It scares me, but I know it's what I need to do to move on and let go.

CHAPTER 29
LIAM

"Thank you all for your dedication and time tracking Pablo and his men. We won't stop until we find him," Chief Moreno says unwaveringly.

We nod and stand, our metal chairs screeching against the tile floor of the meeting room.

"Rodriguez, a moment." Chief Moreno hands me a letter.

I open it up and, to my surprise, find a letter offering me the position I applied for as a detective in Los Angeles. I'm literally speechless, mouth gaping open and all. I applied months ago and never expected to get it.

Chief Moreno pats me on the shoulder. "Congratulations, Liam. They made a good choice. You're a fine young man with a strong work ethic. Manny is dancing with the angels in celebration of his son's achievements."

I swallow the knot in my throat. "Thank you, sir."

He nods and walks off. I'm honored I got the job. It came at the perfect time. I need to get away from here.

Walking out of the station, I sigh. Frustration has been gnawing at me; we've searched Pablo's home and hideout, but the fucker ran again. His son is still in custody, clearly giving us shit for information.

Starting the ignition, my car purrs with the new exhaust I have installed. To say I've been keeping myself busy for the last three weeks is an understatement. The woman occupies my mind, car, house, and even the damn gym. Her sweet smell lingers in my car, and at home. I wish I could bottle it up. She left me with memories, I'll always treasure. The day I walked in the front door and saw the key and her charm bracelet on the coffee table, it hit hard, a blow right in the pit of my stomach. I lost her...because I let her go.

When I enter my front door, I'm not greeted by my boxer anymore. He snarls at me, giving me the cold shoulder even though I'm his owner, the one who feeds him. He wants the woman who filled his heart with belly rubs and cuddles. The house smells of Sophie's candles and her coconut lotion. Despite taking her clothes with her, she left her candles behind in both the bedroom and the living room, leaving me feeling as though she's still present.

I burst into the kitchen, my legs heavy with exhaustion. My fingers fumble desperately for the refrigerator door handle before I yank it open and grab the closest beer. I don't bother finding a bottle opener. I pull off the cap with one sharp tug and chug the cold liquid straight from the bottle. Relief floods through me, easing my tension ever so slightly while I pray that it will dull the piercing pain in my chest.

The honks of horns in the driveway have Duke's ears perking up. He snarls when Dominic, Santiago, and Mark come barging in. I scratch behind his ears.

"Sorry, it's not her. She's not coming back," I whisper in his ear. He jumps up and goes to the spare bedroom. I turn to the three men who are staring at me as if I'm some feral animal.

For the past three weeks, the guys have been calling me and my mother. I haven't had it in me to want anyone's company.

"We've been calling you," Dominic says as he surveys the house: the empty beer bottles, empty glasses, and an empty bottle of tequila. "Let's go outside and drink some beers like the good old days."

Santiago waves the twenty-four-pack of beer at me.

"Yes, and gaze at the stars," he says in a feminine voice.

I snort. My brothers are a bunch of idiots.

Yes, my brothers. It's been true since we were young, but I've never been able to use the words until now.

"How's it going?" Mark asks.

I shrug. "Okay, I guess. And you?"

Mark's girlfriend, April, broke it off with him weeks ago. She's the type who likes to play games. She took advantage of his kind heart. Once she found out what Rachel did, she treated him like shit, as if it was his fault.

"I'm doing good, man. She wasn't the one, anyway."

The one.

Dominic tosses a cold bottle of beer into my hands and then hands out the other three, all of which he had pulled from an old ice chest. We each settle back in our chairs, the cheap metal legs creaking under our weight as we recline. The night air is still and cool, wafting around us like a soft embrace.

Dominic peers at me, shaking his head slowly.

"What?" I bite out.

"What? What do you mean by what? Didn't I tell you to leave her before you hurt her, bro? You got her to fall in love with you and then broke her heart. How fucked is that, huh? I'm sure she will find someone in London. Who knows, she might not even come back. She'll find someone who will love her back."

My heart thuds down to the pit of my stomach. London. She went to London. *Fuck.*

"When did she leave?" My voice comes out raw, thick with emotion.

"Three weeks ago," Santiago answers.

She's been gone for three weeks. What if she never comes back? I'll never see her again. *You fucking let her go, you idiot.*

Santiago deftly inserts a cigarette between his lips. I give him the nonverbal cue that I, too, would like one. He nods and flicks his lighter, offering me the flame. The last time I smoked was in high school. I haven't had any need for it until now. Dominic follows suit and rolls a cigarette of his own.

"You're not supposed to be smoking," I mutter to Dominic. He's been cancer free for six years.

"Just tonight. It's needed for this Delgado huddle we've got going on."

"She left for London?" I say out loud, not intending for them to hear the strain in my voice.

"I enjoy seeing you like this, fucker," Dominic says with a stupid grin.

Taking a gulp of beer, I give him the middle finger. "Fuck you, asshole." He knows me so well.

"I like seeing you like this. For the past years—no, decades —of knowing you, you've mustered a smile and a laugh. I've never seen you show this type of emotion. The desperation and heartbreak you are feeling tells me you're living and feeling it right here." He pats his chest. "Answer me this. Is Sophie on your mind every minute of the day? Is she your priority? Do you picture her and no one else? Did you love waking up to her in your arms? Do you feel like you're dying without her? You want her so fucking bad, and you see a future with her and only her?"

I close my eyes and exhale. "Yes, to all."

"Now all you need to do is admit to yourself you're in love with her. You've lived with a ghost so long, Liam, you're becoming one yourself. Only you can pull yourself out of it. Do it before you lose her completely; before you lose the chance to win her back." He sips beer.

"You gave me this advice with Mila. You said, 'You don't want to live with regret.' Take your own advice and don't live with the 'what ifs.'"

Dominic's words keep playing in my head, *admit to yourself you're in love with her.*

I've never felt my lungs collapse due to a lack of oxygen, not until I lost Sophie. I tried to ignore the tugging in my heart, but I can't deny it. The night we made love was a night that will be forever engraved in my memory. Every inch of her body was explored as I tenderly caressed her soft curves. She deserves the utmost tenderness and gentleness. She's the most wholesome person I've ever met. When my name rolled off her red-stained lips, I want my name to be the only name on her lips.

I'm in love with Sophie Summers. No, I'm madly *in love with her.*

"I'm in love with her," I say, admittedly ignoring the three idiots grinning at me. "But I let her go because I'm in love with her. I'm afraid something will happen to her or if something happens to me."

"I call bullshit," Mark drawls.

"I second that," Santiago says.

"I third that," Dominic says with a stern look.

Seriously, Dom is dad material. He's giving me *the look.*

"You deserve happiness. Don't be like me, Liam. I have to live with the guilt for the rest of my life over how I treated Mila when she moved back. I flaunted another woman in her face, proposed to her, even, a woman my mother arranged for me to marry. Although I never thought I'd see Mila again, I shouldn't have agreed when I knew my heart belonged to the only woman I've ever loved. I hate myself for it—for those words leaving my mouth, for someone else to hear them. I regret not searching for Mila hard enough, and I regret listening to Rachel badmouth the woman I love. I should have tried harder. I lost five years of my son's life. I'll bend on my knees every day for my wife because she deserves it. She gave me a chance when I know I didn't deserve it. Don't let time pass, Liam. By the time you wake the fuck up and emerge from the shallow water, she'll be gone."

I exhale loudly and take a swig of my beer. I've had more alcohol over the past three weeks than I can remember. I've probably got more beer than blood in my veins at this point. I've been drowning myself with.

"It wasn't completely your fault," Santiago says to his brother.

"I love her so damn much I have to let her go. Don't you guys understand how dangerous my job is?" I run my hands through my hair. "When I think about shooting that fucker and don't regret it, I feel sick to my stomach. Sophie deserves more than some sick fuck who killed a man. But most of all, I fear that something will happen to her if she's with me. So many reasons why we can't be together."

"You were protecting your mom and yourself, Liam. You did nothing wrong," Santiago says.

I nod. I know that. I've always felt guilty for being there the night my father died and not being able to do more. I'll never feel guilty for killing the man who hurt my mother. And that makes me feel like a monster.

Falling in love with Sophie came at a price. Letting go of the only woman I'll ever love to keep her safe is the only decision I can make.

Once I sign the offer letter and send it back to LAPD for the detective position in the gang and narcotics division, I check on my dad's truck. I'm getting it painted. It's coming out so well. Juan, the painter, outdid himself. It just needs a final coat. Next, I drag out the lawnmower, fill it with gas, and set to work. Sweat trickles down my forehead as I mow the sparse patch of grass, trimming the edges until they are straight and even. Then I take up the hedge clippers and trim back the bushes, trying to distract myself from thoughts of Sophie. Finally, I grab a hand shovel from the garage and get on my knees to dig in the dirt, planting flowers in a swirl around the edge of the lawn and in front of the house. I've chosen California poppies—the ones that remind me of her. Fuck, I can't even function properly.

I can't drink a cup of coffee without thinking of her, remembering the sound of her New Yorker accent as she would fix my cup in the morning, she says coffee in her accent, cawfee. She would add just the right amount of cream and sugar, sit on my lap in the morning, and say, "Heer-ah ya caw-fee." That's the way it sounded in her beautiful accent. Always made my dick hard.

I stab the shovel into the moist dirt, making a hole just the right size for the plant, but it's too narrow, so I stab, stab, stab, and shovel it out. Dirt flies all over the place. I must look like an angry gardener. Now I understand why people find gardening a good stress reliever. You stab your frustration into the dirt.

I pull out my phone from my pocket and text my mom, telling her I'm on my way. It's time I tell her everything that happened the night my father died. She deserves to know. She's been patient with me for so long.

CHAPTER 30
LIAM

"Hola, Mamá."

She glances over her shoulder at the sound of my voice, but her smile falters when she takes in my appearance.

"Liam, is everything okay? You've lost weight." She runs to me, cupping my cheeks like she used to when I was a kid.

I shake my head. "Sit, Mamá." I gesture to the chair.

My mom constantly told me when I was a kid that when I was ready to talk, she'd be there for me. She stopped pushing around my teens. Now the time has come.

"I'm ready, Mamá."

She sits and folds her hands together. Her eyes are wild with panic and relief. I lay my hand over her shaking ones. Swallowing the thick, burning sensation running down my chest, I peer at her sad eyes.

"Dime," *tell me,* she says in our native tongue.

I take a deep breath and start from the beginning. I tell her the last song he listened to, the one that reminded him of her. Of everything terrible that happened after that. And I tell her what his last words were—words of love for her, for his family.

A tear runs down her cheek, and I take her hands in my own, feeling the trembling coursing through them.

I find the courage to tell her the rest. Running. Being chased. Finding her unconscious on the floor. The blood and the gun in my hand. How my finger pulled the trigger. How the sound of the gunshot echoed through the air like a clap of thunder, how the gun jumped in my hand, and how I can still hear it, feel it, even now, eighteen years later.

Bile rises in my throat, but I know she needs to hear it all. She deserves to know. "I did what I had to do," I say, my voice low but firm. "I saved us."

The ambulance took her, and my dad's partner, Detective Johnson, dropped me off at Abuelita's house that night.

The officers at the scene, chief, and detectives made a statement that Pablo had shot one of his gang members. No one ever confiscated my father's gun or tested the bullet. No one ever spoke of me shooting the man... maybe they were hoping it would appear more like a dream than reality. Or, possibly, they must have known my mom and I couldn't handle court matters when she had lost her husband and unborn children.

"I'm sorry, Mamá," I say, my head drooping. "I'm sorry I couldn't help him. I wish it had been me, Mamá. Then you wouldn't have had to struggle so much on your own to raise Rosa and me—"

"No, no, Liam, look at me."

I peer into her soft eyes.

"You were a child, Liam—an innocent child who didn't deserve this. Losing my husband is painful, but it doesn't compare to losing a child, Liam. I wouldn't have survived without you. When I think of your little brothers, Noah and Daniel, all I have to do is look at you, and I know they would be just like you. And your papá—I see so much of him in you. Your personality, your heart of gold, and the same beautiful eyes as him."

She wipes the tears skating down her face. It kills me to see her cry.

"You can't blame yourself. You can't keep living like this. That man, Pablo, is to blame, not you. Tell me, Liam, why are you not with Sophie?"

"How do you know about Sophie?"

"Inez."

I sigh. Damn, that nosy neighbor.

I shrug. "It didn't work out."

She slams her fist on the table, stands up, then grabs a water bottle from the fridge. My eyebrows furrow. Her too. She sits and takes a sip.

"Why, Liam? You love her, don't you?"

"It doesn't matter—"

She shakes her head. "It does fucking matter, Liam. Why let her go if you love her? I don't understand why you pushed her away."

"I told her everything."

"Did that scare her away?"

"No."

She mutters something under her breath. "Then help me understand, Liam, what is going on in that head of yours? My son, tell me, please. Let me in, Liam. Since the day your father died, you haven't shed a tear. Why?" The pleading in her voice breaks my heart.

I exhale. "Because, Mamá, I promised Papá I would be brave and strong. You didn't need to deal with me. You lost your husband and the babies. I needed to be strong for you. I promised him I would take care of you."

She stands and cups my cheeks so I can look at her. "Liam, no, no. That was not your burden to carry. I'm your mother. It's my job to be strong and brave for you. You were a child. All I wanted was for you to be a kid to move past it and live. Let it all out, Liam. Free yourself."

Her words hit hard. Live. Free yourself. I want to be free. I'm so tired. I want to live.

For the first time in years, I let the tears flow, lean on my mom's shoulder, and cry, reliving the night I lost a part of me. I think about when he taught me how to throw a ball. When he would lift me up in the air, and I'd spread my arms like I was flying. When he'd lie on the floor and play Ninja Turtles with me. Those are the memories I want from today on. I won't think of my father's death as a weight but as a legacy, he left behind for me to follow. From this point forward, I will speak his name with pride and throw off the shackles that have held me captive. The Rodriguez legacy will continue when I take up my position as a detective and bring down Pablo.

After ten minutes of blowing snot onto my mom's shoulder, I lift my head. She smiles through the tears running down her face. "There he is, my son. Your papá would be so proud of you. I raised a fine young man. You and Rosa are my pride and joy. But Liam, honey, you know what would make me happy?"

"Huh?"

"Seeing my son happy with the woman he loves."

I groan and stand up to grab two Tylenol from the kitchen cabinet. My head is pounding from the whirlwind of emotions rolling through me. I swallow them, washing them down with a bottle of water.

"This is the reason I let her go. She means too much to me. You heard what happened at the gala. I couldn't live with myself if something happened to her. My fear is starting a life with a woman I love and losing her because of my job—or what if I get shot? I wouldn't want her to live the life we did, Mamá. I wouldn't want her to be left struggling—watching you struggle, working two jobs, was hard. I don't want that to happen to Sophie—I don't want to leave kids behind."

She jumps out of her chair so fast that I jolt from where I'm standing, and she throws her hands over her chest.

"Kids? Niños. Oh, Liam grandkids!"

"Mamá!" I plead. *Christ*. I didn't realize I said Sophie's name in the same sentence I mentioned kids.

"Una familia? *A family?*"

"Did you hear anything I said?"

She waves her hand, and her beaming smile curves my lips into a similar shape.

"Liam, people die of all different causes. Car accidents, sickness. You can't live your life hiding because you're scared. Please give me a story to tell your father when it's finally my time. I want to tell Manny all about his son, grandkids, and wife. Sophie is your light, the key to your heart you keep guarded. It's time, Liam. Set yourself free and live, hijo mio."

I'd be lying if I said I've never thought about a future with Sophie—with kids. Every time it crosses my mind, I shut it down. But losing her has only made me want her more. I don't know if she'll ever talk to me again, after what I said to her. I wouldn't blame her. She was never just some fuck to me. She was my one saving grace, the only one who could make my heart flutter.

I glance at my watch and see that it's time to leave. I tell my mom and start to gather my things.

"Liam," Mamá calls out as I reach for my keys on the kitchen table.

"Yes?"

"Grovel."

My eyebrows scrunch in confusion. "What are you talking about?"

"You need to grovel like a hungry dog. If a man had said

those words to me, I would have slapped him." She crosses her arms and gives me the stink eye. "Inez overheard you talking to the guys the other night." Of course. Leave it to Inez to hang her ear out the window like she was in a live telenovela.

I pinch the bridge of my nose. "I know. I never meant to hurt her. I said it to push her away. She means a lot to me. Thanks for the advice." I kiss her cheek and take the leftovers she packed for me.

Sophie makes me happy. She's not the reason behind my happiness—she's the definition of the word. I've fallen recklessly in love with her, but after all I've done, can she ever love me back?

———

A LIGHT BREEZE wraps around me, making me uneasy as I walk to my car. The same feeling, I had at the gala. I place the food on the passenger seat and open the glove compartment, where I have my gun. I tuck the pistol into the waistband of my jeans and slowly scan the street. My eyes lock onto a black van parked several blocks away, its windows tinted to impenetrable darkness. I've never seen it before, but something about it makes me uneasy. The hairs on the back of my neck stand on end as I re-enter my mom's house.

"Mamá!" I shout.

"What is it?"

"Lock the door and don't open it, no matter what. There's a van parked outside. Looks very suspicious. I'm going to check it out."

She nods, worry lines creasing on her forehead.

I crouch low behind a small copse of birch trees. My gun is heavy in my grip. The van is tucked expertly between two ancient oaks, and my blood boils when I see Pablo step out of the driver's side door, followed closely by one of his henchmen. They both wear black leather jackets.

"Long time no see, Liam. The boy with the balls of steel who shot a man right in the head. I'm a believer in a life for a life. You took out my brother-in-law. I couldn't care less about the asshole, but my sister, for some reason, loved the man. She wants me to take the life of the man who took her husband." Pablo leans against the van, seemingly relaxed. His age shows with his bald head and a white caterpillar mustache. "Let's make a deal. I let you live, and you release my son."

I let out a short laugh. "Nah, he can rot where he is." Instantly, the atmosphere shifts. "Hands up, both of you," I command. But damn! I have no cuff I can use to restrain them.

"Very well, asshole, a life for a life, sangre por sangre," Pablo sneers, his voice malicious and evil.

The van's sliding door opens, and I understand: they outnumber me. I need to shoot first. The sound of bullets pierces the air as I aim my gun and fire at the man standing beside Pablo. I swivel to shoot at the two men jumping out of the van without skipping a beat. In seconds, they're all on the ground, dead.

A piercing pain hits my shoulder. My body jerks at the impact of the shot. Aiming my gun at Pablo, I shoot, but my aim is off because of the pulsing pain in my shoulder. The shot hits him in the leg as another shot hits me right in the chest. I stumble backward, my vision blurring as a wave of dizziness and a chilling numbness sweeps through me. I look down and see the growing bloodstain on my shirt. I feel the warmth of my blood flowing out of me. He landed a direct hit with his last shot. As my finger tightens around the trigger, I take another shot, and it ricochets off his torso, making a sound like a clap of thunder. I know it's over when my head hits the cold, hard cement.

The sound of my mother's voice is barely audible. What is she doing? My strength is quickly depleting, and I can feel myself close to passing out. I summon the last of my energy to protect my mom, but all of my efforts are futile.

"A life for a life, asshole. Isn't that what I heard you tell my son? You took Manny from us, and I'll be damned if you take my son from me." My mother's voice rings out with rage before she pulls the trigger.

The gunshot echoes around us, and I tumble into a dark abyss.

Sophie...I didn't get to tell her I loved her.

CHAPTER 31
SOPHIE

I sit on the porch of my parents' new ranch house, taking in the fresh air and rolling hills. I've been here for a week now, since returning from London. I stand up from the old rocker and make my way to the bedroom my mom set up for me.

"Hey, sweet pea, do you want to stop for pizza?" my dad asks.

It's been a year since I've been back to New York. I should be happy to be with my parents. But all I want to do is go home to my apartment in California, crawl into bed, and grieve. I've distracted myself from all of it for weeks now. I need to grieve and accept in my heart that it's over.

"Sure, Dad, sounds great." I'll never turn down food, especially pizza.

You. Are. Perfect. Any. Shape. Or. Form.

Five long weeks—the longest weeks of my life. Five days after I arrived in London, Liz was induced, and eight hours later, she had a seven-pound baby girl named Jackie. My niece is adorable. My big brother, whom I hadn't seen in such a long time, was ecstatic, and it was nice to see him that way. My mom and dad have been on cloud nine the entire time. Holding my niece and sniffing her baby scent kept me from breaking down in front of my family. When I had a chance, I would escape and walk around the city, allowing myself to grieve the loss of the man I love. I thought of what Mila had said—maybe he does love me, and he hasn't come to terms with it—but after weeks, I lost hope. He meant what he said.

I spent my time in art museums, my eyes seeping into each art piece. I wondered what was on their minds when the artists created such masterpieces. Were they sad, grieving, happy, in love? Did they combine all their emotions into one piece? Reflecting the past, present, and future? My gaze was drawn to one painting in particular.

It features a young boy no older than eight years old. He kneels on the forest floor, and his face lifts toward an unseen vista with an unreadable expression. His brows are furrowed, and his lips are set in a solemn line that speaks of a sadness that cannot be eased. It's entitled *The Lost Boy*. It's painter, Lacy Vanfreud, is a well-known British artist, and the painting is a masterpiece.

It got me thinking of Liam. He is like this boy—lost. His past tortured his soul, and he couldn't break free. Did he go back to his old ways of sleeping around to numb his past? Images of him with other women churn in my mind, driving me into a jealous rage.

Though it will be difficult for me to witness, I hope the person he falls in love with is his destined soulmate. Only that will heal his broken soul. For most people, unconditional love seems to mean you love someone for a short time only to fall out of love with them or let go of them to fall in love with someone else. To me, unconditional love means...loving someone for life even when they don't love you.

I will always love Liam Rodriguez. He gave me back my confidence and my self-worth.

I reminisce about how his lips felt on mine. How his hot, searing body melted on top of mine like liquid gold. Or how he'd hold me in his arms while I read and he watched *Law and Order*. He would tuck the sheets over me in the morning when he left the bed to go shower. Sometimes I would sleep in a little longer or jump in the shower with him. He would wash my body gently, lavishing me from head to toe. He would pepper kisses along my shoulders, making my body shiver. I etch the memories of those simple moments on my soul, like the wax from a lit candle left to drip. Only the pain remains.

My phone rings, and I sigh once again. Grabbing my phone from the nightstand, I check who it is.

"Hello."

"Hey, bestie, how are you doing? Are you in New York yet?" Mila's soft voice hums on the line.

"I'm doing okay, and I just got home from grabbing some pizza. I'm at my parent's house now."

Mila has been messaging me lately, making sure I'm doing okay. She hasn't brought up Liam in any of our conversations. Presumably, she is trying to spare me from the additional pain of talking about it.

"Umm..." She blows a hot breath. "Sophie, I have something to tell you."

My stomach drops at the sound of her distressed voice. "Is it about him?"

"Yes, umm, Sophie, Liam was shot a couple of days ago."

I can feel the blood drain out of me.

"He was shot twice. He lost lots of blood, and he was in and out of consciousness for three days. He's been awake for two days now. He's doing better. The doctor will probably release him next week, depending on how he's doing."

My heart beats out of my chest. I jump out of bed and begin to collect my suitcases. I need to see him, make sure he's okay.

"I'll take the next flight out," I say.

"No, Sophie."

I drop my stuff. He must not want me there.

"It's better if you stay and take a couple of more days off. He's doing okay now."

"He doesn't want me there?" I ask.

"Umm...I didn't tell you sooner because I wanted to wait just in case."

I get it. She wanted to wait. She knew if she told me I would fly out to him, and he would turn me away.

"I asked him," Mila says, "and he said he didn't want you to know what happened."

I wince. The words hit me like a whip to my back. It's clear he's erased me from his life.

"It's okay, Mila. Thank you for letting me know. He doesn't want me there...he doesn't want to see me. He's moved on. I get it. I'm just glad he's doing better."

She blows out another breath. "I don't think it's that he doesn't want to see you. I think it's that he doesn't want you to see him in the state he's in. Also, Dominic was telling me Liam was offered a position as a detective on the LAPD. And I think he's going to take it."

She attempts to console me, yet her final comments shatter my already-fragmented heart like glass. He intends to stay away from me. He no longer holds any affection for me. I change the subject and ask how Dante and the studio are doing. Once we hang up, I throw myself on the bed and cry into my pillow. This is it—the end. He wanted me out of his life, and he meant it.

We were just fucking. You were nothing more than a good

fuck.

The pain running through my body feels like a bucket of ice water poured into my veins. I ache with the bone-chilling cold. I grab a pillow and hug it for warmth. I cry for the warmth of his touch that I'll never feel again.

As much as I still love him, the pain fades into anger. For months, he led me on, allowed me to fall, only to toss me aside when he was through. I'm angrier with myself for falling so hard and fast, even having known his terms. However, he didn't stick with them when he dragged me to his home, when he proved willing to play the doting lover with me, so domestic-like. In the end, it's my fault for falling for his charm.

I hate that he was hurt and could've died. That thought kills me. I'd rather steal stolen glances than never see him again.

"Knock, knock. Honey, are you awake? Dinner's ready."

I groan and stretch. I must have dozed off, crying myself to sleep.

"Hey, Mom, sorry, I must have fallen asleep. You should have woken me up to help you."

Her blue eyes soften. "Oh, honey, are you okay? Your eyes are puffy and red."

I nod. "I'm fine. Let's go eat." I stumble to my feet like a baby calf.

She smiles, then nods, shutting the door.

I swiftly walk into the bathroom to wash my face and head to the kitchen. My mouth hangs open at the amount of food my mom has made. It's only the three of us, and she cooked as if she were feeding an army—a pile of barbecue chicken, roasted corn, mashed potatoes, grilled veggies, and honey biscuits.

My dad stomps in, covered in dirt like he's been rolling in

the mud with the pigs. I'm not used to seeing my dad so outdoorsy. He's a contractor and used to getting dirty, but never like this. His tall Viking frame fills the doorway. He scratches his blond bushy beard and scrutinizes me.

"How are you doing, sweet pea? Feeling better?"

I raise an eyebrow.

"Good, Dad. I took a nap, and I'm better."

He nods and groans. "If you need me to cut off anyone's balls, you let me know."

I snort and shake my head. "No need, Dad."

My mom walks in and swats him on the butt. I guess that's where I get my butt-smacking from. My dad's brown eyes twinkle as he stares at her with a hint of amusement.

"Go wash up!" Mom hollers at him.

I hear a husky laugh behind my dad. I wrinkle my nose. Who could that be? Mom didn't say we had company.

A tall, muscular man with a ponytail walks in. His arms are pretty meaty. He looks like he gained his muscle by chopping wood and carrying bales of hay. He's wearing Wrangler jeans and a shirt advertising a honky tonk bar. He definitely looks like a country boy—I mean, man.

"This is Ralph, Sophie. He works here with us at the farm. He's been a godsend, helping us out with the livestock." My mom smiles widely at Ralph. "Ralph, meet my beautiful daughter. I think you two are about the same age, twenty-six, right?"

My dad rolls his eyes.

"Hi, Ralph, nice to meet you."

"Hello, there, beautiful. Nice to meet you."

If I had met him before Liam, I would have fallen for his green eyes, sun-kissed skin, and husky body. My heart and mind are not interested. My heart only sees the man who stole my heart. He scoots a chair next to me. I make small talk—nothing to give him the attention that I'm interested.

After dinner, I take a walk around the farm. It's beautiful and peaceful. I understand why my parents bought it. Here, it's easy to unwind and think without the hustle and bustle. On my way to the horse stalls, a couple of chickens run past me. The air smells of fresh-cut hay and manure. On the day Liam took me to the ranch, we rode into the canyon and had sex by the lake. Pulling out my phone, I glance at the photos we took in the field of poppies. My heart thuds, and it bleeds all over again at the sight of his handsome smile. I go through my contacts and hit "block" when I get to his name. I'll always love him, and I'll always carry a piece of him with me. He taught me how to love myself, and I'm forever grateful. It hurts that I was not enough for him to fall in love with me. It's time I stop letting men walk all over me and toss me to the side. It's time I put myself first and take the reins.

CHAPTER 32
LIAM

My eyes flicker open when the nurse walks in for what feels like the millionth time to check my vitals. My body feels like I got run over by a dump truck. Pain shoots to every part of my body, and the pain medication they keep pumping into me makes me feel antsy. I can't handle being here any longer, and it's only been two days since I woke up. I lost so much blood and had so many surgeries that my body remained in a state of shock.

The doctors told my mom I had to get a blood transfusion during surgery. They thought I wouldn't make it, but I kept fighting. I know why. All I kept seeing was her, my Sophie. I couldn't leave this world without telling her how I feel her. Whether or not she takes me back, I want her to know.

The soft snores in the corner make my heart sink. My mom sits in an uncomfortable hospital chair, her head leaning against the wall. She looks so content, so at peace in her sleep. I was worried she'd be as traumatized as I've been. She shot that asshole, after all, but when I asked her about it, she said she'd needed it. If this gives her peace, then so be it.

Dominic walks in with a bag of burgers and fries. Thank the fuck. This hospital food sucks. My mom stirs from her sleep and sniffs the air. I snort. She looks like Duke.

"All right, bro, I got your favorite—two doubles with a side of jalapeños to grow some chest hair." He laughs. "Dante keeps wanting salsa and anything spicy since you explained to him spicy food grows chest hair. He keeps checking his chest for signs of hair growth." He throws his head back in laughter.

"What did my handsome boy bring us?" my mom coos at Dominic.

Dominic wraps her in a hug.

"Burgers and fries, of course, and a side of jalapeños for this guy here. Maybe this will heal those wounds so he can get his ass out of bed."

My mom chuckles and takes a bite of her burger. Just then, Mila comes wobbling in with her hands on her round belly. My mom runs to her and kisses the poor woman to death. My lips curve in a smile when Mila cuddles in my mom's arms for a hug. I can't imagine what it must feel like for her to be parent-less at such a young age, having lost both her parents. She's never known the warmth of a mother. She's a powerful woman.

Mila walks up to me and drops a kiss on my forehead.

"How are you feeling?" She frowns at my patched-up wounds.

"I'm alive, so that's good. The wounds from the blow don't compare to the pain in my chest."

She frowns and sighs. There's a hint of frustration behind those eyes. "I spoke to her last night. I told her you were injured." She lifts her hands up. "I know you said not to say anything, but she's my best friend, and so are you, Liam. She's hurting. I told her you didn't want her to come. I heard it in her voice—she has her guard up. Call her. She's in Manhattan now, but she'll be back in two weeks."

Her guard's up. Of course, it is. That's what I wanted, after all. All this damage...it's all my fault.

"Is she pissed at me?" Dumbass question.

Mila laughs, shaking her head. "Oh, you have no idea. She's pissed and hurt. She's a firecracker, my New Yorker. You have your work cut out for you."

My mom decides to chime in, of course. "Oh, I told him to grovel after what Inez told me. I said he'd better get on his knees."

Mila chuckles, shaking her head.

"I know what I said was hurtful. I only said it to push her away. It fucking hurt saying those words to her. I'll fix it if she lets me," I shout. Of course, the women ignore me. She wasn't just a great fuck. I mean, yes, she was a great fuck, but she's more. She's...*my everything, my woman.*

Dominic glances at me with a smirk on his stupid face because I told the fucker once I would never grovel for a woman as he did with Mila. I give him the stink eye. And he barks in a fit of laughter.

Now I have to figure out how to get my girl back. I'll confess my love to her and drop to my knees.

IT'S BEEN two weeks since they released me from the hospital. My wounds are healing quicker than I expected. The doctor says it's because I'm in good health. I lean back on the sofa and stare up at the ceiling. A sigh escapes me as Duke jumps on the sofa and nuzzles his snout on my lap.

"I'm glad I have you, buddy. I'm going to get our girl back. I just have to do one more thing. I know I'm ready for the next step. I'll go find her." He makes a huffing sound that sounds like a sigh of relief. Ever since I was discharged from the hospital, he has been sticking by my side like glue.

"I have to visit Dad. It's been way too long since I've been to see his grave." He gives me a nudge. "I know. I'm heading there now." I get off the sofa and grab my keys.

Twenty minutes later, I arrive at the graveyard where my father and siblings are laid to rest. I kneel on the grass and carefully place the bouquet of flowers I purchased from a vendor by the side of the road into the vase.

"Hola, Papá, Noah, and Daniel. I'm sorry, Papá, that I stopped coming to see you. The guilt wouldn't let me. It was eating me up. Losing you was hard...I've missed you so damn much. I couldn't unsee you dying on the floor, leaving you there alone." My voice cracks. "Despite my desire to care for others, I felt as though I was not capable or worthy enough to fulfill that role as a man. I was never interested in falling in love, Papá. I couldn't stand watching Mamá strain herself to make ends meet. I'm not mad at you about it. You treated her like a queen, and it was not your fault. I was afraid of moving on from this— and I didn't know how." I take a sharp breath, inhaling the fresh breeze enveloping me as tears roll down my cheeks.

"It took a beautiful woman to shine light into my life. But I went and fucked it all up, saying some cruel shit to her. I pushed her away to save her from this life. I thought I was saving her, but I hurt her. What do I do? I never thought I'd experience love, Papá. I could really use a man-to-man talk. I wish you could meet her. She has this cute accent, oh, and the most beautiful blue eyes that are so memorizing."

I grin, plucking a blade of grass, thinking of Sophie and how I fucked her on the grass next to the lake. God, she has a way of making me smile even when she's not present. I clear my throat.

"Sorry, Papá, my mind went off to, you know...a man's dirty thoughts. So, yeah, she makes me laugh, she has long blonde hair, and she's a firecracker, a big sassy pants. Mamá adores her, and I'm in love with her. She doesn't know it yet. If I get her back—wait, no, *when* I get her back—I'm going to treat her like you treated Mamá, like the queen she is. I'll make her smile and laugh and give her the world, just as you did to Mamá. I've always wanted to follow in your footsteps. I hope I've made you proud, and I'll continue to do so." Another tear strays down my cheek.

"I saw you, Papá, when I felt myself fading. I was dying... you—you brought me back. I thought I dreamed it, but I know I didn't. I remember so vividly your smile—you said it wasn't my time. I knew then that everything would be okay. You're my guardian angel, and I promise to make you proud and continue your legacy. I'll make sure to have lots of stories for Mamá one day for you. Until then, Papá, I'll go find my girl and bring her here so you can meet her. She's beautiful. See you soon. Te quiero, Papá.'"

RISING FROM MY POSITION, I begin walking to my vehicle as I see a white truck drive up. My dad's ex-partner Detective Rick Johnson, steps out. I haven't seen him for quite a while, a couple of years, I'd say. His son, Mike Johnson, took over as a detective once he retired.

"Liam," he greets me.

I nod. "Detective Johnson. How are you doing? What brings you here?"

He pats me on the back. "Ex-detective. Call me Rick, son. Seems more appropriate since I was your father's close friend." He glances at my father's tombstone. "I've been coming here twice a month for the last few years since your father passed away."

It shocks me right down to my toes. I knew he was a good friend of my dad. I remember him coming over a couple of times when I was a kid—they *were* partners—but I didn't think he would still be visiting his grave regularly after all these years.

"Really?" I say, trying not to sound so shocked.

"Liam, do you have a minute? I've been waiting for the right time to talk to you." He scratches his white beard, and his brows scrunch up.

"Sure," I drawl, gesturing to the bench beside us.

He nods. We take a seat.

"Liam, there's something that's been eating me up for years. I come and talk to your father because he's the only one who knows what went down. We agreed that night to keep quiet. Well, he wanted to keep quiet for me—for my sake. I...I just never thought this would happen."

My brows furrow and sweep his face, but his head is down, as if he's contemplating how to go about his confession, if that is what it is.

"What happened, Rick?"

He exhales and looks up at me with sadness in his eyes. "Before he passed away, your father and I worked together on a case. He was an excellent detective. The night at the bust, we didn't just find drugs. Pablo had been trafficking women. Pablo's brother warned he would abduct my daughters and sell them to make up for the women we freed in the bust. I freaked out and shot him in the head. Manny suggested we keep it between us so I wouldn't get in trouble. He said he would have done the same if anyone had threatened his family. I called it in as one though of his own men had shot him." He shakes his head.

Suddenly, it all clicks into place. Pablo mistook my father

for Rick and believed he was the one who had murdered his brother.

"Blood for blood, a life for a life," I say, my voice hoarse. I never understood why Pablo said those words, but my father knew, and he never said a word. He didn't confess who had really killed Pablo's brother, even when his own life was at risk.

"I'm so fucking sorry, Liam. That bullet was meant for me. We never thought they would come after me. My mistake caused your family so much pain. The guilt has been eating me up for years. You went through so much. That night when I arrived at your house and found you with the gun in your hands, I was crushed. I'm not asking for forgiveness, Liam...I needed to tell you—"

Through the shock has come a sense of recognition—I'd always expected something like this. I knew that bullet wasn't intended for my father, but he'd accepted it with dignity. He was never one to back down or turn away. My father was a man of honor, a man many admired.

As much as I want to be pissed at his damn mistake, I can't be. My father wanted it this way, and Rick was defending his daughters. They didn't know the outcome of this. Rick has been punishing himself for decades, just as I have.

"I'm not mad, Rick. I forgive you." I mean it. *I forgive him.*

His head snaps up, and tears begin to flow. Watching a man in his sixties bawling is a little uncomfortable, but I understand he's releasing that pent-up guilt.

The world isn't perfect. We are born to make mistakes and learn from them. We have the power to forgive ourselves, just as we have the power to forgive others. Holding a grudge only makes us bitter, and that's not who I want to be. I want to be free.

"I'm sorry, Liam. I didn't mean to make you uncomfortable."

I shake my head. "No, you didn't. I understand."

"I know for sure Manny is so proud of you, Liam. You're just like him, you know? You're an honorable man. You fill his shoes perfectly."

I swallow the knot in my throat. "Thank you."

He nods and stands. "I'm going to visit Manny for a bit. Is that okay?"

"Of course. I'm heading out. Thank you, Rick, for telling me. Let's keep this between us." We say our goodbyes, and then I get in my car. For the first time in years, I feel lighter. *Free.*

MY BODY MOVES fluidly toward the woman sprawled on a beach towel, lying on her stomach, reading a book with a tiny bikini on.

Fuck me.

The air is alive with the squawking of seagulls, and a cool breeze caresses my face like an old friend. Knots of tension tighten in my stomach, and my heart races like a teenager approaching his crush. My breath heaves as I approach. She's wearing a thong bikini, for Christ's sake. Anyone can see. She sits up, takes a drink of water, then fixes her towel and lies on her back. *Fuck.* My dick twitches, seeing the tiny squares covering her nipples and the flimsy strip of material covering her pussy. The need to roll her up like a burrito in that towel is maddening. I'd like to throw her over my shoulder so men can't gawk at what's mine.

Mila said Sophie recently returned from New York. After calling and sending multiple messages without a response, I figured out she had blocked me. It hurt more than I wanted to admit, and the what-ifs started spinning in my head. Had she moved on?

When I step toward her, my heart stutters. It's been two long months without her. She's so engaged in her book that she doesn't notice me next to her. She lets out a soft moan and presses her thighs together. *Fuck.* I found one of her books at my house, so I decided to read it, not knowing what kind of book it was. I knew it was romance, but not smut. Hell! My eyes bulge out. No wonder she's an animal in bed. It's basically a guide for men on how to fuck a woman properly. I'd say I did a hell of a good job fucking her. I do it better than those other fucks.

"Sophie," I say, my voice coming out raspy and raw. Her body stiffens, and then she closes her eyes tight. "Sophie, baby," I repeat.

Instinctively, she stands and grabs her swimsuit coverup, quickly wrapping it around her waist. Avoiding eye contact as best as she can, she stuffs her belongings into a bag, obviously preparing to make a quick escape.

"Sophie, can we talk?" I plea.

Her brows collide in the center, and she side-eyes me. Her beautiful blonde hair blows with the light breeze. "We have nothing to talk about, Liam. You said plenty that night." She reaches for her bag, but I grab it first. She tugs it from my hold, muttering words under her breath. She looks like an angry Barbie.

"Baby...I need to talk to—"

She turns, and our gazes collide. My breath hitches like always. I bite my lip. That's just how she affects me. I have missed her so damn much. She's been the calmness in my storm and the light in my life. As beautiful as she is...it's who she is on the inside that made me fall in love with her. She taught me the meaning of love.

"I'm happy you're doing better, and that the son of a bitch is dead. But I'm not playing games with you. We are done. You wanted it this way. I'm not some chew toy. I'm worth so much more than just a quick fuck. So why don't you go find yourself a fuck buddy. I'm not it. I found someone who will love me."

I flinch. Her words wound my heart. She found someone else?

"I meant what I said—I don't want to cross paths with you." She whirls on her heels, and angry Barbie marches to her car. A hot tide of jealousy rips through me. I grind my teeth, and my breathing roars with anger.

"Who is he?" I follow her.

"Who?" She doesn't glance back. She keeps walking.

"The guy you're with. You said you found someone who loves you."

"Me! *I* love me, and I won't allow any man to walk all over me again, to degrade me."

Relief washes over me. *Thank the fuck.*

"That a girl," I say.

She growls, pressing on the key fob. Sophie jumps in her car without a word, shutting the door in my face. She peels out, leaving me in the parking lot just like I left her that night I broke both our hearts.

CHAPTER 33
SOPHIE

My knuckles turn white from gripping the steering wheel as I fly down the highway. How dare he show up like a Greek god, the sun glinting off his golden olive skin. His tank top outlined each perfectly sculpted muscle, clinging to his toned body. Every time he flexed, his biceps seemed to ripple with power. Oh, let's not forget his sunglasses. My arousal quickly fades into anger. I turn on the radio at full blast, needing something, anything, to distract me from *him*. "Muscle Memory" by Kelsea Ballerini plays. Oh, goodie. How damn fitting.

Finally pulling up to my apartment, I grab my handbag and make my way to the door.

"Christ, woman, you drive like the devil is chasing after you."

I jump, startled, and my hand goes to my chest.

Liam slams his car door and strides toward me. His car is almost sideways in my driveway, like he pulled in too fast, without a single care except catching me.

"It seems like the devil is chasing me. Again," I grumble, fishing for my keys. "What are you doing here?"

"Can we talk, please, Sophie?" His voice is faintly pleading. What could he possibly want to say?

"Fine," I say through gritted teeth, opening the door.

He trails in behind me, shutting us in together. He swallows and runs his fingers through his silky hair. I've never seen him this nervous.

"Can I take you to my place? I'd like to show you something, then we can talk. I just need ten, maybe fifteen minutes of your time."

Show me what? Maybe he wants to give me the stuff I left behind since he's moving to LA.

"Okay, I'll follow you."

"No, I'll drive."

I give him a haughty stare and nod. I'm not in the mood to argue; surprisingly, I'll just call for a rideshare to bring me back home. I know this is a bad idea. His proximity is dangerous.

"I need to change," I say, making my way up the stairs since I'm still in my bikini.

"Yeah, you do, baby. You wouldn't want my hand to slip into your pussy."

I turn to narrow my eyes at him. "I'd knee you in the balls."

"I'd let you if you would massage them after." The asshole smirks and winks.

I shiver, imagining his large, muscular hands caressing me. *Stop it, Sophie.*

"Watch it, Casanova, before I throw your ass out."

His smirk dissolves. He hates being called Casanova. Fucker.

A FIFTEEN-MINUTE DRIVE seems like a century when you're sitting in the car with a man who makes you feel like a crumb he flicked off his shirt. And I'm starting to regret it. *Dammit, Sophie, you just told the man you would not let anyone walk all over you, and here you are in his car. Pathetic!* I can't help it. I side-eye him. He's grown a short stubbly beard, and it makes him look hotter.

Stop it, Sophie, he's disgusting. I roll my eyes. Of course, he's not. I missed him, and that's making me weak. I can't let him claw me in to toss me out. I'll collect my stuff and leave.

We finally make it to his place after the long drive, sitting in silence. The first thing I notice is the garden bed of poppies in different shades of red, pink, yellow, white, and purple. It looks beautiful.

"You like?" Liam asks.

I nod. "It's beautiful."

"Just like you," he whispers.

He waves me over to follow him to his detached garage.

"I want to show you my dad's truck."

I trail behind him, my eyes on his ass. He opens the garage, and my eyes widen. It's gorgeous. It's painted ocean blue.

"Ask me?" Liam implores, his gaze fixed on mine. His voice is barely a whisper, full of vulnerability. His gaze overflows with vulnerability, too, making a desperate plea without words. He steps closer to me, and I can feel the memory of his breath on my skin.

"What?" My voice comes out barely above a whisper.

"Ask me if I've been in love. Ask me if I've ever had a girlfriend?"

I remember asking him this months ago, what feels like years...before we slept together. My forehead creases. Why is he asking? Could he have lied and fallen in love with someone before me?

"Have you been in love? Have you had a girlfriend?"

"I have." His thumb brushes my cheek. "I'm in love with

you, Sophie. *I'm hopelessly, recklessly in love with you.* I had a girlfriend. She was my first. I was too dumb and fucked in the head to open my eyes and see what was in front of me. I pushed her away because I thought I was saving her. Only then did I realize I went and fucked it up and lost her. I lost the one woman who loved me, saw me at my worst, and still loved me. I painted my dad's truck ocean blue, like the color of the eyes of the woman I'm in love with."

My chin trembles, and I start to cry. His thumb brushes my tears away.

"I'm sorry, Sophie. I'm sorry I hurt you. I never meant those horrible words. You're not some quick fuck. You mean so much more, baby. You mean everything to me—you're my light in my darkness, the key to my locked heart. My woman. Mine. Your mine."

I'm speechless. I wasn't expecting this...his confession. He...he loves me. I don't know how to wrap my head around it.

"You...you didn't want to see me at the hospital," I hiccup, tears coming fast now.

He brushes them away. "Oh, mi bella, I wanted to see you, but not when I was all fucked up on painkillers. I wanted to be clear-headed when I confessed my feelings for you."

I nod.

He pulls a brown leather notebook from the back pocket of his jeans.

"This is the journal my therapist gave me when I was ten. He said for me to write about the most important people in my life, I met along the way. I haven't met anyone worth putting in my journal besides my family, Dominic, and his brothers. I hadn't met anyone—up until I met you. Read it. I have been writing in it since the day I met you."

I take the journal from his hands and inhale—a sweet, musty rich aroma of aged leather. I trace my finger over frayed edges and ink smudges on the corner of each page. "Are you sure you want me to read it?"

"Please," he says.

I open it and read. Each word pumps new blood through me, bringing my heart back to life.

———

Sophie, the woman who will have all my firsts.

I've never met a woman who so completely put a spell on me. Who has made me feel things I've never felt before. She's beautiful. I can't stop thinking about her. I've never wanted a woman more than I want her. She was my first kiss, the kiss that made me want no one else. My lips, my kisses, belong to her only.

I have given her all my firsts that matter.

First kiss, first time holding hands, cuddling, waking up with someone in my arms, first to come over to my house, first to live with me, shower with, first time doing anal, first dance, first girl-friend, first one to make love to. First one to fall in love with.

I'm positive I fell in love with her the minute our lips touched. It took me a long time to figure it out. First one to have my heart. The only woman I want. I hope she will give me many more firsts in our lifetime.

I TURN my gaze back to him, and he lowers his head, looking into my eyes. My heart races, and it's hard to breathe. He wrote all of this in his journal because he loves me.

"You...you love me?" I stutter.

Liam steps closer and cups my cheeks, his thumb caressing my flesh. Apparently, I'm still in shock.

"Sophie, I'm so fucking madly in love with you. I missed you so damn much. There's so much I need to tell you. First, the night of the gala, it scared the shit out of me. If something happened to you, I couldn't live without you. So, when I spilled my past to you that night, I thought I was saving you by pushing you away, after all these years of seeing my mom lonely, sad, and working her ass off to provide for me. I didn't want that for you. I wanted to save you from me. It took losing you for me to see things in a different light. *You saved me.* You saved me from the hole I was drowning in, baby, and you brought me back to life." A tear skates down his cheek. He looks so raw, vulnerable, and beautiful.

"When I was dying, all I could think of was coming back to you, to fight death because I needed to see you and tell you I love you."

I throw myself on his chest and wail. I didn't know he almost died as a result of his injuries, and I never asked Mila because I cut her short. I was too upset.

"Shh, it's okay, it's okay." He rubs my back in soothing circles.

I pull back and wipe my tears. "If something had happened to you, I don't know if I could have gone on living. Please tell me you love me and that this isn't just a dream."

He wipes away the tears before kissing me softly on the nose. "It's real, Sophie. What I feel for you is real. I apologize. I should have called you sooner, but I've been trying to figure things out in my head. I decided to talk to my mom. We had a conversation. That same night, I was going to call you, but then the shooting happened. Sophie, my feelings are different now, peaceful. I'm more sure than ever that I love you. I needed to make peace with myself so I could be the man you need, the man you deserve."

Liam Rodriguez is the man of my dreams. His words are beautiful, real, and sweet as honey. He looks at me with a concerned expression because I haven't responded to him yet— I'm unable to form the words. Cat caught my tongue.

"Do you still love me?" he asks.

I'm about to answer, but he drops to the floor on his knees.

"What are you doing?" I say instead.

"My mamá said I had to grovel."

Holy guacamole, he's so cute.

"If you don't love me anymore, I'll do anything to make you fall in love with me all over again. I want your past, present, and future. I want it all with you, and someday I want you to be my wife and the mother of my kids. You're the woman I want. Will you be my girl again? I can't live without you."

For a second, I thought it was a proposal.

Oh, this man, how can I be angry at him when he's hurting? The man standing—well, kneeling—before me seems lighter. I can see it in his eyes. The darkness has faded, and the light shines from him. There are no more shackles tying him down. I kneel so we are on the same level.

"Liam, I love you, and I want to be your girl."

His shoulders sag with relief. His eyes hold mine as we stare at each other for what seems like forever.

"Say it again," he drawls in his husky voice.

"I love you, Liam."

His lips find mine, and our hungry mouths crash as our tongues caress and explore. His kisses are searing, with an intensity that can barely be contained. Our tongues dance an urgent waltz as we attempt to quench our mutual thirst. My heart races faster as my hands move to his back, feeling each ripple of muscle beneath his shirt. I can't help the soft moan escaping my throat as he deepens the kiss, and we become lost in a world of passionate need.

"I love you, mi bella. Te amo."

God, his voice is like syrup, sweet and thick.

"I was waiting for you to come back to me," I admit. "Don't leave me again."

"Never, Sophie. Forgive me." With a sorrowful expression, he gazes at me with hooded eyes.

"I forgive you, Liam, but please don't ever do this to me again. Don't ever make me feel like I'm less, like I'm not worthy. Show me you love me, Liam. Make love to me."

He sweeps me up in his arms and carries me into the house.

I WRAP my arms around his neck, scattering kisses along his stubbled jaw and down to his neck. Once we're in the doorway, I hear the click-clack of paws running toward us. Duke barks and jumps for my attention. I ruffle his soft ears, scratching him just the way he likes.

"He was so pissed at me. He missed you. We both did. We want you back home." He catches me by surprise, that he wants me back here, but now it's all sinking in. He loves me...I'm his girlfriend. But...no.

He's moving.

"Why are your eyebrows scrunched up?" he asks. "What are you thinking?"

"You said you love me, and you want us to be in a relationship and live together, but you're moving. And I'm happy for you and proud of you, of course—you will be an amazing detective, Liam, but how will we work if you're moving? It won't—"

"I'm not moving. Detective Johnson is moving to relocate. I'm taking his position here, and he's taking the LA position. Okay, baby? I wouldn't leave you, Sophie. Like I said, you mean more to me than anything."

"Show me, Detective Rodriguez." I grin, still scratching Duke, while Liam holds me effortlessly in his arms.

"Oh, I intend to, baby, all night." He walks us to his room —*our* room.

Home is wherever he is.

He slams the door behind us and deposits me gently on the bed. I take a moment to look around the room. It's just how we left it the night we left for the gala.

"I haven't slept in here," he says. "I couldn't. Not without you."

I study the hard planes of his sexy body as if I'm discovering him for the first time.

He slips his tank top off, I let my fingers trace every line until I land on his scar. I kiss it. He shivers at my touch. I like the power I have over him, but something is nagging at me. I have to ask before moving forward.

"Have you been with anyone else? Since we've been apart?"

He groans. "Woman, did you not hear anything I said? I'm in love with you. All I want is *you*. I thought about you every second of every day. No woman comes close to you. Never. I haven't wanted anyone since you." He cups my chin. "Have you?"

I shake my head and remove his hand from my chin. I lick first one of his nipples and then the other.

"No, Liam, you ruined me. I want you only."

He moans as I work my tongue down to the V, then he

yanks his shorts down, revealing his massive, hard erection glistening with pre-cum.

My lips quiver as I kneel, the anticipation building. His eyes are heavy-lidded, and his breath is shallow, his mouth parting in anticipation. His breathing grows more labored as my tongue slowly traces his length. I feel his body tremble, a mix of pleasure and pain emanating from him with every touch. Two months felt like an eternity since I last saw him—his face is the same, but somehow different. My grip tightens on him as I continue, and our eyes lock. He runs his fingers through my hair, his hips bucking in time with each movement.

He pulls me away, stripping me out of my clothes, hastily leaving our clothes in piles, desperate to undress me. He bites his lip, lust hazing his beautiful gunmetal eyes. "You're so sexy, mi bella." He licks his soft lips. "Now spread your legs. I'm dying to taste what's mine." His commands ring with authority, just how I like it in bed, but tonight I plan to change it up a bit. I'll be in control.

Liam bites my inner thigh, making his way up. When his sharp tongue thrusts into my pussy, blood rushes into me, making me tingle. My back arches, and I roll my hips and press deeper against his face. He bites. I grab a fistful of the covers, and my head tips back, my eyes rolling back. It's like I'm possessed by this man. I come so hard, the hardest I've ever come.

"Get on the bed." I try to make it sound like a command, but it comes out syrupy.

He smirks, his lips glistening with my juices. "What are you going to do?"

"Ride you, fuck you, take what's mine," I say as I lift myself up, grabbing his dick and fitting it in.

"Fuck, Sophie, I missed this...us." He swells inside me. "I'm yours, baby, every inch of me. Every part of me is yours, my heart, my soul—it's all yours, mi bella."

God, I love this man. My poor, broken man just needed love, patience, and happiness. I'm honored to be the person who brought him back to life, but he did the same for me. He taught me how to love myself, shining a light on me. He's always had the light in him. He just needed to find it.

My hips buck faster and harder, prompting a deep growl from him. His hands cup my breasts, and his mouth clamps onto my hard nipples, sending sparks of pleasure through me.

Throughout the night, I fuck him, and he fucks me, and I tell him what I want in all different positions. He's giving me control. I've always been embarrassed to take control, but not tonight, and Liam seems to enjoy it. He's one of the good ones, the kind you find when you're not even looking. The kind you never let go.

He ends the night by making love to me just as he said he would. He peers into my eyes as he thrusts into me fast, hard, gentle.

"I love you, Sophie," he says just as his mouth covers mine.

We swallow each other's moans, our bodies glistening with sweat, and my legs tangle and wrap around his waist.

"I love you, baby," I mouth into his just as the power of our orgasms send us into shivering ecstasy.

I still can't believe he loves me. We both were meant to fall recklessly in love with each other. He's all mine, just as I'm all his.

CHAPTER 34
LIAM

I wake up to the woman of my dreams nestled on my chest. Her soft snores vibrate through me. Tucking a loose strand of hair behind her ear, I stare as she sleeps peacefully. She's an enigma, a mythical creature, alluring and exotic, a tantalizing beauty who draws me in, leaving me spellbound, and she's all mine. She'll probably be asleep until noon. Last night, she was a beast in bed. *Fuck*. Being dominated was hot. I've never experienced that, and I'd only like to share that with Sophie.

I asked her what she was reading to make her go all animalistic on me.

She giggled and said, "Oh, I was reading a fantasy romance. It was so steamy. The two faes had wild urges. It was hot." She fanned herself.

My eyebrows lifted, and my lips turned into a smirk. "I, for one, fucking loved animalistic Sophie in bed."

Her cheeks turned bright pink, and she swatted my chest while we lay in bed after the fuck fest we had. "I read one of the books you left here, something about gang banging. I didn't like it. I wouldn't want to share you." Jealousy dripped from my lips.

She giggled and lifted herself up to peer at me. Those beautiful blue eyes twinkled with amusement.

"It's a reverse harem, and it's just a book. But..." She tapped her chin. "What if it was three of *you*—"

I pounced on her and fucked her brains out, claiming her, reminding her it will always be me and me only. She knows, but she enjoys bringing the possessiveness out of me.

I chuckle. This woman will sass me our whole lives. I wouldn't have it any other way. Sliding off the bed, I rest her head on the pillow and tuck her in.

Sophie kicks the sheets down, still in a deep sleep. My chest puffs with pride seeing all the love bites I left on her stomach and between her legs. I lick my lips, wanting more of her sweet taste. I bend down and position myself, tongue swirling in her. Sophie moans in her sleep. I groan with satisfaction. Her sounds of pleasure are for me—only me. I suck, bite, and thrust my tongue to make her purr.

"Liam," she moans.

"Do I make you feel good?"

Her back arches, and she rocks her pussy deeper into my mouth.

"Yes," she breathes out with pleasure.

"You taste so good, mi bella. Come for me."

She does. She comes all over my face, just how I like it. Her eyes go heavy.

"Sleep, baby."

She nods and grins, then falls back into a deep sleep.

I make my way to the shower. I have someplace I want to take her—to our place, Tension Canyon Trails. It will be a start to a new us.

Once I prepared everything and Sophie was still getting ready, I polished my dad's truck. I plan to make new memories with Sophie and me in this truck. When I'm done, I toss the coolers in the back. I thought about asking my mom for advice on how to plan a romantic picnic for Sophie, but I know better. She would act like she was planning a wedding, and then she would tell Abuelita and oof, there goes that. She would take over. Food is a way to celebrate anything. She would load up my truck with all kinds of food, enough to feed an army. She'd probably throw the damn grill in there too.

The front door slams shut, and Sophie steps out in a red summer dress that hugs her perfect curves. She's gained some weight these last two months, and I love it all because she's confident in her own body. My body moves on autopilot, marching right toward her. Sinking my nose into her neck, I sniff her coconut scent.

"Are you sniffing me?"

"Yup, I love your coconut bodywash."

She snorts. "I was wondering why you had a butt load of it in the shower."

"Truth is, I would squirt it all over me and jerk off," I admit and shrug.

She throws her head back and laughs—the little devil.

"I'm sorry. It's cute and sexy. Maybe you can show me sometime." She wags her eyebrows.

Cupping her cheeks, I pull her in for a kiss. Her red lips press against mine, and her kisses are as intoxicating as the finest wine. My hands roam under her dress, grabbing a handful of her ass. She ends the kiss, pulling away and swatting my hand.

A growl vibrates from my chest with disapproval.

"I can feel someone watching," she says.

I glance over at Inez's house, and sure enough, the woman is there. I see the curtains move.

"It's just Inez. Don't mind her. She's my new security system."

Sophie laughs and walks to my garden of poppies.

"These are beautiful. When did you start gardening?"

Taking her hand in mine, I walk her to the truck. "Turns out gardening is great for stress and anger management. You can relieve a load of pent-up frustration by stabbing the dirt." I open the passenger door, and she slides in.

"Good to know. Next time you piss me off, I'll plant a vegetable garden."

"Funny, Ms. Sassy-Pants."

We pull up to the old ranch. The ATV is waiting for me, parked by the horse stalls. I called Jimmy and asked if I could borrow it. I figured it would be a pain to carry our shit on Monkey. I grab the small cooler and blankets.

"So, this is the surprise." She smiles. Sophie has always been easy to please.

"Part of it," I say, tossing the stuff in the back rack and strapping it down. I jump onto the ATV, and she jumps on behind me. Her arms wrap around my chest, and her tits press on my back. My dick stands at attention with the heat of her body.

When we get to the lake, I lay out the blanket. It's just as quiet and peaceful as the last time I brought her here. I acted like an ass. I want to make it up to her.

Sudden nerves rocket through my body. I hope I'm doing this right.

"It's beautiful here, Liam. You should have told me we were coming back. I would have changed."

"Nah, I wanted easy access, and you're going to be naked most of the time."

"Oh, yeah?"

"Uh-huh. We're going skinny dipping."

Her eyes widen.

I can't help but laugh.

"Hell, no. What if something crawls up my ass?"

"Baby, the only thing crawling up your ass is my dick."

She huffs, and the corner of her lips twitch.

Digging into the bag, I take out the bagel sandwich I ordered, similar to what she likes in New York. "I'm not sure if it's the same, but I heard good reviews. They say it's the best bagel you can get outside of New York."

"Thank you. I bet it is."

"Are you happy to be back?" I take a bite of my sandwich—it's not bad.

"Honestly, I wanted to come home. You're my home."

"And you're mine."

If the guys saw me now, they would laugh and call me a pussy. Well, not Dominic. He would laugh and say, "I told you so." I would make fun of him with Mila, and he said one day it will be you pulling out the romantic charm. And here I am, trying to impress this woman of mine. I take out my phone and turn on some jazz music. That day at the bar seems like a lifetime ago—when she mentioned she missed going to jazz clubs and concerts.

"Jazz! This is amazing, Liam." She claps her hands, beaming at me.

Fuck. I can feel my face heat up. I avert my gaze to the duck in the lake. Sophie worms her way onto my lap and kisses my cheek.

"I love you, Liam, so much. I didn't know what love was until I met you."

I'm flushed with emotions, though I hesitate to ask. After all, she had been with him for an extended period of time. She must have cared for him deeply.

"What about your ex?"

"It wasn't love. I was never in love with him. And this... what you did for me, a picnic, the food, music. It means so much to me. No one has ever done anything like this for me. You are something special, Detective. Since the day I met you at the studio, I knew you were the one."

I press my lips against hers hungrily. I can never get enough of her. I always want more. This woman makes me addicted and obsessed. Our tongues intertwine as I hold her close, and soon we're both breathing deeply. When I finally pull away, we gasp for air.

"Say it again?" I plead. "Tell me you love me."

"I love you, Liam."

I'll never grow tired of hearing her say those words. I never thought I would be capable of loving.

"I love you, Sophie, so much. I can't function without you. I felt the same way. I knew you were the one when you came out of your office. No woman has made me feel like you did that day. I fell in love with you the night I pinned you in the restroom and kissed you. It took me a while to sort it all out. I'll never let you go." I kiss her cheek, her nose, her lips.

I'll never let her go. Many say you only find love once in a lifetime. I believe it. She is the woman I'm destined to be with. My forever.

———

AFTER OUR LUNCH, I meant what I said about skinny dipping. I've never done it, and I want all my firsts with her, with us, exploring all our firsts together. I slip off her beautiful dress.

"Liam, what are you doing?" She's left in her underwear and strapless bra. She looks around, panicked.

"You forgot, didn't you? We are going skinny dipping." Turning her around, I unclasp her bra and brush my thumb across her peaked nipples.

"I didn't take you seriously," Sophie says with a moan as my tongue sweeps her nipple. Bending down, I peel off her underwear. Running my hands along her thighs, I work my way up until I'm face-to-face with her.

"You're absolutely beautiful, Sophie, perfect, just the way you are."

She gives me a kiss and then laughs and retorts. "Thank you, Liam. You're the sweetest, but can you undress now?"

I chuckle. "So eager to see me naked, mi bella?" I give her a cheeky grin and begin to undress.

"Yes, of course, and I don't want to stand here naked in case someone shows up."

I unbutton my shorts and slide them down with my boxers. "If anyone so much looks at my girl naked, they must have a death wish."

Running my thumb along her nipples, I suck on one, then the other. My hands roam her soft, creamy body, caressing through all her perfect curves and drawl out, "Your body is only for my eyes, Sophie. No man deserves to see your beauty. I'm not saying I deserve you, because I don't. But you deserve to be treated right. I'll do everything in my power to be the man who deserves you."

I lift her up, and she then wraps her legs around my waist.

"Oh, Liam," she breathes into my lips.

As we kiss, we make our way toward the chilly lake. Another first for me. With Sophie, I find myself exploring all kinds of new sensations. Without breaking away from her kiss, I slide into her. She feels so tight and absolutely amazing. With my hands gripping her thighs, I rock her back and forth harder and faster. Our bodies are so heated by one another that we can't feel the cold water.

The tension in my balls heightens as I press into her with more force, our lips clashing together in a mix of need and fervor.

"Sophie," I moan as I grab her ass, pushing deeper into her until my body shakes with my release. She throws her head back and screams my name as she comes. It's the most beautiful sight.

We spend the rest of the evening lying on the blanket, making love. I still can't believe this woman has fallen in love with me.

For once in my life, the weight I carried for years is now gone. A part of me feels like my dad sent Sophie my way. He knew she was the perfect woman for me. She gave me love, happiness, and life. I'll forever be grateful for the woman who stole my heart. I'd recklessly fall in love with her over and over again.

SOPHIE'S EPILOGUE

Five months later

Today we move into our new studio. We've been needing a much bigger place. Business has skyrocketed, all thanks to Mila's uncle, who handed over so many of his clients and who recommended us to celebrities and models. We hardly do family photographs now, and we've hired two more photographers. Since Mila gave birth to little Luca on Thanksgiving, she's been working part-time; she and Dom have been busy with two kids, two restaurants, and the studio. Liam and I have been helping them out with the kids, giving them a break, and I just love how Liam looks holding a newborn and playing with Dante. I never thought the sight of Liam holding a baby would turn me on, but it does. The way he coos at baby Luca makes my ovaries want to explode.

"Baby, is that all the boxes?" Liam asks, walking in dressed in casual clothing. I miss him in his sexy uniform.

"Yes, that's it for today. We can leave the equipment in the other room. I have a photoshoot in an hour."

"Tomorrow is New Year's Eve. You should just cancel and reschedule after the New Year."

I lean in and kiss his stubbled jaw. "I would, but I rescheduled once already; I felt bad, so I told him we could just do it today and get it over with. It shouldn't take long, then we can go over to your mom's for dinner."

"Him?"

Apparently, that's all he picked up on.

"Yes, it's a *him*. I have the equipment ready—and the oils," I say, trying to hide my smile, but it slips. His jaw clenches, jealousy visible. I add, "He's an underwear model. We have a contract with them... it's a new agency."

He looks like an angry Greek god. "You'd better not rub oil all over his body, Sophie." His arms wrap around my waist. I can feel the possessiveness of his hold and the jealousy dripping from each word.

"Of course not, silly. I'm not going to rub it *all* over. Maybe just his chest," I joke.

He tilts his head back, peering at the ceiling. "Lord, help me."

Taking a bite of his neck, I say, "Mi bebé jealous."

His body shakes in laughter, and he spanks my butt. "Yes, very, and you know how to do it so well."

"I'm sorry. You know I'd never do that."

"I know, even though you've done it before." Of course, he'll never forget that.

"We were not an item, remember?"

"Still," he says, irritated, remembering the swimsuit models. "You're going to get it tonight for messing with me."

I grin. "Promise?"

He shakes his head, laughing. "Oh, I promise, bella." He kisses my lips. "Tomorrow, I'm taking you out for New Year's Eve."

"We're not going to your mom's? I thought since Rosa moved back you'd want to go," I ask.

His thumb brushes my lips. "Rosa moved into her new apartment. Mom's going over to her place to ring in the New Year. I want to be alone with *my girl*."

I love how sweet he is.

The day he took me to the lake, and we had a picnic was one of the most special things anyone has ever done for me—it meant more than words can say. He continues to surprise me every day, showing me how much he loves me. I moved into his place that week and gave up my lease. I've never been happier than I am with Liam. He loves my sassiness, snarky attitude, and lame jokes. And I love everything about my detective, from his possessiveness to his handsome and sexy body to his protective side. I'm so proud of him. He's come along way. We both have.

He's incredibly precious to me.

My parents came down to meet Liam for Thanksgiving. Oh, did they fall in love with him. They clicked with him, just like I thought they would. My mom kept calling him a hunk and telling him stories of my childhood. He laughed, getting a kick out of my embarrassment. My dad fell in love with him, too. They talked about their love for muscle cars and even decided to rebuild a car together. My dad patted me on the back and whispered, "He's a keeper." I think my dad liked him for himself. I don't mind. I'd gladly share Liam with my dad. He deserves to have a father in his life. I saw the warmth in his eyes, how he longed for that.

"I love you," I murmur.

"I love you more." He grinds his erection on my belly.

"Fuck, man, we've been waiting for you outside. You said you'd be right back. We're freezing our asses off," Santiago bites out. He seems to be in one of his moods.

He's been having them a lot now that Rosa is back. I feel the tension.

"As you can see, asshole, I'm busy. What the hell crawled up your ass?" Liam growls.

I love how they bicker like brothers.

"Nothing," Santiago says. "So, are we done?"

"Yeah." Liam eyes Santiago.

"All right, then, I gotta go."

Mark blows out a hot breath. "Fuck, he's been pissy lately. I think it's because the banks are trying to take his shop away."

"Fuck," Liam says.

"Yeah, I know. Well, later, bro. Happy New Year, if I don't see you guys."

We say our goodbyes, and then my undie model walks in, and Liam snorts.

I mouth. "What is it?"

He whispers, "An underwear model with no damn muscle."

I stifle my laugh.

It's New Year's Eve, and I'm unsure where Liam plans to take me. He says it's a surprise. I'm wearing a maroon sleeveless dress with a lace insert on the neckline. It has a side slit that reveals my matching red panties. I slip into the matching heels and walk to the mirror at the end of the hallway. The heels makes my hips sway. I apply ruby-red lipstick.

"I'm ready," I shout, walking into the living room where he sits reading a magazine. He looks up at me with those gorgeous eyes.

"Fuck, Grenade, you're really going to cause an explosion

looking like that, baby." He bites his lip and continues roaming my body. "Fucking sexy."

My cheeks warm. "Thank you," I whisper. Even with all my snarkiness, he still manages to make me feel shy—and that was an unknown feeling for me once upon a time.

"Ready, mi bella?"

"I'm ready." He helps me slip on my coat, and I turn to kiss his cheek. "You look handsome."

He smirks. "Don't I always?"

"Smug bastard," I mumble.

A half-hour later, Liam pulls into the Hard Rock Hotel, where they have their yearly New Year's parties. It's also, where it all started the night he asked me for a deal I couldn't refuse.

"Where it all started, huh?" he says, reading my mind.

"I know. How time flies. So, much has happened in a year."

He nods, unbuckling me. "It has. One of the best years of my life. Because I fell in love with you."

I'm in awe.

Once we take the elevator to the restaurant on the top floor, our server sits us in a private corner booth. It's decorated with a silk tablecloth and a lantern, and rose petals dust the top of the table. It's very romantic.

"We offer samples of wine, if you are interested," the server says, placing our menus in front of us.

"Give us a bottle of whatever top-of-the-line wine you have," Liam drawls, and my eyes bulge out.

The server nods and leaves, and I turn to look at Liam.

"Are you crazy? It could be a five-thousand-dollar bottle of wine."

"It's worth it. We're celebrating tonight." Liam leans to press his lips on mine when the server arrives with a bottle and two glasses. We place our orders and watch the crowd of people flow in. Liam made a reservation. I'm positive he picked a table away from everyone. He scoots me closer to him and wraps his powerful arms around me. I carefully swirl the ruby colored liquid around my glass before taking an aroma-filled sip. The richness of the flavor spreads over my tongue like velvet, and I can tell this is an expensive bottle of wine.

His hands trail up the slit of my dress, sending warmth to my center. His hand moves higher and higher until it loops into my underwear. I gasp when one thick finger inserts into me, then another.

"Liam," I moan. Clawing my nails into his collar and resting my head on his shoulder, my body shakes as he goes deeper and faster.

"I love to see you come undone with just the tip of my finger, baby. Come for me, Sophie. I want my fingers dripping with your cum."

Holy guacamole, this man is going to give me a heart attack.

Thank goodness we're sitting far away where no one can see. He hits the right spot, and I come undone. Fuck.

Liam pulls out his finger when the server arrives with our food. He licks and sucks his dripping finger, savoring it.

"A sample, my love, until we get home."

Who is this man? He's hot as fuck.

Liam orders spaghetti and meatballs, and I order fettuccine. The unexpected orgasm made me hungry.

"This is fantastic," I moan into the creamy pasta. "How's yours?"

He's been a little quiet since the food arrived. I'm not sure if it's because he feels uncomfortable—working in law enforcement does that to you. You always have to watch your back.

"It's good, but the damn meatballs are huge."

"Not as big as yours," I blurt out. *Jeez Sophie.*

Liam throws his head back in a roar of laughter. Well, at least I made him laugh.

"Good to know, Sophie." He wipes his mouth with the cloth. "I'll take that as a compliment. I love that mi bella has no filter." I grin and take a sip of my wine.

The server returns with a sample platter of desserts. My breath hitches when I see it. A black velvet box. Liam takes it and kneels.

"Today marks a year since I had my first kiss, and I'm glad I never gave it to anyone else. Asking you for one crazy thing ended up being the best thing in my life. I never thought I was capable of falling in love, but you made it seem so effortless to do so. You're my soulmate, my other half, and I want to spend it with you for the rest of my life. I want to grow a family. I want it all with you by my side. Will you marry me, Sophie?"

Tears of joy run down my cheek. I wasn't expecting it.

"Yes, Liam, I'll marry you."

He slips the beautiful ring on my finger.

His mouth crashes into mine, taking control of my lips with possessive thoroughness. The noise fades around us. It's only us in our moment. The most unexpected things that occur are the most powerful ones. I never expected to fall in love so hard, so fast. I never expected to find my soulmate. I never expected *to be loved right.*

We pull away, panting and desperate for more. "Let's get out of here, baby. I need to fuck my fiancée."

"I like the sound of that...fiancé." Liam tosses cash on the table and grabs my hand.

"Me too, baby, but I'd like wife more." Goosebumps spread throughout my body. *Wife.* Oh, how I like it.

We leave the restaurant in a frenzy. When we get to the house, and the door slams shut, Liam pins me to the wall, our bodies melting into one. Anxiously, I strip down from my dress, needing to feel the warmth of his body. Liam grinds his erection on me, bruising kisses from my lips to my neck. His hands roam in all the right places. Fireworks pop in the night sky behind the door.

He whispers, just as he hooks his finger in my pussy, "I've heard if you kiss a confident woman at the stroke of midnight on New Year's Eve, it's a sign of good luck."

I smile, remembering how he said this to me a year ago. "Tell me, did it bring you good luck?"

He skims his lips over mine. *"It did. I found my future."* Liam gently lifts me in his arms and carries me to our bedroom. As we enter, he sheds his clothing, and our bodies become one as we melt into each other's embrace.

LIAM'S EPILOGUE

Three years later

I lean up against the wall, sipping eggnog spiked with rum. While watching the kids run around, Sophie made decorations and plastered them throughout the house. Tonight, I want to be alone with my wife, and she promised me I would have her to myself for the rest of the day. But she lied. She invited Mila, Dominic, my mom, and her parents, who are here for the holidays, and her brother and his wife just showed up along with his kids. My beautiful wife is so busy that she hasn't paid any attention to me.

I laugh when Angelica makes a fist at Luca, then points her finger at him. "Don't chase me, or you get it."

My daughter is fierce for a two-year-old. She must get it from her mother. Her golden locks bounce as she shakes her head, showing all her sass. Luca continues to chase her, though, so she puts him in a headlock, and her blue eyes sparkle.

"What did I tell you, Loco? You mess with me, you get it."

"It's Luca...quit calling me crazy in Spanish!" Luca grumbles.

She lets him go and dusts her small hands.

"You created a monster," Dominic says, walking toward me, holding his beautiful eighteen-month-old daughter in his arms.

Yeah, I guess I do wrestle with my kids all the time. I'm positive that's the reason my Angelica is such a badass. That and the fact she clearly inherited her mom's attitude. Yup, we created a monster.

Dante runs out, chasing Diego and Alex's daughter. Diego, who is Angelica's twin, looks nothing like her. He's got my hair and his mom's eyes. The combination makes him look like a badass—a handsome guy. Finding out Sophie was pregnant was one of the most amazing days of my life, along with the day I made Sophie my wife. A year ago, we bought a bigger house, a couple of houses down from where Mila and Dominic live, and as of now, I'm part of the DEA.

"Yeah, I guess I did," I say, taking another sip of eggnog.

"Damn, man, we've come a long way, bro, from being lonely fucks to having wives and houses full of kids."

I nod. "I never saw it coming. You were right—becoming a father is one of the most amazing feelings. We got lucky, man."

"Our wives have been ignoring us," Dominic points out.

Good—I'm not the only one who feels it.

I growl. "Tell me about it. Christmas is not until next week. Why have a gingerbread house party tonight?"

We turn to look at the women laughing and having a good time. Mila and Sophie are laying out candy to decorate the gingerbread houses, and my mom and Clair are wearing matching ugly Christmas sweaters and baking cookies. My mom's face lights up when the kids run to her for a cookie. She has them so spoiled. She's happy, and I'm happy Sophie and I could give her the happiness of becoming a grandmother.

My father-in-law Jerry emerges from the back door. "Are they still at it?" he grunts.

I guess all the men are feeling neglected.

"Yup," Dominic and I say in unison.

"Papá, Papá!" Angelica yells, running to me. I swipe my daughter in my arms and kiss her chubby cheeks. "You see me, Papá?" she says, in her small voice.

"I did. You kicked his ass."

She places her little finger on my lips, keeping me from cussing. I walk out to the backyard patio with her in my arms and Diego following behind. "It's okay. Mamá can't hear now." I scoop Diego into my other arm.

They yawn at the same time.

"You guys tired?"

They nod.

"Tired, Papá," Diego says.

"Your mamá is busy being a host. She forgot all about us." I glance at Sophie through the open door. She's beautiful in her ridiculous reindeer pajamas. She looks beautiful in anything she wears. Her long blonde hair has gotten longer, her breasts are engorged. We just found out she's seven weeks pregnant. I couldn't be happier. Times like these, I wonder what I would have missed out on if I had continued to be bitter, if I still feared bringing a family into the picture and facing the same fate I did as a child.

I'm indebted to this woman who loved me broken and bruised and took a chance on loving me.

"She forgot," Diego whines.

I love my little sidekicks.

"Are you guys having fun playing with your cousins?" I ask.

Angelica wrinkles her nose and shakes her head. "Loco chase me," she says, growling.

I throw my head back in laughter. When she was younger, she couldn't say Luca, so she started calling him Loco, and it stuck. My kids speak Spanish. I make sure to talk to them in

Spanish. My mom speaks to them in Spanish, and Sophie is learning. She's picked up on dirty words—they sound hot coming from her mouth, especially with her accent.

"We play cops," Diego says with a yawn.

"Cops and robbers?" I ask.

"Yes," Diego clarifies. Their little heads jolt when Sophie walks out. I give her a disapproving look as I turn around. I'm mad at her.

She kisses the kids on the tips of their noses and then does the same to me.

"Nice to see you, wife. You've been neglecting us," I huff, turning away from her. I stare at the sunset and the ocean waves crashing in the distance.

She bursts into a fit of laughter. I don't see anything funny about it. I want her in our bed so I can do sinful things to her. I've been so damn horny, and she's neglected me.

"Not funny," I say, still looking at the crashing waves.

"Not funny," Diego says.

Angelica joins in as my side-kick, "Not funny, Mamá."

"Oh, I see my little monsters have turned on me." She gives the kids kisses on their cheeks. "So dramatic, Liam. My possessive, jealous husband."

"I have needs," I say, and it sounds more like a whine. From the corner of my eye, I see her red lips curve. "And the kids are tired—ready for bed."

Once the kids are down for a nap, I can convince her to abandon our guests for a quickie or, if I'm lucky, she'll rap those red lips around me.

"I not tired," Angelica says.

Diego chimes in, sticking with his twin, "Not tired."

Traitors.

"How about we put on our Christmas pajamas on so we can match?" Sophie asks.

They scream excitedly.

"And have cookies with hot chocolate and marshmallows," Sophie adds.

More cheering for their mother, who saves the day. They forget so easily how she neglected them.

Duke runs out, and the kids ask to be put down so they can chase him inside. When we're alone, Sophie wraps her arms around my neck.

"When are they all leaving?" I bite out.

"Liam," she says, pecking kisses.

I remain hardened to her advances. If I don't, I'll give in. I'm mad at her, but my dick swells in my jeans. Her scent and her warmth are not helping.

"What's with you?"

"I want to be alone with you. I want you naked *in our bed.* Once the kids go to bed."

Her thumbs rub my earlobes. It's soothing; no wonder Duke likes it.

"You look sexy when you pout," she says seductively. Hot and wetness laps my neck; she licks up and down, leaving little bites.

Fuck me.

Before I can stop it, a moan leaves me.

"Mmm, I like it when you moan for me." Her hand goes to my swollen dick. She rubs it through the fabric of my jeans. "So hard for me," she breathes out.

Her tongue traces the outline of my lips. Fuck. Then she bites my lip.

"Let's go mingle with our guests for a bit longer. I'll make you some hot chocolate. The grandmas are taking the kids tonight for a sleepover."

That gets my attention. "My parents are staying at your mom's house, and my brother is staying at a hotel.

You'll have me all to yourself. Also, I have an early gift for you."

My eyebrows quirk up. "A gift, you say?"

She nods. "Yes, I'll be wearing it. Red lace for my moody man." She winks, and her beautiful blue eyes sparkle with the sunset. I smirk and agree by kissing her. The instant our lips meet, I feel a rush of electricity. Her lips are soft and full, and I want to kiss her endlessly. The taste of her mouth is like a drug, intoxicating me with desire.

"Can't wait," I say, breathing into her. I return to kissing her. Pulling away, I say. "Okay, let's go back inside. I want to get it over with."

She laughs, taking my hand and guiding me inside.

Every day, I fall more in love with my wife. I never saw her coming. She calms me and centers me. She's the one I can't live without, my grenade, who came in and blew me out of the water, and gave me a family I never thought I'd have.

Acknowledgment

Thank you to my husband Raymond, my muse, who gives me encouragement and supports me. To my daughter Maia, thank you for always supporting my writing and being interested in my stories. To my sons Nathan and Julian, thank you for always hearing me talk about my books.

Tiara, thank you, thank you so much for all your help and for pushing me though the tough times. For staying up late to help me fix all my mistakes. I appreciate all your help.

Thank you to the editors who have taken the time to work on *Recklessly You* with me. Thank you to my street team for taking the time to read Liam's and Sophie's story.

Printed in Dunstable, United Kingdom